With degrees in English and History and a particular love
of Regency and Victorian times, **Deanna Raybourn** is a
committed anglophile, who, at her husband's insistence, gave
up teaching to devote her energies to writing. Clearly her
husband knew what he was doing.

Silent in the Grave is Deanna's debut novel and is the first in
the *Silent* series featuring the effervescent Lady Julia Grey and
the enigmatic private investigator Nicholas Brisbane.

Deanna is currently hard at work on the sequel from her
current home in Virginia. *Silent in the Sanctuary* will be
available in January 2009 from MIRA Books.

Find out more online at
www.mirabooks.co.uk/deannaraybourn

D1513865

SILENT in the GRAVE

Deanna Raybourn

MIRA

DID YOU PURCHASE THIS BOOK WITHOUT A COVER?

If you did, you should be aware it is **stolen property** as it was reported *unsold and destroyed* by a retailer. Neither the author nor the publisher has received any payment for this book.

All the characters in this book have no existence outside the imagination of the author, and have no relation whatsoever to anyone bearing the same name or names. They are not even distantly inspired by any individual known or unknown to the author, and all the incidents are pure invention.

All Rights Reserved including the right of reproduction in whole or in part in any form. This edition is published by arrangement with Harlequin Enterprises II B.V./S.à.r.l. The text of this publication or any part thereof may not be reproduced or transmitted in any form or by any means, electronic or mechanical, including photocopying, recording, storage in an information retrieval system, or otherwise, without the written permission of the publisher.

This book is sold subject to the condition that it shall not, by way of trade or otherwise, be lent, resold, hired out or otherwise circulated without the prior consent of the publisher in any form of binding or cover other than that in which it is published and without a similar condition including this condition being imposed on the subsequent purchaser.

MIRA is a registered trademark of Harlequin Enterprises Limited, used under licence.

MIRA Books, Eton House, 18-24 Paradise Road, Richmond, Surrey, TW9 1SR

© Deanna Raybourn 2006

ISBN 978 0 7783 0137 0

58-0108

Printed in Great Britain by Clays Ltd, St Ives plc

ACKNOWLEDGEMENTS

Because writing is a solitary business, finding kindred spirits is a gift from the gods. This book has been fortunate enough to be touched by two such people: my agent, Pam Hopkins, and my editor, Valerie Gray. Throughout the more than two years that it took to place this book, Pam's kindness and conviction never faltered. And I could not imagine finding a more supportive or enthusiastic editor than Valerie. Pam's diligence and Valerie's elegant turns of phrase are endlessly inspiring in a business where perseverance and style are equally important.

I owe a tremendous debt of gratitude for research and technological support to Dr Susan Korp, Dr G Steve Best, Ian Wright of the University of Edinburgh, and Kelly Stelzriede. Naturally, all errors are mine.

I am also profoundly grateful to the team at MIRA: Adrienne, Dianne, Margaret, Mary-Margaret, Maureen, Miranda, Nicole, Sasha, and Susan. Many thanks to Donna Williams for superb copy editing, as well as thanks to the Proofreading, Production and Sales Departments. Your collective efforts may be unseen, but this book would not have been possible without them.

Also, many thanks to my Jackson girls for moral support. You know who you are and what you mean to me. I am braver for knowing you.

And thanks most of all to my family: to my father and my daughter for their unwavering support; to my mother, who has read and proofread every copy of every novel with the devotion that only a mother could provide; and to my husband, who has given me everything I have ever truly needed, including the chance to write.

This book is dedicated to the memory of my grandmother, Patricia Nile Russell, and my grandfather, John Lucius Jones, Jr.

THE FIRST CHAPTER

London, 1886

Other sins only speak; murder shrieks out.
—John Webster
The Duchess of Malfi

To say that I met Nicholas Brisbane over my husband's dead body is not entirely accurate. Edward, it should be noted, was still twitching upon the floor.

I stared at him, not quite taking in the fact that he had just collapsed at my feet. He lay, curled like a question mark, his evening suit ink-black against the white marble of the floor. He was writhing, his fingers knotted.

I leaned as close to him as my corset would permit.

"Edward, we have guests. Do get up. If this is some sort of silly prank—"

"He is not jesting, my lady. He is convulsing."

An impatient figure in black pushed past me to kneel at Edward's side. He busied himself for a few brisk moments, palpating and pulse-taking, while I bobbed a bit, trying to see over his shoulder. Behind me the guests were murmuring, buzzing, pushing closer to get a look of their own. There was a little thrill of excitement in the air. After all, it was not every evening that a baronet collapsed senseless in his own music room. And Edward was proving rather better entertainment than the soprano we had engaged.

Through the press, Aquinas, our butler, managed to squeeze in next to my elbow.

"My lady?"

I looked at him, grateful to have an excuse to turn away from the spectacle on the floor.

"Aquinas, Sir Edward has had an attack."

"And would be better served in his own bed," said the gentleman from the floor. He rose, lifting Edward into his arms with a good deal of care and very little effort, it seemed. But Edward had grown thin in the past months. I doubted he weighed much more than I.

"Follow me," I instructed, although Aquinas actually led the way out of the music room. People moved slowly out of our path, as though they regretted the little drama ending so quickly. There were some polite murmurs, some mournful clucking. I heard snatches as I passed through them.

"The curse of the Greys, it is—"

"So young. But of course his father never saw thirty-five."

"Never make old bones—"

"Feeble heart. Pity, he was always such a pleasant fellow."

I moved faster, staring straight ahead so that I did not have to meet their eyes. I kept my gaze fixed on Aquinas' broad, black-wool back, but all the time I was conscious of those voices and the sound of footsteps behind me, the footsteps of the gentleman who was carrying my husband. Edward groaned softly as we reached the stairs and I turned. The gentleman's face was grim.

"Aquinas, help the gentleman—"

"I have him," he interrupted, brushing past me. Aquinas obediently led him to Edward's bedchamber. Together they settled Edward onto the bed, and the gentleman began to loosen his clothes. He flicked a glance toward Aquinas.

"Has he a doctor?"

"Yes, sir. Doctor Griggs, Golden Square."

"Send for him. Although I dare say it will be too late."

Aquinas turned to me where I stood, hovering on the threshold. I never went into Edward's room. I did not like to do so now. It felt like an intrusion, a trespass on his privacy.

"Shall I send for Lord March as well, my lady?"

I blinked at Aquinas. "Why should Father come? He is no doctor."

But Aquinas was quicker than I. I had thought the gentleman meant that Edward would have recovered from his attack by the time Doctor Griggs arrived. Aquinas, who had seen more of the world than I, knew better.

He looked at me, his eyes carefully correct, and then I understood why he wanted to send for Father. As head of the family he would have certain responsibilities.

I nodded slowly. "Yes, send for him." I moved into the room on reluctant legs. I knew I should be there, doing whatever little bit that I could for Edward. But I stopped at the side of the bed. I did not touch him.

"And Lord Bellmont?" Aquinas queried.

I thought for a moment. "No, it is Friday. Parliament is sitting late."

That much was a mercy. Father I could cope with. But not my eldest brother as well. "And I suppose you ought to call for the carriages. Send everyone home. Make my apologies."

He left us alone then, the stranger and I. We stood on opposite sides of the bed, Edward convulsing between us. He stopped after a moment and the gentleman placed a finger at his throat.

"His pulse is very weak," he said finally. "You should prepare yourself."

I did not look at him. I kept my eyes fixed on Edward's pale face. It shone with sweat, its surface etched with lines of pain. This was not how I wanted to remember him.

"I have known him for more than twenty years," I said

finally, my voice tight and strange. "We were children together. We used to play pirates and knights of the Round Table. Even then, I knew his heart was not sound. He used to go quite blue sometimes when he was overtired. This is not unexpected."

I looked up then to find the stranger's eyes on me. They were the darkest eyes I had ever seen, witch-black and watchful. His gaze was not friendly. He was regarding me coldly, as a merchant will appraise a piece of goods to determine its worth. I dropped my eyes at once.

"Thank you for your concern for my husband's health, sir. You have been most helpful. Are you a friend of Edward's?"

He did not reply at once. Edward made a noise in the back of his throat and the stranger moved swiftly, rolling him onto his side and thrusting a basin beneath his mouth. Edward retched, horribly, groaning. When he finished, the gentleman put the basin to the side and wiped his mouth with his handkerchief. Edward gave a little whimper and began to shiver. The gentleman watched him closely.

"Not a friend, no. A business associate," he said finally. "My name is Nicholas Brisbane."

"I am—"

"I know who you are, my lady."

Startled at his rudeness, I looked up, only to find those eyes again, fixed on me with naked hostility. I opened my mouth to reproach him, but Aquinas appeared then. I turned to him, relieved.

"Aquinas?"

"The carriages are being brought round now, my lady. I have sent Henry for Doctor Griggs and Desmond for his lordship. Lady Otterbourne and Mr. Phillips both asked me to convey their concern and their willingness to help should you have need of them."

"Lady Otterbourne is a meddlesome old gossip and Mr. Phillips would be no use whatsoever. Send them home."

I was conscious of Mr. Brisbane behind me, listening to every word. I did not care. For some unaccountable reason, the man thought ill of me already. I did not mind if he thought worse.

Aquinas left again, but I did not resume my post by the bed. I took a chair next to the door and remained there, saying nothing and wondering what was going to happen to all of the food. We had ordered far too much in any event. Edward never liked to run short. I could always tell Cook to serve it in the servants' hall, but after a few days even the staff would tire of it. Before I could decide what to do with the lobster patties and salad molds, Aquinas entered again, leading Doctor Griggs. The elderly man was perspiring freely, patting his ruddy face with a handkerchief and gasping. He had taken the stairs too quickly. I rose and he took my hand.

"I was afraid of this," he murmured. "The curse of the Greys, it is. All snatched before their time. My poor girl." I smiled feebly at him. Doctor Griggs had attended my mother at my birth, as well as her nine other confinements. We had known each other too long to stand on ceremony. He patted my hand and moved to the bed. He felt for Edward's pulse, shaking his head as he did so. Edward vomited again, and Doctor Griggs watched him carefully, examining the contents of the basin. I turned away.

I tried not to hear the sounds coming from the bed, the groans and the rattling breaths. I would have stopped my ears with my hands, but I knew it would look childish and cowardly. Griggs continued his examination, but before he finished Aquinas stepped into the room.

"Lord March, my lady." He moved aside and Father entered.

"Julia," he said, opening his arms. I went into them, burying my face against his waistcoat. He smelled of tobacco and book leather. He kept one arm tucked firmly around me as he looked over my head.

"Griggs, you damned fool. Julia should have been sent away."

The doctor made some reply, but I did not hear it. My father was pushing me gently out the door. I tried to look past him, to see what they were doing to Edward, but Father moved his body and prevented me. He gave me a sad, gentle smile. Anyone else might have mistaken that smile, but I did not. I knew he expected obedience. I nodded.

"I shall wait in my room."

"That would be best. I will come when there is something to tell."

My maid, Morag, was waiting for me. She helped me out of my silk gown and into something more suitable. She offered me warm milk or brandy, but I knew I would never be able to hold anything down. I only wanted to sit, watching the clock on the mantel as it ticked away the minutes left.

Morag continued to fuss, poking at the fire and muttering complaints about the work to come. She was right about that. There would be much work for her when I put on widow's weeds. It was unlucky to keep crepe in the house, I reminded myself. It would have to be sent for after Edward passed. I thought about such things—crepe for the mirrors, black plumes for the horses—because then I did not have to think about what was happening in Edward's room. It was rather like waiting for a birth, these long, tense minutes of sitting, straining one's ears on tiptoe for the slightest sound. I expected to hear something, but the walls were thick and I heard nothing. Even when the clock struck midnight, the little voice on my mantel chiming twelve times, I could not hear the tall case clock in the hall. I started to mention the peculiarity of it to Morag, because one could always hear the case clock from any room in the house, when I realized what it meant.

"Morag, the clocks have stopped."

She looked at me, her lips parted to speak, but she said

nothing. Instead she bowed her head and began to pray. A moment later, the door opened. It was Father. He said nothing. I went to him and his hand cradled my head like a benediction. He held me for a very long time, as he had not done since I was a child.

"It is all right, my dear," he said finally, sounding older and more tired than I had ever heard him. "It is over."

But of course, he was entirely wrong. It was only the beginning.

THE SECOND CHAPTER

He heaps up riches, and he heaps up sorrow,
It's his today, but who's his heir tomorrow?
—Anne Bradstreet
"The Vanity of All Worldly Things"

The days leading up to the funeral were dire, as such days almost always are. Too many people, saying too many pointless things—the same pointless things that everyone always says. Such a tragedy, so unexpected, so very, very dreadful. And no matter how much you would like to scream at them to go away and leave you alone, you cannot, even if they are your family.

Especially if they are your family. In the week following Edward's death, I was inundated with March relations. They flocked from the four corners of the kingdom, as mindful of the pleasures of London as their family duty. As etiquette did not permit me to be seen in public, they came to me at Grey House. The men—uncles, brothers, cousins—briefly paid their respects to Edward, laid out with awful irony in the music room, then spent the rest of their time arguing politics and arranging for amusements that would get them out of the house. My only consolation was the fact that, like locusts, they managed to finish off all of the leftover food from the night Edward died.

The women were little better. Under Aunt Hermia's direction, the funeral was planned, the burial arranged, and my household turned entirely on its head. She carried around with her a notebook filled with endless lists that she was forever consulting with a frown or ticking off with a satisfied smile. There was the crepe to be ordered, mourning wreaths, funeral cards, black-bordered writing paper to be purchased, the announcement for the *Times,* and of course my wardrobe.

"Unrelieved black," she informed me, her brow furrowed as she struggled to make out her own handwriting. "There must be no sheen to the fabric and no white or grey," she reminded me.

"I know." I tried not to think of the new gowns, delivered only the day before Edward's death. They were pale, soft colours, the shades of new flowers in spring. I should have to give them to Morag to sell at the secondhand stalls now. They would never dye dark enough to pass for mourning.

"No jewels, except hair jewelry," Aunt Hermia was saying. I repressed a shudder. I had never warmed to the notion of wearing a dead person's hair braided around my wrist or knotted at my ears. "After a year and a day, you will be permitted black fabric with a sheen, and deep purple or grey with a black stripe. If you choose to wear black after that time, you may relieve it with touches of white. Although," she added with a conspiratorial look, "I think a year is quite enough, and you must do what you like after that."

I glanced at my sister Portia, who was busy feeding her ancient pug some rather costly crab fritters laced with caviar. She looked up and wrinkled her nose at me over Puggy's head.

"Don't fret, dearest. You have always looked striking in black."

I grimaced at her and turned back to Aunt Hermia, who was deliberately ignoring Portia's flippancy. As children, we had been quite certain that Aunt Hermia was partially deaf. It was only much later when we realized that there was absolutely nothing wrong with her hearing. The trick of hearing only what she wanted had enabled her to raise her widowed brother's ten children with some measure of sanity.

"Black stockings of course," she was saying, "and we shall have to order some new handkerchiefs edged in black."

"I am working on them now," said my sister Bee from the corner. Industrious as her namesake, she kept her head bowed over her work, her needle whipping through the fine lawn with its load of thin black silk.

"Very good, Beatrice. That will save time having them made up, and I simply could not bear to purchase ready-made for Julia." Aunt Hermia paused, her pencil poised. "You know, the queen has hers embroidered with black tears for Prince Albert. What do you think of that?"

Bee lifted her head and smiled. "I think perhaps plain is best. I mean to get through all of her handkerchiefs before I have to return to Cornwall, and I shall be lucky just to finish the borders."

"Of course, dear," Aunt Hermia said. She returned to her list, but I kept my eyes on Bee. She had not looked at me, and I fancied that her preoccupation with my handkerchiefs was a means of keeping herself too busy to do so. I wondered then how much she knew, how much any of them knew. Marriage is a private thing between a man and his wife, but blood calls to blood, or so my father always said. Was it possible for them to know? I had said nothing, and yet still, I wondered....

"And we should tell Aquinas to prepare the China Room for Aunt Ursula."

I swung round to face Aunt Hermia. The room had gone quite productively silent. Bee was busy with her needlework, Portia and Nerissa were writing out the funeral cards. Olivia immediately picked up a book of hymns to peruse.

"Aunt Ursula? The Ghoul is coming?"

"Really, darling, I wish you children would not call her that," Aunt Hermia said, frowning. "She is a good and decent soul. She only wishes to offer comfort in your bereavement."

Portia smothered a snort. We all knew better than that. The Ghoul's purpose in life was not to give comfort, it was to haunt the bereaved. She appeared at every deathbed, every funeral, with her trunks of mourning clothes and memorial jewelry, reading dreary poems and tippling the sherry when no one was looking. She kept a sort of scrapbook of the funerals she had attended, rating them by number of mourners, desirability of the gravesite and quality of the food. The worst part of it was that she never left. Instead, she stayed on, offering her own wretched brand of comfort until the next family tragedy. We had been quite fortunate in London, though. A spate of ill luck had carried off three of our elderly uncles in Scotland in as many years. We had not seen her for ages.

"Julia?" Aunt Hermia's voice was edged only slightly with impatience, and I realized she must have been trying to get my attention for some time.

"I am sorry, Aunt. I was woolgathering."

She patted my hand. "Never mind, dear. I hear Uncle Leonato's wife is suffering again from her old lung complaint. Perhaps she won't last much longer."

That was a small consolation. Uncle Leonato's wife usually hovered on the brink of death until he presented her with whatever piece of jewelry or lavish trinket she had been pining for, then she made a full recovery quickly enough. Still, there was a pack of hunting-mad cousins in Yorkshire who were always highly unlucky. Perhaps this season one of them might be mistaken for a stag....

Aunt Hermia coughed gently and I looked up. "Olivia was asking about the gravesite. She said there is a very nice spot just beyond the Circle of Lebanon."

The Circle of Lebanon in Highgate Cemetery, perhaps the most fashionable address for the dead in all of London. That would have appealed to Edward.

"That sounds fine. Whatever you think best."

She ticked off another item in her notebook. "Now, what about music?"

What followed was a spirited debate in which I took no part. I tried to appear too grief-stricken to decide, but the truth was, I could not bring myself to care. Edward was gone, there seemed little point in arguing over what the choirboys sang. In the end, my eldest sister, Olivia, prevailed by sheer strength of personality. It did not matter. I never heard the boys sing at all. In the same fashion, I saw the lilies, but I did not smell them. I knew it was cold the day of Edward's funeral because they bundled me into a black astrakhan coat, but I felt nothing. I was entirely numb, as though every nerve, every sense, every cell had simply stopped functioning.

Perhaps it was best that way. I had begun to get snappish and fretful. I had slept poorly since Edward's death, and having no peace, no privacy in my own home was beginning to tell. All I wanted was to bury Edward and send my family home. I loved them, but from a distance. Their quirks and eccentricities, for which we Marches were justly famous, were magnified within the walls of Grey House.

Mercifully, most of them stayed with Father, but a few elected to comfort me in my grief and had moved in, lock, stock and barrel. The least offensive of these was my brother Valerius. A quiet, somewhat sulky youth, he was six years my junior, and I think he found my company marginally less repressive than Father's. Edward's first cousin and heir also gave me little trouble. Simon was sickly and bedridden, afflicted with the same heart complaint that had taken all of his kinsmen. Like Edward he would not make old bones, but it was my lot to care for him until he passed.

The last of my new houseguests was the Ghoul, who had arrived with the expected trunks and a lady's maid half as old as God. Aquinas had installed them in the China Room, which elicited a flurry of complaints. The room was too cold, the exposure too bright—the litany went on and on. I waved my hand, leaving Aquinas to manage, which he did with his customary efficiency. A small heater was installed, the heavy draperies were drawn, and a fresh bottle of gin was placed on the dressing table, sherry having apparently been given up in favor of something more potent. Since then, I had heard nothing from her whatsoever, and I made a note to instruct Aquinas to add a weekly bottle to the household expenses.

But as much as I complained about them, I was glad to have my family around me as I moved through that awful day. I felt like a sleepwalker, being shifted and guided and turned this way and that, but feeling nothing. They told me later that the sermon was lovely. I was glad of that. I had not listened, and I much suspected that the vicar could not possibly have anything comforting to say. He probably quoted Job, that absurd passage about flowers being cut down. They always quote that. And he probably made some innocuous observations about Edward, observations from a man who had not known him. Edward had not been a great believer, nor was I for that matter. We had been brought up to attend when absolutely necessary, and to observe the conventions, but my family was populated with free-thinking Radicals and Edward's was simply lazy.

The end result was, I was certain, a eulogy that could have been spoken over the body of any rich, youngish dead man. I did not like to think of that. I did not like to know that Edward, the boy I had loved and married, was already being lost. He was anonymous to the vicar, to the grave digger, to anyone who passed his grave. No one would remember his charm, his beautiful gilt hair, his sweetly serious smile, his ability to tell jokes, his utter incompetence with wine. I would be the only one to remember him as he truly was, and I did not want to remember him at all.

I tried to imagine, as I stood over his open grave, what I would have carved onto the stone. Nothing seemed appropriate. I ran Bible verses and bits of poetry through my mind as the vicar droned on about ashes and death, but nothing fit. I had a few months yet before they would put the stone in place. They would wait until the ground settled before they brought it. I knew that I had to think of something, some brief commentary on his life, some scrap of wit to sum him up, but that was impossible. Words are simple, Edward had not been.

As I struggled to remember a snippet of Coleridge, a cloud passed over, obscuring the sun and throwing the graveyard into chill shadow. A few of the mourners shivered and Father put his arm about my shoulders. The vicar quickened his pace, cracking through the last prayer. The others bowed their heads, but I looked up, studying the graveyard through the thick black web of my veil. Beyond the grave, where the Circle of Lebanon sheltered its dead, there was a figure, or an impression of one, for all I saw was the dead white of a shirtfront against a tall black form.

I dropped my eyes, telling myself it was a trick of the light, of the veil, that I had seen no one. But of course I had. When I raised my eyes again I saw the figure slipping away through the marble gravestones. No one else had seen him, and he had vanished, silent as a wraith. I might have imagined him, except for the question that burned in my mind.

What had brought Nicholas Brisbane to Highgate Cemetery?

Somehow, I knew I should not like the answer at all.

THE THIRD CHAPTER

And then again, I have been told
Love wounds with heat, as Death with cold.
—Ben Jonson
"Though I Am Young and Cannot Tell"

After the funeral, everyone repaired to March House where Aunt Hermia had conspired with Father's butler, Hoots, to provide an impressive cold buffet and quite a lot of liquor. My relations seemed very pleased with both. And so was I. The more they ate and drank, the less they spoke to me, although I still found myself repeatedly cornered by well-meaning aunts and faintly lecherous cousins. The former doled out advice over shrimp-paste sandwiches while the latter made me dubious proposals of marriage. I thanked the aunts and rebuffed the cousins, but gently. They were an intemperate lot, especially with the amount of spirits Aunt Hermia had offered, and if I offered one of them an insult I had little doubt there would be a duel in the garden by sunrise.

It was a relief when Father finally fetched me to his study.

"Time for the will," he said tersely. "You haven't accepted your cousin Ferdinand, have you?"

He glanced over my shoulder to where Ferdinand was still tipsily proposing marriage to a marble statue of Artemis and her stag, completely unaware of the fact that I had excused myself.

"No, I don't think so."

"I am glad to hear it. He is a famous imbecile. They all are. Marry one of them and I will cut off your allowance."

"I shouldn't marry one of them if you doubled it."

He nodded. "Good girl. I never understood why we Marches always married our cousins in the first place. Bad breeding principle, if you ask me. Concentrates the blood, and God knows we don't need that."

That much was true. Father had been the first to marry out of the March bloodlines and had ten healthy children to show for it, all only mildly eccentric. Most of our relations who had married each other had children who were barking mad. He had strongly encouraged us to marry outside the family, with the result that his grandchildren were the most conventional Marches for three hundred years.

In the study, the solicitor, Mr. Teasdale, was busy perusing a sheaf of papers while my eldest brother, Lord Bellmont, viscount, MP and heir to the family earldom, browsed the bookshelves. He was fingering a particularly fine edition of Plutarch when Father spied him.

"It isn't a lending library," Father snapped. "Buy your own."

Bellmont bowed from the neck to acknowledge he heard Father, nodded once at me, then took a chair near the fire. His manners were usually impeccable, but he hated being barked at by Father. Mr. Teasdale put aside his papers and rose. I offered him my hand.

"My lady, please accept my condolences on your bereavement. I have asked Lord March, as head of the family, and Lord Bellmont, as his heir, to be present while I explain the terms of Sir Edward's will."

I took a seat next to Bellmont and Father took the sofa. He snapped his fingers for his mastiff, Crab, who came lumbering over to lie at his feet, her head on his knee. Mr. Teasdale opened a morocco portfolio and extracted a fresh set of papers, these bound with tape.

"I have here the last will and testament of your late husband, Sir Edward Grey," he began pompously.

My eyes flickered to Father, who gave an impatient sigh.

"English, man, plain English. We want none of your lawyering here."

Mr. Teasdale bowed and cleared his throat. "Of course, your lordship. The disposition of Sir Edward's estate is as follows: the baronetcy and the estate of Greymoor in Sussex are entailed and so devolve to his heir, Simon Grey, now Sir Simon. There are a few small bequests to servants and charities, fairly modest sums that I shall disburse in due course. The residue of the estate, including Grey House and all its contents—furnishings, artworks and equipages, the farms in Devon, the mines in Cornwall and Wales, the railway shares, and all other properties, monies and investments belong to your ladyship."

I stared at him. I had expected a sizable jointure, that much had been in the marriage contract. But the house? The money? The shares? All of these should have rightfully gone with the estate, to Simon.

I licked my lips. "Mr. Teasdale, when you say all other monies—"

He named a sum that made me gasp. The gasp turned into a coughing fit, and by the time Mr. Teasdale had poured me a small, entirely medicinal brandy, I was almost recovered.

"That is not possible. Edward was comfortable, wealthy even, but that much—"

"I understand Sir Edward made some very shrewd investments. His style of living was comparatively moderate for a gentleman who moved in society," Mr. Teasdale began.

"Comparatively moderate? I should say so! Do you know how little he gave me for pin money?" I was beyond furious. Edward had never been niggardly with money. Each quarter he had given me a sum that I had viewed as rather generous.

Generous until I realized he could have easily given me ten times as much and never missed it.

Father's hand stilled on Crab's head. "Do you mean to say that he kept you short? Why did you not come to me?"

His voice was neutral, but I knew he was angry. He was famous for his modern views about women. He favored suffrage, and had even given a rather stirring speech on the subject in the Lords. He made a point of giving each of his daughters an allowance completely independent of his sons-in-law to offer at least a measure of financial emancipation. The very idea that one of his daughters might have been kept on a short lead would gall him.

I shook my head. "No, not really. My pin money was rather a lot, in fact. But there were times, when I wanted to travel or buy something expensive, that I had to ask Edward for the money. I always felt rather like Marie Antoinette in front of the mob when I did, all frivolity and extravagance in the face of sober responsibility. It's just lowering to know that he could have thrown that much to a beggar in the street and never missed it."

Father's hand began to move on Crab's ears once more. She snuffled at his knee, drooling a little. Bellmont stirred beside me.

"Mines in Cornwall. Surely those have played out by now," he said to Teasdale.

Mr. Teasdale smiled. "They are still profitable, I assure you, my lord. Sir Edward would not have kept them were they not. He was entirely unsentimental about investments. He kept nothing that did not keep itself." He turned to me, his manner brisk. I swear he could smell the money in the air. "Now, if your ladyship would care to leave the management of the estate in capable hands, I am sure that their lordships would be only too happy to make the necessary decisions."

"I do not think so," I said slowly.

Beside me, Bellmont stiffened like an offended pointer. "Don't be daft, of course you do. You do not know the first thing about managing an estate of this size. You will want advice."

Father said nothing, but I knew he agreed with me. He would not say so, not now, because he wanted to see if I would stand my ground with Bellmont. Few people ever did. As the eldest son and heir, Bellmont had been entitled since birth, in every sense of the word. Mother had not died until he was almost grown, so he had felt the full force of her far more conventional ideals. It was not until her death, when the raising of the younger children had been left to Father and Aunt Hermia, that the experiments had begun. Bellmont had been sent to Eton and Cambridge. The rest of us had been educated at home by a succession of Radical tutors with highly unorthodox philosophies. Bellmont had never gotten accustomed to thinking of his sisters or his younger brothers as his equals, and of course he had the whole of the English legal, judicial and social systems to back him. He paid lip service to Father's Radical leanings, but when the time came for him to run for Parliament, he had done so as a Tory. Father had refused to speak to him for nearly four years after that, and their relationship still bumped along rockily.

I swallowed hard. "Of course I shall want advice, Bellmont, and I know that you are quite well-informed in such matters," I began carefully. "But I am an independent lady now. I should like very much to make my own decisions."

Bellmont muttered something under his breath. I could not hear it, but I had a strong suspicion Aunt Hermia would not have approved. In spite of Bellmont's elegant demeanor, he was always the one who had contributed the most to the family swear box. The box had been established by Aunt Hermia shortly after she came to live with us. We had fallen into the habit of cursing after a visit by Father's youngest brother, our uncle Troilus, a naval man with a particularly spicy vocabulary. He had taught us any number of new and interesting words and Father had made little effort to curb our fluency, believing that the charm of such words would dissipate with time. It did not. If anything, we grew worse, and by the time Aunt Hermia came to live with us, it was not at all uncommon to hear "damns" and "bloodys" flying thick and fast at the tea table or over the cricket pitch. It only took a day for Aunt Hermia to devise the swear box, which she presented to us at breakfast her second morning at Bellmont Abbey. The rule was that a shilling went into the box every time one of us cursed, with the proceeds counted up once a year and shared among the family. For the most part it worked. We learned that while we could speak more freely in front of Father, Aunt Hermia's sensibilities were more refined, and we curbed our swearing in public almost entirely. Except for Bellmont. The year that he was courting Adelaide we all had a nice seaside holiday at Bexhill on the proceeds.

Now he turned to Father. "You must speak to her. She cannot play with such a sum. If she speculates, she could lose everything. Make her see reason."

Father's hand continued to stroke lazily at Crab's ears. He shrugged. "She has as much common sense as the rest of you. If she wishes to manage her own affairs, under the law, she may."

Bellmont turned to Mr. Teasdale, who shrugged. He had been retained by the family for more than thirty years. He knew better than to involve himself in a family quarrel. He busied himself with papers and tapes, keeping his head down and his eyes firmly fixed on the task at hand.

I put a hand to Bellmont's sleeve. "Monty, I appreciate your concern. I know that you want what is best for me. But I am not entirely stupid, you know. I read the same newspapers that you do. I understand that to purchase a share at a high price and sell it at a low one is unprofitable. I further understand that railways give a better return than canals and that gold mines are risky ventures. Besides," I finished with a smile, "having just acquired a fortune, do you think I am so eager to lose it?"

Bellmont would not be mollified. He shook off my hand, his face stony. "You are a fool, Julia. You know less than nothing about business, and less still about investments. You are not even thirty years old, and yet you think you know as much as your elders."

"Don't you mean my betters?" I asked acidly. He flinched a little. He was always sensitive to criticism that he was playing the lordling.

"I wash my hands of it," he said, his voice clipped. "When you have thrown this money away with both hands and are leading a pauper's life, do not come to me for help."

Father leveled his clear green gaze at Bellmont. "No, I daresay she will come to me if she has need, and I will help her, as I have always helped all of my children."

Bellmont flushed deeply and I winced. It was unkind of Father to needle him so. Bellmont had called upon Father's famous indulgence himself once or twice, but applying for a favor rankled him twice as deeply as it did the rest of us. He felt that, as the eldest and the heir, he should be entirely self-sufficient, which was ludicrous, really. He should and did take his livelihood from the March estate. He oversaw many of the family holdings on Father's behalf, and his future was so deeply entwined with the future of the family that it was impossible to separate them. Even his title was on loan, a courtesy title devolved from Father's estate at Bellmont Abbey. He had nothing to call his own except dead men's shoes, and I think the highly Oedipal flavor of his existence sometimes proved too much for him.

As it did now. His complexion still burnished from his humiliation, he rose, offered us the most perfunctory of courtesies and took his leave, closing the door softly behind him. Bellmont would never create a scene, never slam a door. He was too controlled for that, although I sometimes wondered if a little explosion now and again mightn't be just what he needed. He longed so much for normalcy, for a regular, unremarkable life. We were alike in that respect, both of us rather desperate to be ignored, to be regarded as conventional. We had spent a great deal of time and effort suppressing our inherent strain of wildness. I knew it cost Bellmont deeply. I wondered what it had cost me.

I looked up to find Father smiling down a little at Crab.

"Oh, don't. It's dreadful. I did not mean to hurt his pride—and you ought to be ashamed of yourself. Bellmont cannot abide being made a figure of fun."

"Then he ought not to provide such good sport," Father retorted. He and Mr. Teasdale made a few polite noises at each other and the solicitor, after several more protestations of his willingness to be of service, left us. Father gave me a moment to unbend, but I did not. I kept my gaze fixed upon the window and its rather unpromising view of the garden. For May, it seemed rather unenthusiastic, and I wondered if Whittle was attempting sobriety again. He was a brilliant gardener when inspired by drink, but when he turned temperate, the garden invariably suffered.

"Oh, don't be in a pet, Julia. Monty will come round, he's just having a bit of a difficult patch just now. I remember forty—a hard age. It is the age when a man discovers that he is all that he is ever going to be. Some men are rather pleased at the discovery. I suspect your brother is not."

I shrugged. "I suppose I shall have to take your word for that. But you might be kinder to him, you know. He wants to please you so badly."

Father fixed me with a stern look and I broke, smiling.

"Well, all right, that was a bit thick. But I do think he would like it if you approved of him. It would make life so much simpler."

Father waved a hand. "A simple life is a dull life, my pet. Now, tea? Or something more medicinal, like brandy?"

I shuddered. "Tea, thank you. Brandy always reminds me of the cough preparations Nanny forced us to drink as children."

He rang the bell. "That is because it was brandy. Nanny always said the best remedy for a cough was cherry brandy, taken neat."

That did not surprise me. Nanny had always been one for ladling dubious remedies down our throats. It was a wonder she never poisoned one of us.

Hoots appeared, his long mournful face even more dour in honour of the occasion. Hoots had been with the family for more than forty-five years and often viewed our tragedies as his own. Father gave him the order and we waited in comfortable silence for our refreshment, the quiet broken only by the ticking of the clock and the occasional contented sigh from Crab.

When Hoots reappeared, laden not only with tea, but sandwiches, cakes, bread and butter, and a variety of pastries, we both perked up considerably. So did Crab. She sat politely on her haunches while I poured. I handed Father a plate with an assortment of titbits and laid another for Crab with slivered-ham sandwiches. She ate noisily, her thick tail slapping happily on the carpet. Father toyed with a scone, then cleared his throat.

"I believe that I owe you an apology, Julia."

"For what? The tea is quite good. Cook even remembered a dish of that plum jam I like so well."

"Not the tea, child." He paused and put his cup down carefully, as though weighing his words and the china. "I ought never to have allowed you to marry Edward. I thought you could be happy with him."

I dropped another lump of sugar into my tea and stirred. "I was. I think. At least as happy as I could have been with anyone under the circumstances."

He said nothing, but I could tell from the way he was crumbling his macaroon he was troubled. I forced a smile. "Really, Father. You've nothing with which to reproach yourself. You told me at the time that you had doubts. I am the one who insisted."

He nodded. "Yes, but I have often thought in the years since that I should have done more to prevent it."

A thought struck me then. "Have you talked about it? Within the family?" I remembered Beatrice, bent stiffly over her needlework, not meeting my eyes.

"Yes. Your sisters were concerned for you, especially Bee. The two of you were always so close, I suppose she could sense your unhappiness. She said you never confided in her. I knew that if you had not broached the subject to her or to Portia, that you had not spoken to any of your sisters."

"No, Nerissa is not an easy confidante. Nor Olivia, for that matter. Perfection is a chilly companion."

He grinned in spite of himself. "They can be a bit much, I suppose. But, child, if you were truly unhappy, you should have come to us, any of us."

"To what purpose? I am a March. Divorce would have been out of the question. I offered to release Edward from his marital obligations, but he would not hear of it. So why speak of it at all? Why air our soiled linen for the whole family to see?"

"Because it might have eased your loneliness," he said gently. "Did you never speak to Griggs?"

I put my cup down. I had no taste for the tea now. It had gone bitter in my mouth. "I did. There was nothing to be done. A bit of a shock, really, coming from a family as prolific as ours. You would have thought I could have managed at least one."

Silence fell again, and Father and I both resumed our teacups. It gave us something to do at least. I offered him another scone and he fed Crab a bit of seedcake.

"So, do you mean to keep Valerius with you at Grey House?" he asked finally. I was relieved at the change in subject, but only just. Val was a very sore point with Father and I knew I had best tread carefully.

"For a while at least. And the Ghoul, as well. Aunt Hermia is concerned about the propriety of my sharing a house with Val and Simon without a proper chaperone."

Father snorted. "Simon is bedridden. His infirmity alone should be sufficient chaperone."

I shrugged. "No matter. Aunt Ursula has actually been rather helpful. As soon as she realized that Simon was not expected to live, she settled right in. She reads to him and brings him jellies from the kitchens. They are quite cozy together."

"And Val?" he persisted. "How does he fit into your little menagerie?"

"He comes and goes—goes mostly. I do not see much of him, but that suits us both. And when he is at home, his is quite good company."

Father's brows lifted. "Really? You surprise me."

"Well, he stays in his room and leaves me to myself. He doesn't demand to be entertained. I don't think I could bear that."

"Is he still pursuing his studies?"

I chose my words deliberately. Val's insistence upon studying medicine had been the source of most of his considerable troubles with Father. Had he wanted theoretical knowledge, or even a physician's license, Father might have approved. But becoming a surgeon was no gentleman's wish for his son. It would put Val beyond the pale socially, and close any number of doors for him.

"I am not certain. As I said, I see little of him."

"Hmm. And what is his diagnosis of Simon's condition?" The words were laced with sarcasm, but lightly. Perhaps having Val out of the house was softening his stance.

"Val has not seen him, not medically. Simon is attended by Doctor Griggs. It was only at Griggs' insistence that Simon did not come to the funeral. He would have had himself propped in a Bath chair, but Griggs was afraid the damp air would be too much for him. He continues the same. His heart is failing. It will probably be a matter of months, a year at most, before we bury him as well."

"Has he made his peace with that?"

"I do not know. We have not spoken of it. There will be time yet."

Father nodded and I sipped at my tea. I felt a little better now, but not much. Edward's death had left me with vast financial resources but few personal ones. I had a year of mourning left to endure, and another loss yet to grieve.

"Your Aunt Hermia will expect a sizable donation to her refuge when word of your inheritance becomes public."

I smiled. "She may have it. The refuge is a very worthy enterprise." The refuge was properly known as the Whitechapel Refuge for the Reform of Penitent Women. It was Aunt Hermia's special project, and one that simply gorged itself on money. There was always one more prostitute to feed and clothe and educate, one more bill for candles or smocks or exercise books that demanded to be paid. Aunt Hermia had managed to assemble an illustrious group of patrons who paid generously to support the reformation of prostitutes and their eventual rehabilitation from drudges to proper servants or shopgirls, but even their pockets were not bottomless. She was constantly on the prowl for fresh donors, and I was only too happy to oblige her. She prevailed upon the family to visit occasionally and teach the odd lesson, but I far preferred to send money. It was quite enough that I hired my own staff from her little flock of soiled doves. Enduring Morag was as much as I was prepared to suffer.

"And I am sure a pound or two will find its way into the coffers of the Society of Shakespearean Fellows," I told Father. He beamed. The society was his pet, as the refuge was Aunt Hermia's. It mostly consisted of a group of aging men writing scholarly papers about the playwright and scathing commentaries on everyone else's papers. There was a good deal of re-crimination and sometimes even violence at their monthly meetings. Father enjoyed it very much.

"Thank you, my dear. I shall dedicate my current paper to you. It concerns the use of classical allusion in the sonnets. Did you know—"

And that is the last that I heard. Father was entirely capable of wittering on about Shakespeare until doomsday. I sipped at my tea and let him talk, feeling rather drowsy. The numbness of the morning had worn away and I was simply bone tired. I drained the last sip of tea and went to replace it on the saucer.

But as I put it down, I noticed the spent tea leaves, swirled high onto the cup, curved perfectly into the shape of a serpent. I was no student of tasseomancy. I could not remember what the coil of a serpent meant. But we had known Gypsy fortune-tellers in Sussex, and I had had my future read in the leaves many times. I did not think that snakes were pleasant omens. I shrugged and tried to listen politely to Father.

It was weeks before I troubled myself to discover what the serpentine tea leaves actually foretold. By that time, though, the danger was already at hand.

THE FOURTH CHAPTER

Murder most foul, as in the best it is,
But this most foul, strange, and unnatural.
—William Shakespeare
Hamlet

My family lasted only as long as the funeral baked meats and libation held out. As soon as the platters were emptied and the decanters drained, they left, and Father took me back to Grey House. It looked different now, with its mourning wreaths and hatchments, muffled door knocker and shuttered windows. The mirrors and servants were draped in black crepe—not a particularly useful or attractive addition in either case. It was the most depressing homecoming I had ever known, and as the door shut solidly behind Father, I felt like the Mistletoe Bride.

Thank goodness for Morag. She took one look at my woeful face, handed me an enormous whiskey and put me straight to bed. I had taken a little chill at the funeral, and for a day or so I luxuriated in blissful irresponsibility. Morag brought me meals on trays, nothing heavy or complicated, but simple, well-cooked dishes suited to my feeble appetite. She instructed Aquinas to turn away all callers and even refused to bring me the daily avalanche of mourning correspondence that continued to descend upon Grey House. The only letters she permitted me to read were those from my family, relations too far or too infirm to make the journey to London for the funeral.

Unlike most letters of condolence, these were little master-pieces of originality, full of private family jokes and bits of news calculated to amuse rather than to comfort. My brother Ly sent a highly irreverent epic poem that he had dashed off in the warmth of the Italian sun while sipping a good deal of red wine. His traveling companion, my brother Plum, sent a tiny sketch of me in mourning, with black lace butterfly wings folded in grief. Morag found me weeping over both of them and ruthlessly swept them away with all the other correspon-dence she had forbidden me.

"You'll have time enough to deal with that lot when you're well," she told me severely. "Now finish your pudding and I will read you summat of *Ivanhoe*." I did as I was told. It was just like being back in the nursery—dumplings and pots of milky tea, knightly stories and flannel-wrapped bricks. I was sorely tempted to remain there for my entire year of mourning.

But eventually the tedium defeated me. I finally rose out of boredom, put on my widow's weeds, submitted myself to Morag's stunningly bad hairdressing, and went downstairs to begin answering my correspondence.

And if I had expected that to relieve the boredom, I was entirely mistaken. Unlike those written by my family, these notes were invariably brief and unimaginative. They read like a series of practical applications in a guide to writing letters for all occasions, with the same phrases of hollow sympathy running through them all. I suppressed a snort. The senti-ments were kindly meant, but these were the very people who would conveniently forget my existence now that I had no husband. It was an awkward business having a widow to dinner, so they would not. When my year of mourning was ended and I could respectably accept invitations, they would mean to ask me, but then someone would point out that I had inherited quite a lot of money and some nervous mama would remember the ugly little spinster she had not yet managed to pry out of her nursery and I would be struck from the list—not out of any personal dislike, but as a simple matter of mathematics. There were not enough gentlemen to go around for the young ladies as it was. Why lessen their chances further by tossing a personable young widow with a sizable purse into the mix? I had seen it happen too often to think that I would be an exception. No, once my year of mourning was finished, I would count myself lucky to be invited to Bellmont's house for dinner.

I pushed the letters aside and considered my situation. It was not a pleasant exercise. I had a home, but it was a draughty, gloomy sort of place now that I was alone. It had always been Edward's home rather than mine, and had always reflected his personality. With his charm stripped away, it was a shell, and a theatrical one at that. Edward's taste had been grander than mine, and all of the rooms had been decorated thematically. From the breakfast room with its birdcage stripes, to the drawing room with its Wedgwood-blue walls, Edward had expressed himself exuberantly. There had been no room left for my personality. Even my bedroom and boudoir had been decorated for me, as a wedding present from Edward. They were Grecian, all white marble and blue hangings. The effect was beautiful, but cold, rather like Edward himself, I thought disloyally.

Only my tiny study, tucked at the back of the house, an afterthought, had been left to my whims. I had brought in an elderly red sofa from March House, its velvet beginning to shred at the seams. There were needlepoint cushions embroidered by my legion of aunts, a cozy armchair that had been my mother's. The pictures were not particularly good; Edward had commented with wry humour that they were just the thing for an old cottage in the Cotswolds. They were landscapes and portraits of animals, things I had found in the lumber rooms at Bellmont Abbey. They were not valuable, but they reminded me of the country where I had grown up, and I often found myself daydreaming my way into them, walking the painted green hills or petting the fluffy sheep. It was absurdly sentimental of me, but I was deeply attached to Sussex and the memories of my childhood. My mother had died when I was young, but the rest of my life there had been easy and uncomplicated. It was only in London where things seemed difficult.

So, aside from my untidy little bolt-hole, I did not much like my house. Of course, I still had my family, I thought with some cheer. Ranging from the mildly odd to the wildly eccentric, they were some comfort. I knew that they loved me deeply, but I also knew that they understood me not at all. I had never fought a duel or run away with my footman or ridden a horse naked into Whitehall—all acts for which Marches were infamous. I did not even keep a pet monkey or wear turbans or dye my dogs pink. I lived quietly, conventionally, as I had always wanted, and I think I had been something of a disappointment to them.

That left my health and my fortune—both of which could disappear overnight as I had seen often enough. I rubbed at my eyes. I was becoming cynical, and not doing much for my state of mind, either. I put my head down on the desk.

"Darling, is it really so awful?" called a voice from the doorway. I looked up.

"Portia. I did not know you were here."

"I told Aquinas not to announce me. I wanted to surprise you."

My sister entered, trailing black scarves and feathers and a cloud of musky rose perfume. She was the only woman I knew who could make mourning look glamorous. She settled herself into Mother's armchair, cradling her ancient pug against her chest.

"Did you have to bring that revolting creature?"

She pulled a face and nuzzled him. "You shouldn't speak so of Mr. Pugglesworth. He quite likes you."

"No, he doesn't. He bit me last month, remember?"

Portia clucked at me. "Nonsense. That was a love nibble. He loves his Auntie Julia, don't you, darling?" She cooed at him for a minute, then settled him onto my favorite cushion.

"Oh, Portia, please. Not that cushion. He's flatulent."

"Don't be horrid, Julia. Puggy is nothing of the sort."

I put my head back down on my desk. "Why did you come?"

"Because I knew you would be contemplating suicide in some highly uncreative fashion and I wanted to help."

I raised my head just enough to see her. "No, not yet. But I will confess to being completely anguished. Portia, what am I to do?"

She leaned forward, her March-green eyes sparkling. Portia had always been the most beautiful of my sisters, and she knew just how to use her charms to greatest effect.

"You can begin by leaving off the self-pity. It is unbecoming," she said, her tone faintly reproving. "And don't pout, either. I tell you these things because someone must. You have had a chance to accustom yourself to Edward's loss. It is time you admitted it is not a crushing blow."

I sighed and rested my chin in my hands. "I know. It just feels so awful, so disloyal to admit that I actually feel rather liberated by it."

"Not at all. How do you think I felt when Bettiscombe died?"

"A bit of a different situation, I think," I put in, remembering her aging, infirm husband. "It was a merciful release when Bettiscombe passed away. He'd been malingering for years."

"So had Edward," she said, a trifle acidly. "We both married sickly men, my darling. The only difference was that we all thought Bettiscombe was hypochondriacal."

He had been, poor thing. Always taking his temperature and palpating his pulse. He had been forty-five when Portia married him, and he had seemed robust enough at the time. We all thought his throat drops and chest plasters a charming affectation. But during their first winter together at his home in Norfolk, he had taken a chill and promptly died, leaving Portia a rich widow of twenty.

Of course, Portia was not quite as distraught as she might have been. In London, Bettiscombe had been charming and waggish, ready for any jape, so long as he was well wrapped against draughts. In the country, he was a perfect mouse, rising at six and retiring by eight. He fretted over everything without the whirl of London distraction, and had left Portia too often in the company of his spinster cousin and poor relation, Jane. He died before the true nature of their relationship became apparent, and Portia lost no time in returning to London and bringing dear Jane with her to set up house together in the elegant town house Bettiscombe had left her. I knew my widowhood should not prove half so interesting to my family as Portia's had.

"But you must have felt a tiny prickle of guilt," I prodded her. Portia frowned. She never liked to be reminded of things she had tucked neatly away.

"Not guilt, not precisely," she said slowly. "It was rather more complicated than that. But I had my sweet Jane for compensation. And I think you would do rather better if you counted your own advantages rather than mooning about trying to convince yourself that you have lost your one true love."

"Portia, that is unspeakably cruel."

Her eyes were sympathetic, but her manner was brisk. "I know that you wish to mourn Edward. He was a lovely person and we were all quite fond of him. But the man you buried was not the child you played with. Do not make the mistake of climbing into his grave and forgetting to live the rest of your life."

My fingers were cramping and I realized that my hands were clenched. I rose. "Portia, I do not wish to speak of this now. Not to you, not to anyone. I shall conduct myself as I see fit, not to please you or Father or anyone else," I finished grandly. I swept to the door.

"Hoorah," she said softly, still not moving from Mother's chair. "The little mouse is beginning to roar."

I slammed the door behind me.

I spent the rest of the day in a high sulk, pouting about the evil treatment I had received at my sister's hands and trying not to think about the possibility that she might have been correct. Edward had been my friend and companion when we were children together in Sussex. Our fathers' estates had marched together, and Edward and his young cousin, Simon, had often joined in our games and theatricals and expeditions about the countryside. Like all of my sisters, I had come out into society, but I alone had held myself aloof from the few timid advances that had come my way. I suppose, having been raised on stories of knightly adventures and chivalric endeavors, I had been waiting for my very own storybook hero. But it seemed rather heroic when Edward left off of squiring some lissome beauty about the dance floor and came to sip punch with me where I sat by the potted palms. I was not like the other girls; I had no frivolous conversation or pretty tricks to win suitors. I had forthrightness and plainspoken manners. I had a good mind and a sharp tongue, and I was cruel enough to use them as weapons to keep the cads and rogues at bay. As for the young men I might have liked to partner me, I was far better at re-pelling than attracting. I did not swoon or carry a vinaigrette or turn squeamish at the mention of spiders. Father had raised us to scorn such feminine deceptions. Like my brothers, I wanted to talk about good books and urgent politics, new ideas and foreign places. But the young men I met did not like that. They wanted pretty dolls with silvery giggles and empty heads.

All except Edward. He always seemed perfectly content to sit with me, or even dance with me at considerable risk to his toes. We talked for hours of things other young men would never discuss. People began to talk, linking our names in gossip, and finally, during one particularly painful waltz, Edward smiled down at me and asked me to marry him.

I thought about it for a week. I considered hard whether or not I even wanted to marry. Father said little, but pointed me to the shelf in his library where he housed John Stuart Mill, Mary Wollstonecraft and even, shockingly, some Annie Besant. It was highly discouraging. There were few advantages to marriage for a woman. But there were fewer advantages to spinsterhood. I had already grown tired of the careful whispers behind the fans and the avid eyes that followed me. I was certain that they were saying that I was not the beauty my sisters were, that I would not marry as well as they. Those whispers and glances would follow me the rest of my life if I did not marry, speculating on what frightfulness of mine had driven away any potential suitors. I could not bear that. I was already conscious of how much we were talked about, of how amusing we were to society and how closely to the pale of respectability we walked. Only Father's close association with the queen and the very ancientness of our lineage preserved us from becoming a complete joke. What I longed for most was normalcy—a quiet, average marriage in an unremarkable home where I could raise my perfectly normal children. That notion was more seductive to me than diamonds. And as a married woman I could travel more easily, have male friends without exciting suspicion, have my own home away from a family that was as maddening as they were delightful. A bit of quiet space to call my own, that is what marriage represented to me.

So I accepted Edward on a chilly night early in spring. Father gave his blessing with the proviso that I spend the summer accompanying Aunt Cressida on her travels. It was the only thing he asked of me, and Edward agreed readily enough. He spent the summer with friends in Sussex while I toured the Lake District with a cranky old woman and her assorted cats. Edward and I were married that December in London. I think I was a happy bride. All I could ever remember afterward were the terrible nerves. I dropped things—my bouquet, the pen for the register—and as I came out of the church, I heard a rooster crow, very bad luck for a bride on her wedding day. For a moment I wondered if it was indeed an omen. But then I looked up into Edward's smiling face and I realized how foolish I was. Edward was my friend, my childhood companion. He was no stranger to me. How could I fear marriage to him?

In the end, there was nothing to fear. No great tragedies. Just the small troubles, the little tragedies that can dull a marriage and cause it to fray. We had no child, Edward's health began to fail, we began to follow our own pursuits and spent less and less time together. Edward was pernickety, something I had noted before, but never considered in the context of our life together. It meant that things must be just so for him to be happy. The decoration of the house, the cut of my clothes, the folding of the towels, the laying of the table. I laughed at first and tried to jolly him out of it, but he grew stubborn, and after a while I realized it was easier to let him have his way. The house was kept the way he liked it, my clothes were ordered from his dead mother's dressmaker, in colours he favored that I knew suited me not at all. But it made him happy, and I cared so little. It was easy to convince myself that these things did not matter. We had been married a few years by the time I caught a glimpse of myself in the glass and realized I did not know my own reflection. I was losing myself a bit at a time, and I did not know how to get it back. My only refuge was my study, where I kept my favorite books and furniture discarded from my father's homes. In that room I wore an old dressing gown that Edward detested. He learned not to come there, and I learned to lock myself in when I needed to feel like Julia March again, if only for a little while. It was my little den, my nest of comforts for when I felt unruly and savage and found myself itching to rebel against the normality I had thought I wanted. I went there and calmed myself and found peace in letting him have his way yet again. I was always afraid that if I stood my ground, if I argued for scarlet gowns or purple velvet draperies, I would slip too far down the path toward the very thing I was trying to avoid. There was too much colour in being a March, and Edward, with my willing assistance, did all that he could to paint my life beige.

I think, too, that perhaps I gave way so often because I knew that he would not live long. There was always a sense of waiting in our house, watching for the final attack, for a worsening of his symptoms, for the time when the doctor must be called and preparations made. It had made for an uneasy life, and I dreaded the idea that I should have to live it all again with Simon. True, he was not my husband, but I did love him dearly, like another brother, and to know that his time would be so short was almost more than I could bear. A year at most, the doctor had said. And so little to be done for him in the meanwhile.

But what of afterward? I wondered as I sat in my study, contemplating my mourning. What would become of me then? The life I had fashioned for myself as Edward's wife seemed intolerably small now. And in spite of its size, Grey House suffocated me. The air was dead as a tomb, and the rooms full of memories that I did not wish to preserve. How then to break free of them?

The Ghoul could be persuaded to leave in search of more intimately connected bereavements. Val could simply be told to take rooms for himself or return to Father's. Grey House would be empty, those enormous rooms echoing coldly. It was big, far too big for a childless widow. I could sell it and purchase a much smaller house, something still near to the park, but on a quieter street. Something elegant and discreet, with a tiny staff, perhaps only Aquinas and Morag, with Cook and a pair of maids and Diggory, the coachman. The battalion of maids that it took to run Grey House could be gotten new places. The footmen were a useless extravagance, they too could be given good characters and let go.

The more I considered the idea, the more excited I became. I found myself walking the rooms of Grey House mentally cataloging what pieces I would take with me and which I would send to the auction house, or perhaps sell with the house itself. There was little I wanted. Almost every painting or piece of furniture carried Edward's stamp. I wanted to start afresh, with new things I had chosen for myself. It would take a while to settle matters, I realized. Grey House had so many rooms, all fitted with costly furnishings. To arrange for it all to be sold and to fit out a new house could take months. Months I might spend more profitably abroad, I decided. I could shop for new pieces in Paris and Italy, taking a leisurely tour of the Continent as I went. I had been to Paris before, but never beyond, and the notion of Europe tantalized me. So many shops and museums, so much culture and beauty. Opera, paintings, books, concerts, the ideas spun me around and dizzied me. I could take as long as I liked. And to make matters simpler, my brothers Ly and Plum were still traveling in Italy, having discovered that two could live as cheaply there as one could in London. They were artists, one a poet and composer, the other a painter. They would provide me with companionship, sympathy, laughter. And when I needed to be alone, I could simply move on—Perugia, Rome, Capri, Florence—the possibilities were endless. I need not even plan my return, but simply take things as they came, wandering idly from city to city as my fancy took me. The very idea was more intoxicating than any spirit I had ever drunk.

Stealthily, I raided Edward's library for every book I could find on Italy. I pored over maps, plotting out a dozen different itineraries. I read lives of saints and politicians and princesses and made endless lists of verbs to memorize and temples to visit. Within a few days, I was drunk with Italy and starting to recover quite nicely from the shock of Edward's death. I knew that I had not come to terms with the vastness of it yet, but I also knew that grief takes its own time. I would distract myself with plans and projects, and would pass my first year of mourning with purposeful occupation. And at the end of it, I believed I would be able to think of Edward with something like fondness, perhaps even nostalgia.

Of course, nothing like that happened, but I do not entirely blame myself. I think I might have pottered along quite civilly had Nicholas Brisbane not come to call. It was a week after the funeral and I was in my study, valiantly trying to twist my tongue and pen around an irregular verb, when Aquinas scratched at the door.

I bade him enter and he did, bearing a salver with a caller's card. I glanced at it and felt myself flush with guilt. I had meant to write to Mr. Brisbane and thank him for his prompt resourcefulness during Edward's collapse. At first I simply put it off, dreading the task. After that I had forgotten, enchanted as I was with my paper Italy.

I told Aquinas to show him in at once. I dashed the pen into its holder and thrust my untidy papers into the book of Italian grammar. I was just scrabbling the last stray lock of hair into my snood when Aquinas reappeared with Mr. Brisbane.

I rose, moving around the desk to bid him welcome. I was conscious then of the plainness of the room, its tattered edges that seemed even shabbier when compared to his impeccable tailoring. He was dressed in a town suit that had been cut by a master's hand; his black leather boots were highly polished, and in his hand he carried an ebony cane, its silver head resting in the hollow of his hand.

"Mr. Brisbane—" I began, but he raised a gloved hand.

"You must permit me to apologize before anything else," he said, his expression inscrutable. "I know full well the indelicacy of calling upon so new a widow, and you must believe that I would not intrude upon your grief were the matter not one of extreme importance."

My eyes flew to the desk, stacked high with traveling books, and I felt myself grow warm. "Of course, Mr. Brisbane. I must apologize for my own incivility." I waved him to the chair and perched myself on the edge of the sofa. He seated himself as a cat will, lightly, with an air of suspended motion that seemed to indicate wariness and an ability to move quite quickly if circumstances demanded. His hat and gloves rested in his lap. He kept the walking stick in his hand, rolling the head in his palm.

I rushed to speak. "I neglected to write to you, to thank you for your dispatch and your resourcefulness the night my husband—" I paused, searching for a word that was neither too vague nor too indelicate "—collapsed," I finished. It was a weak sort of word, one I would not have chosen had I been speaking to anyone else.

But something about Nicholas Brisbane intimidated me. It was ridiculous that this man, about whom I knew nothing, whose birth and circumstances were likely inferior to my own, should cause me to be so unsettled. Without thinking, I smoothed my skirts over my lap, conscious of the careless creases. He was watching me, coolly, as if looking through a microscope at a mildly distasteful specimen. I lifted my chin, attempting aloofness, but I am certain I did not manage it.

"Do not think of it, I beg you," he said finally, settling back more comfortably in his chair. "I was gratified to have been of some small service to Sir Edward in his time of need."

I could hear Aquinas, thumping things about in the hall. Like all good butlers, he was usually cat-footed about his work. His noises were a signal to me that he was within earshot if I needed him.

"Would you care for some refreshment, Mr. Brisbane? Tea?"

He waved a lazy hand. His gestures were indolent ones, but affectedly so. He might wear the mantle of the idle London gentleman, but I had seen with my own eyes that he could move quickly enough if the situation warranted action. I found it curious, though, that he adopted a pose of sorts.

Without the prospect of tea to look forward to, I was at a loss. I knew it was my responsibility to introduce a topic of respectable conversation, but in that interminable moment, my breeding failed me. The only event we had in common was the one of which we had already spoken and could not possibly speak of again. Mr. Brisbane seemed comfortable with the silence, but I was not. It reminded me of the endless chess games I used to play with my father when one or the other of us invariably forgot it was our turn and we sat, ossifying, until we realized that we were actually supposed to move.

In fact, the more I studied Mr. Brisbane, the more he resembled a chess king. Polished and hard, with a certain implacable dignity. He was darker than any man I knew, with storm-black eyes and a head of thick, waving hair to match that would have made Byron prickle with jealousy.

But my scrutiny did not amuse him. He arched a brow at me, imperious as an emperor. I was mightily impressed. He did it much better than Aunt Hermia.

"My lady, are you quite well?"

"Quite," I managed feebly, trying to think of a convincing lie. "I have not been sleeping very well."

"Understandable, I am sure," he offered. He paused, then sat forward in his chair with the air of a man who has just made up his mind to do something unpleasant, but necessary.

"My lady, I have not come solely to offer my condolences. I have come to deliver news that I feel will certainly be unwelcome, but must be related nonetheless."

My stomach began to ache and I regretted missing luncheon. Whatever Mr. Brisbane had to tell me, I was quite certain I did not want to hear it.

"My lady, what do you know of me?"

The question caught me unawares. I struggled a moment, trying to reconcile gossip with decorum. What I had heard, and what I could repeat, were not always the same thing.

"I believe you are a detective of sorts. A private inquiry agent. I have heard that you solve problems."

His mouth twisted, but I could not tell if it was meant to be a smile or a grimace. "Among other things. I returned to London two years ago. Since then, I have enjoyed some success in disposing of matters of a delicate nature for people who do not care to share their difficulties with the Metropolitan Police. Last year, I decided to set myself up in business formally. I have no offices as such, nor is there a sign proclaiming my profession at my rooms in Chapel Street. There are simply discreet referrals from clients who have availed themselves of my services and been pleased with the result."

I nodded, understanding almost nothing of what he said. The words made sense, but I could not imagine what they had to do with me.

"The reason I am here today, my lady, is because one of those clients was your late husband, Sir Edward Grey."

I took his meaning at once. I bit my lip, mortified.

"Oh, I am so sorry. My husband's solicitors are handling the disposition of his accounts. If you will apply to Mr. Teasdale, he will be only too happy to settle—"

"I do not require money from you, my lady, only answers." He cast a glance toward the open door. Aquinas was careful to leave no shadow across the threshold, but I fancied he was not far away. Mr. Brisbane must have sensed it as well, for when he spoke, his voice was a harsh whisper.

"Have you considered the possibility that your husband was murdered?"

I sat, still as a frightened rabbit. "You have a cruel sense of humour, Mr. Brisbane," I said through stiff lips. I thought again of Aquinas lingering in the hall. I had only to call him and he would remove Mr. Brisbane from my house. He was no match for Mr. Brisbane's inches, but he could enlist the footmen to throw him bodily out the door.

"It is no jest, my lady, I assure you. Sir Edward came to me, a fortnight or so before he died. He was anxious, fearful even."

"Fearful of what?"

"Death. He was in mortal fear for his life. He believed that someone intended to murder him."

I shook my head. "Impossible. Edward had no enemies."

Brisbane's cool expression did not waver. "He had at least one, my lady. An enemy who sent him threatening letters through the post."

I swallowed thickly. "That is untrue. Edward would have told me."

He remained silent, giving me the time to work it out for myself. I did finally, and it was horrible.

"You think that I sent them? Is that what I am to infer?"

He made a brief gesture of dismissal. "I considered the possibility, naturally. But Sir Edward assured me that it was unthinkable. And now, having met you…"

"I do not believe you, Mr. Brisbane. If Edward did receive such letters, where are they?"

His expression was pained. "I encouraged Sir Edward to leave them with me for safekeeping. He refused. I do not know what has become of them. Perhaps he locked them up or gave them to his solicitor. Perhaps he even destroyed them, although I implored him not to."

"You expect me to believe this fairy story of yours when you can offer not the slightest particle of proof?"

He spoke slowly, as one does to a backward child. "Perhaps your ladyship will be good enough to consider the fact that I was present at Grey House when Sir Edward collapsed. I came at Sir Edward's request. I suggested to him that if I had an opportunity to observe his closest acquaintances I could offer him some notion as to who might be responsible for the letters and for the threat implicit within them."

"Your name was not on the list," I remembered suddenly. "I sent you no invitation card. How did you gain entrance that night?"

"Sir Edward let me in himself."

"Can you prove this?" I asked evenly.

There was the barest flush at his brow, probably of irritation. "I cannot. There was no one present except ourselves. We had arranged that I would come a few minutes early. He wanted to give me the lay of the land, so to speak."

"And no one saw you with Edward? No one can corroborate your tale?"

His lips thinned and I realized that he was holding on to his temper with difficulty. "My lady, my clients come to me because my reputation for integrity and probity is completely unsullied. I had no reason to wish your husband ill, I can assure you." For the first time I heard the faintest trace of an accent in his voice. Scottish perhaps, given his surname, but whatever it was he had clearly taken great pains to conceal it. I took it as a measure of his emotion that it crept out in his speech now.

"And yet, I am not assured, Mr. Brisbane. My husband is dead, of quite natural causes, according to the doctor who treated him all of his life. I have the certificate that states it plainly. But you would come in here, intruding upon the freshest grief, venting accusations so vile I cannot possibly credit them. You can offer me no proof except your good name, and you expect me to find that sufficient. Tell me, Mr. Brisbane, what was your true purpose in coming here?"

His flush had ebbed, leaving him paler than before. He had mastered his temper as well, and his manner was cool again.

"I sought only to right a wrong, my lady. If your husband was murdered, justice should be meted out to the guilty."

"And you would be paid to find them, would you not? You present impeccable motives to me, Mr. Brisbane, but I think you play at a more lucrative game."

His eyes narrowed sharply. "What do you mean, my lady?"

"I think you hope to profit, Mr. Brisbane. If I engage you to finish the task you claim my husband presented you, you will be handsomely paid, I have no doubt. And if I do not wish your allegations to appear in the newspapers, you will expect payment for that as well, I expect."

That stung him. He rose, not quickly as I had expected, but with a slow, purposeful motion that was more frightening than a display of anger would have been. His eyes never left my face as he stood over me, drawing on his gloves and shooting his cuffs.

"If you were a man, your ladyship, I would cordially horse-whip you for that remark. As you are not, I will simply bid you farewell and leave you to your fresh and obviously debilitating grief." He said this last with a contemptuous glance at the Italian books piled on my desk and strode from the room.

I heard the murmur of voices as Aquinas showed him out, and then the resounding thud of the door itself. I felt rather proud of myself for my spirited defense. Father was always claiming that I was too reticent, too easily cowed for his taste. Mr. Brisbane had confronted me with something too awful to contemplate, and I had met him squarely.

I returned to my verbs with a sense of vindication and triumph I had seldom felt. But I noted as I wrote out the words that my hand shook, and after that I was never able to think of that day without the creeping certainty that I had made a dangerous mistake.

THE FIFTH CHAPTER

This busy, puzzling stirrer-up of doubt,
That frames deep mysteries, then finds 'em out.
—John Wilmot, Earl of Rochester
"A Satire Against Mankind"

"Of course you did the right thing, darling. Nicholas Brisbane is the sort of man one takes to bed, and since, clearly, that is not the sort of thing *you* would do…" Portia's voice trailed off, but her meaning was explicit. I was not daring enough; I lacked the dash and the spirit to bed a man I barely knew.

"You would not take him to bed, either," I reminded her sulkily.

"Yes, but for a very different reason. Jane would never forgive me if I went back with men. And I did promise her to remain faithful. You, on the other hand, do not engage in the Sapphic pleasures, so you would be perfectly free to avail yourself of Mr. Brisbane's considerable charms and expertise."

I glanced around furtively. The footpaths in Hyde Park, when deserted, provide excellent opportunities for privileged conversation. But Portia's voice was carrying, and I feared eavesdroppers.

She slapped at my arm lightly, then looped hers through mine. "I was right to call you a little mouse. There is no one about for miles."

That much was true. I had arranged our meeting for eleven

o'clock in the morning, long past the hour when fashionable society exercised itself on the horse paths. There were a few children about with their vigilant nursemaids, but they were far away, near the Serpentine. I could scarcely hear the shouts of the children at play.

"I still have not forgiven you for calling me that," I reminded her.

"Duly noted, my pet. But I am your elder sister. It is my duty to abuse you when necessary."

We shared a little smile and both of us knew she was forgiven. I could never stay angry with Portia for long. Particularly not when I needed her.

"What do you mean 'expertise'?" I asked suddenly. She lifted her brows meaningfully.

"Dearest, you must come to one of my card parties. Caroline Pilkington is the most revolting gossip. As long as she is winning, she will tell you simply everything."

I stared at Portia, remembering Caroline's ample hips and fleshy arms. I could not picture them twined with Mr. Brisbane's. He had seemed so urbane, so groomed and fastidious, that I could not credit him willingly engaged in any intimacy with a woman who was famous for changing her underlinen only once each month.

"Do you mean that Mr. Brisbane and Caro Pilkington—"

"Don't be daft. Her sister Mariah, the pretty one, apparently had a very brief liaison with him. Her husband objected and Brisbane graciously withdrew. Apparently it was all quite gentlemanly. Horace approached him at the club, stated his case, Brisbane agreed, and they shared a cigar and a glass of brandy together. Brisbane broke it off that very evening. Mariah was bereft, according to Caro. She's had scores of lovers and says he was quite something extraordinary. Apparently, he uses disguises sometimes in the course of his investigations. In his liaison with Mariah, he used them for discretion. He came to her once dressed as a chimney sweep. Quite invigorating, don't you think?"

I felt flushed, in spite of the coolness of the morning. "That may well be, but it is considerably off the subject. I need advice."

Portia stopped walking and turned to face me, her expression stern. "No, Julia, you need adventure. You need a lover, a holiday abroad. You need to cut your hair and swim naked in a river. You need to eat things you have never even seen before and speak languages you do not know. You need to kiss a man who makes you feel like your knees have turned to water and makes your heart feel as though it would spring from your chest."

Her eyes were so earnest that I burst out laughing. "I think you have been at my romantic novels again."

"And what if I have? You went from Father's house to Edward's, knowing nothing. You have spent the past five years married to a man who barely acknowledged your existence in his house and who certainly did not provide you with an exciting bedmate. You are free now, rich and healthy and quite handsome. *Do* something with yourself or you will regret it for the rest of your life."

"I had thought of going to Italy," I said hesitantly.

She snorted. "Italy. To point at the statues and buy out the shops? I am not talking about simply a holiday abroad. I am talking about seizing your life and truly living it before it is too late."

She knew me too well. "I am not such a wallflower. I sent Mr. Brisbane off with a flea in his ear," I defended.

"Nicholas Brisbane is an adventure unto himself, Julia. Far too dangerous for you to handle, I can assure you. You were quite right to send him away. If I were not so devoted to Jane, I should be quite intrigued by him myself. You know, absolutely no one knows where he comes from. It is a very great mystery."

"I should think he comes from Mr. and Mrs. Brisbane, wherever and whoever they might be."

"Don't be so literal, dearest. Apparently, he is very great friends with the Duke of Aberdour. The old gentleman sponsored him into his clubs the season before last. But no one knows why. Does he have some hold over Aberdour? Is he the bastard son no one ever suspected? It is quite possible that he is a Scot, given his connection with Aberdour, although no one really knows. Welsh, perhaps? A Savoyard count with a dark past full of misdeeds? Is he a Bonaparte prince in disguise, biding his time until he can claim his throne? It is all quite thrilling, don't you think?"

"It is not thrilling, it is disgraceful. Imagine anyone accusing the sweet old Duke of Aberdour of foisting his bastard on society. And as for being a Bonaparte prince, that is the most ridiculous thing I have ever heard."

Portia snorted. "You have never met Aberdour. *Sweet* isn't the word. And no, I do not really think Mr. Brisbane is a prince, but there is something quite intriguing about him, the tiniest bit uncivilized—like a lion in a zoo. I can well imagine him the descendant of bloodthirsty Corsicans. And he would look rather well in an emperor's robes."

"Why do you think him dangerous?"

"That business last year with Lord Northrup's son." She paused and I looked at her blankly. "Goodness, Julia, will you never learn to listen to gossip? It can be quite useful. Apparently, Northrup's youngest son was cheating at cards. At first he won only modest amounts, nothing to raise too many suspicions. But then he began to be greedy. He started playing for much higher stakes, winning conspicuously. He ruined the Bishop of Winchester's nephew. Someone, perhaps the bishop, engaged Mr. Brisbane to sort it out."

"What happened then?"

"Mr. Brisbane managed to get himself invited into a game

where Northrup's son was playing. Young Northrup won, and Mr. Brisbane immediately charged him with cheating. The young scoundrel had no choice. He challenged Brisbane to a duel and the particulars were arranged."

"A duel? That is illegal," I put in. Portia rolled her eyes.

"Of course it is illegal. And highly dangerous. That is what makes it interesting, ninny. They met at dawn, with pistols. They paced off the proper distance, turned, and Brisbane fired first, clipping young Northrup's curls just over his ear."

"And then?"

"Are you quite all right? You look flushed. Are you over-warm?"

I felt a spasm of irritation. She could not see my complexion through my veil. She was simply trying to draw out the tale, larding the suspense. Although, now that she mentioned it, I did feel a trifle hot.

"I am fine, Portia. Get on with it."

She shrugged. "Well, it was young Northrup's turn to fire, but he thought to provoke a retraction from Brisbane instead. He pointed his pistol at him and told him that if Brisbane would withdraw the accusation, he would not fire. Julia, you are breathing quite fast. I am concerned for you."

I took her firmly by the arm. "Finish the story."

"Very well. Brisbane refused."

"No!"

"He did. He stared down the barrel of young Northrup's pistol and said, 'You are a cheater and a scoundrel and I will say so, even with my dying breath,' or something like that. He stood square to little Northrup, and the young man could not fire at him. He discharged his weapon in the air and left in disgust."

I dropped my hand. "But Northrup might have killed him."

"That is why I said he was dangerous," she said gravely. "A man who cares so little for his own mortality might well play loose with someone else's." Her expression turned mischievous. "But it does make for a rather dashing story, doesn't it? Can't you just see him there, the mist swirling about his legs, the sun just beginning to rise, burnishing his ebony hair…"

I poked at her with the end of my parasol. "Do be serious, Portia. I think I may have made a mistake in sending him away."

Portia sobered. "No, dearest. Nicholas Brisbane is a complicated man. You need simplicity for a while. You must be selfish and think of happy, easy things—like new shoes and a good set of furs."

I opened my mouth to protest, but she went on.

"And as for the threatening letters, I am inclined to think our deliciously devilish Mr. Brisbane was telling the truth. Edward probably annoyed someone at the club with a silly prank and they decided to pay him back in kind."

I felt dizzy with relief. "Of course! That must have been it. A prank that Edward did not recognize for a jest. Then Mr. Brisbane was acting in sincerity," I finished, feeling rather miserable. If he had been sincere, I had behaved appallingly.

Portia put her head to mine. "Be cheered. I am certain he has been harassed by more vituperative women than you. To him, it is probably a hazard associated with his profession. Believe me, he will not think of you again."

For some unaccountable reason, I found this to be less than comforting. I loathed the man and his vile implications about Edward, but I did not like to think of myself as forgettable. Instead, I seized on something she had said earlier that had gone unremarked upon.

"Do you really think I am handsome?"

"Absolutely," she answered at once. She canted her head, studying my face through my widow's veil. "But there is work we could do.…"

I looked at her suspiciously. Portia loved projects. If I

allowed her to undertake me as a project, there was no knowing where it might lead. I might not recognize myself at the end of it.

Then I thought about her remarks—that I needed an adventure, that Brisbane was more of a challenge than I could handle, that he would not think of me again. And suddenly I felt angry, reckless, desperate to do something to change myself and the course I was on toward a staid old age of boredom and bread puddings.

"Then let us begin," I replied firmly.

Portia's eyes sparkled as she began to detail her plans. I was only half listening. I knew that I would give her free rein and that she would do exactly as she pleased with me. Her taste was impeccable, and I had little doubt that I would turn out better at her hands than I had from Aunt Hermia's or Edward's.

She chattered on about coiffeurs and corsets, but I was still thinking of Nicholas Brisbane's dark eyes and cool manners. A year would pass before I saw him again. And it was then that the adventure truly began.

THE SIXTH CHAPTER

For sweetest things turn sourest by their deeds;
Lilies that fester smell far worse than weeds.
—William Shakespeare
"Sonnet 94"

Of course, it did not seem like anything of an adventure at the time. Despite Portia's efforts with my appearance, I still spent most of my time at Grey House, reading to Simon, listening to Aunt Ursula detail her newest remedy for constipation, or waiting for Val to return home from his ever-growing number of social engagements. My year of widowhood was nearly at an end and I was beginning to chafe under the restrictions. I had not been to the theatre or the opera since Edward's death. I had not entertained, and had been invited to only the most intimate of family parties. I felt sometimes as though I might as well have been locked up in a Musselman's *harim* considering how little I was actually outside of Grey House.

As for Portia's suggestion that I take a lover, the very idea was laughable. I saw few men, save those I employed or to whom I was related by blood or marriage. I had only the notion of Italy to sustain me. I had mapped out my plans to the last detail, dispatching letters to delightful innkeepers and receiving particulars on their accommodations. I had applied myself diligently to the study of Italian, and with Simon to tutor me I made rather good progress. He had always had a good ear for languages, and was enormously patient with my mistakes.

"You are a natural," he told me more than once. "I could close my eyes and believe you were Venetian."

"Liar," I said happily.

And we were happy, I think, in spite of his bouts of breathlessness and the fevers that left him too weak to hold a book. I used to look up quickly and catch him, a hand pressed quietly to his chest as he stilled his jagged breathing. But even then he would not forgo our lesson.

"It is all up here, my darling," he said, tapping his brow. "Now, tell me, how would you say, 'these gardens are beautiful'?"

"*Questi giardini sono belli,*" I replied.

"Very good. Now ask what sort of tree this is."

"*Che albero è questo?* But Simon, I'm not terribly interested in trees, I'm afraid."

He smiled up at me, his face pink with exertion and pleasure. "Ah, Julia. You are going to Italy. You must be interested in everything. You must be open to every possibility."

Strange that both he and Portia should parrot the same theme. Change, possibility, opportunity...but as I looked at Simon, I remembered that this particular opportunity would not come my way until he had passed from my life.

I think he remembered it, too, for he looked away then and told me to begin counting, a skill I had mastered a month before.

It did not matter. It was something safe to speak of when we dared not speak of other things.

"*Uno, due, tre...*"

And so the year passed away, dully, though not entirely unpleasantly, until the April morning I decided to clean out Edward's desk. I had not entered his study in months, certain that the maids were keeping it tidy, but now, as the spring sunlight streamed into the room for the first time in weeks, I saw what a halfhearted effort they had made.

Stacks of books and old correspondence remained where Edward had left them, organized in his own peculiar system and bound with coloured tapes. I had leafed through them once to make certain that the letters did not require a response—and for any sign of the notes Mr. Brisbane had mentioned as well. I had found nothing. I had been relieved, so relieved that I had simply shut the room up and left it, much as I had left his bedchamber and dressing room. It had been very easy to turn my attention to more pressing matters, and very easy to convince myself that anything was more pressing than sorting Edward's things. The spring had been a wet one, and I had spent many long hours curled in my old dressing gown, lazing by the fire with a book. But days of chilly rain had given way to watery sunshine, cold, but nonetheless bright, and I was determined to take advantage of it. I ordered a pot of fresh tea and a plate of sandwiches and set to work.

An hour later I had made quite good progress. The papers were sorted, the books organized and the sandwiches almost all eaten. Only the drawers themselves were left.

Briskly, I set to work, emptying the contents of the tightly packed drawers onto the desk. There was little Edward had not saved. Programs from theatre evenings, his private betting book, ticket stubs, letters dating back several years at least. His account books had been given over to the solicitors, but every-thing else was still packed into those five drawers. I went through them all, sorting the detritus to be burned and the few small tokens worth keeping. It was painful and sad to reduce a man to a handful of things—among them a pen with a nub broken to his hand. I should have thrown that away; it never wrote properly for me, skipping and stuttering ink across the page. There was a thin volume of poetry I did not remember him owning, a small sketch he had made of a ruined courtyard long forgotten, a broken watch chain, a molting black feather. A few bits and bobs, and nothing of importance, I realized sadly. The rest was tipped into a basket for rubbish to be hauled away by one of the footmen. The drawers fresh and empty, I prepared to replace them back onto their runners. I had never cared for the desk itself—it was a very large piece, thick with Jacobean carving, but it would likely fetch a good price at auction.

I had just slotted the last drawer into place when I realized that it would not shut. I pushed at it again, but it was caught on something and I pulled it out. My fingers touched a tightly wedged twist of paper, far at the back, hidden in shadow. I worked at it a moment with my fingers and a paper knife before I wrested it loose. A program from the opera, like a dozen others, scribbled over with the names of likely horses. I turned it over, and from inside its leaves fell a small piece of paper, violently creased, as though it had been thrust into the progam in a tremendous hurry and stuffed at the back of the drawer. I smoothed it out, thinking that it was very probably a scrap of a poem that Edward wanted to remember or a note to try a particular wine.

But I was very wrong. It was plain paper, inexpensive, with a bit of verse cut from a book pasted onto it.

"Let me not be ashamed, O Lord; for I have called upon Thee; let the wicked be ashamed, and let them be silent in the grave."

Below it was a rough drawing in pen and ink, only a few lines, but its shape was unmistakable. It was a coffin. And on the stone sketched at its head was a tiny inscription.

Edward Grey. 1854-1886. Now he is silent.

I stared at the page, wishing fervently that I had never found it. Although Mr. Brisbane had never described the notes to me, I felt certain that I had found one. And having seen one, I was also certain that Portia was wrong—this was no jest. Malice fairly emanated from the paper.

I held on to it for a long time, fighting the temptation to throw it into the wastepaper basket and let the footman cart it away to be burned. I could not simply crumple it back into the depths of the desk, pretending I had not found it at all. It would linger there, like a canker, and I knew that my fingers would go to it again and again. No, if I were going to be rid of it, it must be destroyed entirely. I could do it myself, I realized with a glance at the brisk fire crackling away on the grate. No one would ever know—it was a small thing; it would be consumed in a matter of seconds.

But no amount of burning would change what I had seen. And having seen it, I could not forget what it meant. Someone had wished Edward dead, enough to terrorize him with vicious notes, making his last days fearful ones. At the very least, the sender of these notes had harmed his peace of mind.

But what else might this malicious hand have done? Had it done murder? I would never have credited such a thought had Nicholas Brisbane not put it into my mind, but there it was. Edward was a perfect victim in so many ways. He was very nearly the last member of a family famed for its ill health. Neither his father nor grandfather had lived to see thirty-five. Edward was almost thirty-two. He had never been robust, even as a child. And in the year before his death, his health had grown dramatically worse, manifesting the same symptoms that had taken his grandfather and father before him. It would be a small matter to introduce some poison to such a delicate constitution; perhaps it would even work more quickly on one so weakened by poor health. How simple it would have been for some unknown villain to send along a box of chocolates or a bottle of wine laced with something unspeakable.

But why the notes, then? Would they not serve as a warning to Edward? He would have been on his guard, surely, against such an attack. Or would he have been naive enough to believe that his murderer would strike openly, that he would have a chance to defend himself? I knew nothing of his thoughts, his fears during those days. Edward kept no diary, no written record of his days. And he had clearly felt incapable of confiding in me, I thought bitterly.

I looked at my hands and realized that I must have already decided upon a course of action whether I realized it or not. I had folded the note carefully and placed it in a plain envelope. There was only one person to whom I could turn now.

THE SEVENTH CHAPTER

Nay then, let the devil wear black,
for I'll have a suit of sables.
—William Shakespeare
Hamlet

*I*t does me no credit to admit that I had difficulty in deciding what to wear to call upon Nicholas Brisbane. I had thought myself cool and composed, but I kept hearing Portia's voice, reminding me that he would not think of me beyond that first call at Grey House. I also kept thinking of Mariah Pilkington's assessment of him as a lover, but that does me no credit, either.

Portia had been ruthless in her attack upon my wardrobe. Scarcely a garment remained after her onslaught. She began the devastation by throwing out anything she deemed "busy," discarding everything with ruffles, tassels or fringe.

"And above all, no ruching, unless you want to look like some poor misguided woman's parlor drapes," she cautioned.

I gazed mournfully at the heap of clothes I had acquired upon Edward's death. There was several hundred pounds' worth of bombazine and velvet and lace tumbled together on the bed, and not a single garment truly flattered me. "Then what shall I wear?"

She cocked her head to the side, considering my figure carefully.

"Simplicity, my darling. Things that are beautifully draped

and excellently cut need no embellishment. I shall take you to my dressmakers. They are brothers, trained in Paris as tailors, and no one in London cuts a better line. They are frightfully expensive and rather rude, but they are just the ones to take you in hand. Besides, these frowsy things will not fit you when I've had done with you."

"What do you mean they won't fit? What do you mean to do with me?"

"I mean," she said, propelling me toward the cheval glass, "to fatten you up. Look at yourself, Julia. Really look. There's beauty there, but you are a sack of bones. An extra stone will round out your face and arms, give you curves where you have none. You will be lush and healthy-looking, like Demeter."

I grimaced at her in the looking glass. "Edward always liked me thin."

She swung me around to face her. "Edward is gone now. And it is quite time to find out what *you* like."

I smiled at her. "Then why am I letting you boss me about?"

"Because I know what is best," she said, wrinkling her nose. She dropped a quick kiss on my cheek. "Now, pastries for you at teatime, extra gravy on your joints, and as much cream as you like. When you've put on a few pounds, we shall take you off to the brothers Riche and my hairdresser and see what they will make of you."

I agreed because it was simpler and because it seemed to make Portia so happy. Besides, Morag had already spied the discarded clothes and scooped them up to be sold at the stalls in Petticoat Lane. I strongly suspected she would do me some sort of bodily injury if I tried to infringe upon her rights as a lady's maid to sell my cast-offs.

In the end, I quite liked Portia's changes. My hair was cropped, baring the length of my neck and the smallness of my ears. It was an immediate success—Morag's hairdressing skills being fairly nonexistent. Now, rather than struggling to frizz several pounds of stubbornly straight hair, she had only to fluff the little halo of curls that had sprung to life when the length was scissored off.

In the end we compromised on the weight. I gained half a stone, which was entirely ample. For the first time in my life, I had a figure that could be described as feminine, with a soft, curving line I did not recognize. I took to wearing delicate earrings and snug, exquisitely tailored jackets cut like a man's. Sometimes I looked at myself in the cheval glass and I hardly knew who I was anymore. I did not look like my father's daughter or Edward's wife. I was simply Lady Julia Grey now, widow, and she was a person I did not know.

But she was a person who knew how to dress, I thought with some satisfaction as I prepared to call upon Mr. Brisbane. I instructed Morag to button me into my black silk with the swansdown trim. It was a stunning costume, perhaps the most elegant in my wardrobe. It lent me a confidence I did not feel as I drew on my black gloves and motioned for Morag to pin my hat into place. The hat was trimmed with a slender band of swansdown, and there was a muff to match. The afternoon had turned cold and grey and I was glad of my warm finery as Diggory, the coachman, bundled me into the town coach with rugs for my lap and hot bricks for my feet. I had made certain that Simon was napping peacefully and the Ghoul was settled in with a glass of warm gin and a stack of black-bordered correspondence fresh from the post. I felt giddy, like a child let out of school on holiday as the coach drew away from the kerb.

Mercifully, it was a short drive to Chapel Street. I waited while Henry, the footman, jumped down and pulled the bell sharply for me. He stood for a few minutes, preening himself in the glass panel of the door. He was an insufferably vain creature, but there was no denying that he did look rather splendid in his livery. I admired his calves and thought about

Portia's suggestion of taking a lover. There was a family precedent for that sort of thing, my great-aunt had eloped with her second footman, but the idea held little attraction for me. If nothing else, footmen were not noted for their intelligence, and if there was one quality I knew I must have in a lover, it was a quick wit.

There was no reply, and Henry looked to me for instructions, his soulful blue eyes remarkably blank.

"Knock," I called irritably. "There must be someone at home." I said this as much for my benefit as for his. I had steeled myself for this errand once. I was not certain I could do so again. At last the door was opened by a small, plump creature liberally dusted with flour. Henry returned to hand me down from the carriage.

"Ooh, I am sorry," the little woman said, ushering me over the threshold. "I did not hear the bell. I was making a pudding for my gentleman's dinner, I was. What may I do for you, madam?"

She had taken in the presence of the footman returning to the carriage and eyed my clothes with an accurately appraising glance. Brisbane must have had a number of privileged callers, I surmised.

"I wish to see Mr. Brisbane. I am not expected, but I do hope he can spare me a few moments."

She bobbed respectfully, wiping her hands on her apron. "Oh, of course, madam. There is a chair for you. I won't be but a minute."

I was relieved that she did not ask for my card, but it occurred to me that many of his visitors would appreciate such discretion. She was back before I had settled myself comfortably.

"He will certainly see you now, madam. May I bring some tea?"

"That will not be necessary, I do not expect to stay long,"

I said, rising. The plump little housekeeper escorted me up the stairs and knocked once on the door.

"Come!"

The housekeeper bustled back the way she had come and I was left to open the door myself. I twisted the handle and entered, feeling rather like Stanley beating the bushes for Livingstone.

"Mr. Brisbane?" I called hesitantly, poking my head around the door.

"Come in and close the door. The draught will put these seedlings right off."

I entered, quickly closing the door behind me. The room was spacious, and thoroughly cluttered, but not fussily so. A sofa and a pair of chairs flanked the fireplace, with a few tables scattered about and several stuffed bookshelves lining the walls. There was a writing table in the corner, with blotter and inkstand and a litter of correspondence. An assortment of boxes and oddments stood on the mantelpiece. There were a few bits of statuary, not the usual Dresden shepherdesses, but strange, foreign pieces from faraway lands, medieval ivories and bronze bells, jostling with fossils under glass and something that looked horribly like a bit of dried mummy.

A collection of swords and daggers was hung on one wall, and over the fireplace was a small tapestry or carpet with an intricate geometric pattern worked in vivid colours. There were a few pieces of interesting glass, sets of scientific instruments, and even something that I decided must be a camel saddle. In all, the room was fascinating, like a tiny museum storehousing the most interesting bits of a traveler's collection. I longed to poke about, examining everything, ferreting out the secrets this room held.

But I could not. Instead, I turned my attention to the largest item in the room, the long table situated between the large window and the fireplace. It was fitted up as a sort of potting table, and Brisbane was busily engaged with some sort of botanical activity. He was standing in his shirtsleeves, tending a row of little pots tucked under bell jars. He put the last cloche in place and turned, rolling his cuffs back into place.

"What can I do—" He broke off as soon as he caught sight of me. His expression changed, but I could not read it. "Lady Julia Grey. Mrs. Lawson said only that I had a lady caller. She did not tell me your name."

"I did not send it."

He continued to neaten his cuffs, pinning his sleeve links into place and donning his coat, but all of this he did without taking his eyes from me—a curious habit I remembered from our first interview. It was frankly disconcerting, and I suddenly longed to confess that I had stolen my sister's favorite doll for a day when I was eight. I made a note to employ the technique myself the next time I interrogated Cook about the accounts.

"Why have you come?" he asked finally.

I had expected frankness and had decided to answer him in kind.

"Because I need your help. I have discovered that I was very possibly wrong about my husband's death. And to apologize," I went on, my mouth feeling dry and thick. "I was quite rude to you when we last met and I do not blame you if you refuse me."

To my surprise, a smile flickered over his features. "As I recall I threatened to horsewhip you the last time we met," he said evenly. "I can forgive your rudeness if you can forgive mine."

I extended my hand to him without thinking. It was a gesture my brothers and I had always used to seal our differences after a quarrel. He took it, and I felt the warmth of his palm through my glove.

"Sit." He indicated the chair nearest the fire, but I was feeling warm and flushed from the closeness of the room already. I laid aside my muff and removed my gloves.

He watched as I stripped off the kidskin, and I felt as bare as if I had removed my gown. I folded my hands carefully in my lap and he lifted his eyes to my face.

"Why did you change your mind?"

I described the scene in the study that morning, my determination to clear out the detritus, the little wedge of paper caught at the back of the drawer. I removed it from my reticule and passed it to him.

His brow furrowed as he looked it over. He rose and returned with a small magnifying glass, examining every inch of the paper. He was wrapped in concentration, ignoring me completely for the moment. Free from his scrutiny, I scrutinized him.

The past year had left little mark upon him. His hair was longer than I had remembered, with a thread or two of silver that might not have been there before. It was tumbled now, as if he had thrust his hands through it while working over his plants. His clothes, something I should not have noticed before the tuition of the Riche brothers, were beautifully cut, though I noticed his coat strained ever so slightly through the shoulders. In some men this might have exposed a fault; in his case it only emphasized his breadth.

His mouth, which I had entirely failed to notice during our previous meetings, was quite a handsome feature, with a slight fullness to the underlip that lent a sensuality to the slim, purposeful upper lip and hard jaw. There was a small scar, high on his cheekbone, that I had not noticed before, an old one that I only saw now because it was thrown into relief by the firelight. It was shaped like a crescent moon. I wondered how he had gotten it.

He looked up sharply and I felt my face grow hot.

"This looks to be sent by the same hand as the others."

"Looks to be? Can you not be certain?"

He shrugged. "I have not seen the notes in a year, my lady. But the evening of Sir Edward's collapse, he told me that he had received another. He planned to show it to me that night. He was rather agitated about it. I suspect he put it into his desk and died before he had the chance to retrieve it. The typeface from the scissored bit seems to match what I remember of the earlier notes."

He handed it back and I waved it away with a shudder. "I do not want it. What do we do now?"

His expression was incredulous. "We? Now? You will return to Grey House and I will get on with my experiment. Unless you would care for some tea. I am sure Mrs. Lawson would be only too happy—"

"About that!" I interjected, pointing to the note. "What do we do about that?"

He shrugged again, a peculiarly Gallic gesture that, coupled with his dark colouring, made me wonder if he was entirely English. Perhaps Portia's speculations about his parentage were not so preposterous after all. Naturally I did not credit the story of imperial Bonaparte blood, but there was a foreignness to him that I could not identify.

"There is nothing to be done. Sir Edward is dead, the certificate says by natural causes, and you were content to let him rest in peace a year ago. Let him do so now."

I stared at him. "But surely you can see that there has been some injustice done here. You were the one who urged me to have his death investigated. You were the one who first raised the question of murder."

The table at his elbow was layered with objects, a small stack of books, some marked with playing cards to hold his place, a bowl that looked like a solid piece of amber, full of coins and pen nibs and a knot of faded calico. There was a Chinese cricket cage, empty but for a tiny stone statue, and a basket of apples, surprisingly bright and crisp for this time of year. He picked an apple from the basket and began to twist the stem. "It was relevant a year ago, my lady, to an investigation upon which I was engaged. My client died, his widow did not wish to pursue the matter, ergo the case is closed."

The stem snapped and so did my fraying temper. "Ergo the case is *not* closed. You were the one who preached to me of integrity and probity last year. What was it you said? Something about justice being meted out to the guilty?"

He took a healthy bite out of the apple, chewing it thoughtfully. "My lady, what is justice at this point? The trail is cold, clues will have been destroyed or thrown out. You yourself nearly consigned this to the wastepaper basket," he reminded me, flourishing the note. "What do you expect me to do now?"

"I expect you to find my husband's murderer."

He shook his dark head, tumbling his hair further. "Be reasonable, my lady. There was a chance a year ago. Now it is little better than hopeless."

"Little better, but not entirely," I said, rising and taking up my muff and gloves. "Thank you for your time, Mr. Brisbane."

He rose as well, still holding his apple. "What do you mean to do?"

I faced him squarely. "I mean to find Edward's murderer."

I think I would have struck him if he smiled, but he did not. His expression was curiously grave.

"Alone?"

"If needs be. I was wrong not to believe you last year. I wasted a valuable opportunity, and I am sorry for that. But I learn from my mistakes, Mr. Brisbane." I took the note from his fingers. "I will not make another."

I crossed to the door, but he moved quickly, reaching it before I did. His features were set in resignation. "Very well. I will do what I can."

I looked up at him. "Why?"

He leaned a little closer and I felt his breath against my face, smelling sweetly of apple. His eyes, wide and deeply black, were fixed on mine, and I could see myself reflected in them.

My breath came quite quickly and I was conscious of how very large he was and that I was alone with a man for the first time in a year. I thought wildly that he might try to kiss me and I knew that I would not stop him. In fact, I think my lips may have parted as he leaned closer still.

"Because I am a professional, my lady. And I will not have an amateur bungling about in one of my cases."

He smiled and bit firmly into his apple.

THE EIGHTH CHAPTER

I have seen them gentle, tame, and meek
That now are wild, and do not remember
That sometime they put themselves in danger.
—Sir Thomas Wyatt
"Remembrance"

"Blast," I muttered as I returned to the coach, settling myself with an irritable thump against the cushions. Henry closed the door smartly behind me. I gave him a second to reach his perch behind the coach, then rapped at the roof. Diggory sprang the horses toward home.

I stared out of the window and tried to compose myself. I had only met Nicholas Brisbane three times, but each of those occasions had left me entirely unsettled. He had an uncanny ability to raise my temper, an ability I did not fully understand.

Perhaps most irritating was his arrogant insistence upon handling the investigation entirely on his own, his derisive use of the word *amateur*. In the end he had said he would make a few inquiries and promised to send along a report in a few days' time. He had not been optimistic, and as he had ushered me out of his rooms, I had become convinced that he was simply agreeing to this much to placate me. He had no expectation of finding Edward's murderer, and I firmly believed that without an expectation of success, one is rarely successful.

In view of this, I decided to undertake my own investigation. The trouble was, I had no idea of how to begin. What questions did a professional ask? What steps did he follow? What came first? Suspects? Motives? It seemed like a Gordian knot of the worst sort, but if my memory of mythology served, the only way out of such a puzzle is directly through it. Cleave a path straight across and the devil take trying to unwind the wool.

But unlike Alexander, I didn't even have a sword. I cursed Brisbane thoroughly over the next few days, leaving me to make polite chat with my relatives and manage my household while he got to bound about London on my behalf, asking interesting questions and chasing down clues that might provide the answer to our mystery. I imagined him pursuing bandits into the fetid Docklands where Chinamen smoked their pipes and kept their secrets, dashing headlong into a brawl with a gang of cutthroat ruffians, sidling into a midnight crypt to keep a rendezvous with a veiled lady who held the key to the entire case....

Of course, Brisbane was doing nothing of the sort. While I liked to imagine him as the lead character of my most outlandish detective fantasies, he was in fact behaving as any very ordinary inquiry agent might. Instead of making gallant charges against masked villains, he was writing letters to clerks and busying himself in the offices of newspapers and solicitors, patiently searching through dusty files.

According to his report, what he learned was prosaic in the extreme. Sir Edward Grey had died of natural causes due to an hereditary heart ailment at the age of thirty-one. His title and country estate were entailed upon his cousin, Simon Grey; the residue of his estate devolved upon his relict, Lady Julia Grey, youngest daughter and ninth child of the twelfth Earl March. Sir Edward gave quietly to several worthy causes, enjoyed horseracing and was an amateur oenophile with more enthusiasm than skill. He had no enemies, but was widely known at his club as a great prankster and generous friend who could always be relied upon for a jape or a loan to those in need of a laugh or a fiver. The inscription on his headstone, laid in September, was a fragment of a poem by Coleridge, chosen by his widow.

All of this was detailed for me in Brisbane's meticulously written report, delivered as promised, a week after I had engaged him. I read it over, my outrage mounting.

"I could have told you this much myself," I pointed out, waving the paper at him. "What possible purpose did this serve, except to cost us a week?"

We were in his sitting room again, the room unchanged from the previous week, save for the seedlings. They had disappeared, and in their place was an elaborate set of scientific equipment, such as often used for laboratories. A beaker full of greenish-yellow liquid was bubbling away on a burner, but Brisbane did not seem concerned about it, and for all my knowledge of chemistry, it might have been his laundry.

He sighed and settled himself more comfortably in his chair.

"My lady, I did attempt to explain to you last week that inquiries at this late stage would be difficult if not impossible. We have notes of a threatening variety, but a death certified as natural. We know of one person who was cowardly enough to strike with a poisoned pen, but we do not know that he was sufficiently vicious to do worse."

"You think that hounding a dying man is not sufficiently vicious?"

"I did not say that. You have a gift for putting the worst possible construction upon my words," he said, an edge creeping into his voice. He always seemed slightly irritable with me, but I could not tell if it was the result of my company. Perhaps he was just a very cranky man. I liked to think so. I would have hated to think I was responsible for such incipient nastiness.

I adopted a tone of deliberate sweetness. "Oh? I do apologize. Please, do go on and explain how a person could be capable of tremendous cruelty, but not murder."

"That is just what I am trying to explain," he said icily. "People are cruel and horrible to one another all the time, but only rarely do they commit murder. There is a boundary there that most people cannot, will not cross. It is the oldest taboo, and the hardest to break, despite what you doubtless read in the newspapers."

I ignored the barb. "You sound like the vicar at St. Barnabas."

"St. Barnabas?"

"The church at Blessingstoke, the village in Sussex where I was raised. The vicar likes to talk about the great wall that exists in all of us, the end place at which each of us will say 'That is as far as I shall go.' He is very interested in how those walls are formed."

"For example?" Brisbane's brow had quirked up, a sign, I believed, that he was intrigued.

"For example, perhaps a woman would never steal, under any normal circumstances, but to feed her starving child, even she might be tempted to a loaf of bread from a baker's basket."

Just as suddenly as the brow had raised, it lowered, and his nostrils flared a little, as a bull's will when its temper is beginning to rise.

"A very diverting problem for a country vicar, I'm sure, but hardly germane to what we are about," he said. "Now, I have delivered the report, as promised."

"And you mean to leave matters there," I finished flatly. He shrugged. "That is not good enough, Mr. Brisbane. You seemed convinced a year ago that something criminal was afoot. The passing of time does not change that. It simply makes your task more difficult. I would not have taken you for a man to shy from a challenging situation. In fact, I would rather have thought you the sort of man who would relish it."

His expression was thoughtful, but his eyes, watchful as always, gave nothing away. "Oh, very neatly done, my lady. If I refuse to pursue this goose chase of yours, I am either a lazy cad or a coward."

Too late, I remembered Portia's tale of the duel he had fought with Lord Northrup's son. This man was far from a coward. He was headstrong, audacious. Some might even call him violent. And with characteristic March fecklessness, I had just baited him dangerously.

"Did I imply that? I am so sorry. I simply meant that I thought this would appeal to your intellectual curiosity. I was so certain that you were the man to help me, I was perhaps overzealous." I smiled ingratiatingly.

He smiled back, a baring of the teeth that was more wolfish than engaging. "I shall pursue this for you, my lady. Not because you nagged like a fishwife, but because my curiosity is indeed piqued."

Nobly, I ignored the insult. "Edward's murder did not seem to pique your curiosity a moment ago."

Brisbane blinked, like a cat will when it is sunning itself, slowly, hypnotically. "I did not say that it was the possibility of murder that aroused my interest."

Before I could decipher his meaning, there was a scratch at the door. Brisbane did not reply, but the door opened, anyway, and a man appeared bearing a tray. "Tea," he pronounced, looking pleasantly from Brisbane to me and back again.

Brisbane waved a hand. "This is Theophilus Monk, my lady. My factotum, for lack of a better word. Monk, Lady Julia Grey."

Monk was a very superior sort of person, perfectly groomed and very poised. He had an eager, almost educated look about him, and had Brisbane not introduced him, I would have mistaken him for a gentleman, a country squire perhaps, much given to vigorous exercise. He looked robustly healthy, with a very slight embonpoint that seemed the result of the thickening of old muscles rather than too many pastries. His hair was neatly trimmed and silvering, as were his mustaches. His eyes were an indeterminate colour, but assessing and shrewd. He took a moment, as he laid the tray, to take my measure, but he was so quick, so discreet, I almost missed it. I had a very strong suspicion that he assisted Brisbane in his inquiries. I could easily imagine him proving quite resourceful in an investigation.

He bowed very smartly from the neck.

"Do you enjoy being called a factotum?" I inquired, taking the cup he poured. Most bachelor gentlemen would have expected their lady guest to do the honours of pouring. It was a relief to be spared that. I was always rather clumsy around tea things and I fancied Brisbane thought me odd enough without my spilling the tea or dropping the saucers.

"I have suggested majordomo, but Mr. Brisbane finds it too grandiose for such a small establishment," Monk explained in a gravelly Scots voice. "I am in fact his batman, my lady. Feather cake?"

"Ooh, yes, please. Batman, Mr. Brisbane? You were an officer in the army?"

Brisbane stirred his tea slowly. "I have been many things, my lady, none of which would interest you, I am sure."

Monk coughed quietly. I had heard that cough often enough from Aquinas. It was the upper servant's method of tactfully correcting his employer. But if Brisbane was aware of his rudeness or of Monk's disapproval, he did not show it. In fact, if anything, he seemed vaguely amused.

"I shan't need you further, Monk. Her ladyship and I can manage the rest."

Monk bowed again and withdrew.

I faced Brisbane over the teapot. "Did you mean what you said? You will pursue this?"

Brisbane sipped at his tea. "I suppose. I have a few other

matters that I must bring to conclusion, but nothing that cannot wait. And I have no other clients questioning either my integrity or my courage at present."

I bit my lip. He was right to needle me. I had behaved wretchedly. Out of my own impatience and frustration I had offered him an insult that few men would have borne so calmly. I was only surprised that he had borne it at all, considering his bald threat of the previous year to have me horse-whipped for impugning his character.

"Yes, about that," I began slowly. "I spoke in haste. I am truly sorry. I really did not mean it as an insult. I do find the whole matter puzzling in the extreme, and as you are in the business of conundrums…"

"You thought I would find yours irresistible?" he supplied.

Again, his voice was perfectly even, unshaded by even the slightest hint of an ulterior meaning. Why then did I feel he was amusing himself at my expense?

"I thought that it would present a unique problem for you to solve," I corrected with as much dignity as I could muster in the face of his indolent stare.

He shrugged and placed his cup onto the table. "You will find that one problem is very like another, my lady. Only the personalities involved differ, and even then people are very much of a type. That is the greatest asset in my business, and the greatest bore."

"You mean that people are largely predictable? I should think that a rather restful quality."

His smile was small and enigmatic. "It is, and that is what makes it a bore. There is nothing in the world more dreadful than knowing exactly what someone else is going to do, even before he does."

"You would very much like my family, then," I put in with a laugh. "One never knows what a March is likely to do, not even another March."

"So none of your family would have guessed that you came here today?" he asked slowly. He lowered his head, his eyes level with mine. There was something in those dark eyes that had not been there a moment before. Menace? Malice?

I forced a smile. "Of course they would. I told my sister Portia that I was coming here today. And my brother Valerius, who lives with me."

He canted his head, considering me for a moment. Then he shook it slowly. "No, I don't think so. I think you came alone. I think that no one knows the exact whereabouts of Lady Julia Grey."

He moved very slightly forward in his chair and I felt my heart lurch. I learned something in that moment. Fear has a metallic taste, like blood sucked from a cut finger. I could taste it, flat on the back of my tongue as he moved closer toward me.

"My coachman," I said suddenly. "He is circling the carriage. My footman is there as well. They both know where I am."

Brisbane halted his movement, his eyes still intent upon my face. After a moment, he rose and went to the window. He flicked aside the curtain and I felt my toes curling up inside my boots as I prayed that Diggory was at the kerb.

Brisbane resumed his chair, his manner completely altered. "If you will forgive my remarking upon it, the first rule of investigation is discretion. Next time you call upon me, you should come in a hansom, or better yet, a hackney. Anyone who knows you will know that vehicle by the crest on its door. And your footman is a rather remarkable specimen as well. Some lady is bound to remember him."

My heart slid back into its rightful place and I stared at him. "That was a joke, then? That menacing look? The vaguely threatening words?"

He waved a hand and helped himself to a biscuit. "I was

curious. You had just maintained that the Marches were unpredictable. It was my professional estimation that you would have failed to take any precaution regarding your own safety in coming here today, or to make any attempt to conceal your identity. I was correct on both counts."

"My safety! Why on earth should I take precautions on that score in coming here? You are my agent."

Brisbane swallowed and brushed the crumbs from his fingers.

"No, I am not. I was your husband's agent, and he is dead. I have not taken a farthing from you. And as for your safety, you have acted with the most appalling disregard for your own life because you failed to consider one thing, one thing that is staring you squarely in the face."

"And what is that?" I demanded hotly. My temper was entirely frayed by now. I had had enough of his cryptic manner and ghoulish games.

He leaned forward, clamping both hands onto the arms of my chair. I opened my mouth to remonstrate, but he loomed over me, and I knew if I spoke it would come out as a feeble squeak. His face was inches from mine, his voice harsh and low.

"Did you never once ask yourself, my lady, if *I* might have murdered your husband?"

THE NINTH CHAPTER

Break, break sad heart
There is no medicine for my smart,
No herb nor balm can cure my sorrow.
—Thomas Randolph
"Phyllis"

"You needn't have kicked me so hard," Brisbane said bitterly, rubbing at his shin. He had retreated to his own chair and was regarding me much as he might a rabid dog.

"I said I was sorry. Shall I ring for Monk? A wet towel, perhaps—"

"No, thank you," he said, his tone still acid.

"I'm afraid it's going to raise an awful lump," I put in helpfully. That much was a guess. Brisbane had not lifted the leg of his trousers, nor would I have expected him to. Our relationship was quite unorthodox enough without the sight of his bare leg adding to the mix. "Oh, do stop scowling at me like that. It really was your own fault, you know, frightening me like that. Of course I never thought you murdered Edward. Why should I?"

"That was precisely the point," he replied through gritted teeth. "You must consider every possibility. You must realize that no one is above suspicion. You must be willing to scrutinize every person who knew your husband and consider at least the possibility that they were responsible for his death. If you cannot do that, you cannot continue with this investigation."

"But why would you want to murder Edward? You barely knew him."

Brisbane continued to grind his teeth, but I think it was more out of frustration than pain. "I barely knew him according to…"

He paused, waiting for me to catch up. "According to—oh, I do see now. According to you. And if you were the murderer, that makes your information rather suspect."

"Quite," he said grimly.

"Well, did you murder him?"

Brisbane looked at me, fairly goggle-eyed. "I beg your pardon?"

"Did you murder him? It is a simple question, Mr. Brisbane. Kindly answer it."

"Of course I didn't! Of all the bloody—"

"You needn't swear at me. You said I must consider the possibility that you killed him, and I have. I asked you, you said no, and I believe you."

He shook his head, his expression staggered. "You cannot do this. You cannot simply *ask* people if they killed your husband. Sooner or later, you will ask the wrong person. You will be killed in a week, you must know that."

I strove for patience. "Mr. Brisbane, I am not entirely stupid. But circumstances and my own fairly dependable judgment have convinced me that you were not responsible for his death. I promise you that I would not be daft enough to ask anyone I actually suspected."

His look was doubtful. "There are a hundred different ways you could get hurt—badly. You must be very certain what you are about to embark upon. This is no detective story, my lady. There is no guarantee we will unmask this murderer. He could slip through our fingers quite easily. Or worse."

"Worse?"

"Our murderer, if in fact there is one, is comfortable by now.

He has had almost a year of freedom, without even a whisper of murder to disturb him. If he thinks that is about to change, he might well panic, become desperate, even. He might tip his hand."

"How?" I took a sip of tea, cool now, but still refreshing.

"He might try to attack you, for instance."

I blinked at him and he went on, blandly. "I have been assaulted several times in the course of my work. If you were to take an active role in this investigation, you put yourself at risk of harm, even death. I cannot prevent it, you must know that. A clever murderer, one who is determined, desperate, could dispatch you before either of us even realized you were in danger. You must think of that," he finished.

"But you said he is comfortable," I pointed out. "So long as we do nothing to alert him, he would remain so and there would be no danger."

Brisbane shook his head. "Unlikely, at best. Most of the criminals I have encountered have a dog's nose for trouble. They sense when they are about to be found out. And they usually take steps to avoid it. Sometimes they flee, but other times…" His voice broke off and his eyes were distant, as though seeing gruesome conclusions to his other cases.

"That does not frighten me," I said boldly.

Brisbane's gaze dropped to mine. "It should. If you are not afraid, you will not take the proper precautions. That sort of stupidity could get you killed. Or at best, jeopardize the investigation so badly we never catch him. And there are other dangers as well."

"Such as?" I asked with a sigh. I was beginning to feel less than welcome.

"Investigations are rather like snake hunts. Rocks are overturned, hidden places are prodded, and what turns up is often rotten, poisonous and better left undisturbed. Sometimes it is an evil that has nothing to do with the investigation, just something dark and vicious that should never have seen the light of day. But lives are changed, my lady."

"You are being cryptic again, Mr. Brisbane. I have no secrets." Of course, as soon as I said the words, I wished them back. Everyone has a secret or two, however innocent.

He focused those hypnotic black eyes on me for a long moment. "Very well," he said, his voice light. "Perhaps you would like to try a little experiment."

His expression was guarded, but there was anticipation there, something almost gleeful. It made me nervous. "What sort of experiment?"

"Oh, nothing painful. In fact, quite the reverse." He smiled suddenly. "If you wish to be a part of this investigation, you must first provide me with information about Sir Edward, your household, your family. I shall simply ask you a series of questions. Nothing too frightening about that, is there?"

There was the faintest tone of mockery in his voice. I had taunted his courage before, now he was taunting mine.

"Nothing at all," I said roundly. "When do we begin?"

He smiled again, that serpentine smile that Eve must have seen in the Garden. "No time like the present."

He began to make a few alterations in the room. The tea things were dispatched to a far table, jostling a small clock, a set of nautical instruments and a tortoiseshell. In their place he put a single candle, a thick, creamy taper that he lit with a spill from the fireplace.

Then he reached for a lacquered box on the mantel. Out of it he scooped a handful of something that rustled, dried flowers or leaves, perhaps. These he hurled into the fireplace. The change was immediate. There was a fragrance, subtle and soothing, and the flames burned bright green for a moment. He turned to me then, brisk and businesslike.

"Remove your jacket, my lady."

"I beg your pardon?" I clutched the lapels of my jacket together like a trembling virgin. He sighed patiently.

"My lady, I am no Viking bent on pillage, I assure you. You will understand what I am about in a moment. Take off your jacket."

I complied, feeling like an idiot. If Portia had not made it very clear to me that Brisbane would never think of me as a woman, he certainly had. I struggled out of the jacket, regretting that I had instructed Morag to put out the new silk. It was tight and I knew I must look like a wriggling caterpillar trying to get it off. Finally I was free of it and Brisbane took it, tossing it onto a chair. Then, before I could remonstrate with him over the expense of the silk he was creasing, he grasped my ankles and swung them to the sofa.

"Mr. Brisbane!" I began, but he silenced me with an exasperated gesture.

He released my ankles then, but I could still feel the pressure of his hands through skirts, petticoats, boots, and stockings. He thrust a pillow behind my head, causing me to lie back in a posture I had most certainly never adopted in front of an acquaintance before.

"Comfortable?" he inquired, resuming his seat.

"Rather like Cleopatra," I returned tartly. "What exactly is the point to all of this?"

"I told you, it is the beginning of our investigation."

He busied himself taking a notebook and pencil from the drawer of the table beside him. "I know it seems unorthodox, but I need information from you, and I believe that the more relaxed a person is, the more information he or she will relate."

"You believe. Is this your normal practice? Do you do this to all of your clients?"

"No, because most of my clients would not consent to it."

"What makes you think that I will?"

"You already have, my lady. Besides, you are a rather special case."

I felt a warm flush of pleasure. "I am?"

"Yes," he replied absently. "Most of my clients are far more conscious of their dignity to permit such an experiment."

The flush ended abruptly. "Oh."

"But I have great hopes for you, my lady," he continued. The flush began again, a tiny, creeping wave this time, but at least I did not feel quite so low. "I have read a great deal about the techniques used by the police and by those who practice psychology. Some of them seem quite suitable for use in my own work. It is just a theory at this point, but I have had some success in the past."

Of that I was certain. I wondered how many other ladies' ankles he had handled, and promptly dismissed the thought as unworthy of me.

"Begin then, before my neck takes a cramp," I ordered him crossly.

He opened his notebook and made a few comments before he began his questions. When he spoke, his voice had gone soft and mellow, like sun-warmed clover honey. I wondered if he was conscious of it.

"My lady, I need a bit of background information from you. We need a place to begin. So, I am going to take you through some of what Sir Edward told me, and I need you to confirm or correct it."

I nodded, feeling a little sleepy and as relaxed as if I had just had a glass of Aunt Hermia's blackberry cordial.

"Sir Edward told me last year that he had been married to you for five years. Is that correct?"

"Yes," I murmured.

"How did you meet?"

"His father bought the estate next to my father's in Sussex. We knew each other from childhood."

"Was the marriage a happy one?"

I fidgeted a little. My body felt restless, but my limbs were languid, almost too heavy to move. "Happy enough. We were friends."

"There were no children?" he asked, his voice mellower still.

I shook my head sleepily. "Not from me. I could not have them."

"Did he have children by anyone else? Natural children?"

I tried to shake my head again, but now it felt too weighty. "Just lie back against the cushion, my lady," he instructed from far away. I did as I was told, perfectly content to lie there forever.

He made a few notes while I drowsed against the cushions, thinking of Odysseus and the Lotus-eaters. I felt very thirsty, but it seemed far too much trouble to reach out my hand for my teacup. Then I remembered that he had moved it across the room and decided I would wait until he had finished.

"Sir Edward had little family left by the time of his death," he commented.

"Only his first cousin, Simon. He inherited the baronetcy from Edward."

"And you," Brisbane prodded gently.

"I was not Edward's family," I replied. "I was his wife."

"Tell me about your family."

"I have quite a lot of that," I said, feeling a ridiculous and inappropriate urge to giggle. With a great effort, I suppressed it. "My mother died when I was a child. I have nine brothers and sisters. Father is in town just now, at March House in Hanover Square. He lives with Aunt Hermia."

"Indeed. Do any of the other members of your family live with them?"

"None. Most of them live in the country. My eldest brother, Viscount Bellmont, has his residence in London. So does my sister Portia, Lady Bettiscombe."

"Did Lord Bellmont get on well with Sir Edward? Were there problems between them?"

"Only about politics. Monty is a Tory. Edward was apathetic. Used to call each other names. It meant nothing."

"What of Lady Bettiscombe? Did she get on well with Sir Edward?"

"Well enough. Portia does not like many men. She lives with her lover, Jane."

There was a long pause, but Brisbane made no comment.

"And who else lives in London?"

"Valerius, my youngest brother. Lives with me."

Even through the lassitude, I could feel him prickle with interest.

"Tell me about Valerius."

"Wants to be a doctor. Fought terribly with Father over it. That's why he lives with me. He came after Edward died, with the Ghoul."

"The what?"

I explained, in great detail, about the Ghoul, little of which seemed to interest Brisbane.

"Who else lives at Grey House?"

"Simon. Very ill, poor darling. Been bedridden for a year. Inherited nothing but the title and the old house in Sussex. It's almost a ruin, you know. Owls are nesting in the picture gallery."

"Did Simon get on well with Sir Edward?"

"Like brothers," I said dreamily. "But everyone liked Edward. He was charming and so handsome."

"What of your household, the staff? Who lives in at Grey House?"

I sighed, feeling far too tired to give him the particulars. He peered at me closely, then rose and took a handful of dried leaves, this time from a mother-of-pearl box, and threw them onto the fire. They burned orange, with a clean, spicy smell, and after a moment I began to feel a bit livelier.

"Your staff," he prodded gently.

"Aquinas is the butler. You know him."

Brisbane nodded, writing swiftly. "Go on."

"Cook. Diggory, the coachman, Morag, my maid. Whittle does the gardening, but he is employed by Father. Desmond and Henry are the footmen. Magda, the laundress. And there are maids. Cannot keep it sorted out which is which," I finished thickly.

"Have they been with you long?"

"Aquinas since always. Cook four years. Morag came just before Edward died, maybe six months. She was a prostitute. She was reformed at my aunt Hermia's refuge and trained for service. The others at March House quite some time. Renard."

Brisbane wrote furiously, then stopped. "Renard?"

"Edward's valet. French. Sly. Hate him. Stayed on to help with Simon."

This, too, went into the notebook. "Anyone else?"

I shook my head, feeling it throb ominously as I did so. There was a pain beginning behind my eyes and I was thirstier than ever.

"What of Sir Edward's friends? Enemies?"

"No enemies. Everyone a friend, none of them close. Edward was private. God, my head."

He rose again and opened the window a little. Cold, crisp air rushed into the room, clearing out the thick pungent smells from the fire. He left the room and returned a moment later with a wet cloth folded into a pad.

"Here," he said, handing it to me. "Put it on your brow. You will feel better in a minute."

I did as he said, listening to the light scratching of his pencil as he finished writing his observations into his little notebook. Within minutes the lassitude had lifted and the pain had begun to abate. I sat up, swinging my feet to the floor, and watched as the ceiling seemed to change places with it.

"Easy, my lady," he said, pushing me firmly back against the cushion. "You will be quite well in a minute, but you cannot move too quickly."

I lay still, feeling the giddiness recede slowly. When I thought it might be safe, I raised myself by degrees. Brisbane was sipping a fresh cup of tea and had poured one out for me. There was no sign of the notebook.

"What did you do to me?" I demanded, peeling the compress from my brow. I did not want the thing against my skin. God only knew what was in it.

"Drink your tea, my lady. You will feel yourself in a moment."

"How do I know it hasn't been tampered with? For all I know you have laced it with opium," I said indignantly.

He sighed, took up my cup from the saucer and drank deeply from it. "There. It is quite safe, I assure you."

My expression must have betrayed my doubt, for he handed me his nearly full cup. "Take mine, then. Besides, if I were going to lace anything with opium, it would not be tea."

I sipped cautiously at his tea, but it tasted fine. "Why not?"

"Tea is a natural antidote to opium. You would probably vomit it up before it did any real harm."

"Mr. Brisbane, I deplore your manners. Such conversation is not fit for a lady."

He regarded me with something like real interest. "That is quite a little war you have going on in there," he said with a flick of his finger toward my brow.

"What do you mean?"

"You are such a strange mixture of forthrightness and proper breeding. It must always be a battle for you, knowing what you want to say and feeling that you mustn't."

I shrugged. "Such is the lot of women, Mr. Brisbane."

He gave a short laugh. "Not by half. Most women of my acquaintance would never think of the things you do. Much less dare to say them."

"I do not!" I protested. "If you only knew how much effort I take not to say the things I think—"

"I know. That is why I took the liberty of conducting my little experiment. It worked rather better than I had anticipated."

I set the cup down with a crack. "You admit you deliberately gave me something—some sort of truthfulness potion—to get information?"

"Truthfulness potion? Really, my lady, your penchant for sensational novels is deplorable. There is no such thing as a truthfulness potion. Herbs, my lady. That is all. I threw a certain compound of dried herbs onto the fire. They produce a feeling of calmness and well-being, euphoria sometimes, lassitude most often. The result is one of almost perfect truthfulness, not because of some magic power, but because the subject is too relaxed to lie."

I stared at him, clenching my hands into fists against my lap. "That is appalling. No, it is worse than appalling. It is horrible, *horrible*." I could not think of a word bad enough to call him.

"I did tell you I was going to conduct an experiment," he reminded me.

"Yes, but this—this is far beyond what I expected."

He smiled thinly. "Did you think I was going to swing my watch in front of your face and count backward? I could engage in hypnotism if you like. I have practiced it. Mesmerism, as well. But I have found that those methods frequently have more value as parlor tricks than interrogation techniques."

I crossed my arms over my chest, my hands fisted tightly. "I do not care. I still think what you did was appalling."

"Is it more appalling than sending a threat of death to a sick man, making his last days full of fear and doubt?" he asked softly.

Almost unwillingly, I unclenched my fists. "You mean that your methods are justified by the ends."

"I see that you have read your Machiavelli, along with perhaps some Sappho?"

"Leave Portia quite out of this. I would never have told you about Jane without your nasty tricks."

"Indeed."

We sat in silence for a moment, sipping our tea in a state of armed and uneasy truce. I was not happy with his methods, but I understood why he had employed them. If we were to unmask Edward's murderer, we must use every weapon at our disposal, even if it meant occasionally wielding them against each other. But it would be a very long time before I trusted him again.

"Headache better?" he inquired pleasantly.

"Yes, thank you."

"You will be quite thirsty for the rest of the day. It is the only lingering effect I have found."

I nodded obediently and decided to venture a question that had been puzzling me. "Why did it not affect you?"

He gave me a thin, bitter smile. "I inured myself to its effects long ago in China."

"China! How did you come to be in China?"

The smile faded. "I passed through on my way to Tibet. It is a story I do not care to tell, my lady, at least not now. It is sufficient to say that if I did not know how to hold my own against that herb, it would have been more than my life was worth. Now, I believe I have all the major players," he said, rubbing his hands together briskly. "I think the most logical place to begin is with the death itself. Was it murder? If so, it could not have been by bullet, garrote, blade, or any means other than poison. Which means that the first person to consult is—"

"Doctor Griggs," I finished for him.

He gave me a look of grudging acknowledgement. "He knew Sir Edward's health intimately and certified the death as natural. But were there any questions in his own mind about that? Any symptoms that appeared out of the ordinary for a man with Sir Edward's heart condition?"

I shook my head. "I am afraid that Doctor Griggs will not speak to you, especially if he thinks you mean to accuse him of making a mistake. He has connections at Court—lofty ones. He will not thank you for making trouble. I must take him on myself."

Brisbane's eyes narrowed. "I thought we agreed that your involvement was to be largely in a consulting capacity."

"Largely, but not entirely," I replied with spirit. "I shall write to Doctor Griggs. He has known me from my birth. Whatever story I concoct, he will believe it. I will think of some suitably convincing tale, and when he sends his reply, I shall forward it on to you."

He agreed and we made arrangements for meeting again when I had Doctor Griggs' reply in hand. He did not summon Monk, but helped me into my jacket and coat himself. I took my hat from him and pinned it on securely, feeling more myself than I had since I entered the room.

"Oh, and by the way," I said sweetly, my hand on the knob, "if you ever use me in such a disgraceful fashion again, I will use every and all means at my disposal to ensure you get the thrashing of your life. Good day, Mr. Brisbane."

I am not entirely certain, but I think he was smiling as I left.

THE TENTH CHAPTER

He was sad at heart, unsettled yet ready,
sensing his death.
—*Beowulf*

It took me the better part of the next day to write my letter to Doctor Griggs. I had not expected it would be so difficult, but striking just the right balance of wifely concern and abject stupidity was harder than I had anticipated. In the letter, I claimed that although my year of mourning was nearly finished, I thought of Edward more than ever. I told him that he came to me in dreams, mouthing words I could not hear, but that I had read somewhere that this was a clear sign of murder. I begged him to tell me if there had been any indication whatsoever of foul play. I pleaded with him to give me every detail of Edward's collapse and death, especially the few hours I had been kept away from him. I reminded him of the long history between our families and gently hinted that a man of his genius would have easily seen something amiss. I flattered, I cajoled, and in the end, I sprinkled a few drops of water over the ink to simulate tears. I was a little ashamed of myself for enjoying it so much, but that soon passed. I sealed and addressed it and sent Desmond to deliver it by hand. I had instructed him to wait for a reply, but the response was as disappointing as it was succinct.

My dear Lady Julia,
Have read your letter. Cannot reply until I have reviewed
my notes. Please be patient. Will try to respond by tomor-
row's post. I remain your obedient servant,
William Griggs

I questioned Desmond closely, but he could tell me nothing of importance. Doctor Griggs did not appear disturbed by the letter, merely tired as he had attended a confinement late the previous night that had not ended until nearly dawn. He had simply nodded at the letter and dashed off the quick reply Desmond had brought.

"And there was nothing else? You are certain?" I prodded. Desmond was good-looking—as handsome as Henry and almost as thick-witted.

Desmond thought for a moment, his golden brows furrowing together with the effort. "No, my lady. He simply handed me the reply, said that I looked a bit peaky, and recommended a meat tonic."

I peered at Desmond. "You do look peaky. Have one of the maids brew some beef tea for you. I know Cook just bought extra beef to make some for Sir Simon. Tell her to put plenty of blood in it."

He inclined his head. "Thank you, my lady." He made to go, but paused in the doorway, the lamplight shining off of his buttery curls. "You are very good, my lady."

He blushed deeply, a rich rose colour against the pale porcelain of his cheeks, and hurried off, leaving me with a good deal more to think about than Griggs' thin reply. I hoped Desmond was not falling in love with me. It was an extremely delicate proposition to have one's servants falling in love with one. Father's butler, Hoots, had been desperately enamored of Father's elder sister, Aunt Cressida, for years and lived for her annual visits. I could not imagine why—she was not half so pretty as Aunt Hermia and had a thicker set of whiskers than Father.

In any case, the last thing I wanted was for Desmond to cast his lovely clear eyes in my direction. I made a note to speak to Aquinas about him and turned my thoughts to more practical matters. I would not hear from Griggs for another day at least, and I had been neglecting my little household dreadfully. I made up my mind to rectify my laxity. I decided to start with the most distasteful and made my way to the room where we kept the Ghoul.

She was tucked up comfortably in bed, wearing a lace cap festooned with ribbons, the coverlet littered with sweet wrappers and magazines. There was a stack of black-bordered correspondence on the bedside table and I felt my spirits rise. Perhaps someone had taken pity on me and thoughtfully died. The Ghoul had been with us for nearly a year and I was growing impatient waiting for the next family bereavement.

"Good evening, Aunt Ursula," I said, dropping a kiss somewhere near her cheek. She smelled strongly of lavender and blackberry cordial and camphor. And gin.

"Good evening, dearest. How are you today? I have had the most pleasant day. I received a very long letter from Cousin Brutus. His gout is very, very painful, poor dear. I must write to him with the remedy my own lamented Harold used."

"I am fine, thank you," I said, taking a small needlepointed chair by the bed. "I am sorry to hear about Cousin Brutus. Is it very serious?" I asked hopefully. Of course, if Cousin Brutus recovered, there was always Uncle Leonato's wife. I had it on good authority that she had taken a chill at Christmas and the cough had lingered.

She shrugged her thin shoulders beneath the coverlet. "One never knows, that is the trouble with gout. It comes on of a sudden, laying a body low, and it can linger for weeks. Then, one morning, quick as you please, it is gone again. I remember how my poor departed Harold used to suffer with it. But my remedy always seemed to put him right. Of course, it put him so right that he went out riding that wild horse that threw him to his death. My poor darling…" She fished under the covers for her handkerchief, which she applied delicately to her nose.

After a moment she blew it ferociously, then brightened. "Still, as the Bible tells us, 'Man cometh forth like a flower and is cut down.' It was simply Harold's time to be cut down."

I nodded, wondering how on earth we had ventured into such a bizarre conversation. Other people's aunts talked about knitting and forcing paperwhites. Mine quoted Job. I had little doubt she could recite the entire service for the dead from the Book of Common Prayer if asked.

I cleared my throat to reply, but she was still speaking.

"Just like your Edward, poor thing. Such a lovely boy. So little time together! Practically still on your honeymoon. And then to have him snatched so cruelly! Oh, my dear, how can you bear it?"

The question was rhetorical, and it was one she had been asking me almost daily for the past year. At first I had actually answered it, reminding her that Edward and I had been married for five years and that he had always been in delicate health. But then that only brought on some verses from Lamentations, so I learned to keep quiet. I simply put on a mournful expression and nodded solemnly and waited for her to go on. She always did.

"But at least the funeral was properly done. So many people just rush through them these days—no respect at all. But no one can say that the Marches do not respect death. I was very much gratified to see the efforts taken on poor Edward's behalf. Such lovely lilies, and the music was so very moving. I can still hear those little choirboy voices…"

She began to hum then, something I had never heard before and decidedly not one of the pieces sung at Edward's funeral.

I was beginning to think that the blackberry cordial was having an effect on her. Or the gin.

"Aunt Ursula, did you receive any other correspondence?" I asked in desperation. "I note that some of the envelopes are bordered in black. I hope there are no fresh bereavements." Of course I hoped no such thing; I was heartily tired of having the Ghoul settling in my China Room.

Aunt Ursula broke off in mid-verse. "Oh, no, my dear. Those are letters from families still in mourning. Why, dear Cressida's husband has only been dead for seventeen years. It would not do for her to leave off observing the proper signs of respect, would it?"

I sat, dumbstruck, realizing what she had just said. Aunt Cressida, whose husband had been widely held to be a complete monster, had been widowed for seventeen years and Aunt Ursula still expected her to write on black-bordered writing paper. I should be expected to do the same. And I knew it would not be just the writing paper. It would be the widow's weeds as well. Unrelieved black clothing, from the outer petticoat to the gloves. Jet and onyx jewelry. Hair bracelets. Veils.

I excused myself and went to lie down on my bed. I had been marking the calendar, waiting for my year of mourning to end. I had actually been looking forward to putting on gray clothes or adding little touches of white to my collars and cuffs. I was counting off the days until I could wear pearls again, and purple. Now, what was the point? With Aunt Ursula in the house, holding me to the same standards of mourning as the queen, what hope was there? I could either wear what I liked and endure her daily sermons on proper feeling, or I could smother myself in black bombazine for the rest of my life. It did not bear thinking of. So I did not think of it. I rose and went to visit Simon, hoping that his gentle smile would be a balm for my ruffled temper.

I crept into his room, uncertain if he was yet asleep.

"I am awake, Julia," he called. "Come in."

I ventured into the room. It was dimly lit, warm and cozy, and I could see Simon drowsing in the chaise longue by the window. He was propped against a pair of thick pillows and covered with a soft woolen blanket. It was embroidered at the edge with his crest, a Christmas present from me. It had been difficult to choose something for him, so in the end I had opted for something elegant and practical and comforting. He had always loved beautiful things, and the rich dove-grey colour matched his eyes.

The rest of the room had been furnished with his favorite things, framed sketches of his travels, a portrait of his parents, a little china statue of a dog that he had had for so long its tail had been broken off and glued back at a ridiculous angle, more than once.

He smiled at me and I bent to kiss his cheek.

"Ah, violet. My favorite scent," he commented.

I felt a little lance of guilt. "I am sorry. I should have sent up a pot of them in March. Never mind. I will have Whittle grow some for you in the hothouse."

He grinned at me. "Can he do that?"

"Heavens, I don't know. That is Whittle's business. If not, I shall buy you some silk ones, French, and douse them in my perfume."

"Lovely. What have you been about?" he asked as I settled myself on a cushion at his feet.

"Being flayed by the Ghoul," I informed him with a doleful air. "I have just realized that I am expected to keep to my mourning forever. She'll never lie down for me putting on colours again. I shall write on black-bordered paper and drape myself in veils until everyone forgets what I look like."

Simon smiled. "Poor darling. Don't be too disheartened. I'm sure some helpful March relation will die soon and take her off your hands. Loads of lung complaints going around this spring."

"One hopes. Not that I wish any ill on any of my relations, of course. But Aunt Ursula has inflicted herself on us for quite long enough. It is someone else's turn."

"Lucky for you that I am a Grey and not a March. She won't return when you are mourning me," he said, his eyes glinting humorously.

"Oh, Simon, don't," I begged. I had been thoughtless, speaking of such things to him. I reached up and took his hand, willing myself not to feel the bones, brittle and sharp beneath the thin, papery skin. I noticed he had moved his gold signet ring from his smallest finger to the ring finger. Still, it twisted loosely and I wondered how much more weight he could lose before he slipped away altogether.

He touched my hair lightly, pushing it back from my face.

"Ah, I did not mean to upset you. But Griggs was here last week, you know. The man is a fool, of course, but he says it cannot be much longer, and I must believe him."

I felt my eyes fill with tears and I turned my face away so he should not see them.

"Julia," he said softly. "You must have known. I have been sick for so long, I think I will welcome it. I cannot remember what it was to breathe without this weight on my chest."

I nodded. "I know. I am dreadfully selfish. I am thinking of what it will mean to me to lose you. I never think of what it means for you to be here, like this."

He smiled, really smiled for the first time in months. I had missed Simon's smile. It had always been his most engaging feature.

"My poor girl. Promise me this—you will not wear black for me. I have always liked you in colours. Bright, shocking colours. Wear scarlet for me."

I shook my head. "I do not think I could manage scarlet. Edward always said I looked best in pale colours."

His face coloured sharply and his breath came quickly,

wheezing. "Edward was a fool about many things, not the least of which included you," he said savagely.

"We were happy enough," I said feebly, stroking his hand. He gentled then, but I could feel his anger seething just below the surface.

"He never should have married you," he said finally. "That was selfish. He could not appreciate you."

I said nothing for there was nothing to say. We sat in silence for several minutes. I kept stroking his hand, listening to his breathing as it slowed and the wheeze quieted.

"You should not excite yourself," I said after a long while. "Especially about the past. None of it matters now. None of it can be changed."

He turned his hand in mine, grasping my fingers in his. I thought of how familiar his hand was to me. Simon had been orphaned at two and raised by his aunt and uncle, Edward's parents, at Greymoor. He had been a frequent guest in our home, sometimes invited, sometimes not. It had been a bold Simon who discovered the gap in the hedge that provided us with a shortcut between the properties, a gap we were careful never to show to Father, who would have had it repaired instantly.

And it had been Simon who braved the first introductions, interrupting our game of cricket on the broad lawn that swept from the abbey down to the river. Edward, his elder by some years, had loitered rather shyly in the background. We rode and swam and played games together, and if sometimes Simon went home with a glorious marble that didn't actually belong to him, no one really minded. We knew that Simon, unlike Edward or us, with our regular allowances, was desperately poor. We were happy to let him keep the odd book or slingshot—or at least most of us were. My hot-tempered second brother, Benedick, once chased him home and thrashed him for pocketing his favorite tin soldier, the figure of Wellington mounted on Copenhagen from his Battle of Waterloo set. But then Father had felt it necessary to thrash Benedick for hitting a smaller boy and had confiscated poor Wellington, locking him into his desk drawer, where he lay for years. Father kept him as a reminder to Benedick that a gentleman must always guard his temper—a lesson Benedick never entirely learned. And naturally, because of the Wellington incident, Benedick and Simon never quite warmed to each other. Of course, it did not help that anytime Benedick's temper threatened the rest of us would circle him, chanting, "Remember Wellington," which only served to provoke him further.

After that, Simon thought of Benedick as an unrepentant bully, and Benedick branded him a weasel, the worst insult in the March lexicon. But I liked Simon, mostly for his quick wit and ready smile, and marrying Edward only cemented the bond. In time he had ceased to be company, and I had begun to think of him as another brother. I could not imagine losing him any more than I could fathom losing one of them. I had known for months that he was dying, but I was only just beginning to really understand it. In some ways, his death would be more wrenching than Edward's. Edward had been my husband. Simon was my friend.

"You are right, of course," he said, his voice light and mocking, as it had always been. "I should be saving my strength to make a good end." He hesitated, then reached out his other hand to me. "I have something to tell you, dearest." His face was thin now and sharply planed, like that of a fasting monk in an old Spanish painting. "I do not mean to linger forever. When the time comes, I will know it, and I will act."

I stared at him. "You cannot mean it, Simon. You would not—it is a very great sin. You would not be buried in consecrated ground."

He smiled again. "Dear girl, what do I care for that now?" His grip tightened on my hands, forcing me to hear him. "It grows harder to breathe, my sweet. I feel sometimes as though I were living under water, desperately trying to draw one clear breath. Can you understand that?"

I nodded slowly.

"Then you must understand why I will do this thing while I have strength to do it. But I could not act without telling you first."

"Oh, Simon. Must you really?"

His expression was gently rebuking. Of course he must. Who was I to judge what sort of pain he was in? Or what would become of him if he destroyed himself? Like all good Christians, I had been taught that suicide was a sin, that it was unforgivable. But I had long since stopped believing in a God that could not forgive, and I knew I was not arrogant enough to prevent Simon from ending his pain.

"When? How long?"

He rubbed at my wrists, a slow, gentle rhythm that felt strangely calming amidst this new heartbreak. "I do not know yet. I should like to see the summer."

I nodded. "I will bring roses to you. And strawberries."

He looked at me for a long minute, his flecked grey eyes searching my face, memorizing it.

"I have always wondered what it would be like to kiss you," he said finally. "I always wondered what Edward felt."

Wordlessly, I leaned forward. I pressed my lips to his, surprised to find his warm and soft under my own. It had been years since I had kissed a man, and Simon's lips were nothing like Edward's. Simon's were searching and tentative, slowly exploring and remembering mine.

He put his hand to my face and I pulled back, shaken. I had not thought that kissing Simon would be unlike kissing my own relatives. But it felt vastly different, and I realized how vulnerable a woman becomes when it has been a very long time since she has been loved.

Simon lifted my hand to his lips and I saw there were tears in his eyes.

Neither of us spoke. I kissed him again, this time on the brow, and left him. I went to my room and sat on my bed in the dark, thinking of many things.

THE ELEVENTH CHAPTER

There were three ravens sat on a tree,
They were as black as they might be.
With a down derry, derry, derry, down, down.
The one of them said to his mate,
"Where shall we our breakfast take?"
—*Traditional Ballad*

y encounter with Val the next morning was hardly less alarming. Aquinas had just delivered the morning post. Among the usual heap of letters and advertisements, I spotted an envelope with familiar handwriting. Doctor Griggs. I slipped the letter into my pocket and was just about to lock myself into the study to read it when Valerius cornered me, looking uncharacteristically nervous.

"Good morning, Julia. I wonder if you might have a moment?"

I suppressed the flash of impatience I felt to get to my letter and summoned a smile. I saw Val only rarely these days. He was far too busy with his friends and amusements to spend much time at Grey House. Perhaps a few minutes with him would prove enjoyable.

"Of course. Come to my study. Aquinas will have had the fire lit."

He followed me, obedient as a spaniel, and settled himself next to me on the elderly sofa. He took up a pillow and began wrapping the fringe about his fingers. He had always been a fidgety child, though we had all hoped he would outgrow it. Clearly he had not, and his nerves were affecting mine, I realized as I caught myself twisting at a button. There was no imagining what difficulty he might have gotten himself into, and I was beginning to fear the worst.

I folded my hands quietly in my lap. "What is it, Val?" I said finally, my voice a little sharp. I smiled to soften it. "You can talk to me, you know."

He did not return my smile. His eyes, the wide, green March eyes, were clouded with unhappiness and there was the slightest start of a worry line on his brow. "I do know. I would hope that Father will not hear of this, though."

In spite of his sulkiness, I felt my irritation ebb. So that *was* it. He had gotten himself into a bit of trouble over a girl or money and did not want Father's wrath crashing down upon him. Surely it could not be too disastrous if Father's fury was the worst he had to fear.

"He shall hear nothing from me," I promised him. "Now, tell me everything."

He eyed me doubtfully, but plunged into his story.

"I was at the club last night. Playing cards."

My eyes narrowed. I did not much like where this was going. Valerius had always been notoriously unlucky at cards, a fact that our brother Plum had been only too happy to exploit when they were boys. Val's pocket money no sooner came in than it was promptly paid out to Plum to settle some debt or other. For years Val had kept him in paints and canvases. I would have thought that living with such an extortionist would have taught Val a lesson, but apparently it had not. And although I was content to permit Val to live at Grey House, I was not prepared to subsidize his gaming losses.

"It is not what you think," he put in hastily. "I won."

I blinked at him. "Did you really? How extraordinary."

His face relaxed for the first time. "I know. It was quite a lot of money, in fact. But there is one thing that I won that I am not entirely certain…that is, I wondered if you might like…oh, blast, just come to my room and see it for yourself."

Mystified, I followed him up the stairs and to his room, puzzled as to what he could have possibly won that would cause him so much difficulty.

He paused at the door to his room, steeling himself. "Now, do not be alarmed. I assure you, there is nothing to fear."

"Valerius, good heavens! What have you got in there? A lion from the royal zoo?"

I pushed past him to open the door and stopped in my tracks. Leering at me from its perch on the footboard of the bed was the largest, blackest bird I had ever seen. Not daring to turn my back on it, I called softly over my shoulder.

"Is that—"

He closed the door behind us. "A Tower raven, yes. Reddy Phillips apparently stole him for some sort of joke, and I won him last night at the tables."

He moved next to me, keeping a careful eye upon his avian guest.

"You must be mad! That bird is Crown property! Do you have any idea…"

Val put up his hands in defense. "I do, I assure you. I mean to return him to the proper authorities, but I do not want to get Reddy into any trouble. Until I work out how exactly to do that, I wondered if I could keep him here."

"Out of the question," I said, whirling on him. "How could you do something so utterly and appallingly stupid? What were you thinking?"

To his credit, Val looked properly abashed. "I know. But I really did not think I would even win the hand. You know how badly I play. Reddy was so certain he had the cards, and you know, I was, too. I only threw in the last of my money because I wanted to see if he would really put the bird up. And then he did. No one was more shocked than I when I won. I thought Reddy would have an apoplexy."

He was smiling and I fixed him with my sternest elder-sister look. "I never liked those Phillipses. Jumped-up tobacco merchants, all of them. And you are no better. Have you not thought of what this could mean to Father? And to poor Bellmont? It could ruin him in Parliament if anyone discovered that his youngest brother had received stolen property—the queen's stolen property no less! Just having that thing in your possession is a felonious act."

The bird, which had been gazing at us with interest, suddenly hopped from the footboard and skimmed across the carpet, coming to rest near my feet.

"Good morning," he said pleasantly.

I pointed a shaking finger. "It speaks."

Val nodded mournfully. "Yes. Apparently only a handful of them do."

"How on earth did Reddy Phillips get hold of it?" I asked, watching the raven's sharp black eyes watch me.

"His uncle has some sort of post in the Tower. Reddy paid him a visit and managed to smuggle this poor fellow out. He's not one of the public ravens, you know," he finished more cheerfully.

"Not one of the public ravens?" The bird had moved forward again, bobbing toward my shoes, pecking delicately at the carpet.

"Yes, some of them are kept in reserve, solely for breeding. This was one of them."

"And how is it that they have not yet discovered one is missing?" I asked, watching in horror as the creature plucked a long piece of wool from the carpet, unraveling the border.

"Reddy had another raven to put in its place. Apparently the Tower fellows did not much like him and pecked him to death shortly afterward. They buried that raven and still don't realize this one's gone missing."

"Of all the bloody stupid things to do," I murmured. Matters had gone from complicated to disastrous. "I suppose Father could explain it to Her Majesty, but they haven't spoken in years. I daresay she's still angry with him about that Irish business. He will be furious with you, and I cannot think that the queen will be much pleased, either."

Val gripped my hand. "You promised! Julia, you cannot tell him. We have not rowed for nearly six months. He has just consented to let me attend anatomy lectures at university. If you tell him, it will ruin everything. Besides, I did not steal the thing. I want to restore it."

He had a solid argument there. Reddy Phillips was the one who should be whipped.

"Can't you just go to the Tower and say that you found it, walking around outside the wall?" I asked, watching the bird inspect the hem of my draperies.

Val shook his head. "The Tower ravens are all clipped. They cannot fly outside the wall. But if you give me a few days, I am certain I can think of something. Please, Julia."

I looked into his earnest eyes, so like Father's, and knew I would not refuse him.

"Very well. But he must stay here, in this room. Pull up any furnishings he might eat, and see to it that you clean up after him."

Val clenched me into a suffocating embrace. "You are a queen amongst women," he said fervently.

"Victoria Regina" came the croaky little voice from the floor.

I put Val firmly away from my person. "And above all, keep him quiet."

"I will, I will, I promise you." He moved into the room and closed the door behind him.

And through the door, clear as a bell, I heard the croaky little voice say, "God Save the Queen."

THE TWELFTH CHAPTER

Why so pale and wan, fond lover?
Prithee, why so pale?
—Sir John Suckling
"Song"

*I*t was another hour before I managed to seclude myself in my study to read the letter. There were menus to discuss with Cook, laundry orders to give to Magda, and my wardrobe to peruse with Morag. In a fit of industry, Morag had decided that my mourning clothes were beginning to show some wear and that I should order some new ones. This was blatantly false—I had just purchased the black silk and the ensemble with swansdown trim. I strongly suspected she was short of funds and wanted something to sell at the market.

But as we winnowed the garments down to the few items she deemed acceptable, I remembered Aunt Ursula's remarks about widowhood and considered carefully a life spent in that suffocating black. I thought of the queen, a walking effigy in her widow's weeds, and I thought of the Hindu widows with their funeral pyres. There seemed little to choose between the two.

"Leave me the new silk, as well as that heap there," I told Morag, pointing to a pathetically modest pile on my bed. "You may have the rest to sell or make over for yourself."

She stared at me suspiciously. "Are you feeling quite well, my lady?"

"Quite," I returned briskly. "Pack the rest of these up and remove them. I shall need the space for my new things."

She bobbed her head and set to work, still throwing the odd glance at me over her shoulder. I did not care. While she packed away my mourning, I went to my writing table and dashed off a letter containing very specific instructions to Portia's dressmakers, the brothers Riche. In a very few minutes I finished the letter and dispatched it with a footman, feeling absurdly pleased with myself.

That mood lasted until I read the letter from Doctor Griggs. It was a thorough disappointment, from start to finish.

My dear Lady Julia,

I cannot tell you how very distressed I was to receive your letter. It has been my privilege to act as physician to the Grey family for these many years. During this time, I have diagnosed and treated Sir Sylvius Grey, his son Sir Edward, and now his nephew, Sir Simon. It has ever been apparent to me that the men of this family suffer from an illness that is of an hereditary and most vicious bent. I had hoped Sir Edward would escape this curse, but I realized in his youth that this was not to be. This weakness of the heart and lungs was said to be present in Sir Sylvius' father and grandfather, as well. It is for this reason that I say it is a mercy Sir Edward left no issue. Such a weakness in the constitution of such otherwise fine and noble gentlemen is a tragedy of the greatest magnitude, but it is not to be helped by modern medicine. I did all that any man could for Sir Edward and Sir Sylvius, just as I do now for Sir Simon.

As for your ladyship's own difficulties, I should prescribe a sleeping draught of poppy to provide a good night's sleep and all its healthful benefits. Should this not prove ef-

*ficacious, I would further prescribe an interview with the
vicar to offer some spiritual comfort.
I remain your very faithful servant,
William Griggs*

Pooh, I thought, tossing the letter to the desk. Not a scrap
of useful information. He had taken me for an addle-witted,
superstitious ninny.

Or he had poisoned Edward himself and deliberately put
me off the scent. I straightened, feeling quite startled by the
notion. It seemed absurd on the surface, but it was entirely
possible. Who better to help a sick man along to the hereafter
than his own doctor?

I rose quickly. It took only a matter of minutes to slip upstairs
for my things and make my way out of the house unnoticed.
Between Brisbane's lectures on discretion and Valerius' stolen
Crown property, I was very certain I did not wish Brisbane to
call at Grey House. I walked a little distance down Curzon Street
and hailed a cab near the Park. We made quite good time to
Brisbane's rooms, where the plump little housekeeper admitted
me promptly this time, waving me up the stairs with a smile.

I rapped sharply and was greeted by Monk, looking
somewhat strained.

"We did not expect your ladyship," he began.

"I know, but I have something to discuss with Mr. Brisbane.
Business," I said, brandishing the letter. He stepped back, reluctantly, I fancied, and admitted me to the room.

"If you will wait, my lady. I will tell him that you are here."

I nodded absently and made myself comfortable. I removed
my gloves and hat and coat, piling them on a chair in the
corner. There was a copy of *Punch* on the table. I ignored it
for several minutes, but as the time ticked past and I remained
alone, I grew restless. I was more than halfway through the
issue when Brisbane appeared.

"My lady, please forgive my tardiness," he said. I almost did not hear him, I was so surprised by his appearance. He was deathly pale under his usually swarthy colour, and there were faint new lines etched on his brow and on either side of his mouth. His eyes, usually so bright and watchful, were dull and sunken in his face.

I made to rise. "Mr. Brisbane, are you quite well? If I have called at an inopportune time—"

He waved me back to my seat. "Not at all. A trifling indisposition, I assure you."

But I was not assured. He moved slowly, without his usual grace, and I wondered what ailed him. Embarrassed at having pushed in at such a time, I thrust the letter at him.

"This is the reply from Doctor Griggs. It is disappointing, I am sure you will agree."

He read it over, his brow furrowing tightly as he looked at the paper. He held it for several minutes as if he were having trouble making out the words. At length he returned it.

"Disappointing, indeed."

"I wondered if perhaps he might be concealing something."

Brisbane passed a hand over his eyes. "Such as?"

"Perhaps he poisoned Edward. He had as good an opportunity as anyone, and the advantage of being in a position to certify the death as natural."

He nodded slowly. "Yes, but what motive? What profit to him to murder one of his most illustrious patients?"

I blushed wretchedly. Not only had I disturbed him at a time when he was clearly not fit for company, I had done so without having rationally appraised my sudden notion of Griggs' duplicity. "I had not thought that out. I came simply on impulse. I am sorry."

He tugged gently at his collar. "It makes no difference. There could be a hundred motives we have not yet discovered." He paused, as if gathering strength, then went on, his voice marginally less thready. "I have a friend, a surgeon. If we describe the symptoms of Sir Edward's collapse to him, I daresay he could come up with something useful."

"Excellent! Will you write to him?"

He blinked a few times, very slowly. "Yes. I will arrange an interview. We should both be present. I imagine he will have questions about Sir Edward's general health that I could not—"

He broke off then, his eyes fixed upon the fire, his shoulders tightly knotted, his jaw working furiously.

"Mr. Brisbane," I said softly.

He jerked his eyes toward me, seeming almost startled to see me there.

"I think it an excellent idea. Perhaps tomorrow—" I stopped as I watched him lift a hand to his temple.

"Mr. Brisbane, are you unwell?"

I made to rise, to help him, but he waved me off angrily.

"I will be fine. Go now. Send Monk to me." His voice was raspy now, as if the simple act of speaking was a tremendous effort.

I stood uncertainly. Both of his hands were fisted against his temples, grinding into his head. His brow was deeply creased, his mouth white and twisted in pain.

"Mr. Brisbane," I began.

"I said go—now!" This last was a full-throated bellow, ragged with pain and rage.

I will admit to cowardice. I snatched up my things and fled, throwing open the door to find Monk already hurrying to him. He was carrying a flask and some other paraphernalia I could not identify.

I did not stay to see what aid he administered. Instead, I hurried outside, never looking behind me. I walked quickly back to Grey House, making straight for the study. Once there, I poured out a glass of whiskey and took a deep swallow. It burned all the way to my belly, warming me through, but for the better part of an hour I trembled in spite of it.

THE THIRTEENTH CHAPTER

Within himself the danger lies…
—John Milton
Paradise Lost

For the rest of that day, I could not settle to anything. I meant to go over the household accounts with Aquinas, but after he had to explain the wine bill for the third time, he closed the grey leather ledger.

"I think your ladyship is much distracted," he said kindly. "Too much so to bother with the wine merchant. I will inform him that the port was charged twice to your account and that the last bottle of champagne he sent was unacceptably dry. Leave it with me, my lady."

"Thank you, Aquinas," I said with some embarrassment. "I will be more myself later. Was there anything else?"

"No, my lady. Nothing that cannot wait."

He bowed and left me alone with my thoughts, most of them unpleasant. Brisbane was unwell, which was unfortunate both for him personally and for the investigation. Simon had had a bad turn in the night, and Valerius was in possession of a stolen raven. The *queen's* stolen raven.

And I had gotten nothing useful from Doctor Griggs. What sort of detective would I make if I could not elicit information from someone I had known all of my life? I fretted for a while, then decided it was no use worrying about the investigation until Brisbane was feeling himself again. I took my supper tray into Simon's room, pleased to see him feeling a little stronger. He rallied enough from his bad night to take a portion of my lamb and a glass of wine. We even managed half a game of chess before he sent me away, rather to my relief. I had been losing badly.

It was later than I had thought when I left Simon, nearly half past ten. Val was out for the evening, hopefully making some arrangement about the raven, and I was feeling unmoored and wide awake. I poked about downstairs, picking up unfinished knitting, then a book of poetry, but putting them down again only a moment later. Finally, I settled into my study to attempt the accounts again. I applied myself, and this time actually managed to make a bit of progress. I made a few notes on matters I meant to discuss with Cook—she was paying entirely too much to the fishmonger, to begin with. And the amount of butter this household used in a month's time was nothing short of scandalous. I worked on, almost peacefully, relaxing a bit as the numbers spun out of the end of my pen. I could hear Aquinas moving about in the front hall, dousing lamps, when the bell rang. A moment later he came to the study door.

"My lady, a visitor. Mr. Nicholas Brisbane, if you will see him. He apologizes for the lateness of the hour."

I sprang up, upsetting the pot of ink onto a pile of magazines.

Aquinas whipped a snowy cloth from his pocket and wiped at the mess.

"Send him in, Aquinas. The ink has only ruined the magazines. The ledger is quite untouched."

He inclined his head, too correct to question my sudden attack of nerves. He swept the magazines up into a tidy pile and took them away along with his soiled dust cloth.

By the time Brisbane entered the study, I had managed to tidy myself, but I need not have bothered. He was looking rather less than dapper himself.

As always, his clothes were impeccable, but his face was still pale and drawn. He carried his walking stick, the same handsome ebony affair I had seen him carry before. But it seemed to me that he leaned on it rather more heavily now, and the silver head remained clutched in his white-fingered grasp. He was wearing a pair of smoky tinted spectacles that he did not remove as he greeted me. He surveyed the room for a moment, then seated himself with his back to the desk. I could not imagine why he should choose that chair—it was small and badly in need of fresh upholstery.

But as I took my seat, I realized that by choosing that particular chair he kept the bright lamp of the desk behind his shoulder, where it would not cast a glare into his eyes.

I looked at him, apprehensive, but he anticipated my question.

"I took the precaution of loitering until I was certain there was no one about to see me call," he said, his voice thin and brittle.

I smiled my thanks at his discretion.

"Would you care for tea, Mr. Brisbane?" I asked with a glance at the bellpull.

"No, thank you. But a whiskey would not go amiss."

I poured one from the table by the door and took one myself. He drank half of it off quickly, then sat back, his head resting on the back of the chair.

"I am glad to see that your indisposition was short-lived."

His lips twisted into what might have passed for a smile on someone else. "It was not. I daresay I am keeping it at bay— but not for long, I fear. In fact, I may not be available to you for some days' time."

"Indeed?" I took a sip of my whiskey, ignoring the little thorn of annoyance that I felt. I had thought we were compatriots in this together. I had not expected he would leave me to get on with it myself.

A spasm of pain seemed to shake him then. He closed his eyes, his breath coming rather quickly.

After a minute, it slowed and the spasm passed. He opened his eyes slowly, blinking against the low light of the room. "I have contacted my friend, the surgeon. He is very busy at present, but he should be able to meet with us in Chapel Street in a few days," he said.

That hardly seemed likely, given Brisbane's obvious ill health. I felt ashamed of my annoyance. He gave every indication of a man who was truly suffering, and I had pushed myself and my investigation upon him with no regard for his own trials.

"Mr. Brisbane, your indisposition—"

He waved a hand. "Nothing for you to be concerned with. It is an old adversary. As I said, I will be unavailable to you for a few days. I will not write, but I shall send word through Monk when I am ready to resume the investigation. In the meanwhile, I must caution you not to play the sleuth hound. It could well be dangerous."

I sipped at my drink, annoyed once more. Brisbane could not help being unwell, but that was no reason for me to sit on my hands.

And why the air of mystery about his illness? On the whole he seemed perfectly healthy, and yet apparently he suffered from some malady that laid him so low he would not even be able to manage a pen. Of course, he was absolutely correct, it was no concern of mine. So naturally I thought about it—excessively.

He drank off the last of his whiskey and rose, pausing a moment to gather his strength and his walking stick. I saw now that its silver knob was fashioned into a horse's head, with ebony eyes and a deeply chased halter. The neck was strongly muscled, as if modeled when the horse was in full gallop. It was an impressive, heavy piece, unlike anything I had ever seen before, and I wondered where he had purchased it. I walked with him as far as the door. He turned to me then, his eyes blazing black behind the smoked lenses of his spectacles.

"I meant what I said, my lady. You must not endanger yourself. I cannot protect you if you do not follow my instructions."

I nodded, although inwardly I was seething with impatience. Now that we had begun this investigation I wanted nothing more than to finish it.

But I gave him my word and bade him a demure goodnight. He looked at me closely, as if he suspected my rebelliousness. I dropped my eyes and offered him my hand. He took it, clasping it hard in his. It was the first time I had felt the skin of his bare hand against mine, and I was surprised at how warm it was. Overly warm—he was starting a fever. Whatever illness he suffered from, it was real, at least.

"You have given me your word, Lady Julia. Do not disappoint me."

My head went up sharply. He had never used my Christian name. I opened my mouth to remonstrate with him against this familiarity, but I did not. He was obviously in great pain, and yet he had roused himself to come to me and warn me that I would be unprotected until he had recovered. Surely that earned him the right to a little impertinence? And even if it did not, what was the purpose in maintaining pointless formalities? We were partners in this investigation, however junior he might see my role. He treated me like an elder brother might treat a younger sister, with indulgence sometimes, with breathtaking rudeness at others. It was a fraternal sort of relationship, I argued with myself, and entitled to a certain informality.

Brisbane was watching me with interest, no doubt waiting to see if I would protest at this presumption. He was still holding my hand, so I shook his, gravely.

"I will remember. Take quite good care of yourself," I told him.

Just then the door from belowstairs opened and Magda, the laundress, appeared. I was surprised to see her; I had thought her long since abed. I moved to speak to her, but she was not looking at me. Her eyes were fixed upon Brisbane. She came toward us, her bright shawl wrapped tightly about her shoulders.

"Magda? What is it?" She ignored me, coming to stand quite close to Brisbane, peering up through his shadowy lenses. He recoiled from her and I could not blame him. I had warned her about putting on the Gypsy in front of visitors.

"Who is this posh rat?" she asked. There was humour in her eyes and a bright, snapping malice as well.

"This gentleman is a guest of mine, and no business of yours," I said sharply. I turned to Brisbane.

"I apologize. This is Magda, my laundress. She was just going belowstairs," I said with a significant jerk of the head to Magda.

She opened her brown palm to him. "Care to cross my palm with silver? No, I thought not. I will not tell your fortune, though I think I know it well enough." She gave him a laugh and a little push.

"Magda! That is quite enough."

Aquinas appeared then, frowning. I was profoundly relieved; he was the only one in the household who could control her. He took her firmly by the arm and she went docilely, pausing only to throw a meaningful look at Brisbane.

"We will talk again, won't we, little *vesh-juk?*"

The belowstairs door closed after them. Before Brisbane could speak, I rushed to apologize.

"I am so sorry. Magda is usually perfectly well behaved. She can speak the Queen's English as well as I can, but she likes to earn a little extra money by telling fortunes. She thinks it helps business if she puts on the Gypsy."

Brisbane, who had looked perfectly appalled by Magda's little display, seemed to gather himself. He waved my apology aside. "There is no need to explain. I was merely surprised that you employ a Gypsy woman as your laundress."

I spread my hands. "It is complicated. Her people have always camped on Father's land in Sussex. When Magda had some trouble with them, she naturally turned to me. We had closed up the country house, so I could only offer her a position here in London. She works well enough, when she has a mind to. Her life has not been an easy one."

His lip curled in derision. "Do not waste your pity, my lady. I have some experience with Gypsies, and I have found that their lives are just about as difficult as they wish them to be. Good night, my lady."

He nodded shortly and took his leave, letting himself out and leaving me to puzzle over his coolness. I had thought him broad-minded. His obvious distaste for Gypsies surprised me. But in that respect, he was like most other people of my acquaintance. Father was one of the few landowners in Sussex to welcome Romanies onto his property. As children we had played with them, learned their games. But even as they expressed their gratitude at having a safe place to stay, if only for a little while, they kept themselves apart in every way that mattered. We were rarely invited to eat with them, and were strictly forbidden to learn any of their language.

Thus, I had no idea what it was that Magda had just called Brisbane. I only hoped it was not an obscenity, though her tribe of Roma were so fierce about guarding their tongue from outsiders, he would not have understood it in any case. I should have to speak to her about her behavior, something I dreaded. Usually, I allowed her little foibles to pass unmentioned, but soliciting my guests for fortunes in my own home was beyond the pale. Perhaps London was proving too expensive for her modest pay and she was in need of money. Perhaps I should raise her wages.

As I stood in the doorway of the study, pondering the thorny problem of Magda, the bell rang again and Aquinas reappeared to answer it. I wondered if Brisbane had forgotten something, as there was the low rumble of male voices. But another visitor was admitted to the hall.

"Father!"

I went to him and kissed him. "This is an unexpected pleasure. What brings you to me at this hour of the evening?"

He handed his coat and stick to Aquinas and held out his arm, gesturing me to lead the way to the study.

"A letter I received this morning. Come, my pet. You have some explaining to do."

THE FOURTEENTH CHAPTER

As mad as a March hare.
—*Proverb (14th Century)*

I poured Father a glass of port and took nothing for myself. After the whiskey I had drunk with Brisbane, I was feeling addled enough, and I had the notion that this conversation was going to require all of my wits.

Father took a sniff of his wine, then a tentative sip. He raised his brows in my direction.

"Not at all bad. Better than the dishwater you used to serve, my pet."

"I've given over the ordering of the wine to Aquinas. He has a better nose for wine than Edward did."

"Hmm." He took another sip. "Most agreeable. But this," he said, waving my own letter at me, "was not. What the devil did you mean writing this to Griggs?"

I spread my hands innocently. "I meant what I said—I was upset. I thought that Doctor Griggs could ease my mind."

He looked at me shrewdly from under his thick white brows. "Ye gods, girl, if you think I am going to believe that, you are dafter than any child of mine ought to be. Now, if it is a private business, tell me so, and we will not speak of it. I've no wish to press a confidence you do not wish to make."

I thought for a long moment, then shook my head. "No, it is just as well. I could use your advice."

I told him, as briefly as I could without losing any relevant detail, what Brisbane and I were about. When I finished, he whistled sharply.

"So that is your game. Well, I cannot say I am entirely disappointed. No, I cannot say that at all."

Far from looking disappointed, he was happier than I had seen him in an age. His colour was high and his eyes were gleaming.

"You are enjoying this!"

He shrugged, looking only very slightly guilty. "Edward has been gone a year. There is little enough chance of you getting yourself into any real danger. Edward's murderer, if there is such a person, is probably long gone from the scene. This entire exercise is largely academic. It is you I am enjoying, my girl."

"Me? I am as I ever was. I have only cut my hair and bought some new clothes."

He shook his head. "No, it is more than that. You've finally done something daring enough to deserve the family name. You have begun to live up to the family motto."

"*Quod habeo habeo?* 'What I have I hold?'"

Father rolled his eyes. "Not that one. The other."

Audeo. "I dare." It had been our informal motto since the seventh Earl March had married an illegitimate daughter of Charles II, thus linking our family with the royal house of Stuart. Family legend claims that he adopted the motto with an eye to putting his wife on the throne someday, until Monmouth's unsavory end warned him off of his kingly ambitions. It was one of the favorite family stories, although when I was seven I had remarked that the seventh earl had not really dared very much at all. It was the only time I was ever sent to bed without supper. After that I never really warmed to the motto. It had always seemed like a good excuse for irresponsible and reprehensible behavior. I had long thought we would be a far more respectable family if our motto had been "I sit quietly in the corner and mind my own business."

Father would not be put off. "There is more to it than lopping off your curls and buying some new dresses. I always worried about you as a child, Julia. You took your mother's death very hard, you know." He paused, his expression dreamy. "I wonder, do you even remember her?"

I thought hard. "I remember someone who used to hold me, very tightly. Someone who smelled of violet. And I think I remember a yellow gown. The silk rustled under my fingers."

He shook his head, regretful. "Ah, I thought you would have remembered more. That was her with the violet scent. I am glad you wear it now. Sometimes you move through the room and I could almost imagine she has been walking there."

He paused and I think his throat may have been as thick as mine. But he went on, and he was smiling. "The yellow silk was her favorite gown that last summer, when she was expecting Valerius. She wore it almost every day, I think. You stopped talking for just a bit after she died, do you remember that?"

"No." But I did. I remembered the long silences, the feeling that if I spoke, if I moved on, she would never come back. The certainty that I had to stay just as I was if I wanted her to return. I practiced stillness, rarely moving, trying to force myself not to grow without her.

"Of course, you hated Valerius," Father was saying. "Blamed him, I imagine. Most of you children did. I did so myself for a while, although it wasn't the boy's fault. Ten children in sixteen years—too much for her. But she wanted you all. She wanted you so very much."

His voice trailed off, and I knew he was seeing her. She had been beautiful; I had seen the portraits. I had impressions of her, but no true memories. He was right. I had been six when she died. I should have remembered more.

"You are very like her," he said suddenly. "More than any of the others. She was gentle and good, much more respectable than the scapegrace Marches she married into," he said with a chuckle. "She would have understood you with your quiet little places, your desperate need to be normal. Yes, you are very like her." He leaned forward, his eyes bright green in the lamplight. "But she knew how to take a chance, my pet. After all, she married me. You have her blood, Julia, but you are a March as well. There are seven centuries' worth of adventure and risk and audacity in your blood. I always knew it would come out eventually."

I smiled. "I always thought Bellmont must be quite a bit like Mother."

"No. He is the biggest rebel of the lot. That's why he runs Tory."

"And you think I am beginning to live up to the March legacy?"

He gave a satisfied sigh. "I do. This murder business may be just what you need. Although, best to let sleeping dogs lie, I always think."

I snorted at him. "You have never let a sleeping dog lie in your entire life, Father. And surely you are not condoning letting a murderer walk free?"

He shrugged. "You have not found a murderer yet. You may not even have a murder. Perhaps poor Edward ought to lie where we buried him."

I did think about it. It was tempting, the idea of sweeping this bit of possible nastiness under the carpet and getting on with my life. But I knew I could not. I would not be able to sleep nights if I thought that Edward had been murdered and I had done nothing to right that wrong. I smiled at the irony that undertaking this investigation might actually be the one thing in my life that satisfied both my sense of duty and my very secret, very small desire for adventure. I looked at Father and shook my head. "I cannot. It is my duty. If there is any chance that Edward was murdered, then I must do all that I can to bring him justice."

He finished his port. "All right, then," he said, rising. "Do what you must. And I will not ask you what that Brisbane fellow was doing leaving here at such an hour," he said, chucking me under the chin.

My face grew hot. "We were discussing the investigation," I told him quickly. "He was here a quarter of an hour at the most."

Father smiled at me sadly. "My dear girl, if you don't know what mischief can be gotten up to in a quarter of an hour, you are no child of mine. Come to supper on Thursday next. Hermia is having an oratory contest and I mean to sleep through it."

He was gone with a wave over his head, leaving me dumb-struck. Surely my own father was not advocating an illicit affair with Brisbane? But the more I thought about it, the more I realized that was exactly what he was doing. It did not bear thinking about. Well, truthfully, I did think about it quite a lot. At least until Valerius came home covered in blood.

THE FIFTEENTH CHAPTER

If circumstances lead me, I will find
Where truth is hid, though it were hid indeed
Within the centre.
—William Shakespeare
Hamlet

ather had not been gone a quarter of an hour when Valerius came home. I heard him call a brief greeting to Aquinas in the hall, then hurry past the open door of my study and up the stairs.

I called to him, but he did not reply. I followed him up the stairs, catching him up at the door to his room.

"Valerius! Whatever is the matter? I want to speak to you. Father was here this evening—Val? What is it?"

He was hunched over, facing the door, his coat folded over his arm. He was not wearing his waistcoat.

"Are you ill?" I put a hand to his shoulder to turn him, but he threw me off.

"I am well, please." He edged away, but I followed.

"Julia, leave me."

"Valerius, stop being tiresome. Turn around and face me this instant." He went very still, probably weighing the odds that I would go away and leave him in peace. He must have realized how slim they were, for when I reached out for him again he turned. His face was ghastly, pale and lined with fatigue, but it was his shirt that made me gasp. The pure white linen of his shirtfront was dark crimson, crusted with dried blood. I put out my hand.

"Val—you're hurt! My God, what happened to you?"

He brushed my hand away. "I am well. The blood—it isn't mine."

"Whose, then?" I put myself between him and the door and he sighed, knowing he was going to have to tell me the entire story.

"There was a fight outside the theatre. It was quite vicious. A man, set upon by ruffians. They got out his tooth and cut him rather badly about the head."

I raised a finger toward the wide crimson stain.

"Careful," he said, edging away. "There are still some spots that are wet."

I shook my head in astonishment.

"But so much blood, you must have been quite close to him."

He nodded, his face rather grey at the memory of what he had seen. "I sat with him and tried to stop the bleeding while his brother went for their carriage."

"How ghastly for you! What were they about, these ruffians? Did they mean to rob him?"

Val passed a hand over his face. "I do not know. Some private quarrel, I think. But I am out of it now. I want only to change my clothes and get into bed."

I gestured toward his fouled shirt. "Give me the shirt. It must be put to soak or it will be spoilt."

He hesitated, then nodded and slipped into his room. I heard the raven *quorking* at him irritably. After several minutes, he opened the door just enough to thrust the soiled shirt into my hands.

"Thank you," he said shortly. He shut the door before I could question him further. I shrugged. I had no doubt the fight would be detailed in the morning papers. And very likely an enterprising reporter had obtained more details than Valerius had.

Holding the crusted shirt at arm's length, I made my way down the stairs, through the hall belowstairs, past the kitchens and into the laundry. Aquinas was finishing his rounds of the windows and doors, his locking-up ritual for the night. He always carried a lamp with him and extinguished the last of the house lights as he went. The front of the house was in darkness and I could hear him securing the bolts on the garden doors.

I moved quietly, feeling unaccountably timid about explaining Val's gory shirt. If Aquinas saw it he would insist upon soaking it himself and he would doubtless find some fault with Magda's methods of keeping the laundry, his own standards being far more exacting than hers. The absence of a housekeeper at Grey House, though unorthodox, was perfectly adequate in most circumstances. With Magda, it sometimes proved a liability. For the most part she kept to herself, and on the rare occasions when discipline was required, Aquinas was man enough for the task. But Magda seldom went along easily with his corrections, preferring to rage or sulk, depending upon which approach seemed likeliest to garner my support. The two of them were entirely capable of waging a war of attrition that would last for days. Rather than facing a staff row, it seemed far simpler to deal with Val's nasty shirt myself.

Although, I should have brought a lamp or at least a candle, I realized as I barked my shin on the pressing table in the laundry. By all rights I should have summoned Magda to take the shirt herself, but I was far too tired to even contemplate tackling Magda. There was still the question of her appalling behavior toward Brisbane to address, and I was unwilling to speak to her tonight. It was late now, and I was more than ready for my own bed. All I wanted was to dispose of Val's unspeakable garment and put the whole evening's bizarre events behind me.

With any luck, the stains would have soaked out by

morning and there would be little trace of Val's adventure at the theatre. Magda always kept a bucket of cold water at hand for the soaking, and I knew she liked it to be stood below the front windows, those that overlooked the area. It gave her good light, even on overcast days, and a chance to see passersby—if only from the ankle down.

I had just reached the bucket and lifted the lid when I heard voices. I started, thinking I was not alone in the laundry. But as they went on, I realized they were coming from the area above me. The pair had taken refuge behind the potted trees to the side of the front door and were speaking in low, harsh voices. I recognized them at once.

"I will give you one last chance to let go of my sleeve before I break your fingers." To my astonishment, I realized that this was Brisbane. His voice was iron, cold as I had never heard it, and I had little doubt that he meant his threat, though I could not imagine what he was doing there, of all places. He had left Grey House an hour before.

Magda's laugh echoed mirthlessly.

"Oh, I think not. You will not hurt me. There are still some of us who remember Mariah Young."

These last words were a hiss, and they must have struck Brisbane like a lash, for I heard a scrape, like a quick footstep, and her sharp intake of breath. There was a little moan of pain.

"Do not interfere with me," he told her. "I will ruin you if you dare."

"Others have tried," she spat back. "But you remember that I know who Mariah Young was—*and I know how she died.*"

He must have released her then, for there was a sharp clang against the railing and the sound of booted footsteps moving quickly away in the dark. And following him into the night was Magda's laugh, low and throaty, like the rasping call of a raven.

THE SIXTEENTH CHAPTER

Oh, we are lords' and ladies' sons,
Born in bower or in hall,
And you are some poor maid's child
Borned in an ox's stall.
—*Traditional Ballad*

To my surprise, I slept rather well that night. The alcohol I had consumed, coupled with the evening's strange events, proved entirely too much for me. I crept up the back-stairs in order to avoid Aquinas, said little to Morag as she got me ready for bed, and was asleep almost as soon as she closed the door behind her.

But I woke early to the muffin-man's bell, and lay awake, listening to the streets come to life and thinking hard about the previous night. Brisbane's initial call had been unexpected, but not unorthodox. Whatever malady he suffered, it had been considerate of him to make the effort to warn me that he would be incommunicado for some days.

Father's call was somewhat more puzzling. I could well believe him capable of encouraging me in as bizarre an undertaking as a murder investigation. What I could not believe was that he actually seemed to be regretting the fact that I had not taken Brisbane as a lover. That Father had never entirely approved of my marriage was no secret. Just before he walked me down the aisle, he had paused in the vestry and offered to take me away—France, Greece, anywhere I wanted if I had changed my mind. I had laughed, thinking him in jest, but after Edward and I had been married for some time, I began to notice things I had not seen before. Father, always a woolgatherer, became sharply observant whenever Edward was in the room. I watched him watch my husband, and wondered what he was thinking. I never had the courage to ask and he never said, but I suspected I knew already. Edward was the sort of man Father universally despised— wealthy, self-satisfied and utterly incapable of thinking or feeling deeply. Father's sensibilities were so refined, he had been known to lock himself in his study and weep over *Titus Andronicus* for hours. Edward had not even wept when his mother died. Father might deplore Bellmont's stance as a Tory, but he applauded his convictions. Edward had had none.

Whenever the subjects of politics or religion or philosophy arose, generating a heated debate at the March dinner table, Edward would sit with a tolerant half smile firmly on his mouth and say nothing. No matter how fiercely Father baited him, he never rose to it, never offered an opinion on anything more serious than the cut of an evening suit or the vintage of a wine. He let the property at Greymoor decline—the most venal of sins to my own land-mad family. Marches had been taking the notion of stewardship seriously for centuries. We could no more leave a field unploughed or a hedgerow untended than we could keep from breathing. I remembered one conversation in particular. There had been a spirited disagreement regarding enclosure and my brother Benedick had appealed to Edward for his opinion. This was early days yet, when they had not realized that he was never going to take an interest in such things. They had all looked to Edward, eager for his view. He had simply smiled his sweet, sleepy smile and lifted his glass.

"Brother Benedick," he had said, "I cannot think of such things when there is wine such as this to drink. You must tell me the name of your agent," he concluded, turning to my father.

This was a blind, of course. Edward might like to discuss vintages, but he never bothered to keep them straight. His own cellar was a disgrace, not because he lacked the intellect to stock it properly, but because he lacked the initiative. Quite simply, he was the most indolent person I have ever known.

And just then, Benedick must have realized it, too, for I heard him as Father began to discuss the wine, mutter under his breath, "Bloody useless." I raised my eyes just in time to see the tiny smile flicker over Olivia's lips and the way Bellmont was carefully studying his plate. They all thought so. But Olivia's smile was not malicious, and Benedick, for his disapproval, did not actually dislike Edward. They deplored his lack of energy, his casual ways and his refusal to properly manage his land, but they all liked him in spite of themselves. He had a way of endearing himself to people, a manner of charming them with clever conversation and self-deprecating humour that made them in turn feel quite witty. Everyone always felt brighter and sharper and more brilliant when Edward was one of our number.

"He is a diamond-polisher," Portia once told me, and she was correct. He had a gift of being able to take one's feeble little quips and shine them up into real cleverness. He never read books, and rarely newspapers, except to see if his name was mentioned. But he always seemed to know what was being said, and about whom, who was doing what, and to whom. I suspected it was this ability to keep his finger firmly on society's pulse that multiplied the respectable fortune he had inherited into a tiny empire by the time of his death. He listened closely when others talked, and people always talked freely around him. He always cocked his head toward the person to whom he was speaking, enveloping them both in a warm intimacy. He knew just what questions to ask, and did so without anyone ever feeling that he had been intrusive or prying. He always prised just the precise nugget of information he needed, then passed it along to his man of affairs with instructions on how to act upon it.

I knew none of this until after his death, of course. It came out during a long session with the solicitor, Mr. Teasdale. We were making an exhaustive tour of Edward's investments, and I was expressing my astonishment that his affairs had been so sophisticated, so diversified and far-thinking. Mr. Teasdale finally explained to me about Edward's business practices, shamefacedly, as if it was something slightly tawdry. But ingenious, just the same, and behind Mr. Teasdale's demure expression lay more than a little admiration for Edward's abilities. I did not bother to explain to Mr. Teasdale that he might have saved his adulation. Edward had only engaged in his pony tricks for his own amusement. If making money had required anything more demanding than gossiping with friends and penning occasional letters to his agent, he would never have bothered.

It was rather like his pretensions to collecting art. Edward loved landscapes and would often come upon one that he loved at a friend's home. A discreet inquiry would be made and, if his friend was amenable, a quiet sale would be arranged. But Edward would never have troubled to actually visit a gallery, or worse yet, commission an artist for himself. Even his tailor knew better than to require more than two fittings for any garment as Edward simply could not be bothered. He liked things that came easily to him—his inheritance, money, me.

It was highly interesting to me to see that what I always thought of as Edward's little game—spending time quietly drawing people out of themselves—had in fact been an extremely lucrative business practice. I thought of all the people who had said to me over the years that Edward was such a wonderful listener, so very compassionate and feeling. They always envied me, although they needn't have bothered. I was the one person Edward rarely listened to, simply because we were so seldom together.

But everyone else felt the warmth of his sunny attentions, never realizing that there was something slightly chilly and shadowy behind them. I found myself staring at my bedroom ceiling—pale bluish-grey, Edward's choice—and wondering if anyone had guessed that his interest in them had been more calculating than convivial. Had someone been hurt by this? Betrayed, even? Could such a thing drive a person to murder? Possibly, under the right circumstances.

But what were the right circumstances? And what sort of person?

I toyed with that question while I listened to the cabs beginning to rattle down Curzon Street. Traffic was becoming appalling in London and I was longing for the country. I usually decamped by May, but not this year, I feared. Last year, just after Edward's death, I had taken Simon to Bellmont Abbey. The journey was slow, in deference to his failing health, but he had loved it. He felt well enough to have his Bath chair out in the garden where we spent long hours, reading and working on word puzzles together. I painted sometimes, very badly, and we talked or remained silent as the mood took us. His cheeks were brown by the time we came back to London in September, but the city air was a vicious change. He took to his bed again immediately, his cough bad, his colour worse. That summer had been his last rally. Since then his strength had continued to ebb and I knew that if I tried to take him back to Sussex again he would not survive the journey. Even if Brisbane and I concluded our investigation, I would not leave Simon.

But I would regret the summer in the country, I knew. I would miss the fresh, jeweled berries and the sprightly games of croquet, the long sunny afternoons on the lawn stretching from luncheon to tea, the turns on the lake in the ancient rowboat Father kept, the thin muslin gowns that seemed almost indecent after the thick winter garments we had worn in town. Well, I could at least walk in the Park and instruct Cook to purchase berries, I supposed. There was no substitute for the long walks over the Downs, but I made a mental note to order some lighter things from the dressmakers and returned to my ruminations.

Father—and his curious visit. Now that I thought on it, it did not much surprise me that he suggested I take a lover, however discreet he had been. I must have been a sad disappointment to him with my quiet, conventional ways. I had sometimes caught him looking at me with a pensive, almost wistful air, as if he were waiting hopefully for me to do something dashing and romantic and decidedly Marchian. With a legacy of seven centuries of elopements, abandonments, disinheritings, and the occasional execution to spice things up, nothing I did would shock him greatly. And perhaps he and Portia were correct. Perhaps the attention of a man who appreciated me would prove a balm....

One of the maids—Sally, I think it was—came in then with morning tea, and I put aside Father's visit to ponder the more serious events that had followed.

Val's appearance, gore-stained and unprepossessing, had not been a happy development. I had thought he had settled down rather nicely into life at Grey House. Granted, we saw almost nothing of each other, but that suited us both quite well and he had seemed more contented in my house than in Father's.

But he had become almost mysterious of late in his comings and goings. The existence of Her Majesty's raven in my Blue Room was solid proof of that. I should have handed him over to Father before Val returned from the opera, I realized ruefully. Father would have been furious with him initially; I always suspected he harbored some tender feelings for the queen, their having played together as children being one of his fondest memories. But his irritation would have subsided—eventually. He would have seen to it that the thing was taken back to the Tower and restored to its proper place.

And he would have taken up Val's part with the queen, I had no doubt of that. He might rail against the little idiot in private, but no one, not even the queen, would be permitted to speak against one of his own. He might even think of it as one of those high-spirited little japes he was always wishing on us. And surely Val would forgive me for breaking his confidence if everything turned out for the best.

Unfortunately, I had not had the presence of mind to think of it the night before. I had been too preoccupied with Father and Brisbane. And Magda. I sipped at my cooling tea, thinking again of the words she had hissed at him in the darkness.

I know who Mariah Young was…and I know how she died.

Ominous words, chilling even. I had no idea who Mariah Young was, but I did not much think I would like to find out. Was Magda trying to imply that Brisbane knew something about the death of this woman? Or worse, had had something to do with it himself?

I put down my tea and pulled the coverlet to my chin. Had I entrusted myself, foolishly, to a person capable of the very crime we were trying to investigate? Was he capable of violence? Or had Mariah Young died as the result of some tragic accident, perhaps at Brisbane's hands? What did I really know of Brisbane? And, more to the point, what did Magda know?

I was still puzzling over these questions when Morag bustled in with the news that my bath was ready. I bathed and dressed that morning in a state of distraction, still mulling questions for which I had no answers.

And because I was thinking of Brisbane when I took my seat at the breakfast table, it seemed like some sort of sorcery to find a letter from him waiting on the salver next to my plate.

I put out a finger to poke the envelope, not entirely certain it was real. It was, although the handwriting was thinner, less confident than I had seen it. Whatever ailed him, he was clearly in a decline. I opened it, scanning it quickly as Aquinas presented the toast.

My lady,
My friend finds himself unexpectedly available and places himself at our disposal this morning. He will be in Chapel Street at eleven o'clock. I hope that this does not inconvenience you.

Unlike the body of the note, the signature was firm and thick, as though Brisbane had borne down hard with the pen, making an impression in the paper. I ran my finger over it, tracing the loops of his handwriting. If Brisbane's condition was worsening, I did not think I much wanted to call upon him. But only he knew the limits of his strength. I doubted he would have allowed his friend to visit if it was a very great hardship to him.

In a matter of minutes I had penned a quick response and dispatched Desmond to Chapel Street. I sat back, picking at my cold eggs and waving off Aquinas when he offered to fetch me hot ones.

For some reason I could not identify, my appetite had entirely fled.

THE SEVENTEENTH CHAPTER

I have a strange infirmity, which is nothing
To those that know me.
—William Shakespeare
Macbeth

arrived at Brisbane's rooms at ten past eleven, when I was quite certain his friend would have already arrived. Between my father's thinly veiled hint that I take Brisbane for a lover and Magda's less thinly veiled hint that Brisbane was a possible murderer, I was not inclined to be alone with him. In fact, I was not certain which idea made me the more nervous.

The day was pleasant enough—cloudy, but without the chill wind that would have necessitated the carriage. I walked, for the second time in two days, but this time I took careful note of my surroundings. It was liberating, really. I had never been accustomed to walking in London—limiting my exercise to occasional walks in the Park—but I found it exhilarating. Mindful of propriety, I was thickly veiled and I walked purposefully, keeping my head still so that I appeared to look neither right nor left.

But my eyes roved constantly, taking it all in. I was amazed at how different a town it seemed now that there was no carriage window between London and me. My hems were inevitably filthy by the time I arrived at Brisbane's rooms, but I saw so much! There were Mayfair gentlemen, striding with an air of entitlement—these I was careful to avoid. Some of them I recognized, but although a few of them cast glances (appreciative?) in my direction, none ventured to speak to me and none peered too closely through my veil.

These lords did not interest me. I had spent my life packed elbow to elbow with them at dining tables and in ballrooms. No, I was enthralled with the nannies, starched and upright, taking their clean-scrubbed and well-bundled charges for air in the Park. There were becapped maids, scurrying on errands for their mistresses, and less frequently, footmen decked in velvet livery. I wondered at the letters in their hands. Invitations? *Billets-doux?* They were full of their own importance with their elegant braid trim and plush knee breeches and I thought, not for the first time, that I would be rather relieved to sell Grey House and be rid of mine. It seemed silly now to keep a pair of young men in service simply because they were decorative. Loftily they pushed their way down the street, striding amid the flower girls and chestnut sellers and barrel-organ players, shouldering a path through the crowds. I saw one, a tall fellow in sky-blue livery, ruthlessly elbow a flower seller out of his way, jostling her bouquets into the mud. She cursed at him fluently and I took note of some of the words. I gave her a shilling and she handed me a bunch of springy lavender with a smile. I waved her off as she went to find change for me and she bobbed me a curtsey, wishing me well.

I walked along, sniffing the crisp scent of the lavender, trying to remember the last time I had actually paid for something myself. All of the shops I frequented sent their bills to Grey House. And Morag usually carried the coins we required for incidental expenses. It was invigorating to be alone for once, surrounded by so many people, each of them speaking a slightly different English, each of them owning a slightly different London. I realized then that for all my pining for the country, I had come to love the town just as fiercely.

I strode proudly as those lords then, marking my steps with the point of my umbrella and occasionally taking a deep, pungent breath of my lavender. It was one of the loveliest moments of my life, I thought—the more so for having been unexpected.

I arrived at Brisbane's rooms feeling fresh and more than ready to meet whatever challenge lay ahead of us. It seemed ridiculous now, that accusation of Magda's. Whatever she meant, she could not have meant to imply murder. It simply was not possible.

Or so I thought until Brisbane opened the door. He looked wretched, like a man just this side of hell—pale and tight-featured. His eyes were glassy, the pupils pulled in so small that I wondered if he had taken laudanum. My own grand-mother, racked by pain, had taken refuge in a green laudanum bottle herself. She had looked just the same in the days before her death, hollow-eyed and brittle.

"Mr. Brisbane. I hope you are well," I ventured, although I knew perfectly well he was nothing of the sort.

He nodded, then winced. The slight motion must have brought on a shaft of pain, for his face whitened even further.

"Mordecai is already here," he said, his voice thin and rasping.

I moved into the room, lifting my veil. Before the fire stood a youngish man, early thirties, perhaps. He was tall, nearly as tall as Brisbane, and dark, but there the resemblance ended. This man was thicker, almost plump, and his features were marked by the sort of earnest sweetness that one associates with happy dogs. In fact, he put me greatly in mind of a puppy—a very large one, but a puppy still. His hair was floppy and his clothes gently shabby. He looked a comfortable, lived-in sort of person. I liked him instantly.

He turned, smiling at me a smile that extended to his eyes and suffused his entire face with pleasure.

From behind me Brisbane made the introductions.

"Lady Julia Grey, allow me to introduce to you my good friend, Doctor Mordecai Bent. Mordecai, this is Lady Julia Grey, the widow of Sir Edward Grey."

I moved to shake his hand and it engulfed mine warmly.

"I cannot tell you how grateful I am that you are willing to help us," I began.

He waved me off immediately. "The gratitude is entirely mine, my lady. Nicholas knows I love nothing so much as a good puzzle. And poisons are a special hobby of mine."

I felt my eyebrows lift a little. "Oh? How very unusual."

"Not at all," he said, his large, spaniel-brown eyes boring into mine earnestly. "All of our medicines have their origin in plants that are deadly if taken in too great a dose. There is no curative in the world that is not a potential poison in the wrong hands."

"I had not thought of it in quite that way," I replied.

Brisbane waved us to chairs then and I sat opposite Doctor Bent, drawing off my gloves as I cast a surreptitious glance at Brisbane. He had sat slowly, as if the smallest motion was painful to him. I wondered that his friend did not seem more aware of his condition, but it was not my place to ask. Perhaps he was already treating Brisbane for his ailment. I certainly hoped so. Brisbane looked ready for a shroud.

"I assume Mr. Brisbane has given you the particulars of Sir Edward's death?"

Doctor Bent nodded. "He has. I must say that the ability to make a diagnosis with any certainty after this length of time, and with no postmortem, is greatly compromised. You do understand that?"

I nodded. "Yes, but I feel very strongly that this was a case of murder. So does Mr. Brisbane."

Doctor Bent went quite still. "Intuition, perhaps?"

This last seemed directed at Mr. Brisbane, but I could not

imagine why. Indeed, Brisbane did not reply, but kept his eyes averted, toward the shadowy corner of the room.

"I suppose you could call it that, but we do have evidence that someone was threatening my husband before his death. And Edward's collapse was so sudden."

"But not entirely unexpected, I think," Doctor Bent said gently. "I do not think so illustrious a physician as William Griggs would have certified his death as natural if there was not at least a probability that it was."

"My husband was murdered," I said stubbornly. "I know that it will be difficult to prove. I do not ask that you prove it. I am simply asking that you employ your expertise to helping us direct our inquiries to the proper channels."

"I told you so, Mordecai" came Brisbane's voice, rasping through the shadows.

Doctor Bent smiled. "You did indeed, Nicholas." He turned to me. "He told me you are a woman of great strength of purpose, my lady. I will be happy to help you in any way I can. Now, tell me exactly what happened that night...."

I talked for a long time. Mordecai Bent was a very good listener—the sort of person who listens with his entire body and not just his ears. He interrupted me only a few times to ask questions about Edward's collapse.

"And what about his general health before his death? I know it was not good—a history of heart trouble, I believe?"

I nodded. "Yes. His father and his grandfather both suffered from it as well. Doctor Griggs says that it is a congenital weakness, an hereditary one. Edward's cousin, Sir Simon, suffers from it as well."

"And what symptoms does it manifest?"

I closed my eyes, thinking hard. "Edward always had spells. He had them as a boy, I remember." I opened my eyes, noting Brisbane still sitting silently, his gaze unfocused.

"Spells?" Doctor Bent leaned forward, his curiosity piqued.

"Yes. They always came on suddenly, sometimes when he was exerting himself, sometimes when he was quiet. He would have trouble breathing and often his complexion would turn a peculiar shade of blue."

Doctor Bent nodded thoughtfully. "Go on please."

I shrugged. "As I said, he always had these spells. Some worse than others. Often, he could sit quietly and they would pass. Other times he would take to his bed for a few days."

"Had these spells grown worse in the months before he died?"

"Oh, much," I said emphatically. "There were times in which he was not at all himself. He was thinner, visibly so, and had developed a cough."

Doctor Bent's eyes were shining, like a hound's will during a course. "You said he was not himself. How so?"

I spread my hands. "He was usually quite easygoing, very amiable. But in the months before his death he became sharp-tempered, moody. He was very angry at times, but at nothing in particular. He could be perfectly gentle, and then something would trigger his temper."

"Was he ever violent?"

The question was asked without judgment, but I hesitated to answer it. Doctor Bent, sympathetic eyes and gentle manner notwithstanding, was a stranger to me. And some things were too humiliating to tell—or remember.

I was aware of Brisbane watching me then, sharply. I lifted my chin.

"He struck the boot boy, and his valet, I believe."

I flicked Brisbane a glance, daring him to contradict me. Besides, he did not know for certain. He could not know, I told myself firmly.

Doctor Bent was nodding. "This is a very interesting puzzle, my lady. I must do some research before I can offer you anything definitive, and I am quite busy just now at the hospital," he said apologetically.

I rose, extending my hand. "Of course. Thank you so much for your efforts on my behalf."

He shook my hand quite cordially and I turned to leave.

Brisbane rose and took a step toward the door. He got as far as the table next to his chair, then paused, and I watched as the colour simply drained out of his face.

"Mr. Brisbane, are you quite all right?" I asked, but by the time I got the words out, it was very apparent that he was not.

While I watched, he put out his hand to the table, blindly, dashing aside a decanter of whiskey.

"Nicholas!" cried Doctor Bent, bounding past me.

He reached Brisbane just in time to catch him as he crumpled, cushioning his fall with his own body. Brisbane was senseless, his hair tumbling over his brow, completely unaware of his mournful friend, the splintered glass, or the whiskey slowly dripping into the carpet below.

THE EIGHTEENTH CHAPTER

My thoughts are whirled like a potter's wheel;
I know not where I am, nor what I do.
—William Shakespeare
Henry VI, Part 1

or the next three days I heard nothing of Brisbane—either of his health or the investigation. I planned menus with Cook, read to Simon, hounded Val about getting rid of the illicit raven and snapped at Morag. It seemed there were a hundred little domestic problems that needed to be handled—one of the maids quit, one of the footmen was malingering, a stray cat had had kittens in the butler's pantry—but resolving them proved unsatisfying. It was too tempting to wave a hand at Aquinas and delegate. But then I was left with my unruly thoughts and my twitching nerves and that was no better.

I thought many times about visiting Brisbane. Not to actually see him, of course. Just a polite call to offer a token of my concern for Monk to deliver. Surely a little gift to speed his convalescence would not be amiss, I told myself. I could leave it with his man and perhaps glean a few details about Brisbane's condition.

He had recovered swiftly from his swoon. Doctor Bent had applied a little sal volatile and Brisbane had come round quickly enough. But he was still weak and haggard and Doctor Bent had insisted upon putting him to bed—after escorting me firmly but respectfully to the door. I did not blame him. It must have been disconcerting enough to deal with Brisbane in his condition without my gawking like a tourist at the sight.

But I was curious, I could not deny it. To the eye, Brisbane was a healthy-looking specimen—robust, even. I was wildly interested in what sort of malady could fell so vibrant a person. And the thought that Doctor Bent might have sent along some sort of report about Edward that Brisbane was too indisposed to forward to me gnawed at me terribly. I toyed for a while with the idea of a basket of Cook's choicest pastries and a bottle of the best wine in the cellar, selected by Aquinas, but in the end my better instincts took over. Better instincts, or perhaps my cowardice. Twice now I had seen him in the throes of his infirmity, and twice I had fled back to Grey House without a backward glance. There was something quite disturbing about seeing a man like Brisbane in such a state. Inquisitive as I was, I could not quite bring myself to call upon him simply to satisfy my own curiosity.

Instead, I applied myself to the clearing out of my study— a room long overdue for a good turn out. I swept up heaps of unfinished knitting and incomplete watercolour books, bundling them into a cupboard and promising myself that as soon as the investigation was finished, I would bring my little projects to completion. For now, it seemed like a bit of an accomplishment just to get them out of sight.

I moved on to the bookshelves, pulling out piles of unread newspapers and putting them aside for Aquinas to deal with. I straightened the books, flicked a duster over them, and made up my mind to let the maids into the room in future. I was certainly not keeping it tidy, much less clean. The dust was appalling, and I kept sneezing as I burrowed down into stacks of books I had not seen in ages. There were volumes I had brought to my marriage—books of my childhood, much-loved editions with worn covers and jam stains from sticky fingers.

I turned over the leaves, spotting the brown rings from teacups and the occasional pale mark where I had used a leaf as a bookmark. There was my Psalter as well, a gift from the Princess of Wales upon my confirmation. It was marked with the three Wales feathers and her initials in gilt on the leather cover, and inscribed in her own hand on the flyleaf. I turned it over, delighted to see it again. She had been Princess of Wales for only seven years when I was confirmed, and I had been completely in awe of her. She was utterly lovely, and I had been thrilled to own something she had touched with her own pretty hands.

I ran my fingers over the cover, mourning the state of the book. I should have taken better care of it. It had been the most elegant thing I owned for many years. Now the morocco cover was dry and cracking and the gilt cipher flaking. I opened it, almost afraid to look at the silk ribbon, which was certain to be splitting. Really, I did not deserve to own nice things if I could not take better care of them, I chided myself. I leafed through the pages, then bent swiftly over some damage I had not expected. The ribbon was indeed splitting, but it was the hole in the page that was most disconcerting. What sort of worm or moth had done that?

But I knew as soon as the question had formed in my mind that no insect had done this damage. The Psalter had been damaged by human hands—hands with very sharp scissors.

I looked at the book for a long moment, feeling a rush of excitement, I am ashamed to say. For I held in my hands our first genuine clue. The verse that had been scissored from my Psalter was not the one glued to the note I had discovered in the desk, but I had no doubt it had been affixed to one of those that Brisbane had seen. I could not remember how many notes Edward had received altogether—I could not even remember if Brisbane had ever told me. But I was bone certain that they all began with this harmless little book.

I paged through it carefully, almost at arm's length now. It was distasteful, really. Someone else had used this personal volume and it felt polluted. But it was necessary to scrutinize it for more clues and I did so with enthusiasm. There were six holes altogether.

I sat back on my heels, considering. The person who had threatened Edward had taken my Psalter and carefully excised the passages he wanted, then replaced it. This argued that the person had kept it for some time—a person with access to my house, at least twice—once to take the book and once to return it. The implications were faintly horrifying, and I knew exactly what I must do.

I rose and went to the desk in search of a bit of brown paper in which to wrap the book. When it was a neat parcel, I slipped it into my pocket and rang for Aquinas to prepare a basket of fruit. It was time to see Brisbane, indisposition or not.

THE NINETEENTH CHAPTER

Mistress, both man and master is possess'd;
I know it by their pale and deadly looks:
They must be bound and laid in some dark room.
—William Shakespeare
The Comedy of Errors

I alighted from a hansom in front of the house in Chapel Street scarcely half an hour later. The fruit basket was a thrown-together affair, less the tasteful, elegant display that I had imagined, and more a wickerwork coster barrow heaped with fruit that was either not quite ready or just past ripeness and oozing juice. But I had given Aquinas little notice, and for all its shortcomings, the basket was rather pretty. He had instructed the gardener, Whittle, to find a few flowers as well, so here and there a few bright-petaled faces of early roses peered out from behind bunches of cherries or clusters of currants. The Psalter, in its sturdy brown wrappings, was tucked deep into my pocket, bumping lightly against my thigh as I walked.

I rang the bell and it was answered almost immediately, not by Mrs. Lawson, but by a boy of perhaps nine or ten.

I pushed past the child, an easy enough task with an armful of fruit. "Do not mind me. I am expected," I called over my shoulder. Not entirely true, but not entirely untrue, either. Brisbane should have known that I would call if I discovered a clue, shouldn't he? In fact, I distinctly remembered him telling me to do so.

I knocked awkwardly, from under the basket, and waited quite a long time before I heard noise from behind the door.

It opened, a bare crack, and I saw Monk's eye, wary and dull, peering out at me.

"Your ladyship," he began.

"Good afternoon, Monk," I replied, nudging the door open with my boot. "I have come on an errand of mercy." I smiled widely, indicating the fruit.

He hesitated, casting a glance behind him. "I suppose I could admit you for a moment, my lady. But I fear Mr. Brisbane is quite unwell. If you would leave the basket with me, I assure you—"

I edged in through the tiny opening he had left me.

"Actually, I have a matter of business to discuss with Mr. Brisbane. It is rather urgent," I said, pushing on into the room.

The door to the inner chamber, Brisbane's study, I presumed, was slightly ajar, the room itself unlit. Long, dark shadows spilled from its doorway across the carpet where I walked. The main room was brighter and very warm, stuffy even, and in place of the usual scents of leather and tobacco and herbs that usually pervaded the air, was an odour that I had not smelled before and could not place.

Monk hurried to put himself in my path, but I strode on purposefully, stepping around him and heading for the open door that beckoned. Here the scent grew stronger; it seemed sharp, metallic in the nose and on the back of the tongue. From behind the door came a noise, a rustling, gathering sound that for some reason put me in mind of a bear, thawing itself from hibernation. Or something worse, something darker and more sinister, rising from its hiding place at the scent of blood...

It is easy to be fanciful now, but I was not so then. I did not brave the lair of the wolf because I was courageous in the face of danger. I went through the open door because I was too stupid to understand that there was danger at all. I do not know, not even now, if I suspected what lay beyond, but I know that I dropped all pretense at good manners. I brushed Monk aside and forced my way into a place where I did not belong. Was it curiosity? Impatience? Something deeper? Still I cannot say what drove me on. There was only that metallic scent that I did not know, and that strange rustling. I know now that it was Brisbane, rousing from his state of semiconsciousness. I do not know what alerted him to my presence. The sound of my voice? Or was it more primitive than that? Did he catch my scent, over the sharp smell of his own medicine?

I entered the darkened room, heedless of Monk sputtering behind me. I carried the fruit basket in both arms, clutching it gracelessly. It took a moment for my eyes to adjust to the gloom. The room was not a study, as I had supposed, nor was it unlit. It was a bedchamber, Brisbane's bedchamber. There was a tiny fire burning in the hearth, but it was heavily screened. No lamps or candles brightened the corners, and the shadows of the little fire were eerie, atmospheric. There was a small, bare table with a single hard chair and a narrow bed—a campaign bed, probably French, I thought. Brisbane himself sat upon it, wearing only trousers and a shirt open to the waist. The sheets were crumpled damply beneath him as though he had just risen from a restless sleep without bothering to crawl between them.

His hair, usually orderly in spite of its length, was wildly disarrayed, as though he had been tearing at it. His face was half lit by the feeble fire and he sat watching me, Janus-like, as I hesitated just inside the door.

His eyes were in shadow and I did not know if he knew me. I caught a glint from them as he turned his head, restless in the gloom. He lifted his head as a hound will do when it catches a scent, and I thought I saw a flash of sharp white teeth between parted lips.

"What is wrong with him?" I whispered hoarsely to Monk. I had come expecting a fierce headache, a bit of melancholia, perhaps. Instead I had found an animal, unleashed from hell.

"Migraines," Monk replied in a low voice. "Of an unusually virulent variety. He usually manages to keep them at bay—sometimes for months, but then they return with a vengeance. He felt this one coming for a week. We did everything to allay it, but..." He broke off, his voice rough, and I knew that he suffered as much as his master.

"It is so dark," I began.

"The light is like a lance to his head, my lady. He cannot bear it."

"He does not seem to be in pain now." I watched Brisbane uneasily. He was sitting quietly, but rather than seeming serene, he presented a picture of lightly restrained savagery—a lion waiting by the watering hole for an unsuspecting deer.

"He has tried conventional methods of relief and found them lacking," Monk was saying, his tone faintly regretful. "He has resorted to dosing himself with other preparations. Absinthe, for one."

"Absinthe!" I had heard of it, and I had heard what it could do. "Does he know that that rubbish can rot his brain? That it could kill him?"

Monk lowered his eyes. "Better it kills him than he kills himself."

I rocked on my heels a little. "Is it that bad?"

To his credit, Monk did not despise me for the stupidity of the question. "I have to remove knives and glass from his room when he is like this. One of his wrists still bears a scar...."

I did not want to hear more. I could not believe that this self-possessed man whom I had come to think of as my partner in this investigation had been reduced to trying to destroy himself. I looked down at my silly basket, thinking how stupid I had been to bring hothouse fruit. What would that do to cheer him when he was accustomed to the vicious pleasures of absinthe?

Monk touched my arm. "My lady, it is best if you go now. This is the most dangerous time. He has been quite calm as of yet, but I cannot promise you will be safe here."

I nodded, my mouth too dry for speech. Nothing would induce me to turn my back on Brisbane in that moment. He sat, watching motionless as I slid one tentative foot behind me. Before I could even put my weight upon the foot, he was up and across the room, moving with a speed and ferocity I would never have imagined.

I gasped when his hand closed hard on my wrist. He jerked, pulling me into the room. With his free hand he slammed the door in Monk's face and twisted the key in the lock.

It occurred to me then that it was extremely careless of Monk to leave a key in the lock at all, but I realized that this was not the time for such recriminations. I flattened myself against the door, brandishing my basket in front of me—a feeble defense, but the only one I had.

He released my arm and made no other move toward me. He seemed content to stand, staring at me, his eyes clearly bloodshot even in the darkened room.

I heard Monk pounding on the door, his voice muffled through the thick wood.

"I am fine, Monk," I called with more conviction than I felt.

"Thank God for that," I heard him say. "Do not move suddenly, my lady. You must not startle him. I do not believe he will harm you."

I tried to take comfort in that, but I decided it was much easier for Monk to be confident with three inches of stout oak between him and an unpredictable man driven half mad by pain and narcotics. But it was true that Brisbane had had quite enough time to do me harm if that was his intention, and he seemed content to watch me instead, his eyes unfocused and confused.

"Why have you come?"

The sound of his voice startled me. I had not expected him to speak, at least not lucidly.

"I was worried for you. I thought you might like some fruit," I said stupidly, indicating my basket.

He said nothing and I continued to hold it, feeling absurdly grateful that I had at least this flimsy bit of wicker between us. He was quite close, near enough for me to smell again that sharp metallic scent over the lush sweetness of the fruit. It was on his breath, and I realized it must be the absinthe.

"Would you like to sleep now?" I asked softly.

His eyes seemed heavy, like a child's fighting sleep, and I knew he was resisting the effects of his drug. He shook his head irritably, and I saw then the pendant at his throat, gleaming brightly against his skin. It was a small round of silver, threaded onto a thin black silk cord and engraved with a portrait of some kind.

"What is your pendant?" I asked, desperate to make some sort of normal conversation. Perhaps if I kept him talking calmly, Monk would devise a rescue.

Brisbane blinked slowly, then brought a finger to his throat. "Medusa."

I nodded, trying to keep my eyes averted from it. It lay in the hollow of his throat, and in the normal course of events I would never have seen it, or his bared chest. I tried not to look at that, either, although I will admit to a few stolen glances in spite of my fear. Edward had been pale and golden and smooth, like a slim Greek statue worked in marble at sunrise. Brisbane was more deeply muscled, with a spread of black hair over his chest and stomach. The effect was startling and I told myself that it was not at all attractive. I forced myself to look away immediately.

"It is time to sleep now," I said firmly.

He moved and I thought he was going to seize my suggestion. Instead, he seized my basket. It slipped from his fingers to the floor, spilling pears and berries and a rather fat melon across the carpet. He looked at it for a moment, watching the juices ooze into the carpet, then turned back to me. Slowly, he reached out and lifted my hand, curiously, as if it were not attached to my person, but was instead an object for study. He turned it over, looking blankly at the soft leather of the glove, tracing the tiny stitches of the seams as if trying to remember where he had seen such a thing before. He paused briefly at the silk-cord edging, and then moved beyond, slipping a finger under the glove leather at my wrist to rub the flutter of my pulse. He was murmuring in a low voice, something unintelligible but familiar, perhaps an old song or rhyme, I could not tell. I pulled gently at my arm, but he held it fast, his finger dipping down to my palm, stroking the hollow of my hand.

Swallowing hard, I raised my free hand and pushed at his shoulder.

"Time for sleep, Brisbane."

His head came up suddenly.

"Stupid," he said, his voice thick now. "Should not have come, Julia."

His hand still held mine. His free arm came quickly around my waist. He pulled me hard against him. His eyes were dilated, wide black pupil against black iris, giving him an unearthly look. His breath was coming quickly through parted lips. My spine felt rigid, as though he could crack it in two with his hands if he wished.

He dipped his head low, close enough for his mouth to touch mine if he turned ever so slightly. I wondered later what would have happened if I had given him the chance. Instead, I lifted my heel and brought it down viciously on the top of his instep. The pain brought him up sharply and he stared at me, never loosening his grasp. He opened his mouth to speak, hesitated with a shiver, and then closed it on a deep, resonant groan. His eyes rolled back and he collapsed, bearing me down to the floor as he fell.

We landed heavily, his body pinning mine to the carpet and knocking me nearly breathless. I took a few gasping gulps of air, then pushed at his shoulders to shift his weight. He was completely oblivious, and it was only when Monk burst through the door and hefted him off of me that I was free.

"How did you get in?" I rubbed at the back of my head. A lump was beginning to form, but it was not as bad as I expected. Thank goodness for the thick carpet and my own strong skull.

Monk struggled to the bed with Brisbane, a deadweight draped over his shoulders. He laid him down gently and tucked the coverlet around him. He turned back to me. His colour was high, but he seemed otherwise calm and unruffled by the events of the past few minutes. I realized now why Brisbane kept him. A servant with such a cool head was a definite asset in his situation.

Monk reached down to help me up. "A bit of stiff wire, my lady. I knocked the key out of the keyhole and used my own key to unlock the door."

He motioned me toward the sitting room and I followed gratefully, noticing that he did not close the door to the bedchamber.

Monk must have noticed my nervous glance toward the bedchamber door. "In case he needs me," he said simply. "Now, I think a bit of brandy for the shock."

I agreed and took a deep, choking drink, thinking how much better it would have been if it had been a whiskey.

"That was most unpleasant for you, my lady. I can only offer my most abject apologies."

I stared into the depths of my brandy glass, as if scrying for answers. It was a long moment before I answered him, a moment in which he tidied up stray newspapers and poked at the fire. Anyone peering through the windows might have thought it a pleasantly domestic scene. Unless they looked into Brisbane's room.

"That is not necessary, Monk," I said at length. "It was my own fault for coming. I was stupid. I was impatient to show him something," I finished lamely, patting my pocket to make certain the Psalter was still there. "Tell me, Monk, does he show no improvement? Is there no help for him?"

Monk ran a hand through his thatch of silvering hair, his expression grieved. "I used to think he was getting better. There were months, several at a stretch sometimes, when he would be free of them. But since we came back to London…he is getting worse. And so are the cures. He used to take absinthe with an equal part of water. Now I count myself lucky if I can persuade him to put a pipette's worth of water in the glass. He will kill himself with it."

There was acceptance in his voice, but genuine regret as well.

"How long have you known him?"

He gave me a wistful smile. "Since he was a boy. He was a student at the school where I was master. Wild as a moorland pony, he was. A wretched student. He never could abide the rules, the discipline. But a fine mind, the best I ever taught. When they finally threw him out, I went with him."

"Did he have these headaches, even then?"

Monk hesitated, as if he feared to say too much. But I think he realized we shared a bond of sorts, a bond of knowing too much. "As long as ever I have known him. But they are more frequent now, more painful. His usual methods have begun to fail him. I do not know what will become of him."

I set the glass down firmly. "Surely something can be done. There are doctors—"

"He has seen them all. He has been bled and purged like a medieval serf and dosed with things I do not like to think of. They have done things to him that frighten me still, and I am

217

a grown man who has seen two wars. Nothing helps him except oblivion. He tried opium for a while—we had a nasty business getting him off of that. Then he tried morphia, cocaine—every narcotic known to man. We had high hopes for the absinthe, but I think it begins to fail him as well. They all do eventually."

We were quiet a moment, each of us caught up in our thoughts—mine wholly unpleasant ones. There seemed to be nothing I could do, and the helplessness infuriated me.

"At least you could have some help with him," I said finally, taking in Monk's lined eyes and pale skin. Caring for Brisbane was taking a toll upon the portly former schoolmaster. "I think you have not slept in days."

But if Monk was a retired schoolmaster, he was also a former soldier. He raised his chin and shook his head, his spine stiff. "No one sees him when he is like this. Besides, there have been episodes, violent ones. He has never harmed me, but I could not be absolutely certain…"

His cleared his throat, steeling himself, I thought.

"I do hope that he did not offer your ladyship any insult?"

"No. He—he embraced me. I think he was quite delirious. I am afraid that I acted rather stupidly. I stepped on his foot with my heel. That is when he collapsed."

Monk seemed relieved. "It was not your doing, my lady. The oblivion comes on quickly. The last dose should have affected him by the time you arrived. It was coincidence that he should have collapsed at that moment. You do understand he was not himself?" he asked earnestly. "I have known him from boyhood. He would never force himself on an unwilling lady."

I pressed my lips together. There seemed no possible comment to that.

I smoothed my skirts and my thoughts and rose, offering my hand to Monk. "I think you and I must rely upon each other's discretion. If you will gather up the fruit, you may tell him that I sent it with a servant and my compliments. He will never hear from me that I saw him in this state."

Monk's face was suffused with gratitude as he took my hand.

"I will say nothing of your visit, I assure you, my lady. And I must apologize for speaking so freely. I am overtired, as you yourself observed. I would not usually confide, but as Mr. Brisbane has himself remarked, you are a most unusual lady."

Monk pressed my hand. "And thank you for your discretion, my lady. I need not tell you how disastrous it would be if he ever learned you were here."

"Then we shall not speak of it."

He bowed me out of the room and closed the door firmly behind me. I heard the locks being turned and the bolt being shot and I wondered if he was locking the world out—or Brisbane in.

THE TWENTIETH CHAPTER

'Tis such fools as you
That makes the world full of ill-favour'd children.
—William Shakespeare
As You Like It

left the rooms in Chapel Street in a vile mood—so vile that I elected to walk, hoping that the freshening air would blow some of the confusion from my mind and the heat from my cheeks. But exercise was no balm. Rather than being charmed by the bustle of the streets, I was annoyed at being jostled about. I found myself glaring at people and walking too quickly in my agitation. I arrived at Grey House out of breath and perspiring faintly in spite of the breeze. I was tired and cross, more at myself than anyone else. I should have mastered my impatience and my excitement at finding the Psalter and bided my time until Brisbane sent word he was prepared to see me.

Instead I had behaved like a schoolgirl. Brisbane was no performing monkey on display, but I had allowed my own curiosity and excitement to propel me into his sanctum, insulting his privacy. What was wrong with me that I had forced my way into the rooms of a sick man? Such impetuosity was not even part of my character. It was a March trait, one I deplored. And I had allowed myself to be seduced by the thrill of the investigation into acting like a member of my own family.

And worse by far, I had taken advantage of Brisbane's indisposition and state of undress to assess his physique. It was shameful, really. Poor Brisbane, racked by pain and half mad with absinthe, and I had actually taken the opportunity to look at his bared chest.

My only consolation was that I had not enjoyed the experience. Brisbane was not at all the sort of man I admired. He was too dark, too tall, too thickly muscled, altogether *too much*. I preferred a slender, epicene form, with delicately sketched muscles and golden hair. Graceful, aristocratic, like a Renaissance statue. Like Edward.

But if Edward was Donatello's David, in fairness, I must concede that Brisbane was more Michelangelo's. It was the difference between Hermes and Hades, really. The slim, glowing youth versus the dark, brooding lord. Grace versus power, although, if I were entirely truthful, Brisbane had his own sort of grace, nothing so effete as Edward's, but graceful just the same. Brisbane put one in mind of wolves and lithe jungle cats, while Edward conjured images of seraphim and slim young saints. It required an entirely different aesthetic altogether to appreciate Brisbane, one that I lacked. Entirely.

Even so, it was wrong of me even to look at him, especially at so fraught a time. I had acted with a complete lack of decorum and good breeding, and I was thoroughly ashamed of myself.

In fact, I was so preoccupied with my little bout of self-loathing that I did not see the caller lounging at the front steps of Grey House until I had nearly passed him by. I paused and peered closely.

"Reddy? Reddy Phillips, is that you?"

The young man swept off his hat and made me a very pretty bow. "Good afternoon, my lady. I hope that you are keeping quite well."

I surveyed him from his extremely fashionable hat (surely not yet paid for) to the empty watch chain at his waist (certainly the watch was pawned to pay a debt). He had always been a handsome creature, but I looked at his too-carefully brushed hair and meticulously shot cuffs and found myself growing impatient, my lips thinning in disapproval. Not my most attractive expression, but I could not help it.

"What brings you to Grey House, Reddy? I am not in the habit of receiving callers in the street."

He had the grace to blush a little, but it was not as charming as I had once thought.

"I have come about a matter of honour," he said, leaning toward me with a conspiratorial little smile. He glanced up and down the street, as if to make certain we were not overheard. He needn't have bothered. The only passersby were on the other side of the street and Curzon is wide enough that low voices and clandestine glances are more for effect than necessity.

"What matter of honour? Are you referring to that ridiculous bird in Val's rooms?"

He blanched, either at my forthright conversation or the audibility of my tone.

"Well, Reddy?"

He smiled again, licking his lips. I noticed that they were peeling. I glanced down at his hands and saw that the nails were bitten to the quick, one thumb bleeding discreetly around the nail. Surely he had not pawned his gloves, as well.

"My lady, I am certain that you will appreciate the need for discretion in this very delicate situation. Perhaps we could go inside...."

He moved toward the door, but I stepped neatly in front of him, squaring my shoulders and lifting my chin. Really, this was too much. I had complained to Val that the Phillipses were all jumped-up tradesmen and it was only too true. Two generations of money cannot compensate for the complete neglect of a gentleman's social education. No other person of my acquaintance would have presumed to invite himself into my home, particularly when I was still observing my period of mourning. But I was rather relieved at Reddy's pushing rudeness. It absolved me of being nice to him.

"No, we cannot go inside, Reddy, because it is nearly teatime, as you would know if you still owned a watch, and I have no intention of inviting you to stay."

Stunned, he opened his mouth, but I put up my hand.

"Silence, please. Clearly you have come because you think that you can prevail upon me to intercede with Val on your behalf. I can assure you that such efforts on your part would be entirely futile. Do you deny that you put up the bird as a wager?"

"N-no." I raised an eyebrow at him. He had very nearly insulted me by leaving off my honorific. I was beginning to get annoyed.

"No, *my lady*," he amended swiftly.

"Do you deny that Valerius won the wager fairly?"

"No, *my lady*, but the Honourable Mr. March—"

"There is no but, Reddy. Either Valerius won the bird fairly, in which case you have no business trying to get it back as you well know, or he cheated you of it. Which is it? Is my brother a cheat and a liar or are you just a particularly poor loser?"

If I had thought him pale before, it was nothing to the colour he faded to now.

"I had no intention of calling his honour into question," he managed to say, his voice tight with panic. I think he had some dim idea that aristocrats still dueled with swords at dawn. Of course, Marches *did* still do that sort of thing from time to time, though none within my memory. And for all I knew, Valerius would indeed call him out over the matter if pressed. He was an odd, unpredictable child, even for a March.

"Good. Because if you did—" I leaned closer to him, lifting my veil so that he could see my eyes clearly "—if you did accuse my brother publicly, I should have to inform the earl at once. And if there is one thing his lordship will not brook, it is the malicious slander of one of his own. He would take action, Reddy, swift and entirely merciless, I assure you."

I was referring to legal action; Father was nothing if not litigious. But Reddy did not know this. He was doubtless imagining himself shot dead at twenty paces on Hampstead Heath in the faint light of some misty dawn while his seconds looked on. He gulped and I counted silently to ten before I dropped my veil.

"Now, let us hear no more of this." I moved to enter my house, then turned back.

"Oh, and Reddy?"

"Yes, my lady?" He shied like a pony.

"The word 'Honourable' is never spoken, only written. You would properly refer to my brother simply as Mr. Valerius March."

His face went a dull, sullen red and I knew that I should have left off toying with him, but I could not. It felt obscenely good to torment him. He had behaved badly, and after my call in Chapel Street I was feeling volcanic. Besides, if I had loosed my anger at my staff, I would have paid for it for the next year with cold meals and poorly laid fires. I could abuse Reddy and send him on his way with a fine story to tell at the gaming tables.

"And remember, Reddy, if I catch the slightest breath of a rumour about this, I will assume you have been talking indiscreetly. And I will not go to the earl with the matter. I will deal with you myself."

I would swear the boy actually shivered. I swept into Grey House, feeling powerful and strong and capable of anything.

Then my hand touched the Psalter in my pocket, and I realized that I was a good deal less capable than I had thought.

THE TWENTY-FIRST CHAPTER

Go and catch a falling star,
Get with child a mandrake root,
Tell me where all past years are,
Or who cleft the Devil's foot,
Teach me to hear mermaids singing,
Or keep off envy's stinging,
And find
What wind
Serves to advance an honest mind.
—John Donne
"Song"

For the next several days I mooned about the house, brooding and regretting my horrid treatment of Reddy Phillips. Everything had seemed rather safe before that fateful visit to Brisbane's rooms. The brief minutes I had spent there seemed to have unbalanced something within me, leaving me unsettled, wobbling like a child's spinning top, and the worst of it was that I did not know why. I had behaved wretchedly, and in consequence found myself rattling around Grey House, starting every time the bell went, imagining that now Brisbane would write and something resembling normality would resume.

But the days stretched on into a week and the bell rang many times, but he did not write. In the end, I found myself in my study, taking up the books I had disarranged the day I found the Psalter. I had it still, locked snugly in a drawer beneath my costliest lace for safekeeping. But the rest of the study was still a wreck and I thought a bit of physical labor was in order. I sorted the books carefully, grouping poetry with poetry and alphabetizing novelists, rather than my usual haphazard method. The books of my childhood I gathered on the last shelf, smiling to myself as I touched them again, these treasured, yellowing friends from my youth.

Persuasion. Wuthering Heights. Jane Eyre. Pride and Prejudice.

The rest were much the same, romantic stories with dark, brooding men with mysterious pasts and scornful glances. Some of them were good novels, by proper authors. Much of it was complete rubbish. I groaned as I shoved them back onto the shelf. How many summer days had I whiled away tucked in the apple tree at Bellmont Abbey with one of these books, dreaming of the day when a darkly handsome man would sweep me away to his castle on the moor? How many winter evenings had I huddled in bed, reading by candlelight until my eyes ached just to see if all turned out happily for the beleaguered lovers?

Why on earth had my father permitted me to read such muck? It had left me with an overactive, overromantic imagination, I thought furiously. As a girl, when I had imagined my future husband, I had always thought of someone dark and masterful, lord of some crumbling estate, hopefully with a mad wife tucked away in the attic for effect. I had never looked to marry a fair man, preferring instead to dream of someone mysterious and saturnine. No one was more surprised than I when I married a man with golden curls and bright blue eyes, a slender and graceful man, with a sleepy smile and beautifully-shaped hands.

Once I married him, I ceased to think of my girlhood heroes, carefully shelving the books I had once adored. I somehow felt it disloyal to Edward to read them and spend hours conjuring thoughts of other men. Not that Edward would have minded. He never troubled about such things. I sometimes wondered if he would have cared if I had taken a real lover, someone flesh and blood to replace him. But he never said and I never had the courage to ask. And I remained faithful to him, even in literature.

This time, though, after carefully shelving the other volumes, I kept back *Wuthering Heights* and carried it to my room. London was no cloud-scoured moor, and I was no Cathy, but at least I could thrill to Heathcliff in the privacy of my own bedchamber. That Yorkshire moor was a far sight more entertaining than the rest of my activities. I spent many quiet hours reading to Simon or taking the Ghoul for drives in the Park. Unfortunately, Simon often fell asleep just as I was getting to the interesting bits, and the Ghoul wanted only to talk about her current bout with constipation.

The high point of my week came when the boxes from the dressmakers were delivered. Messieurs Riche had outdone themselves. The costumes I had ordered were even better than I had anticipated, so daring in their simplicity, so eye-catching in their stark purity that I felt almost naked, even when Morag fastened the last button. There was not a single ruffle or bow or rosette to draw the eye—only the pure line of severely perfect tailoring and the elegant curve of a draped bustle.

Morag stepped back and said nothing, her gingery eyebrows higher than usual.

"Say what you like," I snapped. "I can smell your disapproval."

Her brow puckered in surprise. "Not me. I think it suits you."

I stared at her. Never, in all the time she had spent in my employ, had Morag ever complimented anything I had worn. The best I could hope for was a grunt of approval that I looked respectable. But open admiration was something entirely new.

"You do?" I turned, observing myself as many ways as possible in the cheval glass. "You don't think that it is too—"

"Oh, yes. That's why I like it," she said seriously.

Considering Morag's penchant for garish colours and blowsy feathers, I was not completely certain I should be pleased. But I was. Approval is pleasant, no matter from what quarter.

"But the others are just the same," I said, waving at the boxes yet to be opened. "And this is the only black one. All the rest are colours."

Morag shrugged. "It was a year last week, my lady. It is time enough to put off your mourning."

I stared at her reflection in the cheval glass. "Last week? You must be joking. Edward has not been dead a year—he cannot."

She said nothing but went to my escritoire and retrieved my diary. She opened it to the previous week and pointed.

I looked at the little boxes with their printed dates, trying to make sense of the numbers. "Good Lord," I said finally, "it was."

Morag continued to unpack the boxes, lifting rich violet and chocolate-brown silks from the crackling tissue.

"There is a note here. From the elder Monsieur Riche himself," she told me. I waved at her to read on. "He says you are an appalling creature to order the gowns without allowing him to fit them personally and he will come to Grey House whenever you like to alter them. He begs that in the meantime you will not tell anyone they came from his establishment. He does not like to think that anyone will know he let them go without a perfect fitting." She finished the note with an air of satisfaction. She had only learned to read at Aunt Hermia's refuge and the skill was one she was rightly proud of.

I nodded absently, admiring the set of a particularly luscious bottle-green sleeve. "I will reply later. He can come tomorrow if he likes, although I don't see why he bothers. You are just as handy with a needle as any of his soubrettes."

Morag preened herself a bit as she laid out the rest of the gowns, but I ignored her. How could I have let Edward's anniversary slip by unmarked? It was thoughtless and disloyal and I made a note in the book to take flowers to his grave soon. It did not seem enough, but I could not think of anything that would serve better.

I glanced again in the glass at my new reflection, but the bloom had gone off it a little.

"I will try the rest of them on later," I told Morag, her hands full of bottle-green and claret silks.

Her face fell, but her eyes went to the book still clutched in my hand and nodded. She left me then, surrounded by my extravagantly simple finery and I sat for a long time, uncomfortable both with the person I had been and the person I was finally becoming. Caught between the two of them, I felt rather lonely, as one often does with a new acquaintance.

I remembered quite suddenly a stream at Bellmont Abbey, broad and swift, rushing each spring with clear, icy water. There were only a few flat rocks between the banks and picking one's way among them was a tricky undertaking. Once, when I was perhaps seven, I had managed to follow my brother Benedick. I had skipped blithely across the rill, leaping from rock to rock. But when I reached the middle, surrounded by dark, tumbling water, I had frozen, too frightened either to move or to remain where I was. I hesitated, half turning back toward the bank I had started from. Benedick, who had reached the other bank, turned and saw my predicament.

"You've come too far to go back, Julia," he had shouted at me. "Be a man about it and come on."

And I had. He had been so calm, so matter-of-fact, that I had obeyed, slower and more cautiously than I had begun, it was true. But I had made it and Benedick had rewarded me with the first bite of the cherry tart he had stolen from Cook's larder. Be a man about it. Good advice then and now, I supposed. Doubtless Father would have made some Shakespearean reference to Caesar and the Rubicon, but the idea was the same. Begin as you mean to go on and do not look back. No sniveling, no quivering. *Audeo*.

I thought for a long time about what that might mean in my particular case. I could continue the investigation, leave off my mourning, express my opinions freely and with vigor. I could dance with whomever I chose, travel alone, to Italy or to Greece and beyond. I could take a lover if I wished, albeit discreetly, and unlike Lot's wife, I would not look back.

The question was, was I capable of it? I had always sympathized with Lot's wife. Serving as the family salt cellar for all eternity seemed a rather stiff price to pay for a little understandable curiosity. My own consequences would not be so extreme. Certain people would give up my acquaintance, I was sure. I would no longer be invited to the endless round of tea parties, card parties, music parties, dance parties that had bored me for years—parties, I reminded myself, to which I had scrupulously not been invited during my year of mourning. I would no longer be viewed as a suitable chaperone for young virgins in some quarters, but as young virgins were usually monumental bores, I was not unduly distressed. The people who would hold themselves too respectable to associate with me were the very people who had neglected my acquaintance during my widowhood. Widows were skeletons at the feast, dampening everyone else's pleasure, so they had not asked me.

But neither had they called on me privately. The visits and letters of encouragement that had deluged Grey House in the first weeks had trickled to nothing. My acquaintances in society would accept me readily enough back into their set if I wore grey and married again, someone dull and sober and not interesting or suitable enough for their own daughters. That was what was expected of me.

But what if I did the unexpected? People would whisper behind their hands about me, there might be one or two veiled references in newspapers—nothing actionable of course, but everyone would know who they meant. In short, I would lose a little respectability among those whose good opinion mattered not at all to me, and I would gain my freedom. It seemed a bargain I could live with.

I did not rouse until Morag returned, bearing a note written in a flowery hand and smelling strongly of attar of roses mixed with something else. Musk, I think.

"What is this?"

"It is a note," she said, exasperated. I knew why she was annoyed. I had been sitting so long she had been unable to dust my room and would have to explain to Aquinas why it had not been attended to. Like most of the staff, Morag made a point of avoiding Aquinas whenever possible. For a fundamentally gentle soul, he could be quite unnerving when roused.

I took the envelope and paper knife, slit the envelope and waved Morag away just to complete her annoyance. She always took a healthy interest in my correspondence. The signature I did not recognize, but the message was direct.

> *My dear Lady Julia,*
> *I beg you will forgive my impudence at writing to you without an introduction. Our mutual friend, Nicholas Brisbane, begs me to write to you on his behalf as he is still too much unwell to undertake correspondence. He wishes to know if you will call upon him here at my house where he is convalescing. Naturally, you must come at your convenience. You are most welcome at any time.*

It was signed with a scrolled flourish of flowery ink— Hortense de Bellefleur. I turned over the envelope, running my fingers over the heavily embossed crest. Not just an Hortense, but probably a Comtesse Hortense. Perhaps even a duchess. The note was gracious, but its syntax seemed foreign, French, if memory served. I had heard of the lady, of course, most of London had. But I could not place her correct title. That was not surprising, I supposed. She had been married so many times to so many different Continental aristocrats that it was impossible to remember whose title she was currently using.

But it was not her title that intrigued me. Brisbane had chosen to convalesce at her home, which led me to one extremely diverting question: what precisely was Brisbane's relationship with London's most notorious courtesan?

Later that afternoon, to my astonishment, Hortense de Bellefleur opened the door to her house herself. The address was a good one and the home so beautifully appointed that I could not believe that financial troubles precluded her from employing staff. The explanation was quick in coming.

"My dear Lady Julia," she enthused, wrapping her hands about mine and tugging me gently into the foyer. "I was so eager to meet you that I could not wait for my poor old Therese to hobble her way to the door and back. You will forgive my impatience, will you not?"

I had stared at her all through this unorthodox little speech as she flitted about me, taking my swansdown cape from my shoulders and putting it carefully aside with my umbrella. She was older than I had expected, well past forty.

In another woman this might have marked the end of real beauty, but not Hortense. Bellefleur, indeed! For she was a beautiful flower, not with the blowsy obviousness of a rose, but rather with the lush grace of a wild lily. The bones of her face were so eloquently sculpted that the years had merely honed them, mellowing them to something more arresting than mere loveliness. There was good humour there and kindness, as well as an elegance no Englishwoman could ever match. I took her in from her barely silvering dark hair to her pure, rose-tinted complexion, discreet jewelry to embroidered lace slipper tips, and I thought how easy it would be to hate this woman.

But in fact, it was impossible to hate Hortense. She chattered like a between-stairs maid, praising my costume—the fabric (heavy Lyons silk), the colour (bittersweet chocolate), and the artful cut. Morag had applied her needle discreetly to the hem, but nowhere else. In spite of Monsieur Riche's protests, the dresses required little alteration.

"A Frenchman has had his hands on this," she proclaimed, turning me around like a marionette. "You have an excellent eye, Lady Julia, far better than most Englishwomen. Are your people French?" she asked, searching my face for clues to a Gallic ancestor.

"Only distantly," I replied, thinking of Charles II's fractious mother, the dainty Queen Henrietta Maria. She was the closest French relative I had, being my eighth great-grandmother, but it seemed inappropriate to share this with Madame de Belle-fleur.

She was smiling at me. "But of course! Even a drop of French blood would give you a certain élan that your compatriots lack. Blood always tells, *madame,* do you not think?"

Without waiting for a reply, she looped her arm through mine like a schoolgirl and led me down the hall.

"Now, you will forgive Brisbane," she advised. She pronounced his name "Brees-ban" rather than the usual "Brisbon," which from anyone else would have sounded backward. From her it was simply charming. She was so close to me that I could smell the same fragrant mixture that had scented her writing paper. Roses and musk, innocence and earthiness. I wondered if it was a metaphor for the lady herself.

"He is in a sulky mood. He did not want to come to me," she confided, her voice low. "He is stubborn, like all men, but like all men, he needs pampering when he is unwell. They are all little boys at heart, don't you think?" she asked, nudging me familiarly.

Again, I did not reply, but this time it was because I simply could not think of anything appropriate to say. It seemed insulting to comment that she should know, but I did not doubt that she *did* know far more than I on the subject. I smiled instead.

She patted my hand. "You will ignore him and I shall make you very welcome. I do not often get callers, and I am so charmed that you have come."

Her eyes were long and thickly lashed, the startling blue of a pansy. The expression in them was utterly sincere, and I realized that her attraction was not just her actual prettiness. It was this sincerity, this gift of making a person believe they were utterly necessary to her happiness. I wondered if the dustman felt this way when she looked at him.

But that was a cynical thought. By her reputation, Madame de Bellefleur had set herself beyond the boundaries of most of polite society. Gentlemen would call often, ladies almost never. I found myself wondering if I was the first, and I felt a little stab of pity for this charming and perhaps slightly lonely woman.

She threw open a door and gestured for me to enter. My first impression was one of serenity. The colours were soft, as were the lights, and it occurred to me only later that these were the most flattering for an aging beauty.

But for now they served to soothe Brisbane's eyes, I realized as he rose slowly to greet me, still wearing his smoked spectacles. I would have waved him back, but there was something ferocious about the set of his jaw that stayed me. He was still struggling with the notion of his own weakness and I was not surprised. I loathed being ill. How much more must a strong, otherwise healthy man hate his infirmity?

I smiled at him and offered my hand. "Mr. Brisbane. I am so glad to see you up and about. I hope you are well on the way to recovery."

I was rather proud of that little speech. I did try to make it sound casual, but the truth was, I had rehearsed it in the carriage all the way from Grey House to Primrose Hill.

He resumed his seat after I had taken mine, a lovely little Empire piece upholstered in pale blue bee-embroidered silk. He did not look as bad as I had feared. He had shaved and his hair was orderly, though still untrimmed. Other than his pallor and the darkened lenses and a few lines still bracketing his mouth, there was little trace of his ordeal. It seemed incredible that a man could recover so thoroughly from the wreck that Brisbane had been a mere week before. I made up my mind to ferret into a few of Val's medical texts when I returned home to learn more about Brisbane's condition.

"My lady?" he said archly. I jumped, realizing with a dart of embarrassment that I had been staring.

"I am sorry. Building castles in Spain, as my grandmother used to say," I told him with a fatuous smile.

His mouth turned down slightly at the corners. He seemed guarded, although whether because of his condition or Madame de Bellefleur's hovering silken presence I could not tell.

"I am recovering," he said at last. "Thank you for the basket of fruit. It was kindly done."

I started, thinking of the last place I had seen that basket, tumbled on the floor with cherries spilling out, crushed juicily underfoot as Brisbane leaned into me, his arm laced about my waist. Deliberately, I pushed the thought away.

"Think nothing of it, I beg you." I hesitated, a bit reluctant to produce the Psalter in Madame de Bellefleur's presence. As if reading my thoughts, Brisbane lifted his eyes to the lady.

"Fleur, I think Lady Julia would like a cup of tea. Do you think that Therese—"

"Of course! I shall go and supervise her myself." She gave me a conspiratorial smile. "Therese is old and very set in the French way of doing things. Sometimes her tea is not to Brisbane's liking. His taste in coffee is that of a Turk, but he is a proper Scotsman about his tea. Have yourselves a pleasant tête-à-tête and I will return in a little while with refreshment."

She withdrew and I watched Brisbane watch her leave. His eyes lingered, but not hotly, and I found myself wondering again the precise nature of their connection.

"I appreciate your willingness to come here, my lady," he said, his voice pitched too low for her to hear through the closed door. "Not every lady would feel comfortable calling at so notorious a house."

"Is it notorious?" I asked him with a nonchalance that fooled neither of us. "I had no idea. I had only heard Madame de Bellefleur spoken of as a great beauty, and I am glad of the chance to make her acquaintance."

His lips lifted very slightly, almost but not quite a smile. "You are a better liar than I would have thought. But thank you for that."

I inclined my head. It would be pointless and stupid to contradict him. I knew that I was in fact playing fast and loose with my reputation by coming to the Bellefleur home, but then I was beginning to realize that I was not altogether comfortable with my reputation in the first place.

"She is your friend, Mr. Brisbane. I trust that if she were a truly objectionable person, you would not bring us together in this fashion."

"No, rather the opposite. For some reason, I have always thought that you and Fleur would get on rather well. You have one or two qualities in common that most women lack."

I edged forward, wildly interested in what those qualities might be, but he disappointed me. He chose that moment to cough a little and reach for the tumbler of water that sat on the table near his elbow. By the time he had swallowed a good part of it and caught his breath, he had lost his train of thought or abandoned it on purpose. Instead, he stared at me through those strange smoky lenses, scrutinizing my face until I could bear it no longer.

"What is it, Mr. Brisbane? Have I left the house with my hat on backward?" I asked, smiling to relieve the touch of asperity in my voice.

He passed a hand over his brow. "Forgive me. I have a

strange sense that I have seen you, quite recently, but I cannot place it. A dream, I think."

My heart began to drum so loudly that I thought he certainly must hear it. I was grateful then for the high collar that hid the pulse at my throat.

"It must have been. Perhaps you took some medicine while you were ill. They can often provoke strange dreams."

His eyes fell briefly to my mouth, his fingers twitched, and I wondered if he was smelling ripe cherries, remembering the feel of a supple glove against his finger.

"Yes, they can," he said finally. I dared to breathe then. Apparently he had convinced himself that I had been an apparition, conjured by his drugged fever. Would God he always thought it so, I prayed fervently. The thought of prayer caused my hand to move to my reticule.

"Mr. Brisbane, while you were indisposed, I discovered something—something rather remarkable."

I drew out the Psalter and handed it to him. He took it, and to my surprise, did not open it at once. He inspected the cover closely, running those sensitive fingers over the binding, the edges, the stamped crest and Prince of Wales feathers. He even lifted it to his nose to sniff lightly. Curiously, he closed his eyes, pressing the book to his brow. I thought for a moment that he might have relapsed into migraine, so intently still did he become.

After a few seconds the spell seemed to pass, and he opened his eyes. He paged through the Psalter, pausing to read the inscription in the princess' hand and my own childish scrawl beneath it. He thumbed on, stopping at the page I had marked with the splitting silk ribbon, the page defiled by the sender of Edward's notes. He leafed through it slowly, taking note of each neatly scissored hole.

When he reached the end, he rifled through it slowly again backward, but found nothing new. He sniffed it again, carefully, but either detected nothing of interest, or did not see fit to share it.

Finally, he spoke. "Where did you find it?"

"In my study. It was tucked into a stack of books that I have not looked at for years."

"Was it dusty?"

I hesitated to admit the slatternly state of my bookshelves, but I knew that it might be important.

"Yes. That is, the top book was dusty, those below it, including the Psalter, less so."

"Could the stack have been disturbed recently?"

I closed my eyes, picturing the pile of crumbling volumes. "No, I do not think so. The maids never clean there, they are forbidden. And I'm afraid that I haven't done it myself for quite some time. There were a few newspapers in there as well, old ones, quite creased, but only folded once. I think they might have been creased more if the pile was disturbed."

"Not necessarily, not if our villain was quite careful. And I think he must have been."

My ears pricked unexpectedly. "He? You think it definitely a man, then?"

Brisbane was examining the book again. "No, I simply grow tired of multiple pronouns. You may take it as given that I do not know the gender of the perpetrator."

Prickly, indeed! I pursed my lips in displeasure at his tone, but I might have been a potted cactus for all the notice he took of me. He was too busy comparing the holes and measuring them with his fingers.

"Seven passages of the Psalms, all cut at the same time, then the book was returned to your study—but why?"

"How can you be certain they were cut at the same time?" I interrupted. His tone had been thoughtful, as if he had been posing his question more to himself than to me, but I did not care. I had found the clue, after all, and I deserved to know what he had deduced from it.

He regarded me impatiently. "What villain in his right mind would take the book seven times, and risk apprehension each time he retrieved it and put it back?"

I bit my lip again, now thoroughly chagrined. How stupid I was! No wonder he treated me like a slow-witted child.

"Besides," he added, his tone somewhat milder, "the passages all appear to have been cut with the same scissor—a short one, perhaps a nail scissor. In the longer passages there is an overlap where the blade was moved."

He opened the book for my inspection and I saw that he was correct.

"So the question is, who had access to the book, and more important, access to replace it, a year ago?" he mused.

I spread my hands. "Anyone! The Psalter has been there since Edward and I moved into Grey House. We entertained frequently—it could have been taken by anyone and returned at any time and we would not have noticed."

"But would just anyone know that?" he asked softly.

It was my turn for exasperation. "What do you mean?"

He leaned forward, his long fingers tapping the cover of the Psalter. "Many people use the books given at their confirmation for spiritual comfort. One would think a volume given by the Princess of Wales would be even more prized. Most people," he went on, "have the downstairs maid clean their bookshelves, on a regular if not a daily basis. Now, who among your circle would know that not only did you not use this Psalter, but that in fact, you never even permitted your staff to clean the study where it was kept?"

I stared at him blankly. "Brisbane, what are you on about? If you are criticizing my housekeeping skills, I will admit I have been less than—"

"I do not give a damn about your housekeeping," he said

sharply. "I am talking about someone in your own house who just might be the villain."

"You are quite mad," I said evenly. It was unthinkable that he could be right.

"Am I? Think about it," he said, not bothering to be kind. His tone was harsh, his words unutterably painful. "The person who took that Psalter had to know that you did not open it often, or he risked detection. It must have been someone with little access to another such book—this points either to someone who has little money or whose time is not their own. They needed your Psalter because it was handy and would not implicate them, but also because it was unlikely to be discovered. And if it was, whom would it implicate? No one except the lady of the house. So, whom does that suggest to you, my lady? Someone inside Grey House with little time and little money to call their own. *Whom does that suggest?*"

I saw what he was saying and I hated him for it.

"One of my staff."

He nodded slowly, then pushed the book toward me. I snatched it from him.

"You cannot honestly believe that one of my own staff has done this. Think about what you are saying."

He leaned forward swiftly. "No, you must think about what you are denying. What I have just given you is the only explanation that makes sense. And it means that you could be at risk if you continue this investigation. Someone in that house hated your husband, perhaps enough to kill him. If you try to unmask him now, he might kill again, and this time it will be you."

I shook my head angrily. "I cannot believe that. I know them—"

"Do you? What do you know of Aquinas? You may have had references for him, but what about his life before that? Before he came into service? What of Morag? What of the footmen, the maids, Diggory? What do you know of any of them? Think of it the next time one of them brings you a pot of tea or lights the fire or scrubs the floor or laces your corset. One of them might be responsible for murdering your husband. And they might simply be waiting for their next chance...."

I rose then, icily calm, stuffing the Psalter into my reticule. "I am sorry to have wasted your time, Mr. Brisbane, when you are so clearly still in the throes of your indisposition. We can discuss this again when you are more clearheaded."

He muttered something under his breath, something faintly obscene, so I pretended not to hear it. He did not rise as I left, and as I closed the door behind me I heard the high, splintering sound of breaking glass.

Madame de Bellefleur met me at the door, her face anxious.

"My lady, must you leave so soon? But we have not had tea."

Her tone was pleading and I felt chagrined. She had been very hospitable, and I was behaving badly by running away. Impulsively, I put a hand to her arm.

"It is as you said, Madame de Bellefleur. Mr. Brisbane is in a nasty temper. Too nasty to do business with, I am afraid. But if you would invite me again, just the two of us, I would be delighted to take tea with you. Or," I added recklessly, "perhaps you would care to come to Grey House."

Her face suffused with light. "How lovely you are! Yes, that would be very nice. Come, I will walk you out."

She escorted me to where Diggory was waiting at the kerb. I settled myself against the grey satin upholstery and asked myself for the thousandth time why Edward would have chosen such an impractical fabric for a carriage seat. Velvet would have been just as opulent, but at least then I would not have had to hang on to the edge of the seat by my fingernails to avoid slipping off of it.

Madame de Bellefleur put her hand into the window to shake mine. "It has been most charming making your acquaintance, my lady. Thank you for coming."

"You were very kind to invite me. I am only sorry that I have to leave so suddenly. And I fear I have left him rather more difficult than I found him," I said with a rueful glance toward the house.

Her laugh was merry and light, like the trill of silver bells. It was a Frenchwoman's trick; I had never known an Englishwoman to laugh like that.

"*La*, my lady, I have seen him far worse than this. I have ways of handling him, do not fear."

Of that much I was certain.

THE TWENTY-SECOND CHAPTER

Truth is truth
To the end of reckoning.
—William Shakespeare
Measure for Measure

was depressed that night, as I had not been since Edward's death. Mindful of Brisbane's warning, I started every time Aquinas spoke to me. I waved Henry off when he would have lit the fire in the study, and I dismissed Morag as soon as she had unlaced my corset, pleading a headache. The only peace I had had the entire evening was the hour I spent with Simon, chatting and reading the newspapers.

But even that had been tinged with regret. His face had grown thinner still, and his hands, when they held mine, were like twiggy bundles of bones under his skin. I left him, feeling desperately sorry for myself. When he passed and the Ghoul moved on, I would be alone in a mausoleum of a house with a staff I no longer trusted and a brother I never saw. I heard an occasional *quork* from behind Val's door, so I knew the raven was still in residence, but I did not have the heart to scold him. I paced a good deal, and found it difficult to get to sleep, the more so because I now refused the little remedies that Morag was so proficient at concocting. I took to reading, far into the night, until my eyes burned and the words swam on the page. When I did finally sleep, my dreams were ragged and dark and I woke often, cursing Brisbane and wishing I had never found the threatening note in the drawer.

Even as I muttered the words, I knew I did not mean them. However difficult, however impossible, I wanted the truth, even if it meant unmasking one of my own. Yet I could not believe that an inhabitant of Grey House had harmed Edward, was capable of harming me. I firmly believed that the danger had come from outside.

But how? I had tried to convince Brisbane that the house was frequented by guests and family, but he had been disinterested, preferring to focus his accusations upon my own staff. How could I possibly get him to direct his attentions outside Grey House, where the true perpetrator lay?

After a good deal of rumination, it came to me. In order to force Brisbane to look outside Grey House, I had to prove to him that there was nothing of interest *in* it. I would undertake to prove the innocence of my staff, and in doing so, I would eliminate my own people as potential villains. Then Brisbane, seeing the error of his ways, would be properly abashed, apologize prettily, and we would pursue the true perpetrator.

I liked this plan very much. It was neat, tidy, and above all, it permitted me to score over Brisbane. The only trouble was devising a method of actually proving the innocence of my staff. There was only one means that came to mind, and I did not like it at all.

Unfortunately, Brisbane was quick to point it out to me when I saw him the following day.

"You will have to search Grey House," Brisbane said flatly. He was watching me closely, waiting for my impassioned refusal. But I surprised him.

I sipped coolly at my tea. "Of course. I had already planned to do so."

His expression was wary. He had not expected to find me

so tractable. And I had not expected to find him so much improved. He was looking so much better, in fact, that if I had not seen him so ill with my own eyes I would never have known he had been unwell. We were on the terrace of Madame de Bellefleur's villa, taking tea while she busied herself inside, tactfully out of earshot, although neither Brisbane nor I had asked her to leave. Her own natural delicacy dictated her withdrawal while we discussed business. I was rather sorry to see her go. She had greeted me even more warmly than before, and I found myself very glad to see her.

"I am surprised that you are amenable to the suggestion, considering your earlier vehemence."

I raised my brows lightly at him. "Was I vehement? I don't recall."

"You questioned my sanity," he returned with a touch of asperity.

I smiled sweetly. "Yes, I do recall that. As a matter of fact, I do still think it a daft notion. However—" I put up my hand to stem his interruption. "However, I am willing to concede the *possibility* that someone at Grey House was involved. I fear the only way to put that particular suspicion to rest is to establish without question the innocence of my staff. And the only way to accomplish that is to search their rooms."

"All of Grey House," he corrected.

I suppressed the little ripple of irritation I felt at his bossiness. He was still recovering, I reminded myself, and though his temper was vastly improved, he was still a trifle prickly.

"I do not see the purpose—" I began.

"The purpose would be clear if you applied your considerable intellect for even a moment," he said coldly. "If the perpetrator is an inmate of Grey House, he may share his quarters with someone else. That means that any evidence of his wrongdoing—poison, glue pots—would best be hidden in some neutral part of the house, someplace that would not implicate him if it were discovered."

I sipped again at my tea, torn between my pleasure at the slightly peachy undertones of the Darjeeling and impatience at my own stupidity. Really, I was going to have to start thinking things through before I opened my mouth. I was going to have to start thinking like a criminal.

"That's it," I said suddenly.

"What is it?" Brisbane's voice was weary and I wondered if his strength was beginning to flag.

"I do not know how to think like a criminal," I said with some excitement. "If I knew how to think like one, I could probably unmask one."

"It does help," he returned dryly.

I tipped my head and regarded him from crisply shined boots to clean, waving hair. "You seem to have no difficulty with that. Have you a criminal past?" I asked, joking.

To my astonishment, he flushed. It was almost imperceptible, but I watched the edge of dull crimson creep over his features.

"What a perfectly stupid question," he commented, his voice as controlled as ever. But in spite of the even tone, his colour was still high and I knew that I had struck a nerve.

"Your past is your own concern, of course," I said lamely. I had never been so socially inept as I managed to be with Brisbane. How exactly did one extricate oneself from an apparently valid accusation of criminality against one's investigative partner? There were no rules for this in the little etiquette books with which Aunt Hermia had drilled us. I stumbled on the best I could. "I mean, who among us has not stolen a sweet from a shop as a child?"

Brisbane's complexion returned slowly to normal, but his hand had gone to his throat and he was rubbing absently at the spot where I knew the Medusa pendant hung beneath his shirt.

I had just opened my mouth to mention it, when I realized that I was not supposed to know about that pendant. I gulped at my tea, now gone stone cold, aghast at how nearly I had given myself away. He was irritated enough with me as it was. I did not think he would ever forgive knowing I had been with him during his illness.

"I will of course search all the rooms of Grey House," I said quietly. "Even my own. I take your point. You are quite correct."

He was silent a moment, his black eyes thoughtful.

"This is more difficult for you than you had anticipated."

I nodded, tears springing suddenly to my eyes. I blinked them back, determined not to let them fall.

"I warned you when it began. But you thought I was simply being cruel."

I bit my lip in silence. The tea had grown scummy. I placed it on the table, careful lest my trembling fingers upset the porcelain.

"I underestimated the difficulty, yes. And you were cruel."

"And correct." His voice held no trace of triumph, only certainty. He had known from long experience what this would cost me, and I had not listened.

I shrugged. "It does not matter now. I have thought how easy it would be to put an end to this, to resume my life and pretend none of this ever happened. But I cannot. It is changing me, has changed me. And I do not know yet if it is for the better."

He did not pity me, and I blessed him for that. Had there been any sympathy, any kindness in his eyes, I would have crumpled. But that cool, appraising stare pricked at my pride. I raised my chin, determined to retain my dignity at least. And as always, he told me the truth, unvarnished and plain.

"You will not know until it is done. And then, only you will know if the cost has been too high, if the change has been too great."

I nodded, and our eyes met. We were comrades now, bound more closely than lovers, it occurred to me. Lovers may quarrel and part company. We were linked, irreparably, until this thing was finished. And in one of those rare moments of harmony, I knew that he felt it as well, this bond that we could neither explain nor break. I did not know if he was comfortable with the knowledge, or if perhaps he resented it. But he knew it as clearly as I did.

He moved quickly then, putting his cup on the table and bringing out his notebook. His manner was crisp as he outlined the places to which I would have to pay careful attention, the details I must not overlook. It was awkward to read upside down across the little table, so I went to sit beside him on the sofa. He talked briskly, turning once to make certain I was paying careful attention to his instructions. We were sitting in close proximity, his leg very nearly pressing against mine on the tiny sofa, the black wool of his sleeve brushing my silk as he sketched on the paper. I caught the scent of his soap and something else—something that made it rather difficult to breathe. It reminded me of bay rum, but smoother, without the sharpness of the spice. It was a mellow scent, perhaps it was the smell of Brisbane himself. It was warm on the terrace, the air heavy with rain that had not yet fallen and voluptuous with the fragrance of Madame de Belle-fleur's syringa. Together, the lowering sky, the combination of scents, were a heady mix. I could not focus clearly on what he was saying. Instead I watched his hands, one penciling broad, sweeping strokes while the other gripped his notebook. They were large hands, and not quite a gentleman's. The nails were short and clean, but there were a few scars crossing the knuckles, and a callus or two, possibly from riding without gloves. They were deft, competent hands, and I could not imagine a single task they could not perform.

The wind rose then, blowing a shower of syringa petals

onto his black hair, spangling the shoulders of his coat like confetti. Some dropped onto my lap and I gathered a handful, crushing them to release the thick fragrance into my fingers. Had I been with anyone else, it would have been an achingly romantic scene. And for the space of half a heartbeat, I wondered...

But then he turned, his expression forbidding.

"You have petals in your hair," he said, gesturing toward my cropped curls.

I reached up and brushed at them, sending a flurry of petals over his hands.

He tore the page he had been filling out of the notebook and thrust it at me, almost angrily. He rose, dripping petals onto the stones of the terrace.

"Mind you do not fail," he said severely. "Everything depends upon this. I cannot like leaving this in your hands."

Stung, I clutched at the paper. "I can do this," I protested. "You have told me what to look for, and I assure you I can be discreet."

He regarded me for a long moment, then gave a little snort of disgust. "What choice do I have?"

He turned, crushing the flowers beneath his heel, and went inside, to fetch Madame de Bellefleur, I expected. I folded the paper carefully and placed it inside my reticule, thinking that I had been quite stupid to wonder, if only for a moment. Apparently Brisbane only found me attractive when he was out of his senses.

To my credit, I managed to comb the petals from my hair and compose myself before Brisbane returned with Madame de Bellefleur on his arm.

We talked idly for a few minutes, about nothing in particular, when Brisbane rose suddenly.

"I have business to attend to at home," he announced. Despite Madame's protests he left us, bowing coolly to me and giving Madame's hand a dryly affectionate kiss. The difference could not have been more marked. But he need not have bothered. I was firmly in my place. I would not think of stirring from it again.

The atmosphere lightened a little after he left, and Madame and I remained on the terrace, watching the failing light cast long shadows over the garden.

"This is a charming house, Madame, and so prettily situated. You must be very comfortable here."

She nodded eagerly. "Oh, it is so. I am so very grateful to Nicholas." She pronounced it "Neekolas."

I blinked at her. "Oh, I should have realized. Brisbane has provided the house."

"He provides me with an annuity, as do a few other of my friends," she corrected me. "But Nicholas found the house for me and arranged the purchase. It was exactly what I wanted after all those years of wandering. A house of my own."

She stretched a little, catlike, her limbs supple and sleek. She moved like a dancer, and I wondered if this was part of the courtesan's repertoire.

"So many cities, so many rented rooms," she reminisced, her expression dreamy. "I did not even know where I was sometimes. I would have to tell Therese to ask the maids. Always living on someone else's sufferance…" Her tone was not bitter, but I caught a trace of something akin to it. Regret?

"But surely your husbands…that is, you married, did you not? Their homes would have been yours."

She laughed her light, musical laugh. "Spoken like an Englishwoman! You have never married a Continental, my dear, or you would know better. My third husband, a Russian prince—never marry a Russian, my darling. They are the gloomiest husbands. Always complaining about the money, the leaking roof, the furniture being sold to pay for the repairs. Serge once sold my favorite bed literally out from under me.

They came to take it away while I was sleeping in it. They carried it off with the bedlinen still warm."

"Good heavens!"

She shrugged. "Well, I suppose he thought it justified. I did have a lover in the bed with me at the time," she added with a wicked gleam in her eye.

In spite of myself, I laughed. She was so frank about her adventures that it was difficult to be judgmental. I relaxed and listened to her stories, each more colourful than the next. She sent Therese to a chophouse to buy our dinner and we ate there on the terrace, wrapping shawls about our shoulders and sharing a bottle of remarkably nice Burgundy. By the time we had finished pudding, she was calling me Julia ("Zhuleea") and begging me to call her Fleur.

"It was my childhood nickname," she told me. "But I always thought it was pretty."

I agreed that it was. "Fleur," I said, gargling the vowels a little like she did.

She clapped, her eyes bright. "That was very good! Ah, it has been so long since I have enjoyed the company of another woman. I have Therese, of course," she confided, "but she is an old woman, so set in her ways. You are young. I like to be around young people. It reminds me."

I cut my eyes at her, thinking she was looking for a compliment. I was not that much younger than she was—perhaps a dozen years. Well, I would not give her the satisfaction of balming her vanity. I sipped at my wine and found myself suddenly emboldened to ask a question that had been niggling at me.

"How long have you known Brisbane?"

She tilted her head, counting on her fingers. "Oh, goodness, it must be nearly twenty years. Something like that."

I choked a little as my wine struggled to go down. Twenty years. No great wonder they were so familiar or that he had come to her when he was ill. No great wonder he trusted her.

"It was in Buda-Pesth," she said, drawing her shawl about her more closely. The stars were beginning to peep out and she tossed her head back to look at them.

"Buda-Pesth? Hungary?"

"Yes. I was with an Hungarian count at the time—very fiery those Hungarians. Deliciously so, but it becomes tiresome after a while, I assure you."

I took her word for it, but I was still trying to make sense of what she had told me. She and Brisbane had met in Hungary, when he was little more than a boy.

She smiled at me, understanding my confusion. "Yes, he was very young. I was his first real love," she said, yawning discreetly. "It did not last, of course. My Hungarian would not permit a rival, even a boy, but Nicholas was delightful. Very ardent."

I was not certain that I wanted to know about Brisbane's ardor. I was just trying to decide how I could tactfully change the subject when I grasped what she had said.

"Did not last? Do you mean that now…that is to say…"

"Am I his mistress now?" she supplied frankly. My face was burning, and I was glad the terrace had grown so dim. But she was not offended. In fact, she laughed.

"Oh, my dear child, I have not shared his bed since that summer in Buda-Pesth. I am his Pompadour, if you understand the reference."

I did. I adored history, not the dry dates and boring battles, but the stories and the people who populated them. I knew that Madame du Pompadour had been mistress to Louis XV for only a short while, but had reigned as his dearest friend for many years after their physical liaison ended. The fact that Louis XV was my cousin, though only of the most distant variety, had only spiced the story for me.

"I understand. Forgive me, I assumed…"

She patted my hand. "Forgive? Child, I appreciate the compliment. I am far too old for such frolics now."

I took her in, from her dark hair, only lightly laced with silver, to her limber figure and exquisite carriage.

"Too old at forty?" I teased.

She laughed again, this time without a trace of silver bells. It was a hearty belly laugh, and she reached for her handkerchief, wiping at her eyes.

"Oh, *chérie*, thank you for that. Forty indeed! My dear girl, I will be sixty on my next birthday."

I stared at her, at the unlined complexion and firm, high bosom. "Witchcraft," I said distinctly.

She hooted again. "Nothing like that. Cosmetics of the most precise kind," she said. "I mix them myself, with Therese." She put the tip of a pointed finger under my chin and raised it, looking closely at my skin. "Very nice, very lovely. Only the English have such complexions. But too pale sometimes. You must let me give you a jar of my rose-petal salve. It will bring the fresh pink roses to your cheeks, you will see."

"Do you—" I indicated her own delicately tinted complexion.

"Of course. Rub a little into the lips, as well. It heightens the colour and will taste of roses when someone kisses you."

I bit my lip against telling her how unlikely that would be. We sat a while longer, gossiping like old friends, and I realized that, except for a few suppers with Portia, I had not done this in a very long time. Not since before I married, when I still lived at March House with my sisters. It felt so natural, so effortless to be in Fleur's company. I realized, too, that if I had followed the conventions dictated by society, this evening would have been forbidden; Fleur would have been forbidden. I watched her as we talked, aging so gracefully, so happily. She was a bit lonely, I could see, but apart from that, she seemed quite pleased with her lot in life. She did not have regrets, which was the most one could expect of life at her age.

I thanked her when I left. She pressed a jar of the rosy salve into my hands, advising me on its use.

"If you like it, I will give you more," she promised.

Impulsively, I embraced her. She held stiff a moment, and I remembered that the French did not care for physical affection.

But before I could withdraw and apologize, she threw her arms around me and squeezed tightly.

"You must come again, anytime," she said, her blue eyes sparkling almost violet in the lamplight.

"I will. And I hope you will come to Grey House. In a few days," I temporized, remembering the distasteful task Brisbane had set me about.

She nodded and I left her then, profoundly grateful to have spent such a lovely evening in such delightful company. But before I was halfway home my thoughts had turned to Brisbane. And for that I was not grateful at all.

THE TWENTY-THIRD CHAPTER

There's small choice in rotten apples.
—William Shakespeare
The Taming of the Shrew

It occurred to me as I began my search of Grey House that size is entirely relative. I had always thought it a modest sort of town house. But when I began to pace it thoroughly, methodically, and above all surreptitiously, it seemed enormous.

The most difficult part was inventing plausible excuses to be in rooms I had scarcely even seen before. I murmured that I was thinking of changing the wallpaper when Aquinas found me in the butler's pantry, and I very nearly insulted Cook by delivering the day's menus to the kitchens in person. Cook did not like even Aquinas setting foot in her domain. I was strictly persona non grata belowstairs.

For a while I walked around with paper and pencil, ostensibly making an inventory of furnishings to be sold when I left Grey House. That ruse got me through Edward's rooms, but by the time I finished, my hand was cramping and the inventory had grown to an unwieldy length. The search saddened me, more than I had anticipated. I had not ventured into Edward's rooms since his death. The sight of his things, freshly dusted but undisturbed, brought quick, hot tears to my eyes. The rooms looked cold, unused, unfriendly even, like a set piece in a rather forbidding museum. I wandered about for the longest time, touching things, picking up little treasures and peering into photographs. I touched the beautiful candlesticks on the mantelpiece, Sèvres, with a design of roses and lilies, copied after a pair made for Madame du Barry. They had been his mother's, the only really decent pieces she had ever bought. There were a few other bits with them, not quite so beautiful, but still pretty enough: a little clock with a shepherdess and a porcelain box decorated with a picture of Pandora opening the legendary box. There were only a few books, the histories he liked to read when he could not settle to sleep, a few volumes of poetry, that sort of thing. On the walls were a pair of rather good paintings with mythological subjects—one of Narcissus gazing into a brook and the other of Achilles mourning the death of Patroclus. I had never much cared for them, but they were very much to Edward's taste—refined, fashionable, serenely coloured with his favorite blues and greys. I moved from item to item, opening boxes and drawers and peering into vases. I found nothing except a little dust and a few ghosts. It was a disturbing experience, and I realized then that I had no wish to search Grey House by myself. In the end, I convinced myself I had no choice. I told Aquinas.

"You wish to search Grey House, my lady," he said, his voice carefully neutral. Like all good butlers, Aquinas would never dream of offering an overt criticism.

"That is correct."

"For the purpose of discovering evidence of some wrongdoing."

"Exactly."

"Perhaps I might offer a suggestion or two that would be of assistance."

"I rather hoped you might."

"If your ladyship could possibly postpone the proposed

search until tomorrow, I think it would be immeasurably easier to arrange."

I blinked at him. "Why?"

"Tomorrow is the Sabbath, my lady," he said, without a trace of impatience.

"Oh, very good. How many of them go to church?"

"All, my lady. And afterward they have the afternoon free to avail themselves of the pleasures of town, such as they are." Aquinas had been in service in Paris and was always bitter about the solemnity of a British Sunday, even in London.

I stared at him. "Really, how very extraordinary. I never noticed. But I always have luncheon on Sunday, the fires are always tended to."

"I do not attend services myself, my lady. It is my privilege to stay behind and make certain that you are taken care of."

I did not know what to say. Aquinas had always shown such deft, quiet concern for me that I was not surprised that he should have given up his own Sunday so that I should not be inconvenienced. What surprised, and saddened me, was my own blindness to his devotion.

"Thank you, Aquinas. You are most diligent."

He bowed from the neck. He never sat in my presence, with the result that our conversations were always slightly awkward, and I usually finished them with a crick in my neck. But I respected his insistence on decorum.

"Now, I have undertaken to solve a problem with the assistance of Mr. Nicholas Brisbane. Perhaps you will remember that he has called here?"

"I remember all callers, my lady." A lesser servant would have noted my callers in a book. Aquinas, I was certain, simply filed them in his head.

"Yes, well, Mr. Brisbane has suggested that I search the premises for our culprit. I may tell you the wrongdoing in question was a peccadillo itself—one of the books in my study was vandalized and the snipped passages were fashioned into anonymous notes. Mr. Brisbane's intention is to prove that one of the staff here at Grey House was responsible, but I intend to prove him wrong. Unfortunately, the only method for doing so is to search the house for any clue, however trivial, that might point to the guilty party."

Aquinas nodded thoughtfully. "Might I suggest that your ladyship pay particularly close attention to the public rooms? I do not think one of the staff, if he is a clever villain, would leave evidence of his guilt in his own rooms."

"Good Lord, Aquinas! You, too? Mr. Brisbane said much the same thing. I thought it indicated he had a criminal mind."

Aquinas said nothing, but his colour deepened, staining his neck a ferocious scarlet.

"Oh, really, not you as well!"

"I beg your pardon, my lady?" he asked innocently.

"Nothing, Aquinas. I do not wish to know," I said firmly, and I meant it. In spite of Brisbane's allusions, I trusted Aquinas more than anyone else in Grey House. I did not care what youthful escapades might have brought him to the wrong side of the law. All that mattered to me was that he was on the proper side of it now.

"Naturally your ladyship will wish to search my room as well," he said smoothly. "It will be at your disposal whenever you wish."

"Oh, no, really, I could not—"

For the first time I could remember, Aquinas interrupted me. "You must. I would not like there to be a shadow of suspicion clouding my name, my lady. I value your good opinion too highly."

I said nothing, but I could hear Brisbane's voice, insidious as a snake. *Well, of course he would say that, wouldn't he? Especially if he has already hidden the evidence.*

Resolutely, I put Brisbane's nasty voice from my mind, but

it came creeping back when I opened the door to Aquinas' room the next morning. The bells had already summoned the faithful to church and I was surprised at how quickly the house fell silent. Renard, usually kept on duty to look after Simon on Sundays, was given one day free per month. Usually, he took it in the middle of the month, but Aquinas had made some excuse for requesting that he take it this first Sunday, and Renard had been too eager to question it. The Ghoul had left on her customary Sunday tour of the churchyards. She left quite early each Sunday morning, swathed in mourning veils and crepe, and did not return until late in the evening, quite as rested and relaxed as if she had just taken a holiday.

Even Magda had gone, although I knew better than to expect her to have gone to worship. She would pay a visit to her own people, no doubt, catching up with the aunts and sisters who had opposed her leaving, and who continually pressed their menfolk for her return. The others would likely go to the parks, meeting up with friends and would-be lovers. From my post in the study, I had listened to them, chattering happily as they crowded down the backstairs, liberated for the better part of the day. It seemed a little insulting really, that they should be so glad to be quit of Grey House, and of me. But I tried to imagine myself in their places and I knew I would have been the first one down the stairs. Even poor Desmond, recovering from a cold, had managed to rub enough camphor on his chest to make an outing worth his while. I could still smell him, along with the cheap perfume the maids had splashed on when I crept out into the hall, feeling for all the world like an intruder in my own house.

I began with Aquinas' room, for no other reason than guilt. I was ashamed at having to do it while he was in the house, but he had tactfully taken himself upstairs to tend to Simon. I made a quick but thorough search of his effects. I learned that he was a lapsed Roman Catholic, which I had always suspected, and that he was a widower, which I had not. I found a bit of newspaper in an envelope in his washstand drawer, its edges soft with age, detailing the acrobatic exploits of the Amazing Aquinas and his beautiful wife, Gabriella, of the Gioberti troupe of Milan. There was a sketch below it, crude but recognizable, of Aquinas balanced atop a wire with Gabriella perched on his shoulder. There was a second clipping as well, this one almost too painful to read—a gust of wind, a bit of ribbon snagged onto the wire.

I thrust it back into the envelope, sorry I had seen it. I had known that he had trained as a circus acrobat, but I had always thought it amusing. I had believed it a youthful escapade, given up for a secure job in service that would see him taken care of in his dotage. I had never imagined the circumstances that drove him to leave the vagabond life. I thought of the countless times I had plagued him to tell me stories of the circus, and how he had always put me off, saying they were dull. I should have known better.

But those were the only surprises in his room. He was neat and tidy to the point of obsession, his effects few and beautifully kept. Of course, Aquinas was far too clever to keep any scraps of his crimes hanging about if he were the villain, but I preferred to think him innocent instead.

I moved to the top of the house, and collected Aquinas to help me search the maids' dormitory and the footmen's room. I had told him of the notes, but not of the poison. He would help me search for anything suspicious, but I kept my own lookout for small boxes or vials that might yet hold the means of Edward's murder. He showed me the way to the staff quarters as I had never ventured there before. The maids shared a largish room that overlooked the garden; the footmen were in a slightly smaller room that faced the street. Both were nastier than I had imagined. Between Betty's sodden heap of used and crumpled handkerchiefs and Desmond's collection of drippy patent medicines, I felt rather queasy. The maids' dormitory revealed nothing of interest, though, besides a rather childish attachment to cheap mementos and fairings. They each had bags of ginger nuts and little fair dolls dressed in gaily coloured scraps. They were old enough to earn a living in service, but none of them was more than nineteen, children really, in so many ways. There was a single pot of rouge, cracked and almost empty, that I fancied they shared between them on their days out, and a large bottle of very cheap perfume that was nearly empty. The entire room smelled of it, heavy and sweet, and I was glad to move on to the austere quarters shared by Desmond and Henry. The air was little better than in the maid's room. Here it smelled of camphor and liquorice and a few other medicinal things I could not identify.

Aquinas raised a brow at the collection of bottles arrayed on the windowsill next to Desmond's bed.

"He is homesick, my lady. He pines for the country."

"Then what is he doing in London?" I asked, exasperated, although I knew well the answer. "There are no jobs in the country, I know, Aquinas. You needn't look so repressive. But really, one would think something could be done for him. I know—I shall ask Father to send him down to the Abbey. A spell in Sussex should put him right, what do you think?"

"I should think the country would be exactly what he requires, my lady. He is a capable young man, diligent and amiable in discharging his duties. I think he would prove most satisfactory to his lordship. You might suggest something with dogs, my lady."

"Dogs?" I was moving on to the chest at the foot of Henry's bed.

"Yes, my lady. He is very fond of them."

I heaved back the lid and began to poke the untidy contents with my finger.

"Well, Father is always looking for someone he can trust

with his mastiffs. Especially now that poor old Crab is finally about to throw a litter. Good God!"

I had found an album, bound in cheap leather and tied with a black cord. I opened it, expecting the usual postcards from seaside resorts. What I found was something entirely different.

Aquinas looked discreetly over my shoulder and coughed. "French, I should think, my lady."

"How can you tell?" I asked, wide-eyed.

"The caption around the edge."

"Well done, Aquinas. I had not even noticed there was a caption." This was because I had been too occupied with the photograph of the young woman in a provocative state of undress. She was staring at the camera with a saucy expression, apparently oblivious to the young man touching her.

I flipped through the album hurriedly. There were more of the postcards, dozens of them, all featuring subjects of a prurient nature. But toward the back, there was something different. The first postcards had been cheeky, almost funny. Most of the young women were draped, exposing only their bosoms. The young men in the pictures were entirely clothed. One could imagine small boys tittering over them in groups behind the privy.

But the others—I stared at them, feeling faintly sick to my stomach. These were not photographs. They were drawings printed on heavy paper, the edges raw as though they had been bound once and torn free. They were thoroughly obscene, not because they were sexual, but because they were violent. They depicted things I had never imagined, never wanted to imagine could happen. I stared at them until Aquinas lifted the album gently from my hands.

"Some things are best left unseen," he remarked, his voice cold with anger.

"I do not understand," I said stupidly.

"You would not, my lady, because you have been raised with dignity and with grace." He ranted softly for a moment in Italian.

"But why would Henry have these?"

Aquinas averted his eyes and I flushed painfully.

"I mean, I can imagine *why*, but where did he get them?"

Aquinas shrugged. "There are places…"

I did not press him, but simply made a note to tell Brisbane of my discovery and pressed on. There was a small viewer, of rather good quality wood, inset with a disk of glass to magnify the cards mounted behind it. It was grouped with a pack of cards, their subject matter much the same as the pictures in the album. I shoved them aside. There was nothing else of interest in the chest, and I was grateful when we moved on, closing the door behind us. The atmosphere in that room at the top of the house had grown close and airless. The hall seemed a little cooler and I breathed deeply for a moment before we moved into Morag's room.

If Henry's things had been a shock, Morag's were a revelation. The small room was packed with items as a magpie's nest, some things I had discarded, others bought with her modest wages. I recognized a vase that had been chipped slightly when one of the new maids had handled it carelessly. I had told Aquinas to dispose of it, but Morag had interceded, asking if she might keep it. I had shrugged, sublimely disinterested in what became of it. I saw now that Morag had filled it with dried grasses and placed it almost reverently on a starched mat of Brussels lace that had once been a shawl of mine. She had turned the vase so that the chipped edge did not show and tucked the snagged threads of the shawl out of sight. Everywhere I looked in that room I saw care and thrift and an almost painful determination to make good use of whatever came her way.

"I think our Morag is the proverbial thrifty Scot," I said with a smile. "She throws nothing away."

Aquinas was studying a framed sketch that I had come across months before. It was a courtyard, thick with fallen leaves and broken statuary. Edward had sketched it himself, before we married. It was well done, but melancholy, I always thought, and we had hung it in a back hallway and forgotten about it. I noticed it one morning, shortly after Edward died and had taken it down. I had been ready to consign it to the dustbin when Morag snatched it, saying she had a frame that needed a picture. I recognized the frame as well. It was a gaudy, heavy, scrolled thing that once belonged to Edward's mother. I had never liked it, and when the corner had broken off, I had been delighted. Now it hung paired with the sketch, wildly inappropriate for such a humble subject, but Morag must have liked it. It took pride of place over her bed.

"She came to us with only the clothes on her back and a sewing basket," Aquinas reminded me.

I said nothing and busied myself with her chest of drawers, feeling rather abashed. I had known what Morag's life was like—Aunt Hermia had made certain of that. She had described for me the existence of an East End prostitute in terms that could only be described as brutally frank. I had known that Morag once lived largely on the street, sleeping in a bed only on the nights when she made enough money to pay for a doss. All of her possessions were carried on her person, tucked into pockets and sewn into hems. I had thought it would seem like paradise to her to have her own furnished room at the top of the house.

But why had I never thought to hang proper pictures on the wall or give her an unbroken vase or frame? Immediately I thought of a dozen things in Edward's room that I could pass on to her. A few were valuable, but not wildly so, and I did not need the money they would bring. Why not give them to Morag, who would enjoy them? I turned to Aquinas, shrugging to indicate that I had found nothing.

He nodded. "All I found was a half-empty box of barley sugar sweets, for her sins."

I preceded him out of the room, making up my mind to give her a large box of the best candy I could find. In spite of her ragged edges, Morag had been a comfort to me through my widowhood. I should make rather more of an effort to tell her so, I thought.

Next we ventured into Renard's room, a task I was not anticipating with any great joy. His room was untidy as a lord's, strewn with soiled clothing and discarded footwear. There were newspapers and cigar ash underfoot and a plate that had been sitting around long enough for the remains of the food to become truly revolting.

"I thought the French were supposed to be fastidious," I complained, waving a handkerchief over my nose.

"I never thought he was French," Aquinas replied. He had taken up an umbrella and was using it to tentatively shift the dirty garments.

"Really?" I whirled to face him, my hands full of magazines.

"The accent is too affected, *too* French, if you take my meaning, my lady. If you will forgive the observation, he sounds very much like your ladyship's dressmakers."

I laughed, thinking of the Riche brothers and their exaggerated accents, their conspicuous use of simple French words in every conversation. "Of course! Where do you suppose he comes from?"

Aquinas wrinkled his nose at a particularly malodorous stocking. "Kent. I never trust a Kentish man."

"I am sure there is a very good reason why, but I will not ask you now. I suppose his real name must be Fox, and that is why he uses that ridiculous sobriquet," I mused, flipping quickly through the magazines. They were old ones, Edward's castoffs. There was nothing more interesting in them than a mildly scandalous article regarding the Chancellor of the Exchequer. Aquinas had given up on the clothes and was poking about under the bed with an umbrella.

After a moment he gave a grunt and reached as far as his arm would stretch, hooking the handle of the umbrella around something. He crabbed backward, collecting a fair amount of dust and cobweb, pulling a small portmanteau with him.

I dove after it, although I cannot imagine why. Did I think I would find scissors and a glue pot secreted inside? Actually, I rather liked the idea of Renard as villain. I had always found him distasteful, and the notion of dismissing him without either pay or character was wildly appealing.

The portmanteau was locked, but it was a moment's work to find the key, hanging on a hook behind the mirror over his washstand. Aquinas stepped back and allowed me to fit the key myself. It turned easily and I threw back the lid, feeling a surge of profound disappointment. There were only books, old ones by the look of them, with moldy, crumbling covers and the choking smell of dust and mildew.

Aquinas lifted one out and opened it. We stared at the illustration for a long moment.

"Well, I suppose that explains where Henry managed to find such filth," I said finally.

Aquinas nodded thoughtfully. "Renard must strip the pages and sell them to him, perhaps to others as well."

I picked up another book, noting the French title and the owner's coat of arms embossed on the leather cover.

"Are they valuable, do you think?"

Aquinas made a little moue. "Perhaps. There are collectors—a comte I once served in Paris, for example. They would pay rather a lot for a volume such as this from an illustrious library. But to cut the pictures and sell them alone, either he is eager for the money—too eager to find a dealer, or he does not recognize the value."

"I do not think Renard is the sort who would overlook

the possible value of anything," I said slowly. "Where do you think he got them?"

"France," he said firmly. "He probably worked for this gentleman, or his family, and took them when he left. One would think he took them because they were easy to steal, easy to sell off—a few pictures whenever he wanted a little money."

"But why pretend to us that he was French?"

Aquinas smiled at me, a little sadly. "Because there is a prejudice about French servants, a notion that they are superior to Italians, even better than English ones. Better pay to pretend you are French."

"But that is ludicrous. If he were a good valet, it would not have mattered to Edward if he were a Chinaman."

"To Sir Edward, no. But there are others to whom it matters very much."

"Nonsense. All that matters is that one does a good job and can speak the language well enough to be understood. I should not care if my staff were Albanians."

"You are different, my lady." I must have looked doubtful, because he went on. "Do you remember the dinner here, a few weeks before Sir Edward's death? You hosted Lady Thorncroft? Yes, well, as I was bringing in the roast, I clearly heard her ask if you counted the silver after I had polished it to make certain it was all still there."

I looked away, squirming a little. "I had hoped you did not hear that."

"But I did, and I heard your ladyship's reply. I do not think you will be invited again to Thorncroft Hall, by the way."

I looked up at him, and his eyes were twinkling in his sad face. "Well, what else could I say to her? She was insulting and rude."

"She only said what many other guests at Grey House have thought. How can you trust your valuables to an Italian?"

I closed the book and put it back into the portmanteau.

"I do not know why everyone persists in thinking of you as Italian, you are half English. You don't even have an accent. Most of the time," I amended, thinking of the rare fits of anger that rendered him incapable of communicating except in passionate Italian.

"Come, I want to get out of this room and wash my hands," I said. He shoved the portmanteau into its hiding place and replaced the umbrella.

At the door, I paused. "Aquinas, has Mr. Brisbane ever said anything to you? Ever made any sort of remark about the fact that you are not English?"

Aquinas smiled. "Yes, my lady. The first time he called at Grey House, when I showed him to the door. He told me how much he admired Italian acrobats and asked me if I had ever seen the Giobertis perform in Milan."

I stared at him, openmouthed in astonishment. His smile widened.

"I know, my lady. That was precisely the reaction I had to him. A very remarkable gentleman, Mr. Brisbane."

"Remarkable indeed, Aquinas."

By three o'clock, we were tired and dusty and had turned up almost nothing. No diaries with heartfelt, murderous confessions, no glue pots except where they belonged. And I had found no poison in my surreptitious searches when Aquinas' back was turned. We had tiptoed past Simon's room, although I had given the room a cursory glance the night before. It was not entirely impossible that the culprit had hidden something away in Simon's room, Brisbane had warned me. It was almost as neat a solution as hiding something in mine, and he had instructed me to take note of anything that might seem out of the ordinary. I had peered into corners under the guise of looking for an earring I had dropped, but I found nothing and Simon had begun to look at me peculiarly. It was on the tip of my tongue to take him into my confidence, as well, but in the end I decided against it. Brisbane would be annoyed enough that I had told Aquinas as much as I had; explaining that Simon also knew would leave him apoplectic.

Aquinas brought Simon's luncheon tray while I prodded the skirting boards outside his room. They proved sound, and Aquinas joined me shortly to finish our search. To my relief, my own rooms turned up nothing. It was irrational, really, *I* knew that there was nothing there. But it made me feel immeasurably better, and I decided that I would tell Brisbane I had enlisted Aquinas to act as an impartial observer during my search of my own things. He would not believe it for a minute, but I thought it sounded very professional.

The public rooms on the main floor took very little time. They had been furnished by Edward in his favorite Empire style—all cleanly designed and uncluttered. No hiding places among all those bare legs and stripped floors. That left only the belowstairs—kitchens, offices and the private rooms I had not yet searched. The kitchens were pristine, with perfectly ordered utensils and graduated copper pots ranged on hooks. There was not a fork out of place, and I was not surprised. Cook was more ferocious than any battlefield general; no one would have dared leave her kitchen until every last saucer was stowed in its place.

The laundry was marginally less tidy. It was under Cook's nominal authority, but it was Magda's actual responsibility. She had left a cake of soap melting in a puddle of water and a brass can of water standing nearly in the doorway, so awkwardly placed that I nearly fell over it. I muttered, shoving it aside with my foot. The rest of the room yielded nothing, no cupboards or trunks where something suspicious might be lurking. There was only the bucket under the window where I had left Val's shirt several nights before. I moved toward it, surprised to find the water again reddened, as if someone had stuffed something bloody into it.

And they had, I realized, peering into the bucket. I asked Aquinas for a stick and he found me a bit of long, thin pipe that Magda used to stir the boiler. I levered it under the water and heaved. A lump of sodden linen tumbled to the floor with a splash.

Aquinas was on top of it before I could stop him. He was not so fastidious as I. He unfolded the dripping garment with his hands. It was a man's shirt, as I had known it would be, stained streakily across the cuffs with blood. There was a handkerchief this time as well—a woman's, from the look of the pansies embroidered garishly in the corner.

I stared at the bloody, soaking mess, wondering how I could have been stupid enough to believe Val's story about a fight at the opera. He was a medical student, not permitted to practice. It was apparent that he had found somewhere to continue his studies, somewhere he could not speak of, somewhere that would provide him access to people who were profoundly in need of his attentions, I thought as I fingered the handkerchief. It was slashed in places, the edges of the cheap cotton curling back on themselves like the petals of a gruesome flower.

I shoved the handkerchief back into the shirt and rolled the bundle back into the gory bucket.

"This has nothing to do with what we are about. I will deal with it myself," I told Aquinas firmly.

He said nothing but simply threw fresh water onto the pinkened puddle and took up a mop, swabbing at it until it was gone.

But it lingered in our minds, and I knew we were both thinking of it as we made our way to Cook's room. There the mood lightened. We both smiled at her harmless indulgence in cherry brandy and fashion magazines. But even as we neatly tucked her bottles back under the bed, I found myself wondering about Magda. As the laundress, she could hardly have overlooked Val's bloody shirts. I had rinsed the first bloody one clean for him, but I had little doubt now that there had been others. He had not bothered to rinse this one, and yet he had to know she would see it. Did he pay for her silence? This possibility worried me. Val never had much money. Father's allowance was generous, but Val was, too, always giving money to causes he deemed worthy and friends who were not. I found myself rushing to search Magda's room. I felt certain that I would find something there that tied her to my brother, and I was very much afraid of what that might be.

But even I never expected that it would be arsenic.

THE TWENTY-FOURTH CHAPTER

My duty pricks me on to utter that
Which else no worldly good should draw from me.
—William Shakespeare
The Two Gentlemen of Verona

Of course I was not certain that it was arsenic when I found it. I was not even certain that it was anything of importance. But I suspected.

And when I looked at the little box of grey powder, I felt sick. I had wanted so badly to give Magda a chance. Aunt Hermia had warned against it. She had never been as warm in her acceptance of Gypsies as Father had, and she was eloquent on the folly of bringing one into the house.

"You won't have a stick of furniture left by the time she's done with you," she had warned me. "She'll sell it all from under you. And you'll not get a proper day's work from her, either." Privately, I rather agreed with Aunt Hermia. I knew Magda too well to expect she would settle easily to life inside four walls. I had a somewhat higher opinion of her honesty, and indeed in the time with us nothing more significant than a teaspoon had gone missing. But Magda had not fit in happily with the staff, preferring to keep to herself, occasionally engaging in violent, shrieking quarrels with one of the maids, which usually ended with the maid stalking off with a stellar reference and a handsome pay packet from me, and another trip to the domestic agency for Aquinas.

But I could not turn her out, any more than I could explain to Aunt Hermia why I had taken her in. Why Magda had turned to me in her time of trouble, rather than Father, or someone else with the authority to help her, I could not imagine. She had, though, and I could no more abandon her than I could neglect any other responsibility. Father may have been a bit slapdash in the raising of his children, but he managed to instill in us the essentials, and duty was one of them. We were charged with taking care of those to whom our money and our blood made us superior, and it was an obligation we neglected at our peril. When Magda had come to me, cast out and penniless, I had not wanted to give her a place at Grey House, but I had no choice in the matter. She was in need and had asked for my help.

I had given her cold refuge, I thought as I looked around the little room. It was bare as an anchorite's cell, and I felt a stab of anger, not at Magda, but at myself. She was like Morag, a creature without a home, but I had given her little more than four walls to call her own. The room was uncarpeted, furnished only with a narrow bed and a single hard chair. Her meager possessions were divided between a carpetbag and a discarded, crumbling old hat box. There was not even a proper curtain at the window. I looked at those four dull grey walls and the cold stone floor and the cheerless window, and I realized then what a prison it must have seemed to her, a Gypsy woman with rolling moors and tumbling rivers in her blood. She had roamed freely with her people before coming to me, winding from one corner of the kingdom to another. From Kentish summers making hay to the foggy winter London campgrounds, she had spent her entire life out in the fresh air, sleeping in a low tent, and later a painted caravan. Now she was confined to pavements and coal dust, as unnatural a being as the raven locked in Val's room.

I pocketed the box and turned to Aquinas.

"There is nothing else here. I do not think we need search Diggory's quarters. He has no access to the house."

Aquinas nodded solemnly. "I think there is more at hand here than anonymous notes, my lady," he ventured, without a hint of reproach.

"Yes," I said. I hesitated, then squared my shoulders. I had trusted Aquinas this far. It seemed pointless and insulting not to tell him the rest. "Mr. Brisbane suspects, as do I, that Sir Edward may have died by poison."

"I thought as much," he said blandly.

I blinked like a hare. "I beg your pardon?"

"In Italy such things are more common, even in France it is so. It is not unheard of for an unhappy wife or husband to remove the cause of their sorrow. Or for a young nephew to help a rich and elderly uncle along to his grave for the sake of his inheritance. And it is not impossible that a man with poor health would take his own life rather than linger on in pain."

I stared at him, remembering suddenly what Simon had told me about his own intentions. Why had it never occurred to me that Edward might have done the same?

But I patted the tiny box of mortality in my pocket and I knew better. Edward had been genuinely terrified of the anonymous notes, according to Brisbane. A man bent on self-destruction would not have been so troubled by them. Besides, if Edward had engineered his own death, he would not have left the means secreted away in some innocent person's room to cast suspicion where it did not belong.

"I shall have to deliver this to Mr. Brisbane. I think sooner rather than later."

Aquinas withdrew, leaving me alone in Magda's room. I sat for a long moment, trying to put things together in my mind, but nothing seemed to fit. Every thought I had seemed to end with a question mark. What was Val about and how much did

Magda know of it? Did she have cause to harm Edward? And would she? Had she?

I shook myself finally and prepared to call upon Brisbane. I had questions, to be sure. And perhaps he had answers.

I should have thought that I would have felt rather smug handing over my little box. Instead I felt only miserable. I was implicating a woman I had known since childhood, a woman I trusted, after a fashion. I was putting her fate into the hands of a man I knew very little about. I still did not know the cause of his terrible headaches, but knowing the cures he had sampled did not reassure me. Everyone I knew had taken opium in some form, but I had never met anyone who had dosed themselves with absinthe. It had left me wildly curious and a little wary. Of course, this was largely due to the fact that I had recently sat up late, reading the story of Dr. Jekyll and Mr. Hyde by guttering lamplight. I did not seriously believe that Brisbane had somehow caused his own suffering through scientific experiments gone horribly wrong, but it was enough to make me look at him closely as he surveyed the contents of the little box.

Suddenly, he surged up out of his seat. He went to the long table under the shuttered windows where his scientific equipment was arrayed. I followed, watching as he spooned a small sample of the powder into a little crucible. He lit it and a strong, garlicky aroma filled the air.

He turned to me, his eyes lambent with a sort of savage satisfaction.

"I shall send it along to Mordecai to be fully analyzed, but this test indicates arsenic."

I felt my heart sink a little at the words. There were plenty of good reasons for possessing arsenic, but Magda had none of them. I knew she did not use it for cosmetic purposes, nor did she kill rats. Brisbane, of course, was sensing my thoughts.

"There is only one reason to have arsenic in this quantity and in this concentration," he said flatly. "She has poisoned someone, or at least intended to."

"You do not know that," I argued feebly. "Doctor Bent has not even finished his report on what may have induced the symptoms Edward suffered."

The black eyes narrowed unflinchingly. "Then can you explain why a Gypsy laundress in your employ keeps enough arsenic to fell a battalion tucked in her spare petticoat?"

"You do not know that is arsenic!" I returned, angry. I do not know why I was enraged, only that I was. He was so eager to believe the worst of her. Perhaps I was angry with myself because I could think of no proper defense for her. Or perhaps I was angry with him for demanding one.

Brisbane folded his arms over his chest, his shirtsleeves brilliant white against the dark wool of his waistcoat. I had called without sending ahead—rather foolhardy in light of how I found him the last time I did such a thing—and found him reading quietly by the fire. He had seemed pleased enough to see me, and delighted when I told him what I had brought. But I had felt every inch a traitor.

"My lady, I know what that is, even if you do not. I will send it to Mordecai simply to confirm my own analysis. Now, sit down and tell me everything you know about Magda."

Miserable and defeated, I did as I was bid. He rang for tea and I took a cup and a biscuit from Monk simply for something to do with my hands. Monk was careful not to make eye contact with me, and I wondered if he regretted the intimacies he had shared during my last call. He left quickly, and Brisbane did not wait for me to finish my tea before launching into his interrogation.

"How long have you known Magda?" The notebook was on the table at his side, but he did not open it.

"All my life, I think. I told you that Father permits the

Gypsies to camp on his land in Sussex. Magda's people have been coming there since my father was a boy."

"And has she always gotten on well with your family?"

"Oh, yes. Father would pay her to tell fortunes at the harvest ball. He always bought horses from her brothers and told the tenants to buy the clothes-pegs and harnesses they made."

Brisbane was thoughtful. There was an expression, almost of distaste on his face, as if he did not like peering too closely into their transient lives. I remembered suddenly the ragged bit of conversation I had overheard from the laundry room, and my certainty that it was Magda taunting Brisbane.

"Who is Mariah Young?" I asked.

His face did not change, at least not in any way I could define. It seemed to go flat, though, as if his features were no longer flesh and blood, but paper and ink, technically correct, but utterly devoid of animation. He sipped at his tea and then looked at me, his eyes strangely hooded. I had never seen quite that expression in them before, although his face betrayed no emotion whatsoever.

"I thought I heard someone crashing about. What is down there? The laundry?"

I nodded, my hands a little clammy. I patted them surreptitiously on my napkin.

"Mariah Young is my business," he said evenly. "And she has no bearing on this case."

"But you were there, talking to Magda—"

He did something then, something I had not seen him do before. He put down his teacup and brought out a little wooden box. From it he took a slim, very dark cigar. He lit it in an unhurried fashion, taking a few deep draws to make certain it was smoldering properly. He had not asked my permission, but the tobacco had a sweet, musky smell that was actually quite appealing.

"Spanish," he said with a thin smile. "I find they help me think. Mariah Young," he said, his tone thoughtful. He was silent a moment, as if weighing within himself how much he could or should reveal. I sat very still, trying to look more trustworthy than curious, but I did not deceive him. He simply shook his head and said, "I can only tell you that the conversation between Magda and myself has no bearing on this case except in one respect." He blew a soft blue cloud of smoke over his head. "I think that your laundress might very well be capable of blackmail. And if that is so, it is a short step to murder, don't you think?"

"And that is all you are going to say on the matter?" I demanded.

"That is all." The words were softly spoken, but underpinned with iron, and I did not doubt he meant them. I would learn nothing from approaching him directly. I decided to leave it—for now. But I made up my mind that before I was done with Brisbane, I would know the full story of Mariah Young.

"How does a Gypsy teller of fortunes come to be employed as a common laundress?" he asked, taking back the reins of the conversation.

"Her people were encamped at Bellmont Abbey when she got into some sort of trouble. She became unclean, according to their laws. You see, the Gypsies believe—"

"I am familiar with the mythology," he said dryly. Of course he was. I had deduced from my conversations with Monk and Fleur that Brisbane was extremely well traveled. Doubtless he had encountered many wanderers in his own journeys. Likely that accounted for his antipathy toward them.

"Yes, well, Magda was deemed unclean for a period of a year or two, I am not certain of the precise rules. It meant that she could not travel with them and would probably have starved. She came to me and I told her she could work for me, here in town. She has only just now been allowed to visit her brothers. They are encamped in London at the moment, and I think she may rejoin them soon."

Brisbane sat and puffed, staring at a point some inches above my head. I might have been a bowl of fruit for all the attention he paid to me.

"If you did not want a biscuit, you did not have to take one to be polite," he said finally.

"I beg your pardon?"

He gestured with the glowing tip of the cigar. "You have crumbled that biscuit to bits. You had only to decline."

I looked at the wrecked remains of the little pastry mounded on the plate. I put it down hastily.

"Did Magda have any reason to bear a grudge against Sir Edward?"

"Absolutely not. If Edward had objected to her employment, she would never have been given a post at Grey House."

"And yet she brought poison into that house," he mused. There was another interval punctuated only by the soft exhalation of his breath. I sat quietly, mentally redecorating the room. It was quite nicely proportioned with good moldings, but I thought the chairs were a little dark, a little heavy for my taste. And the green of the curtains was entirely too grey.

I had just moved on to the artwork, replacing his stark sketch of an Eastern mosque with my own rather good copy of Jupiter and Io when he spoke.

"Why was she found to be unclean?"

I began to toy with my rings. "It is really quite distasteful, Brisbane. It has no bearing on the investigation, I am certain of that."

"But I am not," he rejoined with a smile.

I fumed a little, but I told him. "It has something to do with the dead. She touched a dead person. Apparently that violates their greatest taboo."

He took up a small china dish figured in gold dragons and ground out the remainder of his cigar. "What were the circumstances?"

"Really, Brisbane, must I—"

"Yes, you must," he said, his tone hard. "I will know everything."

I drew a deep breath. "Very well. Her daughter, Carolina, had died. My father arranged for her to be buried in the village graveyard at Blessingstoke. Magda was found there the next night. Her daughter's body had been dug up. She was embracing the corpse."

"Good God." He sat back heavily in his chair, and I felt a childish sort of satisfaction at having shocked him. "I am surprised they only banished her."

"They pitied her. She was ranting, half out of her mind with grief. They put out her things and packed their own. They were gone by daylight. Within the space of a few short days she had lost her only child, her entire family, her whole way of life. Now perhaps you can find some pity for her."

His eyes lifted to mine, cool and black as a night sea.

"Pity is a luxury I cannot afford, my lady. For anyone."

"How can you be so unfeeling?" I demanded. "What is your heart made of that it can remain so wholly untouched by the suffering of another human being?"

"Stone. Steel. Flint, if you like. I am sure that is what you think."

"What I think does not matter at all," I retorted. "I simply cannot comprehend how any person can live as you do."

"That is because your ladyship has the advantage of a clean conscience and an untroubled past," he said, his words tinged with ice. "If you had to live with what I do, you would understand it well enough."

A sudden image flashed into my mind of Brisbane, drugged and in agony, and I felt ashamed of myself. I inclined my head.

"You are right, of course. I should not have judged you. I apologize."

He blinked. "I beg your pardon?"

"I have just apologized," I said, smoothing my skirts. "You were right and I was wrong. I spoke thoughtlessly. Shall I make amends, or do you forgive me?"

I waited coolly for his reply, but he simply stared, dumbfounded. He was shaking his head, his expression entirely astonished.

"Now I do not understand you. One minute you are passionately attacking me for my cold heart, the next you are craving my pardon."

I lifted my shoulder in a genteel shrug I copied from Fleur. "A lady's prerogative. We are widely believed to be the less logical sex."

"Not you," he said. "I am suspicious of you now."

I smiled guilelessly. "You have no reason to be."

"That I do not believe."

I did not reply and he moved on, rather reluctantly, I thought.

"Is there anything else I should know about Magda?"

I thought, then shook my head. "I have told you everything, as far as I remember. If I recall anything else, I shall write to you."

He rose and walked me to the door. "I will send the ars— powder," he amended hastily, "to Mordecai in the morning. As soon as he sends word I will let you know."

He paused, his hand curved around the knob.

"I am very impressed, my lady," he said quietly. "You turned up a piece of evidence that makes a needle in a haystack seem like a winning proposition. And you did not permit sentiment to dictate your actions. I know how easy it would have been for you to conceal this from me."

"It would not have been easy at all," I remarked, pulling on my gloves. "As you observed, I have the advantage of a clean conscience. I should like to keep it that way."

THE TWENTY-FIFTH CHAPTER

They love not poison that do poison need,
Nor do I thee, though I wish him dead.
—William Shakespeare
Richard II

The next day my spirits were low. I could not bring myself to question Val about the second bloody shirt or even scold him for failing to get rid of the stolen raven. I cringed every time Henry came near me, remembering his foul collection of French pornography. And I had a ferocious headache, the result of spending several hours copying my observations during the search into legible form for Brisbane's records. After my surprising success in Magda's rooms, he had sent word that he would require a full list of the contents of the house, particularly personal possessions. It was tedious stuff, and I strongly suspected he had requested it simply to keep me occupied with something dull while he had the more interesting task of taking the grey powder to Doctor Bent's for analysis.

After three hours of writing, painstakingly listing the contents of every room I searched, I threw down my pen, spattering the page with a temperamental spray of ink. I had been cooped up in the study long enough. It was time for some physical labor to stretch my limbs and clear the cobwebs from my mind.

I instructed Aquinas to send boxes and tissue to Edward's

room and give me the loan of one of the servants—anyone except Henry. I had no desire to be alone with the mad pornographer. To my surprise it was Magda who came, clinking her gold bracelets and swishing her taffeta petticoats. I cringed a little—it was the same red petticoat that I had found wrapped around the box of powder.

"Magda, I have decided to clear out Sir Edward's clothes and personal effects. I would like to box them all up and send them along to Lady Hermia's refuge. They should be able to make quite good use of them."

I was chattering, but Magda did not seem to notice. She simply shrugged and began shifting the stacks of shirts from the wardrobe. Without being told, Magda wrapped the garments into neat parcels, putting a shirt, collar and cuffs with each suit of clothes to make a complete ensemble. After a long moment of watching her, I remembered something I had meant to ask her for several days.

"Magda, what does it mean when there is a serpent in the tea leaves?"

Her inky eyes narrowed. "You have let another Gypsy read the leaves for you?"

"No, of course not. I was just wondering."

She regarded me a long moment, then shrugged.

"Sickness. Bad luck. Spiteful enemies."

"Oh," I said feebly.

The dark gaze narrowed still further. "Are you certain the leaves were not yours?" she demanded.

I gave her a thin smile as I lied. "Of course. But, I wonder, speaking of fortunes, why could you not tell Mr. Brisbane his fortune?"

Her hands did not hesitate but moved smoothly along as she wrapped the next shirt. "I cannot tell you, lady. He can."

We worked another minute in silence.

"Who is Mariah Young?"

There was a reaction at this, a tiny jerk of the hands and a bit of the paper tore. She smoothed it, regaining her composure. "I cannot tell you, lady. He can."

"But he won't."

"Then it is not my place," she said calmly. She was fetching hats now, crumpling paper to fill out the crowns.

I twisted one of Edward's neck cloths in my hands. "Magda, how can you be so stubborn! Don't you realize that I am only trying to help you?"

She continued to work deliberately and slowly, moving with a certain deft precision that I had often seen among the Roma. I moved closer, determined to make her understand.

"He means to see you hang for murder, do you hear me? He has the poison."

She turned, her dark eyes wide with surprise. "He took my arsenic?"

I groaned and dropped Edward's neck cloth to the floor. She bent to retrieve it, fluidly, with none of the creaking and snapping one would expect from a woman of her years. A life spent traveling had kept her supple and strong, stronger than I.

"It *was* arsenic, then. He thought so. He has sent it to a doctor to be tested."

I reached out and took her hand. It felt cool and wrinkled, like the top of a blancmange left too long in the larder.

"Magda, I know that you must have had some innocent purpose for the arsenic. I must believe that you wanted it for a cosmetic, a face cream. But Mr. Brisbane believes Sir Edward was poisoned. I cannot help you if you do not tell me the truth."

Her face was utterly blank. No emotion, just the calm, fatal acceptance of her race.

"I always tell you the truth," she said. "Not all of it, not at once, but what I tell you is never false."

I nodded encouragement.

"I did not kill Sir Edward."

I felt my spine sag. I had never actually believed her guilty, but it was a profound relief to hear her deny it.

She looked at me curiously, her eyes snapping with emotion. "You know why I am unclean to my people. But you have never asked me why I went to Carolina's grave. It was because she called me."

My breath caught painfully in my throat. "Called you? Magda, how can that be?"

"I was sleeping, and I dreamed of her. She came to me and said that I must go to her, that she was in danger. I rose and I went to her. My brothers found me there, sitting on her grave with her body in my arms. My brothers understood, they knew that I had to protect her, but the taboo had been broken. I was unclean and I had to leave them."

Magda fell silent, but her words echoed in my head. Why had she felt the need to protect her dead child? The graveyard was a quiet country place, with no one to disturb her. And why should anyone want to? Granted, graverobbing had been a lucrative occupation fifty years before, but there were laws now, providing for the legal use of cadavers for medical study. Schools no longer needed to rely upon unsavory villains to retrieve the newly dead for their anatomical dissections.

But there were others, I thought with a thrill of horror, others who might have need of a fresh corpse, others who had no access to proper medical schools. I thought of my poor, misguided brother, and it was almost more than I could bear.

"Magda, did someone else remove Carolina's body from her grave before you reached the churchyard?"

She nodded and began to rock slowly, her arms crossed over her womb.

"I was too late to stop him disturbing her rest, but I chased him away. He could not take her."

I had read before, in lurid Gothic novels, of one's blood running cold. Until that minute, I had thought it an exaggeration. But as the implication of her words took root, a monstrous idea began to grow, and with it, a cold, creeping certainty.

"Did you have that arsenic because you intended to kill the man who defiled her grave?"

She looked directly into my eyes. "Yes. I waited. It is almost time for me to return to my people. I did not want to kill him and remain under your roof."

I clamped my hand around her arm and shook her hard.

"Do not speak. Do not say another word. Your intentions are enough to buy you a noose."

I stopped a moment, thinking with an icy clarity that should have surprised me.

"Are any of your brothers in London?"

"Jasper. He is at Hampstead."

Jasper, he would do. He was a horse dealer, and a good one. During the season, he could usually be found in London, peddling prime horseflesh to the pinch-purses who would not pay the prices at Tattersall's. I moved swiftly to the mantel, sweeping up the nearest bibelots.

"Take these," I ordered, thrusting the Sèvres candlesticks and the porcelain Pandora's box into her startled hands. "Go to Jasper. He will know where to sell them to get money for you to live on. I haven't any banknotes in the house and I dare not ask Aquinas. Once Jasper has gotten some money for you, get straight out of London. Go anywhere, but not into Sussex. Stay as far away from me and mine as you can, and above all, do not send word where you are. In a few months, you should be able to rejoin your people, up north would be best."

She tightened her grip on the pieces of porcelain, nodding slowly. "You understand that I would never harm you, lady."

I regarded her coldly. "You were prepared to poison a

member of my family, my own kinsman. You have already harmed me."

She nodded sadly and turned to wrap the objects in paper. I instructed her to cushion them with waistcoats and shirts, and in a very few moments she was finished. She reached into her pocket and drew out a piece of knotted calico.

"Do you know what this is?"

I shook my head.

"It is a charm, made from the graveclothes of a dead Rom. This comes from Carolina. It is the strongest magic I can give you."

I took it with reluctant fingers. "Magda, I do not—"

"You will need magic. Because of him, the dark one. I cannot tell his fortune, but he brings death. He brings ruination and despair. I hear weeping when he walks and the screams of the dead echo in his shadow."

The words might have been a trifle melodramatic, but the effect was ghastly. Her voice was low and her eyes glowed conviction. Whatever she had seen, or thought she had seen in Brisbane, she believed it.

"Thank you," I said, clutching the small charm.

She nodded and moved heavily to the door, cradling her parcels.

"You will see me again, lady," she promised me solemnly.

"Not for a very long time, I hope," I said as the door closed softly behind her.

I opened my hand and stared down at the knot that carried so much powerful magic. And I tried to remember where I had seen one like it only recently.

THE TWENTY-SIXTH CHAPTER

Sharp violins proclaim
Their jealous pangs, and desperation,
Fury, frantic indignation,
Depth of pains, and height of passion,
For the fair, disdainful dame.
—John Dryden
"A Song for St. Cecilia's Day"

$\mathcal{P}$erhaps the last activity to promise any diversion that night was an evening with my family. But almost as soon as the door closed behind Magda there was a knock at the door and I could hear the too-cheerful voice of the Ghoul.

"Julia, dear, are you in there?"

I was tempted, sorely tempted not to answer her. But I knew she would run me to the ground eventually.

"Yes, Aunt Ursula."

She entered, black skirts swishing, and surveyed the scene—me, woebegone and bewildered, surrounded by a load of Edward's things, half-packed and tumbled about the room.

"Oh, my dear girl! Why didn't you call me to help you? Packing up a loved one's effects can be so very trying."

Especially when one's laundress admits to wanting to kill your brother in the midst of it, I thought sourly.

"I thought it was time," I said.

"Of course you did. It is only one of the many tasks that you will have now that your first year of mourning is ended."

Trust the Ghoul to mark the anniversary of Edward's death

when I had not. Really, she was a better widow to him than I was. I smiled feebly.

"Yes, I suppose so."

"After all, you will need new clothes to observe this new stage in your mourning."

I widened my eyes. "I beg your pardon, Aunt? I thought you expected me to observe strict mourning in perpetuity."

She gave me a sympathetic cluck. "Oh, no! Well, I admit I did think of it at first, but then I realized how much there would be to do if you put on half mourning. And I thought perhaps it might be best if you had something to occupy your days. Besides, there will be time enough to put your weeds back on when Simon passes."

She began to burrow through Edward's effects and I sat, trying to digest what she had just said. Naturally the arrangements of half mourning would appeal to her. There would be all sorts of doleful things to attend to, all manner of fresh new grimness to inflict upon me. I could well imagine what pleasure she would take in draping the house in purple and ordering new writing paper and candles. I opened my mouth to blast her, then stopped. Her intentions were appalling and her remark about Simon had been utterly cruel, but she was harmless enough. I complained loudly about her, but the truth was I minded her rather less as the months went by. Besides, one look at the wardrobe I had selected for my "half mourning" would likely put her into her own early grave.

I dragged my attention back to the Ghoul, who had been chattering happily the whole time, poking through Edward's bits and probably marking out something she would ask for as a "memento." That was another of her favorite tricks. No matter how far removed she had been from the deceased, she always asked for some small token to remember them by, usually the most expensive bibelot or costliest jewel in the house. Few people had the courage or cruelty to resist her, with the result that she had amassed a collection of jewels and objets d'art to rival the queen's.

"And I told dear Hermia that I would be coming with you tonight."

I jerked to attention. "Tonight?"

"Yes, to Hermia's musical evening. Don't tell me you have forgotten," she said with a trill of laughter, sharp and brittle, nothing like Fleur's silver bells.

Of course I had forgotten. I had begged off of her oratory contest, pleading a headache, but Aunt Hermia was nothing if not persistent. She had sent me a note more than a week before regarding the musicale, a note I had thrust aside and promptly dismissed. Aunt Hermia's musical evenings were legendary within the family. Absences were rarely tolerated, and performances were strongly encouraged—or extorted if necessary. Occasionally other guests were invited, which made for hilarity and a boisterous evening. Other times it was just family, and those could be deadly. I wondered which this was to be and I was strongly inclined to send my regrets.

But I could not. I had missed the oratory contest and the last two musicales; a third and Aunt Hermia herself would come to Grey House to drag me out of it. Besides, I was not much enthused about spending another evening alone, reading and answering correspondence. For all their faults, my family were gregarious and animated, which I could not say for my books and letters. And as an added incentive, it was very possible that Val might be there. I longed to observe him without his being aware of it. He was so seldom at Grey House that Aunt Hermia's entertainment might be the only chance I would have to engage him.

And do what? I asked myself later as I pondered Morag's selections from my wardrobe. She had laid out a deep-necked, delicious violet velvet and a beautifully cut, tight crimson silk. I dithered between them, trying to imagine how I could possibly accuse my youngest brother of the attempted robbery of a new grave. Perhaps I could ask him to pass the gravy and make a dreadful pun…no, that would never do. I would simply have to go and keep my eyes sharp and my ears sharper. Perhaps I could delicately probe our family for their opinions on his sanity. It made me not a little nervous to think of sharing a house with a person capable of exhuming a young corpse simply to cut it open.

Shivering, I settled on the crimson and permitted Morag to dress me. I think we were both startled at the result. I had thought the violet revealed a bit of décolletage, but the crimson was nearly as flagrant. In fact, I felt it was a bit much for a family party, but as Morag reminded me, it was *only* a family party. Who else would be there to see and be shocked by the rather sumptuous display of bosom? I agreed with her, only because it was too late to change, and I made a note to myself never to wear the violet outside of my own home. What on earth had Monsieur Riche been thinking? Honestly.

I had just a few moments to spare and decided to spend them with Simon. The valet, Renard, was just collecting his dinner tray and he stepped aside at the doorway to let me pass.

"Good evening, my lady," he said, casting an approving glance at my bosom. I drew back, ensuring that even my skirts would not touch him.

"Renard," I said coolly. I could not help it. Every time I saw him, I thought of the odious drawings he had supplied to Henry and my skin crawled. He slipped past me, brushing as near as he dared, and I closed the door firmly behind him. I moved to Simon, my lips set in a deliberate smile.

"How are you this evening, dearest?"

His face brightened. "Julia! You are the very picture—turn around and let me see you properly."

I pirouetted obediently. He watched, nodding in appreciation.

"Lovely. I did tell you bright colours, didn't I?"

"You did," I said, dropping a kiss to his brow. "I feel rather unlike myself, though. I've never worn anything quite so…"

He smiled, reaching for my hand. "You have never looked lovelier. Where are you bound?"

"March House."

"Ah! One of Lady Hermia's musicales, am I right?"

"You are. Shall I plump your pillows for you?"

"Please do. I should far rather have you do it than Renard." He leaned forward and I busied myself fluffing the feathers. "I remember those evenings," he said, his voice tinged ever so slightly with nostalgia. "Edward played the most awful piano, but your singing was quite—"

"Vile," I put in helpfully. He gave me a reproachful little look.

"I was going to say original, but all right. You are frightfully tone-deaf, my darling."

"I know. Pity that I love to sing, isn't it? But you must have paid better attention than Edward to your piano master. Your melodies were always so lovely."

He gazed down at his hands, swollen a little about the knuckles. "I doubt I could play now. Doubt I even remember a note of anything," he said ruefully. "Funny how we spend our entire adolescence learning skills that are supposed to serve us in society, then spend our entire adulthood forgetting them."

"Not all of them. The last time we danced, you still remembered how to do that quite well."

"Well, dancing is different. I always enjoyed that. Music and gaiety and breathless promises to meet in darkened gardens—so much intrigue." He raised a brow meaningfully.

I settled him back against his pillows. "Ass," I said affectionately. "When did you ever make assignations in the garden?"

He waved an airy hand. "Loads of times. I cannot tell you how many lovely memories I have of fumbling with buttons under the cover of leafy darkness...." His voice trailed off and his eyes were dreamy.

I slapped lightly at his hand. "You are a beast, Simon Grey."

"Yes, but a discreet one. You never knew I was off misbehaving, did you? Did you never once see me slip back into a ballroom, cravat askew, face dewy and flushed with rapture?"

"No, thank God. What of the poor creatures you were deflowering? Were they ever discovered?"

"No, not one, mercifully. But as I say, I was discreet. Edward used to get up to the same, did he never tell you?"

There was a flash of excitement in his eyes, an avidity that comes with truly succulent gossip.

"No!" I leaned forward, heedless of my neckline. "Do tell."

He smiled and wagged his finger. "I shall not. Some secrets should be kept. But the stories I could tell…"

I wrinkled my nose at him. "Very well. Keep your secrets. I don't care a bit." I kissed him again and bade him good-night.

"Good night, Julia. You really do look quite delicious." I blew him a kiss and slipped out, thinking about Edward as a youth, cavorting in the garden with some innocent maid, and wondering why he had never asked me to step outside with him.

Probably because he knew from the first he wanted to marry me, I thought reasonably. Gentlemen do not propose to girls who lift their skirts, Aunt Hermia had warned me, and in this case, she appeared to be correct. Edward had had trysts before me, but had not touched me until our wedding night. Although, if he had ever seen me in this scarlet, he might not have kept his hands so politely to himself, I thought wickedly, with one final glance at the glass.

Wrapping my black cloak tightly around me, I collected the Ghoul and we set off, arriving at March House punctually— no one ever had the courage to do otherwise. Aunt Hermia was legendary for her insistence upon promptness. Most people thought she was a stickler for manners, but the truth was, she had a horror of leathery meat. Rather than hold the meal to accommodate tardy guests, she simply struck the unpunctual from her guest list and harangued the rest of us into promptness. We were greeted at the door by Hoots, Father's butler. There was no sign of Aunt Hermia.

Hoots reached to help me off with my cloak and I asked after her.

"She is attending to Cook, my lady. Some accident concerning a knife and a sprout."

His eyes fell to my exposed bosom and he averted them quickly.

"It is very good to see you out and about again, my lady," he said without a trace of irony. I looked at him suspiciously, but his face was perfectly correct.

"Hmm. Yes, thank you, Hoots."

I turned and Aunt Ursula got her first unimpeded view of my gown. She blanched and reached for her salts, but said nothing. There was a commotion behind me as Portia and her companion, Jane, appeared from the drawing room.

"Portia, Jane, good evening," I greeted, going to kiss them.

"Julia, dearest, I am so glad you are here!" Portia exclaimed, returning my kiss with enthusiasm. "All of you," she murmured with a lift of the brow toward my gown. She was dressed in blue, a delicious cerulean shade that flattered her wide eyes. "Father is just now gone to change and Aunt Hermia is bandaging up Cook in the stillroom. Jane and I were simply aching for conversation. Oh, good evening, Aunt Ursula." Portia went to make polite noises at the Ghoul and I turned to Jane.

As usual, she looked as though she had been dragged through a bush backward. She was wearing one of her favorite shapeless dresses. Usually they were made up in heavy cottons, but she had a few in thick, unattractive fabrics for evening. She wore them with heavy ropes of dull, lumpy beads that could not hope to match the sparkle of her fine eyes or the exquisite colour of her complexion. She put a hand to her untidy red hair. "I know," she said mournfully. "I look a fright. I had put my hair up, I promise. But I seem to have lost the pins."

I smiled at her. "Nonsense. I was just thinking that you look like Daphne, the moment she metamorphosed into a laurel bush."

She looked very happy at the allusion, and I tucked my arm through hers. "Now, what shall you play for us tonight? I am quite out of practice, so I shall not perform, but I always look forward to hearing you."

This was entirely true. Jane was a gifted musician with a remarkably sweet, clear singing voice and a talent with three different instruments. This was perhaps the most significant reason behind why we loved Jane so. The family, and occasionally, friends, were pressed into performing at Aunt Hermia's evenings, usually something we had all heard a hundred times before, and usually done quite badly. We had our gifts, we Marches, but I do not think we numbered music among them. Having Jane with us was rather like having Sarah Siddons stride into the midst of an amateur theatrical.

"The harp," Jane said promptly. "I have a new Irish air I have been practicing. It is very melancholy, very atmospheric. You will smell the peat fires and damp wool, I promise."

Her eyes were bright with enthusiasm, and I shivered playfully. "Sounds quite intriguing. What of you, Portia?" I called over my shoulder. "Will you play, or is simply giving us all something beautiful to look at contribution enough?"

She raised a brow at me. "Good Lord, Julia, what has come over you? You are positively giddy. Well, I am glad you are in high spirits, because if I am not mistaken, that is a footstep upon the walk."

A moment later Hoots opened the door. The thing I remember most clearly from that moment are Portia's eyes, dancing with amusement, and Father appearing just at that second, still straightening his necktie. He, too, was looking highly amused, and I wondered if that is how the gods of Olympus looked when they were meddling with people's lives, for they were certainly meddling with mine.

There upon the doorstep stood Brisbane, beautifully dressed in evening clothes, and with him was an elderly gentleman I had never seen before. They were returning Hoots' very civil greeting, and I took the opportunity to hiss at Portia. "What do you think you are doing?"

She smiled back, dazzlingly. "Stirring the pot, darling. But it isn't my hand on the spoon. Father invited them. Mind you speak up, the Duke of Aberdour is rather deaf."

Father had moved forward and was welcoming the pair of them. According to precedence, he presented us to the duke.

"You remember my daughter, Lady Bettiscombe, your Grace." He motioned to Portia.

The duke murmured something, but his old eyes were sharp, noting Portia's beauty, I had little doubt.

"Your Grace," she said loudly, dropping an elegant curtsey as she dimpled up at him. "I am so pleased you could come."

The duke patted her hand and seemed reluctant to let it go.

Portia stepped back and Father waved at me. "I don't believe you know my youngest daughter, Lady Julia Grey."

I made a proper curtsey, and his Grace reached for my hand, taking in an eyeful of my displayed bosom.

"Enchanting. Why have I never met you before?" he asked in an accent slightly blurred with Scottish vowels. He was as perfectly turned out as Brisbane, but with much better jewels. I nearly goggled at the size of the ruby in his cravat.

"I have been in mourning this past year for my husband, your Grace," I said. He was still holding my hand, his eyes wandering over my décolletage in an openly appraising manner. I should have been insulted by such treatment from anyone else, but from him it was merely amusing.

"You have my condolences, my dear, but your husband is more deserving of them. I cannot imagine what a loss he suffered at leaving you behind."

I smiled in spite of myself. "You are too kind, your Grace."

"Not at all. I simply like good-looking women." He tucked my hand through his arm. "You will help me in to greet my hostess, won't you? I do not need the help, but I will pretend to in order to keep you close to me." He finished this with an exaggerated leer and I laughed. Father and Brisbane had greeted each other quietly as Hoots closed the door, and now they stood, watching my exchange with the duke.

"I would be honoured to escort you, your Grace, but I must warn you, your reputation precedes you. I shall be on my guard with you."

He cackled and motioned toward Brisbane. "She is clever as well. I like this one. Say hello, boy. I believe you know the lady."

Brisbane smiled thinly and did his duty. I would have thought it impossible for anyone to speak to him in such a fashion and emerge unscathed, but the duke apparently had the gift of charm. It was clear that Portia thought him adorable.

The duke turned back to me. "I do like you. I might make you an offer of marriage before the evening is over. What do you think of that? Would you like to be a duchess? I'm very rich, you know."

"I do know it. But I am entirely unworthy to be your wife, I assure you, your Grace. Perhaps, if it is not too presumptuous of me, we could just be very good friends."

"How good?" he asked, edging his elbow into my ribs.

"Not quite that good," I replied, patting his arm. He roared with laughter and allowed me to introduce him to Aunt Ursula and Jane. He greeted them in a perfunctory fashion, dismissing one of them as plain and the other as older than Moses, no doubt. He clung to my arm and I led him into the drawing room, where Aunt Hermia had just arrived, breathless and patting her hair. I flashed Father a smile to let him know he was forgiven. He might have broadsided me by inviting Brisbane without my knowledge, but he had ensured my good will with his Grace. It was not every day that I received a proposal of marriage from a duke, even if he was more than eighty years old.

For her part, Aunt Hermia was delighted with her unexpected guests.

"Your Grace! How lovely that you could join us this evening," she said. "It is only a family party, though, and I am certain you will be quite bored with our feeble entertainments."

"Not at all, dear lady," he said, bowing over her hand. "The reputation of the beauteous March women is as widespread as it is accurate. I shall simply admire the view. I believe you have met Nicholas?"

Brisbane stepped forward. "Lady Hermia. How good of you to include me."

Aunt Hermia's face was pink with pleasure. "Ah, we owe you much, Mr. Brisbane." She turned to the duke. "My niece Julia's husband passed away last year under most unfortunate circumstances. Mr. Brisbane was very helpful during that trying time. I am so pleased to see you under more pleasant circumstances, Mr. Brisbane, but I must insist on a forfeit for your supper," she added waggishly.

"Oh, God," I said, sotto voce, to Portia.

"A forfeit?" Brisbane smiled down at her. "I cannot think that I possess anything that would be worthy of your ladyship."

"Heavens!" Portia whispered back. "Did he learn that from the darling old duke?"

"They must be relations," Jane put in. "Charm like that runs in the blood."

"Our evening is a musical one," Aunt Hermia was explaining. "We each of us contribute something to the entertainment of the group. Do you play? Or sing, perhaps?"

The duke snorted, lifting his bushy white brows. Clearly he intended something by the gesture, but the moment was smoothed over by Aunt Ursula's petulant inquiry about dinner. Aunt Hermia bustled forward, suddenly realizing that there were far too many ladies for the men to escort.

"Never mind!" cackled the duke, taking Aunt Hermia firmly by the arm. "We'll be here until Michaelmas if you insist on precedence. Let the young people sort themselves out."

To her credit, Aunt Hermia obeyed, leading the way to the dining room and leaving the rest of us to follow behind in a haphazard fashion. Blessedly, Aunt Hermia favored a round table and precedence there was not an issue. True, the round table created a bit more confusion, but it ensured general discussion, rather than lots of indistinct murmuring. It usually made for more spirited and interesting conversation and this night was no exception. In spite of the duke's presence, Father and Aunt Hermia engaged in a heated debate about the use of Biblical images in Shakespeare's sonnets. It ended with Aunt Hermia throwing walnuts at Father and the duke offering her marriage instead, claiming that spirit was as important a requirement in a wife as beauty.

"That's what I keep telling the boy here," he said, jerking a thumb at Brisbane. "He's got no interest in marrying, he tells me, because he cannot find a woman who interests him for more than a fortnight. He's got a twisty mind, that one, and he wants a woman that's got the same."

Brisbane sipped thoughtfully at his wine. "All women have twisty minds, sir, or so you told me."

Aberdour laughed his dry, creaky laugh. "That I did, boy, that I did. This one gets it from his grandmother," he said, pointing a knobbly old finger. "She was just the same, always turning a word back on you, bending an argument to suit her end. She was a wily bitch. I was glad to see the last of her."

Jane gasped, which did not surprise me. I have often found that the most outspoken liberals are secretly the most conservative in small matters. For all her open thinking, Jane was deeply shocked at the duke's plain speaking. Father simply went on cracking nuts, Brisbane kept deliberately at his wine, and Aunt Hermia looked up curiously.

"His grandmother? Is there a family connection, your Grace?"

"My sister," he said, his lips thin. "She ran off with a footman when she was fifteen. She died in childbed eight months later. We had the raising of her son, and did a dog's job of it. He no sooner grew up than he—"

Brisbane coughed sharply and some understanding passed between them, for the duke simply muttered, "Then he bred this one and died on us." I fancied that was not how he intended to finish that sentence, but it must have appeased Brisbane. He had tensed at the mention of his father, but now he uncoiled slightly.

Aunt Hermia cocked her head. Anyone who did not know her might mistake the shine in her eyes for sympathy, but I saw it for what it was—rampant curiosity.

"That accounts for the different surname," she said, "but I do not remember hearing of your father, Mr. Brisbane. Surely he is not in Debrett's." This was simply a conversational gambit. The Shakespearean society's quarterly journal was the only publication she perused for names. In itself, her line of inquiry was only mildly intrusive. But I had felt Brisbane tense again next to me, and I knew he did not like it.

I rose, dropping my napkin. "I think the champagne would

best be served in the music room—after the entertainments. Forgive me, Auntie. I am simply too eager to hear Jane's harp."

I smiled innocently to the table at large as I collected my napkin.

As I had expected, Aunt Hermia pricked up like a pointer. "Jane! Have you a new piece? Splendid! Nothing I love quite so well as a moody Irish harp. To the music room!"

Aunt Hermia never permitted cigars and port on her musical evenings on the grounds that they thickened the voice. There was a general flutter of movement as people rose, gathering wraps and stretching discreetly. Father whistled for the mastiff, Crab, who had been lying quietly under the table, snuffling for crumbs during dinner. Amid the chaos, Brisbane leaned near.

"It seems I shall be obliged to sing for my supper," he murmured, his lips disconcertingly close to my ear. "What would you like to hear?"

"Bach," I said without hesitation. I had the irrational notion that he was thanking me somehow for deflecting Aunt Hermia's impertinent questions.

"A little old-fashioned, don't you think?"

I shrugged. "I don't care. I have loved Bach since childhood." I did not tell him my first clear memory of Bach was from my mother's funeral. I was six years old, too young for the church, Father had said. I had been left in the nursery with Nanny and Val, that awful, screaming baby who came when Mother died. It had been quite an easy thing to slip out when Nanny's back was turned. She had left me to go and quiet the baby, something she was doing far too much of, I thought. I followed the mourners, hiding outside in the churchyard, listening to the music that flowed out of the open windows. It was a warm day, with late roses giving off a thick perfume and bees buzzing drowsily near my face as I listened to the choirboys singing "When Thou Art Near." It seemed as if angels were singing her to sleep, I thought sleepily, and I promptly curled up behind a gravestone and took a nap. Father found me there some time after Mother's burial. I woke when he pulled me onto his lap and we sat together for a very long time. He stroked my hair and rocked me and I listened to the ticking of his watch through the wool of his coat. Or perhaps it was his heartbeat—I never knew. I only knew that this was a very special moment, and that Mother had left me, but Father was still there and that although Nanny and everyone else seemed to like that awful, screaming baby, Father still loved me, probably much more. The choirboys sang again, practicing for evensong, and Father began to talk to me, about Mother and about music, and all manner of things that I did not pay attention to. But I remembered the feeling, and from that day I always associated Bach with consolation and comfort.

Brisbane had not answered. I lifted my chin a little and arched a brow for effect.

"Bach it shall be," he promised.

I was pleased, but a little surprised. "Can you sing?"

He smiled, that tricky smile he had that touched his lips, but not his eyes.

"I can, but never in public. I mean to play for you. I assume there's a violin?"

"A rather good one. Made in Cremona."

"Excellent," he said, turning his attention suddenly to Jane. For no good reason I felt cast aside, and in favor of a woman who wore doughy beads and curtain fabrics, I thought irritably. I turned and left them, trailing into the music room on my own, a little dispirited. What difference did it make to me if Brisbane found Jane interesting? She was a delightful person, and an amusing conversationalist. At least, that is what I told myself, but I still felt nettled by the notion of Brisbane chatting with Jane, and that little annoyance disturbed me greatly.

And worse, Val had not deigned to make an appearance.

"Oh, no, dearest, he had a previous engagement," Aunt Hermia answered in reply to my question. "The opera, I believe. With that Phillips boy. The one who always looks as though he's picked one's pocket."

A succinct and perfect description of Reddy, I thought as I took my seat. I would have to wait up for Val, no matter how late, and collar him with what I had found in the laundry—and with his choice of companions. Reddy Phillips was quite enough of a nuisance without encouragement. I had not told Val that Reddy had accosted me in the street demanding the return of his raven, but I hoped fervently that they would settle the matter between them. The wretched bird was beginning to take a toll on my nerves.

"Well, if Val is not coming, what about Bellmont?"

"Downing Street. He is dining with the prime minister. By the way, dearest, I see you have given up mourning, and with quite a spark," she finished, eyeing my crimson with a smile.

"Believe me, Auntie, I wouldn't have worn it if I had known this wasn't a family party."

Aunt Hermia gave me an affectionate pat. "Don't be feeble, Julia. How do you expect to attract another buyer if you don't display the wares?" She moved off, leaving me to follow speechless in her wake. I took my seat, marveling that so vulgar an analogy could come from such a harmless-looking old lady. Portia nudged me.

"What did Aunt Hermia say? You look bilious."

I shook my head, mindful of Brisbane, settling himself into the seat on my other side. "Nothing of importance. Tell me, why is it that old people are allowed to be so ghastly and say all sorts of things that we would never get away with?"

"Privilege of age," Portia returned, raising her eyebrows in the direction of the duke. He was creaking himself down into a chair next to Father, bending and folding his frail little body until he was at last seated.

The musical evening began, as they always did, with Father reciting a soliloquy. He always played them well—his resonant voice and firm delivery would have served him well on the stage. He loved amateur theatricals and gloried in the applause. He did Lear that evening, or perhaps not, I confess I did not pay him much attention. I was too busy wrestling with my own thoughts, not the least of which was the guilty realization that I had sent Magda away without telling Brisbane. Sooner or later I should have to confess my guilt, and I was not anticipating the event with any good feeling. Brisbane was technically employed by me in this investigation, but I had a strong suspicion that he would be quite severe with me when he discovered what I had done.

Thank the heavens for Jane. Her sad Irish air was as soothing as a lullaby and twice as sweet. I felt comforted when she had finished, though I saw Aunt Hermia dash away a tear.

"That was utterly moving, Jane, dear. Thank you," she said, turning to face us as we sat, arrayed in our little gilt chairs.

"Your Grace, would you care to favor us?" she asked. There was a gentle snore from the duke's chair. "Ah, perhaps not just now. Portia?"

Portia rose and went to the piano where Hoots was waiting quietly to accompany her. It was perhaps unusual to allow one's butler to join in the family entertainments, but Hoots was a rather fine accompanist. He gave a little trill of introduction and Portia began, singing in her adequate soprano. Something Italian. I did not listen much to her, either. Of course, Portia's talent did not lie in her singing. It must have been some aria to do with lost love or a broken foot or some other tragedy, because there was a great deal of posturing and dabbing at her eyes with her shawl. I think it must have ended with a suicide because she suddenly clasped her fisted hands to her bosom and drooped onto the piano. Crab let out a pitiful sound and crept as far as she could under Father's chair. Hoots pounded out a few more mournful notes and Portia rose, triumphantly taking a bow.

She took her seat next to me, fanning her reddened cheeks.

"You are far too fat to play a consumptive," I whispered through a smile.

She smiled back. "Yes, but I am going to marry a duke, so I do not care what you have to say. When I am very rich, I shall hire you for my maid."

I put out my tongue at her only to find Brisbane watching me coolly. I blushed and looked away, Portia snickering in my ear. Aunt Hermia rose again. "Mr. Brisbane?"

Brisbane rose and went to the centre of the room. There was an array of instruments for performers to choose from. An old harpsichord, a rather unhygienic-looking flute, and an oboe that no one remembered bringing into the house. Among this motley group was the violin—the one true and pure thing in the room. Brisbane looked at it a long moment before picking it up. He ran his hands over it, slowly, reverently. And then he held it to his nose, briefly, as if using its scent to gauge its wanderings. He stroked the inlay of the wood and handled the bow, trying out a few strings. He frowned, plucking at the strings and adjusting them slightly. I heard no difference, but he must have, for his frown eased and he positioned the violin under his chin.

He played softly at first, then with growing vigor. I recognized it at once. I had asked him to play Bach, rather as a joke. The greatest Bach devotees were usually keyboard aficionados and singers. I myself preferred him simply because unlike other composers he actually wrote interesting music for alto sopranos to sing. I had not expected Brisbane to rise to the challenge. And once again I had underestimated him.

He played a unique version of "Sleepers Awake," a bold choice for a solo violin. It was a credit to his proficiency that I never missed the violas, basses or horns. I sat, amazed. He must have played it before, that much was certain, and yet I had not seen a violin in his rooms.

The piece rose and fell in arching phrases, by turns sweet and soaring. I heard Jane's breath catch and I glanced at Portia, unblinking beside me. The duke was still snoring gently, but it did not matter. The music was enchanting. It felt true and pure and I gaped at Brisbane. He was a genius. Why had I not realized it before? Surely talent like that must leave its mark on the face? In the eyes?

I was still gaping when he brought the piece to its high, triumphant close. I moved to clap, but before I could bring my hands together, Brisbane—whose attention had been fixed upon his instrument—threw a look at his uncle. The old gentleman, intent upon his snores, missed it entirely, but it made my blood run cold. There was a chill in that look, a malevolence that I would never have credited had I not seen it. It vanished quickly, replaced by his usual cool mask, but I wondered at the antipathy between them—at least, I wondered until Brisbane began to play.

From the first note I knew it was different from anything I had ever heard before. This was no church piece. It began simply, but with an arresting phrase, so simple, but eloquent as a human voice. It spoke, beckoning gently as it unwound, rising and tensing. It spiraled upward, the tension growing with each repeat of the phrasing, and yet somehow it grew more abandoned, wilder with each note. His eyes remained closed as his fingers flew over the strings, spilling forth surely more notes than were possible from a single violin. For one mad moment I actually thought there were more of them, an entire orchestra of violins spilling out of this one instrument. I had never heard anything like it—it was poetry and seduction and light and shadow and every other contradiction I could think of. It seemed impossible to breathe while listening to that music, and yet all I was doing was breathing, quite heavily. The music itself had become as palpable a presence in that room as another person would have been—and its presence was something out of myth. It was apart from Brisbane, this melody he created, spun from dreams and darkness.

I dragged my eyes from him and realized that I was not the only one so affected. Jane was sitting with her mouth agape, her handkerchief in shreds under her nails. Portia was squirming in her chair, and both of them were blushing and moist as June roses. I did not dare look at Aunt Hermia.

I told myself I was disgusted by them. A fine pair of Sapphic lovers they were, getting themselves pink and panting over a man and his violin. But in truth, I was the worst. My palms were damp, my face hotly red, and I found myself staring at those long, nimble fingers, thinking very unsuitable things. I told myself it was natural. I had been a widow for a year, had not known the affectionate touch of a man for much longer. It was expected that I would find an attraction to a handsome gentleman of my acquaintance.

But I was not interested in pragmatism. I was too busily engaged with fragrant fantasies stretched out on red velvet. I dug my nails into my palms, but my gloves prevented any real pain. Instead I bit the inside of my cheek until I tasted the metallic salty redness of my own blood.

If Brisbane sensed anything of his audience's reaction, he did not betray it. He played on, or perhaps the music played him, for he performed as one possessed. The music arced and twisted, tightening and coiling upon itself, rising faster and faster, almost shrieking with pitched emotion, until—at the very height of its ecstasy—a string snapped with a mandrake scream. The violin itself seemed to sob at the echo of the sound, which had the report of a gunshot. Brisbane remained perfectly still, his bow poised until the echo died away. Then he turned coolly and laid the injured instrument down upon the piano.

"My apologies, my lady," he murmured to Aunt Hermia. "I shall of course make arrangements for the repair."

She replied, something suitable I am sure, as she patted herself discreetly with her handkerchief. Conversation was roused and people began to stir. I heard my father complimenting the performance, and Brisbane's quiet reply. Father must have been sincere, for he introduced Brisbane to Crab, a singular honour. Portia shot me a speaking look, and Jane was moving toward Brisbane to add her accolades. I acknowledged none of it, taking a moment instead to regain my composure and waiting for my knees to stop trembling.

I rose after a moment and decided to fetch myself a glass of champagne. Brisbane waylaid me.

"Ah, Mr. Brisbane. You are a virtuoso. You should have warned me. You must think us frightfully unsophisticated in our little family entertainments."

His look was impenetrable. I could not tell if he were pleased or embarrassed or merely bored. "Not at all. I play only rarely these days, and never for so appreciative an audience."

He leaned near, ostensibly to reach past me to pick up a glass of champagne. But as his sleeve brushed my arm, he said softly, "I must see you tomorrow. Mordecai has news."

My eyes flared with interest, then dropped demurely. "When?"

"Five o'clock. My rooms."

He pressed the glass into my hands and I smiled my acceptance, giving him a single short nod. He moved away then, approaching Aunt Hermia. I watched him for a moment, thinking that this was a man whose depths I would never begin to plumb.

And for some reason, my gaze fell, quite by accident upon the duke. He, too, was watching Brisbane, but his expression was not one of admiration. He had awakened during his great-nephew's performance, his features twisted with irritation at having his nap disturbed. But now they betrayed more than mere annoyance. There was frustration there, and something worse—something that looked frighteningly like hatred. I would not forget that look for a very long time.

Much later, as I lay awake, late into the night, I heard the faint scrape of footsteps on the stair. There was a long pause and then the unmistakable slither of stocking feet on a polished floor. Valerius had stopped to remove his shoes before moving past my door to his room. I put my hand to my dressing gown. I meant to rise, to go to him and demand an explanation for bloodied shirts and despoiled graves.

But I thought again of what Magda had told me and what I had deduced for myself, and I lay back down, too cowardly to do what must be done. Soon, I promised myself. Soon I would go to him and lay out what I knew, and tell him what must be done. But not just yet. It would mean disgrace for Val and banishment from the family. And in spite of our troubles, I could not bear to lose him yet. He was still my youngest brother, still the tiny, squalling infant who had been left motherless so many years ago, in need of his family's protection. So I would protect him, I decided, staring sightlessly into the dark. I would say nothing, and I would keep him as long as I could.

THE TWENTY-SEVENTH CHAPTER

Our fears do make us traitors.
—William Shakespeare
Macbeth

I did not sleep well that night. I remembered the hateful look that Brisbane had cast his great-uncle, and the vicious one he had received in turn later. I wondered, late into the darkness, why malevolence in the elderly should be so much more frightening than in the young. Is it because they were supposed to be wiser? Nobler? Or simply because we liked to believe they were past such passions? It was comforting to think that the sharper emotions could simply dull with time, taking the worst of our suffering with them.

But the duke did not seem dulled, I thought with a shiver. Between his salaciousness and his inexplicable malice toward Brisbane, he seemed as ripe as a youth of eighteen. Even if he did resemble the desiccated husk of an old fruit, I thought with a snicker. I had heard once that age stamps character on the face, that one's passions were slowly etched over time, limning both experience and desire upon the features. If this were true, the duke's face told a rather alarming tale, especially when compared to Father's. Where the duke's visage was a memoir of thwarted passion, Father's was a love letter, creased and soft with much appreciation. There was good humour in Father's eyes, while the duke's bore the slightest sinister cast.

In spite of this, or perhaps because of it, I hoped to see more of the old gentleman—and not the least because he was Brisbane's kinsman. If the affection between them was interesting, the antipathy was much more so.

Yet even the puzzling old Duke of Aberdour could not dampen my spirits the next morning. I rose as soon as Morag appeared with my tea tray, surprising her as well as myself. I hummed a little as she drew my bath and instructed her to lay out one of my new costumes—a striking striped ensemble of black-and-white silk, fixed with discreet, ruby-set buttons. There was a new hat as well, all black ribbon and red taffeta roses, with pure white ostrich plumes waving above. I was more than a little in love with that hat. But it was the new scarlet stockings that drove Morag to question me, her long rabbity nose quivering with curiosity.

"Are you feeling quite well, my lady?"

I smiled broadly at her. "Quite. Put out Madame de Belle-fleur's rose salve, will you? I shall dress after luncheon. I am going out this afternoon."

She did so, eyeing me the way a nervous rider will a skittish horse. She was waiting for me to bite or bolt. I continued to smile at her as she brushed my hair. She stripped out the fallen hair from the brush and shoved it into the hair receiver.

"Not hardly worth bothering about with that crop of yours," she muttered.

I ignored her and picked up a nail buffer. It was silver, one of a set. I inspected my nails, pink and healthy compared to Morag's ridged grey ones. Without a thought, I handed her the second buffer.

"What is this?" she asked with a fair dollop of suspicion.

"A nail buffer. You haven't one of your own, have you? I thought you might like it."

I rose and went off to put on my loose morning gown. I

knew Morag was desperate to question me, but she was careful to slip the buffer into her pocket first.

"There are colds going round," she said with a doubtful look at me. "Are you feverish?"

I sighed as I wrapped the sash into a loose bow. "No, I am happy, that is all."

And the surprising thing was, I was speaking the truth. I could not imagine why it should be so—I was mired in an investigation that I did not particularly want to continue. I had a partner I did not fully trust. And it could well be that the appointment I was to keep that afternoon would bring everything crashing down on my head.

But at least my head would be prettily hatted, I thought that afternoon as I tipped the rose-strewn chapeau at a rakish angle. I put my hand out for my plain black silk parasol and twirled it. I felt confident that whatever the news Doctor Bent would bring, whatever the answers Brisbane and I unearthed, all would be well.

If I have not said so before, let me say now—I was sometimes very stupid. My exhilaration that afternoon only proves it. Why did I have no inkling of the danger? I had seen all the signs—I could have put the thing together even then had I known how to read them. But how does one learn to read shadows? I think of that morning as the last truly innocent time of my life. I wonder sometimes if I would have trod another path had I known what lay in wait down the one I had chosen. It is painful to lose one's illusions. I like to think I would have chosen to learn, even through extreme danger and despair, whatever lessons life has to teach. But every now and then, I wonder what my life would have been had I broken that appointment with Brisbane, had I never gone back to Chapel Street, had I never learned the truth about Edward's death. It would have been quieter and simpler and more peaceful, I know that much. And I like to believe I would have scorned these placid virtues in favor of adventure, in favor of life itself. But even still, every now and then, I wonder...

I arrived on Brisbane's doorstep at the same moment as Doctor Bent. He lifted his battered hat, smiling his charming, puppy-dog smile.

"Lady Julia. I hope you are well."

"Very much so, Doctor. And you?"

He grimaced. "I am behindhand as usual. I sometimes despair of ever catching up with my work."

I took him in from his unpolished shoes to the bit of jam that had dribbled down his shirtfront. Doubtless he had eaten on the fly and his clothes bore the unmistakable rumpled air of being slept in. He made an interesting contrast to Brisbane, I thought as the latter admitted us to his rooms.

There was no sign of Monk, for which I was mildly grateful. I had seen him just once since that unimaginable scene in Brisbane's bedchamber, and the feeling between us had been strained. People often regret confidences given in a time of trouble, and I suspected that Monk might well resent me for receiving his.

Brisbane bade us be seated, offered us refreshment, and seemed pleased when it was rejected. I understood his satisfaction at this. He had on his bloodhound look and he was ready for the trail. Doctor Bent seemed aware of it, too, for he began without preamble.

"The powder was arsenic."

I felt myself deflate, like a child's pricked balloon. I had known it, of course. Magda had confirmed it herself. But I suppose somehow I had held out hope that Doctor Bent would find otherwise. Impossible, I knew, but still I had hoped.

Brisbane gave a little animal sound of satisfaction, something like a grunt. But Doctor Bent held up his hand.

"But it does not matter in any case. Sir Edward was not poisoned with arsenic."

I could not speak. I felt a ferocious surge of joy. Magda had told the truth. She had not murdered Edward.

Brisbane had opened his mouth to remonstrate, but Doctor Bent was handily holding his own. "I am sorry, Nicholas, but it is a matter of scientific fact. I have compared your account of Sir Edward's symptoms with her ladyship's. They tally perfectly, yet they do not match any recorded case of arsenical poisoning that I can find. Sir Edward experienced symptoms that are inconsistent with arsenical poisoning, while the symptoms that are most indicative of arsenic were simply not present."

Brisbane said nothing, but sat looking mightily displeased, the muscles of his jaw working furiously. Doctor Bent turned to me to explain.

"My lady, you described convulsions, vomiting. You say he had pains in his chest and that he was sweating freely."

"So he was," I agreed.

Doctor Bent plunged on. "You also told me that he complained of feeling cold, a sensation of iced water flowing in his veins, although the evening was warm."

I nodded, confirming this as well.

"And you say he had difficulty in speaking, although he remained conscious."

"As far as I know," I reminded him. "My father sent me from the room shortly after Edward's collapse."

Brisbane stirred slightly. "He was conscious, giddy even. What does that signify?"

"It signifies that it was not arsenic," Doctor Bent said, with only the faintest air of triumph. "Did he pass blood?"

Brisbane frowned. "Mordecai, I hardly think that Her Ladyship wishes to know—"

"But I must!" Doctor Bent countered fiercely. He tugged at his hair, leaving it standing electrically on end. Brisbane sighed.

"No."

"And was there an odour of garlic?" the doctor demanded.

"No."

"There would not have been," I put in suddenly. "Edward could not abide garlic. He would never have eaten it."

Doctor Bent's face was shining evangelically. "The odour of garlic is not from the plant itself," he explained. "It is from the arsenic. Do you not see, Nicholas? Victims of arsenical poisoning almost always sink into a coma before dying. There is—" he paused with an apologetic glance in my direction "—usually considerable bloody offal, smelling heavily of garlic."

Brisbane fetched out one of his slender brown cigars and lit it, smoking energetically. "That is acute arsenical poisoning—a massive dose, administered all at once. What if he were poisoned slowly, over some months?"

"You are determined to see Magda hang," I burst out.

"I am determined to find the truth," Brisbane returned coldly. He fixed his attention on the doctor, who was looking uncomfortably from one of us to the other.

"When arsenic is administered in small doses, over a long period of time, it produces jaundice and episodes of gastric distress. From those symptoms one might make an assumption of gradual arsenical poisoning, although I must warn you, those findings are my own. I hope to publish them one day, but they are not universally accepted in the medical community."

"It does not matter," I said, jubilant. "Edward did not suffer from gastric distress, and he certainly was not jaundiced. Magda is acquitted," I finished with a jerk of my chin at Brisbane.

He ignored me, which was probably for the best. "What could it be, then?"

Doctor Bent shrugged. "Without a proper postmortem, I can only offer the broadest suggestions. Perhaps some sort of plant poison. But I cannot tell you how it was administered. If I had seen the contents of his stomach, or the pallor of his skin…" He threw up his hands helplessly.

"What about Doctor Griggs?" I put in. "Surely he would know those things. I mean, not the stomach, of course—" I felt slightly queasy discussing this, but I pressed on "—as there was no postmortem. But he might have noticed something during the examination that would shed some light on matters."

Doctor Bent and Brisbane shared a look.

"What is it?" I demanded.

"Mordecai wrote to Doctor Griggs regarding another patient. I had him test the waters a bit to see if perhaps he could form some sort of professional relationship. A means to eventually questioning him informally about Sir Edward."

"And?"

I looked from one to the other. Doctor Bent did not meet my eyes. Brisbane's handsome mouth had curled into a sneer.

"Doctor Griggs does not associate with Semites, professionally or otherwise," he said flatly.

I swore softly and Doctor Bent's head came up. He smiled.

"Thank you for that," he murmured. "But really, it is nothing new to me. Besides, there are many others who do not share his views. The real difficulty is that it means we are at a loss. We have no way to proceed without some detailed knowledge of the state of Sir Edward's body."

I looked again from one to the other.

"Why not ask Mrs. Birch?"

Brisbane pulled lazily at his cigar. "Who is Mrs. Birch?"

"The parish worker who washed his body, of course," I said impatiently. "Really, you didn't think I did it, did you?"

Slowly, dazzlingly, a smile—a real, bone-deep expression of violent joy spread across Brisbane's face. It was perhaps the first time I had seen him really smile. I had been so accustomed to his scowls and frowns that the effect was rather unsettling.

"And you know how to find this Mrs. Birch?"

"I should think so. She is on the charity list for Grey House."

"The charity list?"

I waved a hand. "Yes, of course. There are a number of people within the parish who are what the vicar calls the 'deserving poor,' you know, people who work, but who still half starve. Those of us who have the means send along blankets, meat, soup, clothes for the children, that sort of thing. Mrs. Birch has been receiving baskets from Grey House for years."

Brisbane stubbed his cigar out slowly. "Then we shall call upon her at once. Well done, madam."

I preened a little. Doctor Bent rose, a trifle uncertainly. "I suppose I had better be off, then. I've left a clinic full of patients. They'll not thank me if I stay away longer."

I rose and extended my hand. "Doctor Bent, I know you are quite busy, but I wonder if you could perhaps see your way to taking on another patient? I am in need of a doctor, my own has proven unsatisfactory."

He patted his coat, finally extracting a creased, grimy card. "There is the address of my rooms," he said, flushing a deep, becoming red. "I know you will not wish to go there, but if you will send for me, I will come."

I smiled. "You are very kind."

The blush deepened and he stammered a little as he let himself out. Brisbane sat, regarding me thoughtfully.

"I rather think you've made a conquest of poor old Mordecai," he said finally. "Pity you are not a daughter of Leah. You might have made him a rather fine wife."

"Do not be nasty, Brisbane," I returned, refusing to rise to the bait. "It does not suit you." I rummaged in my reticule. "Here is the completed inventory of Grey House. It is the only copy."

He took it from me and scanned it quickly, thumbing through the pages. "Good. Not that I think it will lead us to anything, but one never knows."

I felt a rush of irritation. That inventory had taken hours to complete, dreary, dull hours of copying out endless lists of what Aquinas and I had found in every room. To have those interminable hours referred to so lightly was more than I could stand. I would not be made to feel like his pet clerk.

"Brisbane, you are being churlish. Now, if you mean to call upon Mrs. Birch, get your coat. I will wait."

He arched an imperious brow at me, but obeyed. I had not liked his little jest about Doctor Bent. I knew it was intended flippantly, but why then had I felt a thorn beneath the smooth words?

He returned a moment later, shooting his cuffs. "My lady?" He lifted his hand, indicating the door. I preceded him out and into the hansom that he hailed. I gave him the address to give to the driver and we proceeded in silence, the air thick with questions that went unasked. Brisbane said not a word, but sat like a great black bird of prey, watching out the window of the cab. His pose was relaxed, but his hands were tensile, clenching his walking stick until the knuckles went white.

In the end, I could not bear the silence.

"You are angry."

He sighed. "I am not. I am intensely irritated. If a quantity of poison is discovered amongst the private possessions of a suspect, it should bloody well be the murder weapon, don't you think?"

It was a symptom of his mood that he swore. Brisbane had frequently been quite rude, but he rarely cursed in my presence. Most ladies would doubtless have been horrified by such a breach in manners. I did not mind. It made me feel more of a comrade-in-arms. "Don't be peevish. I know you wanted Magda to swing, but you will simply have to knock your arrow in someone else's direction."

He flicked me a cool, almost dismissive look.

"Your metaphors are deplorable, my lady. I assure you I had no evil intentions toward your laundress."

"Former laundress," I said without thinking.

His gaze sharpened, and I spoke quickly to extricate myself.

"She left Grey House. So it is just as well that she is not the murderer," I said lightly. "As a Roma, I imagine she could hide herself quite handily. I would not have relished smoking her out once she's run to ground."

"Indeed not," he said finally. "Were you planning to keep that little nugget of information to yourself?"

"Of course not," I said sharply. "Had the arsenic been the cause of Edward's death, I would have told you instantly. But it is all very much moot, as Doctor Bent has just informed us."

He was silent a long minute, and I began to feel uncomfortably warm in my new finery. He was staring out of the window again, but I felt quite certain he was not seeing the streets outside. When he spoke, he kept his face turned toward the glass.

"If I find that you have hidden anything else from me, hindered me in any way," he said softly, "I will not be responsible for my actions."

I did not reply, but merely turned my head to look unseeingly out of my own window. And between us the silence grew thick again. He did not speak when I ordered the hansom to stop at a bookshop, nor did he say a word when I returned to the cab a moment later with the parcel I had purchased. He kept silent until we reached the modest home of Mrs. Birch, and it occurred to me then that Brisbane might be a prodigiously good holder of grudges. Yet something else to worry about, I thought irritably as he reached out to knock at the peeling door.

The fact that Mrs. Birch washed the bodies of the dead of the parish speaks eloquently to her financial necessity. She was a widow of little means, with seven children to bring up, and she applied herself diligently to whatever work could be found for her. Mending, charring, brewing and a little baking kept her children fed and clothed and with a dry roof over their heads. She was not above any honest work that might purchase a scrap of beef or crust of bread for them or, to my delight, a book.

Once I discovered her determination to educate her young, I made a habit of tucking an inexpensive volume or two into her baskets from Grey House. A costly book would have brought with it the temptation to pawn it for the cash. A cheap edition could be kept for the pleasure of reading alone, by Mrs. Birch as well as her children. She spoke plainly, her speech liberally sprinkled with the profanity she had learned from her sailor husband. In all, she was rough and crude and common. I liked her immensely.

And most of all, I liked her for her naturalness. It would have been a great day for her if the vicar himself called, rather than sending the curate. But faced with a gentleman of Brisbane's elegance, and myself, she did not turn a hair. She simply threw open the door, smiling and motioning us inside.

"Good day to you, my lady—that is quite a fine hat if I may say it."

"You certainly may, Mrs. Birch, and I thank you. I hope you are well?"

She stepped aside, letting Brisbane enter the narrow hall.

"As well as God ever made a body," she said heartily.

"Mrs. Birch, please forgive the spontaneity of our call," I began, but stopped when I saw her brow begin to crease. "That is, we have called without sending ahead, unforgivably rude, I know. I hope you will understand when I tell you it is a matter of some importance to us. Otherwise I would not dream of interrupting you when I know you must be very busy."

She flapped a plump hand. "Don't you worry about that, my dear lady. Always welcome you are, it is true. And whatever I can do for you, you've only to ask."

She looked at me expectantly and I hastened to make introductions.

"Mrs. Birch, this gentleman is Mr. Nicholas Brisbane. Mr. Brisbane, this is Mrs. Birch, a widow of this parish."

Mrs. Birch thrust out a thick hand. Brisbane, taking her in from untidy cap to worn shoes, did not hesitate. He took her hand warmly in his own.

"I am pleased to make your acquaintance, Mrs. Birch. You are very kind to see us."

Mrs. Birch turned and led us down the passage. "I've all the time you like, so long as I can keep on with my stitching. I've a dozen more shirts to get to the tailor, so I must not stop."

We followed her into the overheated kitchen, which was the heart of her little kingdom. Unlike its mistress, the kitchen was spotlessly tidy. The few utensils were gleaming, as were the pots and floor. A few small children were scattered about, learning their letters on a slate wielded by their elder sister, but Mrs. Birch made short work of shooing them out. As the last one—the eldest girl—was scuttling out, I handed her a package in brown paper. She looked at me inquiringly.

"A few new books. Some Shakespeare and a volume of fairy stories. Some of them are rather gruesome, so mind you don't read them to the little ones."

She did not smile, but her expression was one of pure rapture. She held the books close to her body, ignoring her mother's admonition to thank me.

I waved it aside. "Never mind, Mrs. Birch. I was shy myself as a child." Brisbane coughed, I think to cover a snort.

The girl threw me a grateful look and scurried out. I made a mental note to inquire when she would be ready to go into service. Another employer might mistake her shyness for backwardness and shove her into the scullery. But she had a good mind, that much was clear from the flicker of quicksilver intelligence behind her eyes. With a proper hand, such as Aquinas', she might make a good chambermaid, perhaps even a housekeeper in time. She could learn enough there to keep her own shop someday if she had ambition.

But I had more pressing matters to attend to, and I turned my attention back to Mrs. Birch, who was bustling about, putting the kettle on the hob and cutting off a few slices from a new loaf. She spread them with thrifty scrapings of fresh butter and assembled miscellaneous bits of crockery, some of it chipped and carefully mended, together with a small packet of sugar and a tiny pot of jam.

Brisbane held a chair for me near the fire and I seated myself, pleased to find that the chair cover, while faded and shiny with use, was perfectly clean.

Mrs. Birch watched as Brisbane settled himself, her hands busy with the tea things. She looked him over with the appraising eye of a woman who has seen a good number of naked men, both dead and alive. She seemed appreciative.

By the time the bread was cut and the cups assembled, the kettle was boiling. While she busied herself with the teapot and packet of tea, I took careful stock of the room. It was a home that had known hardship, that much was evident from the furniture, worn with polishing and hard use. But the walls were cheerfully, if cheaply, papered, and the floor was spotted with a few rugs of an unlikely shade of green. Garish but happy, rather like Mrs. Birch herself. I realized that she must be a woman of some sense and great resourcefulness to have made a pleasant home for herself and her children under trying circumstances.

Beside me, Brisbane was silently watchful, and I imagined he was making much the same assessment of Mrs. Birch and her little home. Finally, the tea things were ready and Mrs. Birch presented them to us with no apologies.

"I've cut a loaf of new bread, and that's fresh butter, mind you, straight from my sister's farm—none of that dyed muck they try to sell up at the shop. I don't know where that comes from, but you mark my words, a cow had nothing to do with it."

She gave us thick slices of bread with butter and hot mugs of strong, perfectly brewed tea. It was like being in the nursery again, and I ate with abandon. For all her fancy ways, Cook had never sent up a tea tray half so tempting. Mrs. Birch settled herself and took up a gentleman's shirt, finished but for the buttons. Her nimble needle whipped through the linen, stitching buttons into place while she talked. She scarcely looked at her hands, but the needle never missed, setting stitches so tiny, so precise they were almost invisible.

After my second piece of bread and several minutes of desultory conversation between Brisbane and Mrs. Birch, I came to the point.

"I believe that you attended my husband, Sir Edward Grey, after his death."

She nodded. "I did, and I hope you will permit me to offer my condolences. It's a hard thing to lose one's man, I know, my lady."

I did not speak for a moment. Her simple expression of sympathy had touched me more than the elaborate condolences I had received from her betters.

"Thank you. Although, I have at least had the consolation of a comfortable living and no young ones to worry over. I know your own lot must have been very difficult."

She stared at me, her expression pitying. "No, my lady. You've got it backward. The young ones are my consolation."

I took up my tea to swallow down the lump in my throat. Sometimes I simply wanted to disappear through the floor. Naturally her children were precious to her. I had seen them only as a pack of mouths to feed. No wonder I had not been blessed with children, I thought bitterly. I did not deserve them.

"It were a pleasure to wash Sir Edward," she said. She paused and took a thoughtful sip of her tea as Brisbane threw me a quizzical look.

"Pleasure?" he put in softly.

"Oh, yes. I never mind scrubbing the quality. Such nice, clean ways they have—well, most of them. There's some that would better suit a barnyard than a ballroom, but you'll hear no scandal from me. Sir Edward was a nice, clean gentleman."

"Mrs. Birch, I must beg your discretion for what I am about to reveal," I said.

She nodded once. "You have it."

I believed her entirely. She did not seem the sort that would sell my secret as a bit of gossip over the wash line. Besides, she was country-bred, and in the country there was still a strong tradition of loyalty to the gentry. Some might call it feudal, but as it served my purposes, I was not about to argue with it.

"We have reason to believe that my husband's death might have been hastened. Do you take my meaning?"

"Oh, was it murder, then?" Her tone was as casual as if she had just offered me another slice of bread. I stared at her.

"Mrs. Birch, you astonish me."

"Oh, I am sorry. Did you not mean murder?"

"I did, as a matter of fact." I had the strangest sense that Brisbane was trying to hide a smile behind his mug.

"I believe that Lady Julia is simply surprised at your quick grasp of the situation, Mrs. Birch," he said smoothly. "She does in fact mean murder."

Mrs. Birch sipped contentedly at her tea. "There's nothing to be embarrassed about, my lady, indeed there isn't. It does happen in the best of families, you know."

Her voice was reassuring and I felt almost as if she had just patted my hand. The entire conversation was taking an extraordinary turn.

"Thank you. Am I to understand that you have had some experience with such matters?"

"Of course I have, my lady. I have washed the dead of this

parish for nearly twenty years. I've seen stabbings and slashings, garrotings, stranglings, head-coshings…" She trailed off, doubtless reminiscing pleasantly.

"Have you ever seen a poisoning?"

She put a hand under her cap and scratched, thinking hard. With the cozy glow from the fire, and the lines of her face soft with thought, I could see that she had once been a handsome girl. A handsome girl of good sense and an excellent constitution. Her only liability had been a lack of fortune and good birth, and because of that, she lived in a tiny set of rooms, existing hand-to-mouth as she raised seven children, patching and darning her things to make them last from year to year. I, too, had been born handsome and sensible and healthy, but because my father sat in the Lords and had an annual income in excess of more than a hundred thousand pounds, I had every advantage while Mrs. Birch washed the dead to feed her children. Murder might be an interesting puzzle, but Fate is by far the greatest mystery of all, I mused.

"Poisonings," she said thoughtfully. "Yes, I have had a few. There was the poor girl who came from Leeds. Her man topped up her ale with arsenic when she got with child…then there was the old lady in South Street. Her nephew, I always thought, slipped her a bit of belladonna." She shrugged a sturdy shoulder. "Hard to say. So many of them just look like normal dying, if you take my meaning. But I suppose some of them might be poisoned."

"Might one of them have been Sir Edward?"

She smiled, showing an almost complete set of strong teeth.

"*Might* is a large word, my lady. Anything is possible."

I sighed, wondering how on earth I had come to be discussing philosophy with a charwoman of Jesuitical bent.

Brisbane inserted himself seamlessly into the conversation.

"A woman of your considerable experience would doubtless have noticed if something were amiss," he began.

I almost snorted into my tea. If he managed to achieve by flattery what I had failed to gain by appealing to her intellect…

"Now that I think of it, there was something," she said slowly.

Brisbane and I leaned forward as one man, so to speak.

"Yes?"

She looked carefully from one of us to the other, weighing her response. "I will tell Her Ladyship. You will have to go, sir," she said firmly.

Brisbane rose, placing his mug carefully upon the table.

"Of course. I will await Her Ladyship on the front step. Mrs. Birch, thank you for your hospitality. I will see myself out." Over her head he shot me a look that was unmistakable. He expected me to wring every bit of information out of her, and the look had been a warning. I had better not fail this time.

I stared at the fine tailoring of his retreating back while Mrs. Birch ogled something else.

"That your man?" she asked after the door closed behind him. Her expression was friendly, and I did not take offense.

"No."

She clucked her tongue. "Pity. He's got lovely legs. My Jimmy had lovely legs. Long and—"

"Mrs. Birch," I said sharply. She laughed, and this time she did pat me on the arm. She poured herself another cup of tea and I allowed her to fill mine for the sake of companionship.

"It's all right, my lady. It's just us hens. You can tell me. Do you fancy him?"

I could feel my rings beginning to cut into my hands. I forced myself to relax.

"Mrs. Birch, you said you would tell me what you noticed about my husband's corpse."

She regarded me a moment, judging my humour, I think. Something of my edgy mood must have shown itself, for she settled down at once. She told me what she had seen, to the last detail. I questioned her closely, but she did not vary her story, and in the end, I realized I believed her entirely.

"Thank you. I appreciate your assistance," I said, rising. "But I must warn you. You cannot repeat this to anyone—not what you have just told me, or even that I called. If my husband was murdered, anyone who possesses knowledge of the crime must be in danger."

She waved me off. "I am an oyster, I am. I've too much to think about, keeping the little ones fed and clothed to waste my time with idle gossip. Besides, it would be a poor thanks for your kindnesses to tell your business on the street."

I gave her a surprised look and she laughed. "I know it is you, my lady. No butler would think to put books in the baskets for the kiddies. And there's always a packet of hair ribbons for my girls, pretty new ones. And good leather shoes for the boys. Most ladies leave the baskets to their servants and they never know if we get the scrag end of beef and the burnt-down ends of candles. You always send us good meat, and a bottle of wine at Christmas. I do not forget it, my lady."

I could not think of a reply. I had always instructed Aquinas to prepare the baskets, only occasionally troubling to add something myself. She was praising Aquinas' generosity, not mine. I must remember to commend him.

Mrs. Birch saw me to the door. "If that Mr. Brisbane should die soon…" she began hopefully.

"I will send for you at once," I promised, smoothing my skirts.

"Oh, that is kind of you, my lady."

"Not at all. And to answer your question, I suppose some would find him fanciable."

She sighed and pulled open the door. "Just as I suspected, my lady. We are not so very different after all, if you will pardon the observation."

I thought of the society ladies I knew and how outraged they would be by such a statement coming from a woman of Mrs. Birch's ilk.

I smiled at her, knowing that if I had been born poor and disadvantaged, I would have ended my days rotting in a ditch, rather than mistress of a tiny, cozy home and proud mother of seven.

"On the contrary, Mrs. Birch. I take it as a compliment. A very fine one."

THE TWENTY-EIGHTH CHAPTER

If you fear the wolf,
Do not go into the forest.
—*Russian Proverb*

𝓑risbane had hailed a hansom and was waiting for me at the kerb. He handed me in and gave the direction of Grey House to the driver. I fussed with my reticule, pretending to search for a tin of lemon pastilles, then my handkerchief. Anything to avoid revealing to Brisbane what Mrs. Birch had disclosed.…

I had just begun burrowing about for a bit of lip salve when his nerve broke. "All right, I know it must be something fairly awful. You might as well tell me now."

"I'm not entirely certain that I can. How do you know it is awful?" I asked mildly.

"You've fidgeted so violently that you have managed to rip the cording of your reticule completely off. Tell me."

"Very well, but you must look out of the window."

I sensed his eyes rolling in exasperation, but I would not turn my head.

"I beg your pardon?" His voice was even—quite a good effort, I thought, given how annoyed he must have been at this point.

"I simply cannot say it if you are looking. I know that we are supposed to be quite grown-up about such things, but I cannot help it."

"About what such things?" he asked with deliberate patience.

"You are still looking at me."

This time the eyes definitely rolled, punctuated with an audible sigh. But he turned, edging his broad shoulders toward me, his gaze clearly fixed out of the window.

"I am not looking now, nor shall I."

I cleared my throat. "Very well. Mrs. Birch said that when she washed Edward she noticed that there was some discolouration—some rather violent discolouration."

"What sort of discolouration?"

My cheeks were warm and I fanned my face with my hand.

"How explicit must I be? Something was not the colour it should have been. It was *dis*coloured."

"I am conversant with the meaning of the word, my lady. I am inquiring as to the location and the extent of the discolouration," he said coldly. "In plain words, what part of his body and in what manner discoloured?"

"Oh, you are beastly. Very well, if you must know, it was his—his manly apparatus."

Brisbane gave a little choking noise. I do not like to think that it might have been a laugh.

"His what?"

"His *penis*, Mr. Brisbane. His stem of fertility, his manly root."

By this time his shoulders were definitely shaking, but to his credit, there was not a trace of amusement in his voice.

"She is quite certain? I mean, it is quite customary for the, er—manly apparatus to be of a different coloration than the rest of a gentleman's skin."

"Is it quite customary for it to be the colour of a vintage Bordeaux?" I asked venomously. "Mrs. Birch has washed more bodies than you or I have had hot meals. I take her opinion as the valuation of an expert."

"No doubt," he said gravely. He fell silent, ruminating as I recovered my composure. My cheeks felt marginally cooler, and by the time he straightened in his seat, gripping the head of his walking stick, I was almost myself. His face was lit, his expression rapturous, like St. Paul's on the road to Damascus, I imagined.

"What? What are you thinking?"

He was fairly quivering. The hound had once more picked up the trail.

"That was how the poison was introduced."

I stared at him, not bothering to conceal my scorn.

"You are barking mad. How could someone possibly introduce poison to a man's...well, his...*person* without his knowledge?"

He gave me a slit-eyed stare. "Perhaps it was with his knowledge."

"Are you saying it was suicide? That I find very hard to believe, and I must warn you that if you intend to pursue that particular line of investigation, I will stop this hansom right now and leave you here before I will have my husband's good name—"

He grabbed at my hand, squeezing hard, then dropped it suddenly, as if remembering himself. "I am suggesting nothing of the sort. I believe Sir Edward was murdered by a person with whom he was intimately connected."

"Oh, God, you think I did this!" I sagged against the seat, regretting with every atom of my being the day I had engaged him on this case.

"You will have to learn not to take such flying leaps of imagination if you ever hope to make an investigator, my lady," he said, rubbing at his temples. "I believe it must have been someone who knew his most intimate habits. It is the only way it all makes sense. He must have used a contraceptive machine—a sheath. A condom."

I was finally beginning to grasp what he was saying.

"And this sheath was poisoned? On the inside?"

"Precisely. It would account for the discoloration of his genitals, while no other part of his body bore traces of poison."

"What sort of person would do such a thing? *Could* do such a thing?" I murmured.

Brisbane shrugged. "Someone who hated him, that much is obvious. Someone who knew he would possibly use a prophylactic device during his amours. His valet, possibly, but far more likely it was a lover."

He seemed to have forgotten entirely that I had been Edward's wife. We were colleagues now, and I was not certain if I minded this or not. "His amours. That is quite a leap, is it not? You assume that he had mistresses, but you have no proof. Your entire theory hangs on the question of my husband's fidelity."

Brisbane turned to me, his eyes cool and pitiless. "I do not suppose it, my lady. I have proof. I have had ever since you gave me the inventory of his rooms."

I returned the cool stare. "Of what are you speaking, Mr. Brisbane?"

"The inventory listed one object that proved your husband had carnal relations with other women."

"Impossible. What object could possibly reveal that?"

A smile crossed his lips. It was feline, almost cruel, and I knew he was thinking of the case and not of me at all.

"There was a small porcelain box, painted with the image of Pandora, opening her own legendary box, the gift of the gods."

My lips went dry. "What of it?"

"If it is the one I suspect, I know those boxes. They are made to order for one of London's most notorious brothels. And they are only given to the most illustrious and profitable of patrons."

I said nothing. He settled back against the cushion, basking a little in his brilliant deduction. I felt my upper lip begin to grow moist. I blotted it discreetly with my gloved finger and waited for what I knew must come next.

"All we need do now is retrieve Sir Edward's box from Grey House, and I will use it as entrée to the brothel, where I shall discreetly question the inmates."

I swallowed hard and steeled my nerve. "Except that the box is not at Grey House."

He went very still. "Where is it?"

"I gave it to Magda. I knew she did not kill Edward, the very idea was ludicrous, and yet I feared you meant to hang her. I sent her away."

"With the box." His even, measured tone was far worse than any shout would have been. He reminded me of a cat that Cook had kept at Bellmont Abbey when I was a child. It would sit for hours, quite still, quite harmless-looking, but always watching with ravenous eyes. The poor, doomed mice never even saw the pounce. I licked my lips.

"And a pair of Sèvres candlesticks. I did not have any cash to hand and I knew she would need money."

"So," he said in a dangerous, silky voice, "your Gypsy laundress has taken our single best clue and pawned it, somewhere in a city of five million people."

I gave him my most abjectly sorry look. "I do apologize. I see that I have made rather a muck of things. But you must understand, I only did it to save Magda. I knew she was innocent, but I heard the way she spoke to you, the way she taunted you. I feared that you would be less than impartial."

"You mean that you did not trust me," he said flatly.

I lifted my chin. "No, I did not. But it cannot matter that much. You believe that you know the source of the box. Surely you do not require the box itself."

"That box is evidence, and I will have it."

"I cannot think how," I pointed out reasonably. "After all, London is a rather large haystack, and Magda such a small needle." I gave him a feeble smile, which he quite rightly ignored.

He did not speak until we drew up in front of Grey House. He alighted and held the door, but just as I made to exit the cab, he pounced, thrusting his arm across the opening, barring my path.

"That needle has, I imagine, hidden herself in a very small, very specific part of the haystack," he said, his voice low. "Do not underestimate me, my lady. I will have that box."

He had not taken his eyes from mine, and I understood from that unflinching gaze that we were no longer partners in this endeavor. He would know exactly where to find Magda, of that I had no doubt. What I did doubt was his ability to recover the box with his limbs intact.

He stepped back sharply, dropping his arm.

"Good day, my lady."

I gathered up my skirts and my dignity and swept past him and into Grey House. It was not until I had gained the privacy of my own home that I picked my skirts up into my hands and began to run.

Through some miracle that I still cannot credit, Valerius was at home. I found him in his room, his nose buried in a book, idly feeding the raven titbits from the tip of a pencil. I burst in without apology.

"Val, you must help me. He's going to the Gypsy encampment on Hampstead Heath. He'll be killed, I know it."

Val rose, sending the raven scuttling off irritably to the bedpost, where it glared down at us, muttering. Val put an arm around me, leading me to a chair. I did not sit.

"Julia, calm yourself. Who is going to the Gypsy camp?"

I took a deep breath, pressing my hand to my corset. "Mr. Brisbane."

Val's eyes widened, in fear, I thought. "Nicholas Brisbane? You know him?"

"Yes," I said, throwing off his arm impatiently. "He was here the night that Edward died. Father met him. He is investigating a matter for me. I stupidly gave a piece of evidence to Magda and now he means to get it back. She's gone to her people, and if he goes there and tries to take it from her, or to make trouble—"

I did not have to finish. Val knew the Roma as well as I did. Any infringement of their freedom by the English was met with hostility at the very least. More than once we had witnessed exchanges of some violence when they had been interfered with by villagers who should have known better. We had left them largely alone and they had been good to us. But I had always suspected that if we pushed them too far they would turn on us as well. Their friendship was like the good will of any wild thing—a gift not to be taken lightly.

"We must go, Val. It will not be dark for a little while yet, but we must hurry."

I was tugging at his coat, but he held my hands fast.

"You cannot go like that," he pointed out, taking in my extravagant costume with a glance. He was right, of course. No one with a scrap of sense flaunted their wealth in a Gypsy camp. To do so was to invite robbery—or worse. Smart visitors dressed discreetly and did not wager large amounts at their games. If we meant to blend in, we would have to do the same. I think the idea occurred to us both in the same instant, for no sooner had I looked at him than he was rummaging in his wardrobe, tossing out garments that might serve.

Within moments I had gathered them up and disappeared behind the screen to transform myself. It took me ages to wriggle out of my clothes, but in the end I managed, tearing only a few of the costly ruby buttons off in the process. I retrieved them, taking a few precious seconds to tuck them into my pocket. It would have gone much faster with Morag, but I dared not take her into my confidence. She would have insisted on coming along, and I was dubious enough about accepting Val's help.

A few moments more and I stepped out, rigged as a boy, from proper tweed trousers to choking necktie. Val had slipped into my room and fetched my own boots and a hard black hat. He gave me his wide woolen scarf to wind about my chin and stepped back to appraise the effect.

"At least you have a crop, so we do not have to worry about your hair giving you away," he said finally.

I scrutinized myself in his glass, rubbing at Fleur's rosy salve with my handkerchief. "Passable, I think. With any luck it will be full dark by the time we arrive. Get some money, will you?"

He scooped up his notecase and gloves and we departed, slipping down the stairs and out the study door, into the back garden. In a very few minutes we were through the gate and into the mews. I was breathing a little easier then, wondering if we might actually get away with our deception. We scurried around the corner and into the street where Val hailed a hackney. I muttered a little, wishing he had found a speedier hansom, but there was no help for it.

"Where would you and the lady like to go, sir?" the driver inquired amiably.

"Damnation!" I said softly. "What gave it away?"

"If you don't mind my saying, love, it's the walk. All hips and bum, nothing like a bloke at all. Where to?"

"Hampstead Heath, the foot of Parliament Hill," I muttered, and subsided into a sulky silence. All during the lengthy, creaking drive I tried to imagine how I was supposed to walk without using my "hips and bum," but at length I gave up. Darkness had fallen and we were climbing, almost to the Heath, when Val spoke.

"Julia, I wish you would confide. What is this all about?"

I looked at my hands, fisted against my unfamiliar, tweedy lap.

"Why should I? You have not confided in me," I said simply. "There was another bloody shirt in the laundry. Not another fight in front of the opera this time, I think."

"Oh." That was all he said. I knew that I should collar him about Magda, as well, demand an explanation for the despoiling of Carolina's grave, but I did not. I realized how close Magda had come to destroying him. I could not have borne that. He was my flesh, and I loved him for all his faults, for all his misdeeds. I would protect him, in the end. But for now I did not want to know.

The cab alighted at the fringe of the Roma camp. There were a few private carriages, a fair number of horses, and another cab or two standing or tethered. Val gave the driver an extortionate amount of money to wait for us. I doubted our ability to find another cab so far out. Besides, although I did not like to think about it, there was the chance we might have need of a quick escape.

Mindful of the cabman's criticisms, I pulled my hat low and made a concentrated effort to walk flatly, my hips held firmly in check.

"What is the matter with you?" Val hissed.

"I am walking like a boy," I explained, pitching my voice as low as I could.

"No, you are walking like a perfect imbecile. For God's sake, Julia, you're *clumping*."

I straightened my knees a bit. "Is that better?"

"A bit."

"You had best call me something else. Julian, I suppose. And get your hand away from my back. God only knows what people might think."

Val shied violently but kept his hands to himself. Without thinking, he had reverted to his inbred courtesy and been guiding me with a hand to the back. A mistake like that could be lethal in these surroundings.

For a while we simply skirted the camp, keeping half in shadow as we ambled along. The ground was dry and hard, well-packed from the wheels of the Gypsy caravans and the hooves of their horses. The wind carried the sharp smoke of their wood fires, laced with the fragrant spice of the cook pots. Over it all lay the thick odour of horse, the pungent smell of money to the Roma. There was music as well, lively and bold, and threading through it all the strange, exotic lilt of their language, drawing us along. A half-naked girl tried to pick Val's pocket and failed, running back to her mother. The woman cuffed her lightly, smiling and scolding her gently in Romany. I had no doubt she was being reprimanded—not for the attempt, but for its failure. The woman leaned over her cook fire, stirring an iron pot, and I smelled something rich and spicy, a stew of some sort, I supposed. My stomach gave a rumble of protest.

"Blast."

"What is it, *Julian?*"

"I should have thought to bring food. Did you dine?"

He shook his head. "No. Even a few sandwiches would have served."

"Never mind. I'll stand you to dinner at Simpson's when all this is done. Roast beef with all the trimmings."

"Splendid. Only promise me you will wear a dress. This masquerade is playing hell with my nerves."

"Done."

We slipped in and out of the jostling crowds, sometimes following groups or pairs as a new bit of entertainment would lure them on, sometimes holding back and peering into the shadows near the caravans. There were fortune-tellers, scrying with crystal balls and cards and palms. There were dancers with tiny, high-arched feet, stamping and yelling to the rhythms scraped out by the violins and guitars. And there were the men, beguiling the English to wager on a roll of the dice or perhaps the purchase of a new horse. There were smiles and shouts and groans, all well-lubricated with money and liquor. I might have enjoyed myself had it not been for the coil of fear knotted in my stomach.

Val had no such scruples. I caught him ogling a dancer, her wide skirts flaring up to reveal a ripe brown thigh as she turned. She winked at him, doubtless in hope of a generous coin, which he was quick to throw. She blew him a kiss then and I tugged at his sleeve as he so often used to do to mine, urging him on toward a little group gathered around the blind old man who told lengthy tales in Romany with great, theatrical gestures.

"I was looking for Mr. Brisbane," he protested.

"He is not under that dancer's skirt, I can assure you," I returned sharply. "In fact, I do not see him here at all. Or any of Magda's people. Where have we not looked?"

Val scanned the encampment. "The caravans."

I shook my head. "Too dangerous. We might edge near if we were to have our fortunes told, but if they caught us skulking about…"

He nodded grimly. "They are dealing horses that way," he said, inclining his head behind me. "And there is a boxing tent as well. Perhaps he is watching a match."

We decided to try the horse ring first, then the boxing tent, but before I could move, I heard the Gypsy story-teller's voice rise and fall and I stood, captivated by the sound of it. It was a beautiful language, with an Italianate, musical quality to it. It was an expressive tongue, a perfect vehicle for the richness of the Roma emotions. It was a language contrived to woo or to lament, to seduce or revile. I, of course, knew none of it. For all Magda's affection for me, she had never permitted me to speak a single word of her language. I had gleaned a few bits here and there, con-textually, but never more than a handful of words, and I had forgotten them along with so many other scraps of child-hood. I had never been allowed to ask if I even understood them properly. The one time I had ventured to use the Romany word for Englishman, *gorgio,* Magda had turned her back on me and walked silently away. Later she relented, but only enough to explain her anger.

"Romany is ours, lady. It is a powerful language, with great magic. We do not give our power or our magic away," she had told me. It made a curious kind of sense, although I still did not see the harm it would do if an English girl could count to ten in Romany. But Magda's message had been plain. I would not be allowed into their camp if I trespassed on their language. I never attempted to speak Romany again.

But I drank it in whenever I listened to them talk, marveling at the smooth, liquid sound of it. I began to think it impossible that an English-speaker could ever learn it. It was a very unbuttoned sort of tongue, demanding enthusiasm and passion and a liveliness that those with cold northern blood could not muster.

I relaxed a little as the old man rambled on, and after a few minutes I allowed Val to lead the way toward the horse ring. A deal was in progress, with an Englishman, protesting the price, ranged against a Gypsy horseman who was holding firm. They were each backed by a dozen or so men of their own kind, shouting and jeering as negotiations moved back and forth. Several times the buyer named a price and put out his hand in the traditional manner of Gypsy horse-dealing; scornfully, the dealer slapped it away and named a better one. Between them the horse stood placidly, his head hanging low, his eyes shifting from his Gypsy master to his prospective buyer. He looked handsome, and sound enough, and I wondered how many times he had been sold and found his way back to the Roma.

My father often bought horses from Magda's people and

had never had any difficulty with them, finding their horse-flesh to be of the highest quality and their prices fair. But he always maintained that this was because Magda's people knew and liked him. They were permitted to camp on his land, and so treated him fairly when horse-dealing. But other Gypsies, he warned us, were far too clever and tricky for us. He had always instructed my brothers to purchase their horses at Tattersall's if Magda's menfolk were not to be found. My second brother, Benedick, had neglected to follow this good advice once, purchasing a solid-enough looking animal from a traveling group of Roma when he was in Cornwall. He had been particularly taken with its glossy coat, I remember. It washed off during the first good sweat. Benedick had tried desperately to get his money back, but of course they were long gone, doubtless laughing themselves sick over the stupidity of the young *gorgio* lordling too stupid to spot a bit of dye in a horse's coat. I looked as closely as I dared, but this horse seemed genuine enough in his colour, if a bit spavined. And if the prospective buyer did not look to that before the sale was completed, he deserved to be fleeced.

We slipped past them and toward the boxing tent, where a match was in progress. According to the hawker outside, the Gypsy champion, an enormous brute, was fighting all comers for a pound. We listened to his patter for a moment, rather impressed at the fighter's credentials. His record was a prodigious one, and it occurred to me that they might attract more challengers if they did not stress so openly the number of men he had knocked down.

Val paid the entrance fee for both of us, grumbling as he did so. I reminded myself to reimburse him for the night's adventures. His allowance was generous, but so were his expenditures. The remainder might not run to an evening's entertainment.

My eyes watered as soon as we stepped inside and I fought

against the urge to cough. It was close in there, with three or four dozen men crowding around, smoking and cursing at the combatants. The rank smell of sweat and horse, sawdust and stale beer clung to the canvas, and I could hear quite distinctly the sounds of solid fists slamming into bare flesh. Val shot me a doubtful look.

"Are you certain you're up for this?"

I nodded, but he continued to look dubious. He needn't have bothered. I had seen a number of prizefights as a child. Father adored them, and if he happened upon one, he had not been terribly fussy about bringing me along. I had only to promise not to tell Aunt Hermia and he would bribe me with ginger nuts. I had rather enjoyed those illicit outings. The fighting was brutal, but Father carefully explained the finer points and I always enjoyed the little wagers we placed. The summer I backed seven winners was the summer he stopped taking me along, I remembered wryly. He had begun taking Valerius instead, but he always said wistfully that Val lacked my appreciation for watching grown men thrash each other.

I was surprised now at how quickly it all came back. It seemed that one bare-fisted fight was rather like every other. A few sharp-eyed men would make money on the affair, and several dozen men, largely inebriated, would not. The crowd, ever in danger of having their pockets picked, ringed a beaten-down area thickly laid with sawdust tamped hard by booted feet. It even smelled the same, I remarked to Val. He grimaced, which I thought rather weak from a student of anatomy.

He kept us carefully to the back of the spectators while he scanned the crowd, looking for Brisbane. I had difficulty seeing over the heads in front of me, and for the briefest of moments I regretted my disguise. Had I come in skirts they would have all made way for me, I thought ruefully. But then if I had come in skirts, I would have doubtless attracted un-welcome attention, women being scarce at such events.

A few of the men shifted and I realized the crowd was a bit thinner on the other side. I motioned to Val. We edged past, keeping to the back of the tent as we made our way around. There was a crunching hit suddenly, and a roar went up as the crowd surged forward. I was very nearly knocked off my feet, but I kept my wits and shoved hard against the man who had jostled me.

He turned, his face fat and moistly red in the light of the hanging lamps.

"Watch yourself, sonny. Mustn't get trampled, now, my lad."

He turned back to the match and I gave a little sigh of satisfaction. Finally someone had owned me for a boy, even if it was only a drunken lout at a prizefight. I threw a little look of triumph at Val, but he was staring straight ahead, over the man's head at the fight itself. I nudged at him, but he simply stared. He jerked his chin toward the boxers.

"Look," he hissed finally.

I edged around the fat man, thoroughly annoyed. He had probably seen a broken nose that had intrigued him or something else perfectly useless, I thought irritably. I rose up on the balls of my feet, peering over the fat man's shoulder, and got my first proper look at the boxers.

There was indeed a broken nose. Both of the fighters were stripped to the waist. The touted champion stood facing me, streaming blood freely from a pulpy pile in the middle of his face. He was dashing blood out of his eyes with his fists, his expression murderous. Then he smiled, horribly, revealing teeth bracketed in blood. He spit a tooth into the sawdust, but continued to grin like some demented creature. Slowly, deliberately, he raised his fists—enormous, meaty things, the size of hams. He swung heavily, but his opponent darted back lightly, just out of reach. There were bruises beginning to darken the side of the slighter man's torso, and I wondered if his face was undamaged. It did not seem possible that he could have inflicted such damage on the champion and sustain only a few bruises himself.

But as I watched them battle, I began to understand why. The Gypsy had size on his side, but that was his only advantage. He was heavy and slow, his feet moving as if stuck in treacle.

I pursed my lips, madly disappointed. From a champion I expected more than brute strength. There should be finesse and even a certain elegance of movement. Father had taught me that fist-play was no different from swordplay, demanding skill as well as strength. This Gypsy was nothing more than a machine, hammering whatever lay in his path.

His challenger, on the other hand, was something else entirely. He held himself like a horse will at the start of a race, lightly, ready to spring. His head moved quickly, luring blows that he avoided with a catlike nimbleness. It was so delightful to watch that I nearly laughed out loud. He was a natural, and I regretted bitterly that we had come too late to place a bet on him.

I was just beginning to anticipate a nice long bout when the challenger did something that ruined it all. He moved back again, this time canting himself sideways, forcing the champion to move off balance. Then he raised his fist, and with one quick, brutal blow to the jaw—so fast the eye could not follow—it was done. The Gypsy took a moment, rocking on his heels, eyes rolling back white. Then, without a sound, he fell to the sawdust. A great cloud of it went up with the cheer and money began to exchange hands. The fat man in front of me threw his hat down in disgust.

"Have you lost, then, sir?" I asked, too amused to be careful.

He fixed me with a baleful look. "I have, indeed. The bastard knocked him down in less than two minutes!"

He stomped on his hat and stumped away, cursing fluently.

I turned back to what was left of the match, laughing. The crowd had dissolved into a flood of curses and barbs, in Romany and English, and the challenger turned to accept them, as well as his share of the winnings. For the first time I was able to see his face, which surprised me in two ways. First, there was no blood. And second…

"Good Lord," I said to no one in particular. "Brisbane has rather a nasty right."

THE TWENTY-NINTH CHAPTER

Quit, quit, for shame! This will not move;
This cannot take her.
If of herself she will not love,
Nothing can make her:
The devil take her!
—Sir John Suckling
"Song"

he revelation that Brisbane was a skillful prizefighter was not the only one disclosed that night. As he pulled on his shirt, collecting the approbation of those who had profited from his victory, he talked with them, his voice clearly audible to me, even over the crowd. But it sounded strangely unlike his voice, and it took me almost a full minute to realize why.

Brisbane was speaking Romany. He was speaking, my addled brain told me, a language that he could not possibly know. But of course he did know it. Fluently and idiomatically, to judge by the laughter of his companions. His hands moved as he spoke, sketching the dramatic gestures that every Roma uses to punctuate his speech. He knew this fluid tongue, and there was only one way he could have learned it.

As Brisbane paused in his conversation to reach for his shirt, Val made to raise a hand in greeting. I slapped it down, motioning him to silence. "We must go. Now," I said through clenched teeth. "Before he sees us."

"What the devil is wrong with you? We've been scouring the Heath for the better part of the evening, looking for him, and now that we have found him, you want to leave?"

"I will explain it all later. Just come with me—*now*."

To his credit he came, although still muttering about the inconsistency of women. I did not much blame him. I was busy cursing my own stupidity. How could I not have seen it? I had repeatedly remarked to myself upon his swarthiness, his *unEnglishness*. I had thought him French or perhaps even a Jew. But I had never once imagined the truth.

We made for the tent flap, moving quickly and quietly behind the crowd so as not to attract attention. But just as I put my hand to the flap, it was brushed aside by a man entering. Magda's brother, Jasper. I pulled back hard, slamming into Val, but Jasper did not see either of us. His gaze was focused on Brisbane, who swung his head around as if on a wire. Jasper gave him a perceptible nod and melted out of the tent as quietly as he had come.

"Oh, no," I breathed. Val put a questioning hand on my shoulder, but I shook my head and slipped out of the tent, careful to move in the direction opposite to the one that Jasper had taken. We had walked only a few steps when Val seized my arm and dragged me behind a caravan.

"What is the matter with you? You have insisted we must find Mr. Brisbane, and there he is. You wanted to find Magda's people, and we have just seen Jasper. What is it you want?"

I jerked my arm out of his grasp. "I want to get out of this place without Brisbane knowing I've come. I should not have followed him here and I have seen something I was not meant to see."

"His business with Jasper?"

I rubbed at the place on my arm where he had gripped me. I had not realized Val's fingers were so strong. I would have a bruise there.

"No, not entirely. Well, yes, that is part of it. Jasper has apparently decided to give Brisbane what he came for."

"And what is that?" he asked.

"The rope to hang you with."

"What?" His voice was incredulous. "Julia, what are you talking about? This has nothing to do with me. You said you engaged Mr. Brisbane on a matter of business. How does that involve me?"

"It is too complicated to explain now. I thought I had taken care of it, and it seems I have done nothing but complicate matters to the utmost. I do not yet know how I will put it right, but I will. I must get home, though, and quickly."

I heard the imploring note in my voice and so did Val. He relented. He gave me a quick nod and we turned for the far side of the camp, where I prayed the cabman would still be waiting. It would be a long ride back to Grey House, but at the end of it I could count on a hot meal and a hotter bath.

I stepped out from behind the caravan and into the fitful light of a crowded campfire. And at just that moment Nicholas Brisbane moved out of the shadow of the boxing tent, lifting his head, sniffing the air like a dog. His eyes roved past the firelight, skimming lightly over the figures moving between us. They came to rest on me, peering through the gloom. His eyes narrowed, his teeth bared, and I took to my heels.

I had something of a head start—perhaps an eighth of a mile. But it did not matter. I had known almost as soon as I began to run that he would catch me up. I did not dare to imagine what he might do to me once he did. But I was soon to find out.

I suppose I expected him to beat me. Some might have even said he was justified. I had discovered that which was never meant to be known. Most Englishmen held Gypsies as lower than dogs. Less than a Jew, better than an African? No, I knew ladies who kept blackamoor pages quite happily, but would never let a Roma set foot in their house. They were thought to be capable of any treachery, cunning and malicious and black-hearted as devils. I could not blame Brisbane for not confiding in me. I, too, would have hidden my bloodlines under the circumstances.

But I did not think my sympathy would win me any points this night. So I fled, dashing past campfires and under clotheslines, dodging onlookers and mocking laughter on my way across the camp with Brisbane in furious pursuit. I put on a burst of speed as we neared the carriages, hearing him closing behind me with every stride, Val wheezing along somewhere behind. And then I realized that Brisbane had eased into a lope. He was keeping pace with me, but deliberately he did not close, allowing me to lead him to the hackney where he could catch me up easily and have at me in private.

Gasping, I reached the door and had just grasped the handle when his hand came down hard upon mine. His shirt was open, sweat-stuck to his sides. Absurdly, I noticed his pendant, lying in the hollow of his throat. I noticed, too, that I had lost my hat somewhere along the way. I should have to order a new one, I mused. If I lived so long.

Val skittered up, a hand pressed to his side.

"Mr. Brisbane, what are you about, chasing my sister all over God's own creation?" he demanded loudly.

Keeping his hand firmly anchored upon mine, Brisbane turned to Val. He might have omitted the precaution. My side was burning from the run, and he looked barely winded. If I decided to flee I would not make it three steps before he caught me again.

"Have a care for her reputation," Brisbane advised softly. "Do you have any notion of what would become of her if it became known that she visited a Gypsy camp dressed like that?"

Val flushed angrily. "You think I should have prevented it."

Brisbane's face was expressionless. "I think that is beyond the reach of your abilities, Mr. March. But I think you might have provided a better escort."

Val's hands tightened and he stepped forward.

"Don't be stupid, Val. He's quite right. I was a fool to come and you were a fool to come with me."

Brisbane did not look at me. "Now, if you will oblige me by getting into the cab, Mr. March. I have some business to discuss with your sister." Val hesitated, but Brisbane's features were stony. Val threw me a look, of supplication I suppose, but I flicked my eyes toward the cab, indicating he should do as he was told. I doubted Brisbane intended to murder me on Hampstead Heath, but if he did, it was probably no more than I deserved.

Brisbane stepped aside, pulling me with him, so that Val could enter the hackney. With Val and the cabman looking on, there was little privacy there, so I was not entirely surprised when he put his hand under my elbow and directed me to a stand of trees some short distance away. They were a bit of a screen at least, and would offer some protection from Val witnessing the humiliation of what I was certain would be the dressing-down of my life.

"You needn't bother, really," I said as he pushed me against a tree. He had an arm above me, clamped to the rough trunk, ensuring I could not escape. "I will not run away. I deserve everything you care to throw at me. I have been vile and stupid and completely untrustworthy. You may shout as much as you like."

I admit that I had hoped that this abasing little speech would win me a little pity. But Brisbane's eyes were murderous. I had never seen him so completely in the grip of strong emotion, not even when he had been drugged. I swallowed hard and licked at my lips.

"Brisbane, say something. If you wish to strike me, do it and get it over with. I know you are frightfully angry, and you have every right…"

I stopped then because he made me. He did not strike me; instead he did something I had never expected. He reached for me. It was some time before he let me go.

When he did, I was breathing far too fast and I tasted blood on my lips. Without a word he grabbed my arm and half dragged me back to the hackney. He wrenched open the door and thrust me toward Val, who caught me, wide-eyed with surprise.

Brisbane turned and gave a little whistle to the cabman, who whipped up the horse, turning the hackney toward town. Brisbane did not look at me as we drew away. I sat very still, aware of Val's scrutiny. He handed me a handkerchief. I touched it gingerly to my mouth.

"Did he hit you?" His voice was even, but I thought I detected a little ragged edge at the end.

"No."

"Ah."

He turned away then and for once did not ask questions. I was grateful for that at least. I had no answers. For Val, or myself.

THE THIRTIETH CHAPTER

Trust not the physician.
—William Shakespeare
Timon of Athens

I was awake the next morning when Morag brought my tea. I had been awake the better part of the night, considering my course of action. Confront Valerius with what I believed to be proof of his truly abominable deeds? Force my way into Brisbane's rooms in Chapel Street and demand that we mend matters between us? Turn the entire matter over to Father? Or, most tempting of all, forget the entire mess and leave at once for Italy?

Morag put down the tray and peered at my face. "You're green, you are."

"Oh, Morag, you do say the sweetest things."

She pursed her lips. "There's no need to be churlish, my lady. I was simply inquiring after your health. You look as if you could use a tonic."

I sighed and took the cup she thrust at me.

"I am sorry, Morag. I am unfit to be around other people today."

She sniffed over her shoulder as she went to draw back the drapes. "Some might think that you've little enough to be unfit about—a rich lady, of good family, with not altogether unattractive looks. It's spoilt you are, not appreciating the blessings the good Lord has given you."

I took a deep, restorative breath of the tea-scented steam, then sipped, wincing at the touch of the cool porcelain against my swollen lip. "Very likely. And of course I am so very fortunate in my choice of domestic help."

She bent to gather the clothes I had dropped on the floor when I had undressed myself the previous night. I had dismissed her as soon as I arrived home. She had blinked at my costume, but for once said nothing. Apparently Aquinas' frequent lectures on the imperturbability of a good servant were beginning to take effect.

"You are about to be more fortunate. I happened to overlisten when that Frenchie gave his notice to Mr. Aquinas."

"Renard? He has given his notice?"

Morag's lips were thinned with satisfaction. "He has. Good riddance, I say. Filthy creature, that Frenchman. Now, Mr. Diggory, that's a good man to have about the house."

I listened with half an ear as she chattered on about the coachman's virtues. A house without Renard would be very pleasant indeed. But perhaps complicated. Brisbane might have questions for him, and I could not take the chance that another member of my staff would slip from his clutches.

"Where is he bound?" I asked casually.

"Lord Crayforth. The brewer," she said with a meaningful arch of the brows.

"Morag, you've become a thorough snob, do you know that?"

"It is true and well you know it, my lady. A jumped-up brewer with dirty habits. I hear he don't change his underlinen but once a month."

I pushed my toast away uneaten. "Good Lord. I suppose Renard will not perish of overwork, then, will he?"

But I felt better at this bit of intelligence. Lord Crayforth was a fixture in London. He was famous for his hatred of the country. His summer house was only as far away as Chelsea. If Brisbane wanted to find Renard, he should not have far to look.

"We shall have to find someone else to tend to Sir Simon, I'm afraid."

"Won't have him to worry about much longer, either," Morag put in darkly. "He's had a bad night and his cough is worse."

I pushed back the coverlet and swung my feet to the floor.

"Why did you not say so? I will go to him before breakfast."

By the time I reached the breakfast table, my appetite was well and truly gone. Simon had indeed had a rough time of it. There was a little blood now when he coughed, and I sent word to Aquinas to send for Doctor Griggs. The prospect of seeing him again, and of bearding Brisbane in his den afterward, robbed me of any hunger I might have had.

Aquinas brought food, anyway. There was always enough to feed a regiment keeping warm in the chafing dishes, and Aquinas always made a point of entering the room with a rack of fresh toast and a basket of rolls precisely when I appeared.

"Good morning, my lady. I have dispatched Henry with your note to Doctor Griggs. He has replied that he will be here very shortly. Also, I have had Renard's resignation this morning. He wishes to enter service with Lord Crayforth."

I buttered the toast to give myself something to do. "I know. Morag happened to overhear something to that effect."

We exchanged a conspiratorial smile. Morag's habit of "happening to overhear" was famous. And though Aquinas' demeanor was perfectly neutral, I knew he would miss Renard as little as I did. "I have no objection. When does he mean to leave us?"

"As soon as possible. I gather his lordship is eager to secure his employment. His own valet left rather abruptly."

"Ooh, do tell. I smell scandal," I said, moving on to the jam pot.

"His lordship struck his valet with a riding crop."

"Goodness! Whatever for?" I took a bite, anyway. The jam was extraordinary. Cook had put up dozens of jars from the tiny strawberries my father sent from his hothouse.

"I understand his lordship's shaving water was tepid."

"Indeed. Well, his lordship and Renard should get along rather well together." I took another bite and chewed thoughtfully. Aquinas busied himself at the sideboard, testing the temperature of the eggs and kidneys and so forth, although I do not know why he bothered. Simon barely nibbled at food these days, and my appetite was wildly variable. Val was the only other person in residence, the Ghoul having taken herself off to Twickenham for a few days' holiday with her constipated niece—a protest against my abandoned widow's weeds, I suspected—and I doubted he would bother with breakfast. I wondered briefly what would become of the piles of leftover ham and rashers of bacon, but decided I would rather not know. Surely someone would eat it. They would not just throw it out. Would they?

"We shall have to see about finding someone to care for Sir Simon," I said. I glanced down, surprised to find only crumbs where my toast had been.

"I thought Desmond, my lady. He is rather peaky and I do not like to send him out. Perhaps if he stayed in, taking care of Sir Simon until other arrangements can be made…"

He did not finish his thought, but I did. He meant until Simon died and Desmond could be moved to the country to handle Father's dogs. Well, it was not pleasant to think of, but it did kill two birds rather nicely. Desmond was cutting a rather poor figure in his livery. Unlike Henry, he had never preened in it, lording his finery over his lessers. He was a quiet, modest boy, in spite of his strikingly delicate good looks, and I was glad we had found a means of keeping him. I had little doubt he would thrive in the country. I would have been sorry to lose him altogether, although I admit I was beginning to mark the weeks until I could dismiss Henry.

"Tell Desmond he needn't bother to wear livery as he will no longer be going out or greeting callers. A plain suit should be sufficient for tending Sir Simon. Father will want him in something serviceable at the Abbey in any case."

"Very good, my lady. Will you be going out this morning?"

"Yes, I'm afraid I am."

A question flickered in his eyes, but he suppressed it.

"Tell Diggory I will need the carriage in an hour. There is no need for Henry to come. He will have more duties here now that Desmond has been shifted to the sickroom. Call me when Doctor Griggs is ready to leave, will you? I should like a word with him."

Aquinas bowed from the neck and turned back to the chafing dishes as I left the breakfast room. I stepped back into the room.

"Aquinas, don't think me very odd, but I was wondering, what happens to all the food? What the family does not eat, I mean."

"The meats are turned into luncheon for the staff, my lady. Kidney pie, ham croquettes, that sort of thing."

"And the eggs?"

"The eggs, kedgeree, rolls and toast are given to the poor."

"Thank God for that," I murmured.

"I beg your pardon, my lady?"

"Never mind, Aquinas. Never mind."

I should have dressed with care that morning, arming myself for battle. But I was in a hurry to speak with Griggs before he quitted Grey House, and in the end I simply stood still while Morag dragged on something green she had unearthed from the wardrobe.

"Oh, feathers," I said, peering into the looking glass at my sallow skin. "You have gone and picked the one colour that I could not stand up to today. Best hand me some of that rose salve of Madame de Bellefleur's."

She passed over the little jar. "Only a thumbnail's worth left, I should say. You'll be wanting more of that, I wager."

I rubbed a bit into my cheeks and lips. There was immediate improvement, although I was beyond real help.

"I cannot ask Madame de Bellefleur. What is in it? Could you make it?" Morag often pottered about the stillroom, concocting soaps and cosmetics and even proper perfumes. She had never made anything as sophisticated as this rose salve, but it was certainly worth an effort.

Morag gave it a sniff, then rolled a bit between her fingers. "Aye. Bit of beeswax, I should think. Some crushed rose petals. Cannot say for the rest, but I could try."

"Then save the rest of it. You'll want that for comparison." I smoothed my hair and gave a final tug to the waist of my jacket. The green seemed almost regal now, or at least less like a weedy pond. I gathered up my reticule and umbrella.

"Morag, I will be going out as soon as I have spoken with Doctor Griggs. You may have the afternoon free to do as you like."

She blinked at me, a little suspicious. "My afternoon is Wednesday."

"I am aware of that, Morag. But my wardrobe is in order and I shouldn't think it would take you very long to tidy up in here. You might see if there is anything Sir Simon requires if you go out."

"Aye, my lady." She did not move, and I stared at her, faintly exasperated.

"Is there something wrong?"

She shook her head slowly, but her expression said otherwise.

"Well you look mightily put out to me, although I cannot think why. If there is a problem, we will have to discuss it later. I am late."

"My lady." She bobbed me a curtsey, rare for her, and said nothing more. But I caught her look as I turned away and it was speaking.

My interview with Doctor Griggs was brief and unhappy.

In short, Simon's heart was beginning to fail and Griggs had prescribed laudanum to ease his pain and help him to sleep. He thought it might only be a matter of a very few weeks now and encouraged me to spend as much time with him as I could.

"Although, I see you are dressed to go out," he finished with a touch of disapproval.

A flash of anger rose and I beat it back with an effort. It took all the control I possessed not to tell him exactly what I thought of him. I dared not, for Simon's sake. I had little doubt that Doctor Bent could give him better care, but what difference would it make now? Simon was comfortable with Griggs, he did not see him for what he was. To me, he was anathema. His stupid prejudices, his blindness, his thoughtless dismissal of me as a mere woman…he represented everything I hated most in an Englishman. Narrow, biased, unfeeling and snobbish. But snobbery was a two-edged sword for the daughter of an earl.

I drew myself up and fixed him with the coldest look in the repertoire Aunt Hermia had passed on to me.

"My business is my own, Doctor," I said, stressing his title. If there was one thing Griggs hated, it was being reminded that he was little better than a tradesman.

He gawped at me, his jowls wagging. He would have liked to have told me what he thought of me as well, I imagined. But he did not dare, either. The power of the March name cut too deeply for him to risk that. Attending Sir Simon Grey on his deathbed was simply another feather in his professional cap.

"I meant no offense, my lady. I simply thought that Sir Simon should have the comfort of his family at so critical a time."

I checked the clasp of my reticule and smoothed my jacket.

"You have just said that you gave him laudanum. He will be sleeping. He will not know if I am out or not," I pointed out reasonably.

"But if he should wake, he would doubtless welcome the sight of your face," he put in. There was something sly in his manner, something I did not like. "Besides, I am sure it is not my place to say, but there is beginning to be some talk…"

He let his voice trail off suggestively, intimating God only knew what. But I had some idea. I had relaxed my vigilance in my calls to Brisbane's rooms. I had not bothered with incognita when I called at Madame de Bellefleur's. Anyone might have seen me and put the worst construction upon it. And Griggs was a popular enough figure in society thanks to his penchant for the latest gossip. It would not have been long before some patient poured the story into his eager ears.

I fixed him with the sweetest smile I could, taking care that it did not reach my eyes.

"I have no doubt of that, Doctor. There are always those unfortunates who have nothing better to do than gossip about their betters."

A dull red flush crept up his cheeks. I doubt anyone had ever had the temerity to speak to him so. I picked up my umbrella and gave it a little twirl.

"You see, Doctor, aristocrats are rather like tightrope walkers. We simply do not notice what is beneath us."

I swept out, leaving him speechless in my wake. It was one of the most childish things I had ever done. But one of the most satisfying, I thought as I settled myself in the carriage. Most satisfying, indeed.

THE THIRTY-FIRST CHAPTER

I have unclasp'd
To thee the book even of my secret soul.
—William Shakespeare
Twelfth Night

I was regretting the jam I had eaten at breakfast by the time Mrs. Lawson waved me up to Brisbane's rooms. It sat bitter on my tongue, and as I rapped and waited for the door to open I sucked a cachou to sweeten my mouth.

Monk admitted me at once. "Good morning, my lady," he said, civilly enough.

I gave him my warmest smile. "Good morning, Monk. How are you today?"

His expression was correct, but his gaze dropped instantly to my bruised lip.

"Better than most, my lady."

It was an effort, but I held my bright smile fixed in place.

"Mr. Brisbane is not expecting me, but I wonder if he could spare me a few minutes of his time?"

Monk stepped backward and gestured for me to enter.

"I shall see if Mr. Brisbane is available to callers, my lady."

He gestured for me to take a chair and I sat, willing my knees to stop trembling. I was frankly nervous at seeing Brisbane, and I wished fervently that I had worn something more flattering, something to give me a bit of dash and a bit of confidence. Yes, I should definitely have worn the scarlet walking suit. Either that or taken a very stiff whiskey before I had come out.

Monk offered me tea or coffee and withdrew when I refused both. I did not look at *Punch* or peruse the bookshelves. I sat instead, staring at the little calico knot in the bowl on his side table. A knot very similar to the one Magda had given me, doubtless fashioned from the graveclothes of a dead Rom. One of Brisbane's Gypsy relations? Did he keep it for protection, as a talisman? Or simply as a reminder of someone he had loved and lost? Or was it a bit of detritus, flotsam he had collected on his travels and neglected to discard?

So deep was I in my musings, I did not hear Brisbane come in—it was only a moment later and he was treading like a cat. Or a Gypsy. I remembered from childhood how soft-footed they were. From years of eluding trouble, I imagined, but I suppose it served Brisbane well in his chosen occupation. He took the chair opposite mine and simply regarded me, saying nothing. There were a few bruises from the fight darkening his jaw, and a little cut on his lower lip that I was very much afraid had not come from the fight at all. I felt a wave of heat break over my face, doubtless leaving me unattractively ruddy under his scrutiny.

"It was good of you to let me in today," I began, my voice a good deal steadier than it had a right to be. The tips of his nostrils were flaring white—not a good sign. I had always been undone in the presence of angry men.

"I did not," he pointed out coolly. "Monk did."

"Ah, yes. Well, I suppose it would be too much to ask for you to make this easy for me. Why did you agree to see me, since you so obviously do not wish to?"

He lifted one shoulder in a bland shrug. "Curiosity. It killed the cat and no doubt it will be my undoing, as well."

"I suppose that is fair enough. What do you wish to know?"

He gave a short, mirthless laugh that was probably intended

to make me feel stupid. It succeeded wildly. "Everything. To begin, how could you, a woman of such obvious intellectual gifts, not realize the danger of a Gypsy camp?"

"I did realize the danger. That is precisely why I went."

He passed a hand over his eyes. They were shadowed today, and I wondered if he felt another headache coming on.

"I do not understand you. Most women would go fleeing in the opposite direction of such a situation."

"Oh, and so would I, under other circumstances. But you see, I did not have a choice."

Brisbane's eyes were sharp and wolfy. "Because you wanted to find the box before I did."

"Yes. Or no, I mean I wanted the box, but I went to find you, really."

"To ask me to give up on Magda, I expect."

"No, of course not," I said, growing exasperated. Why were men so impossibly obtuse at times? "If I were so worried about poor Magda, I would hardly have told you where to find her. Come to think of it, why did you even tell me that you were making for the camp?"

"Because I did not think you would be daft enough to follow me," he returned, his temper rising.

"But how else was I supposed to make certain that you were all right?"

He went quite still then. I would have sworn that even his pulse did not beat in that quiet moment. "Explain," he said finally, his voice quite low.

"As you pointed out, Roma camps can be dangerous places. I thought you meant to tear off and accuse Magda of something dreadful—something her menfolk would not stand for. To be honest, I would not have given a farthing for your chances if you hadn't known the language. As it was, you were really quite lucky, you know. Magda's family are very private, even for Gypsies. They don't mix very much with their own kind."

He was staring at me with an expression that would have been dull-witted on any other man. I waited while he gathered his thoughts and closed his mouth.

"Let me see if I understand you," he began slowly. "You went along because you thought you were on a mission of rescue?"

"Something like that. I mean, I doubt Val and I could have done much against a tribe of angry Roma, but we do know Magda's family. We could have vouched for you, that sort of thing. I rather think they feel they owe me something for taking care of Magda, which is utterly backward when you think about it, because they are the ones who turned her out without so much as a cook pot—Mr. Brisbane? Brisbane, are you quite all right? You look very queer."

He rose and went to the window. He was thinking, apparently something too electric to share. I shrugged and sucked another cachou, waiting for him to get hold of himself.

After a minute or so he resumed his chair. "Forgive me, my lady. I was simply struck by the irony."

"Irony?"

He waved a hand. "Never mind. I sent word to Mordecai about Mrs. Birch's observations. He wrote back this morning. He seems quite encouraged by her information and tells me that he hopes to have discovered the source of the poison within a few days. Then we shall be one step closer to finding our man."

"Our man. You still think the murderer a man?"

He shook his head slowly. "No. I meant the word figuratively. Poison is often a woman's weapon, and the method…it speaks of love gone wrong, does it not?"

I nodded slowly. "I suppose the brothel, then. Perhaps he had a relationship with a particular girl…"

Brisbane was watching me closely.

"Do not think that I enjoy this, Mr. Brisbane, but it is only logical."

"Yes. Especially when you know the purpose of the box."

He reached again into his pocket, this time producing the little porcelain box that was the source of so much trouble. It was rectangular, fitted with gilt or perhaps even gold fastenings. It was slim and elegantly proportioned, but the colours of Pandora's portrait were rather garish. Gilt, I decided finally.

He opened it, but it was empty. "Do you know what this is?"

I shrugged. "As you said before, a rather tacky souvenir of my husband's distasteful adventures."

He placed it carefully on the table. "It was designed to hold condoms—contraceptive sheaths."

I stared at the pretty, tawdry little box. "You mean that that actually—"

"Held the murder weapon. Yes. At least I am as certain as I can be. I intend to have Mordecai test it eventually. Perhaps traces of the poison remain."

The sweet cachou turned sour in my mouth. "Put it away. For God's sake."

He did, slipping it into his pocket.

"How did you persuade Jasper to get it from Magda?"

"I offered him money."

I lifted a brow at him. "Is that really all it took?"

"She had given it to him to pawn. It saved him a trip. My greatest trouble was persuading him that I only wanted the box. I almost had to take those bloody candlesticks as well."

I looked up at him and he was almost smiling. He knew I would not take offense at his language, and I think he was trying in some small way to put things right between us. I was still miserable, but not as bleakly so as I had been a moment before.

"I am sorry, you know. Clearly you meant to keep your Gypsy blood private and I blundered in where I had no right to be."

He waved an indifferent hand. "Perhaps I did not mean to

keep it so private as I thought I did." He paused, canting his head at my incredulity. "You're blinking at me like a rather curious owl."

"Forgive me. You seemed angry enough at me last night for discovering your secret."

"I was angry...for a variety of reasons. Not the least because I distrusted your motives. I thought you meant to take the box before I could retrieve it."

"Oh. Well, I hope you understand now that that was not my intention."

"I do." His gaze was firm and clear, no shadow of a headache, I thought now. "But you are quite correct. I told you where I intended to be. I opened myself to the possibility that you would find me speaking Romany."

"Quite fluently, I should say." I caught my breath, comprehension beginning to dawn. "Magda knew, didn't she? The first time she met you, she spoke Romany because she intended you to know that she had discovered your secret. She called you a posh rat."

Brisbane's eyes gleamed. "The word is *poshrat*," he corrected me, giving it the same inflection Magda had used. "It means half-breed. And yes, she knew me well enough for what I was. My mother's people all bear a strong resemblance to one another." His mouth twisted into a bitter little smile. "You will note that I do not resemble His Grace of Aberdour in any respect."

"Thank God for that! Is that why he looked at you so viciously when you played the violin?"

He nodded. "It reminds him too much of the wild little half-breed he took in. Especially when I play Romany music."

I felt my heart quicken. "The second piece?"

"Yes. Did you like it?"

"I did." I swallowed thickly. "I had never heard it before, but I should have known it for what it was. I heard enough Gypsy music as a child."

He waved a lazy hand. "So, you see? I must not have intended to keep my secret from you for very long."

His gaze narrowed and focused now, tightly upon my face, my eyes, and I began to feel flustered. I have seen the terrible excitement of chickens when a fox comes creeping too near the hen yard. I felt my feathers beginning to ruffle.

I cleared my throat primly. "You may be certain that I shall keep it."

"It does not matter. One of these days my great-uncle will get too old or too tipsy and that particular cat will come streaking out of the bag. And I will be finished in society."

"You do not know that." I felt suddenly argumentative. I did not like him like this, quiet and acquiescent. Combative and difficult was his normal manner. I had grown accustomed to it. "Many Jewish men are accepted in society. Why not a Roma?"

"The Jewish men in society all have a great deal of money that they are happy to lend to their impoverished peers."

"That is horribly cynical, Brisbane. But probably true," I admitted. "Still, you are only half a Gypsy. Half Scot as well."

He laughed. "Slim redemption, that. With the exception of the duke, all of my father's family still refer to me as 'Jack's filthy Gypsy bastard.' I doubt they would sponsor me should I lose my entrée into the best houses."

"Don't be self-pitying. It isn't becoming," I said sharply.

He shrugged again. "It is true. That they say it, I mean," he said with a grin. "Not that I am. My parents were married very properly some seven months before I was born."

"Your father was quite something else," I observed mildly.

"Quite," he agreed.

He seemed so reconciled to the thought that he might lose his standing, his reputation, that I had to ask, "Why do you pursue society clients, then, if you do not seem to mind about losing them?"

"Money, of course. The wealthy are able to pay far more for my services than the middle class. Why not take fewer, more lucrative investigations and leave myself more time for my own pursuits?"

I did not wish to probe too deeply into this. I had a vague notion that some of these pursuits might be unsavory.

"What will you do if the clients do not come?"

"What I did before. This and that. Do not mind about me, my lady. Like all cats, I land on my feet."

I started. I had so often thought of him as feline, that I wondered for one mad moment if he had read my thoughts.

"Ah, good. Well, I suppose we had best discuss the investigation and how we shall proceed."

"*We* shall not proceed, my lady," he said matter-of-factly. "I must do the rest alone." He raised a hand to stem my angry protest. "Listen, before you screech at me. You went to that camp last night because you feared for my safety. I shall not forget that. But in return, you must allow me to have a care for yours. The next step must be tracing this box to the person in the brothel who knew Sir Edward. You might have gotten away with your little masquerade in a dark Gypsy camp on a moonless night. But there is no possible way, I repeat, *no possible way* that you could do the same in a West End brothel. There are men there whose sole occupation is to beat and torture those who make trouble for the proprietors. Do not think they would scruple to hurt you if they discovered the truth about your identity."

"But you cannot—"

He sat forward sharply in his chair.

"This issue is not open to discussion," he said sternly. "You have assisted me as far as possible, but it must end now. I will report to you what I discover, but I will do this alone, are we quite in agreement?"

It really was not a question at all. He did not expect an

argument and I did not give him one. I nodded, dry-mouthed. He had let me off quite lightly from my faux pas of the previous evening. I should keep very quiet and be grateful, I supposed. Besides, there was Simon. I had a duty there, and Brisbane's insistence upon working alone would permit me to honour it.

I rose. "Then there is nothing more to discuss." I extended my hand and he touched it briefly before dropping it. He followed me to the door. I thought he had reached to open it, but he flattened his palm against the wood, keeping it closed. I did not turn, but I was conscious of him, just behind me, his breath stirring the hair at the base of my neck. I remembered what he had done the last time he was so close to me and I felt rather giddy, sick even.

"I was angry with you last night," he said softly, "but it was nothing, *nothing,* compared to what I will be if you interfere now."

I reached out and turned the knob sharply, forcing him to step back.

"Good day, Mr. Brisbane," I said, flinging my shawl over my shoulder.

He did not reply, but I felt his eyes boring mercilessly into my back all the way down the stairs.

Upon returning to Grey House I went directly to Simon. He was moving a little in his sleep, tossing under his embroidered coverlet. Desmond was sitting with him, sponging his brow from a basin of warm water laced with lavender.

I smiled as I entered and he rose, spilling a little of the water on the carpet. He started, blushing. With his Titian colouring, it was entirely charming. I thought of Portia's insistence that I take a lover and blushed a little myself.

"Do not mind that," I said softly as he bent to blot the water spots. "It will dry soon enough and the scent is pleasant." I beckoned him away from the bed. "How is he?"

"H-he was sleeping peacefully until perhaps a quarter of an hour ago, my lady. I asked Mr. Aquinas and he thought a bit of lavender water might ease h-his sleep."

His eyes were round with apprehension. He had seldom had cause to speak to me directly, but when he had, his speech had always been laced with a boyish stammer and the slightest lilt of a country drawl. I could not imagine how he had come to Mayfair.

"You have done quite well, I am sure. Did Doctor Griggs leave instructions about the next dose?"

"Oh, yes, my lady." He crept to the night table where he collected a piece of paper. There were a few directions given, but only general in nature.

"Blast, nothing about what to expect," I murmured.

The round blue eyes, anxious and wide, fixed on my face. "I beg your pardon, my lady?"

"Nothing. I suppose Aquinas has told you that Sir Simon's health is failing completely now?" He bowed his head, dropping his eyes to the carpet. "I doubt that your stay in the sickroom will be of any long duration," I said softly. "I simply want him comfortable. I will be here often myself. I see that you have left off your livery. I will tell Aquinas to have a bed made up here for you so that if he wakes, he will not be alone."

Desmond inclined his head further, assenting.

"You did well referring your question to Aquinas. You must not hesitate to tell him, or myself, if there is anything you think Sir Simon requires. You'd best go and have your supper now. I will sit with him."

He withdrew and I took his chair by the bed. I slipped my hand into Simon's. It was warm and damp with sleep, like a child's. After a while he opened his eyes and turned to me, blinking slowly.

"You were moaning. Are you in pain, dearest? I could give you some more laudanum."

He waved a hand. "No. I've had the most appalling dreams." He licked his lips and I poured out a glass of water. I held his head while he sipped. When he was done I laid him back against the pillows, settling him gently as an infant.

"Not long for it now, am I, Julia? No, don't look like that. I won't be brave and make speeches. I will be so glad to go."

I picked up Desmond's basin and began to sponge his brow, wiping it slowly.

"You are not afraid?"

His expression was dreamy. "How can I be? You should have learned by now, darling, it is life that holds all the terrors, not death." Something clouded his eyes then, and his hand tightened on the coverlet. "I used to be afraid of it. So afraid. I cannot think how it changed."

I wrung out the sponge and put it into a saucer.

"Perhaps because you have seen others pass."

"Edward," he said softly. I nodded. I resumed my seat and picked up his hand again.

"Perhaps it makes us brave when we have watched others."

He nodded slowly. "Perhaps. I was so terrified, I used to think I would do anything to save myself. But there is no way. I have come to know that, Julia." He was growing animated now, almost feverish, and I could hear the rattle beginning to sound in his chest. A few weeks, Doctor Griggs had said. I was beginning to think days, instead. "Do you remember the stories, the myths we used to read together as children?"

"Yes, of course. I always fancied myself as Artemis."

He gave me a feeble smile. "Is that why you always ran around with Benedick's castoff bow?"

"Of course. Lady of the Wild Things. I used to pretend my grandmother's moth-eaten old spaniel was my faithful hunting hound, don't you remember?"

This time he laughed, but I was sorry I made him. A painful

interlude followed, with much gasping and coughing. I gave him more water and persuaded him to let me order some broth from the kitchen. We talked of nothing in particular while we waited, and then I held the bowl as he spooned it into his mouth, spilling a little on the coverlet. After a very few sips he waved me away and patted his mouth with the napkin.

"The Fates," he said suddenly.

"I beg your pardon?" I resumed my seat.

His fingers were plucking at the damp patch on the coverlet, but his expression had grown dreamy again, perhaps an after-effect of the laudanum. "I was thinking of the Fates. When we used to read myths, they always frightened me. Those three old crones, spinning and measuring and cutting the thread of life. What were they called? Clotho spun, I remember that, and Lachesis measured, but the last…"

"Atropos," I supplied. He nodded.

"That is the one. Atropos. The cruelest Fate of all. There is no bribing her, you know. No putting her off when she decides you are done. Snip!"

His voice was growing loud and I half rose, but he shook his head at me, angrily I thought.

"What does it matter now? Let me shout a little, Julia. What harm will I do?"

I sighed. "None, I suppose. I feel perfectly helpless, you know. I keep thinking there is something I could do, should do, but there is nothing. Is there?"

But Simon could not give me absolution. He had retreated deep into himself and was brooding. Probably on the cruel Fates and their obsession with the men of his family. I rose and kissed him on the brow, smelling lavender and sweat.

"I will return later. I will send Desmond up to you now."

He heard me, his eyelids flickered, but he said nothing. He

was angry, and with good reason. His thirtieth birthday was two weeks away. He would not live to see it. I would have been angry, too.

THE THIRTY-SECOND CHAPTER

Mother, I cannot mind my wheel;
My fingers ache, my lips are dry;
Oh! If you felt the pain I feel!
But oh, who ever felt as I!
—Sappho

I spent the next two days sulking around Grey House. I worked on the household accounts, tidied the stillroom, read and wrote letters. Or at least I pretended to. The truth is, I often found myself staring at a book I did not remember picking up or writing such utter gibberish that in the end I tore the pages into tiny pieces and dropped them into the wastepaper basket. I was utterly useless, waiting for Brisbane to send a report and for Simon to expire. I went often to the sickroom, intending to read to Simon or simply sit with him, but he had settled into a routine with Desmond and seemed easier with him. I made Simon uncomfortable and, if I am honest, I was uncomfortable as well. Edward's death, while horrible, had the saving grace of being quick. Simon would not be so lucky. It was torture to watch him suffer, and I was craven. I made every excuse I could to avoid the sickroom, until my conscience prickled and I knew that I could put it off no longer. I always felt a guilty sense of release when I slipped out again, like a child on holiday from school.

To assuage my guilt I spent hours closeted with Cook, concocting menus that I thought might tempt him to eat. I needn't have bothered. He ate little, sometimes barely tasting the delicate morsels we sent up. Each day I saw the plates go by, often untouched, and each night I prayed to a God I no longer wholly believed in for Simon's deliverance. But he lived on and I added that to the score I had to settle with God.

To add insult to injury, it was at about this time that I was adopted. One morning, as I sat muttering obscenities over Cook's outrageously extravagant food accounts, I heard a sound from the floor. A distinctive, wholly unwelcome *quorking* sound. I edged around my desk and glanced down.

"Good Lord, how did you get loose?"

The raven looked up at me and cocked his head. "Good morning," he said, quite civilly.

"Yes, good morning to you, too, I suppose." He continued to regard me thoughtfully and I returned the favor. He was too big for me to wrestle back to Val's room were I so inclined. But even if his size was no deterrent, his beak and talons were. We enjoyed our impasse for some minutes, but at length I grew bored and returned to my accounts.

Immediately, the wide black wings whirred and the raven flapped up and settled himself on my desk. I froze, but he did not move again, apparently content to perch there, watching me. He was rather gentlemanly, all things considered. He did not disturb my papers or inkwell, keeping himself carefully out of my way. His round, shining eyes were focused steadily on my pen, watching with great interest as I made my sums.

After a minute, I opened a box of sugared plums and held one out to him.

"Are you hungry?"

He made a sound I had not heard before, something very like Aunt Hermia's sigh of pleasure whenever she is offered a box of violet creams. He plucked the plum from my fingertips and tore into it. It was not particularly pleasant to watch, but he seemed very contented.

"Sweeties," he said when he had finished.

"Hmm, yes, sweeties. Whatever shall we do with you?" I asked him rhetorically. Val had made no progress with his scheme to return him. I had scanned the newspapers every day, but there was no mention of a scandal regarding the Tower ravens. For all intents and purposes, I supposed the fellow belonged to us now.

Or perhaps to me, I thought with a flutter of alarm as he toddled across the desk. He lowered his head, bobbing it toward me. After a moment, I realized he expected something and I lifted a hand to scratch his handsome feathers.

"You are no better than a dog," I said repressively. But he was busy making his little *quork* and bobbing for more scratches on the head. When he was finished, he flapped down from the desk and busied himself inspecting the room. He walked the length of it, poking his shining head into the nooks and crannies, occasionally chattering at me. I responded, feeling rather stupid, but at least he said a word or two in return, which is certainly more than a dog would have done. By the time I had finished the accounts we were rather good friends and I was feeling a bit less bleak than I had before.

"You are a very companionable creature," I told him. "But you really ought to have a name. I suppose Hugi or Muni is too expected. I wonder what they called you."

He looked at me with gem-bright eyes, and for one mad moment I thought he was going to tell me. But he kept his secret and did not speak again for the rest of the afternoon.

To my delight, Portia called that evening. I nearly wept with relief. I greeted her warmly, too warmly, I suspect, for she pulled out of my embrace and looked at me suspiciously.

"Darling, do you feel quite yourself?"

I shook my head. "No, it's been quite dreadful, really. Simon is worse, nearly at the end, according to Griggs."

She divested herself of her hat and gloves and other trappings, heaping them in a bright, shifting pile of expensive, misty blue. She kept Puggy, settling him onto a purple fringed cushion as she took a chair. We began our usual duet.

"Oh, not that cushion, Portia. It's rather a favorite."

She gave me an injured little pout. "Puggy is very well behaved. What do you expect him to do to it?"

"Flatulate," I said plainly. "Or worse."

"Nonsense. You wouldn't do anything so frightfully common, would you, Puggy-Wuggy?"

She blew him kisses, which he ignored. "There, you see? He is a perfect lamb. Order up something decadent from the kitchen and have Aquinas open some champagne. We will be very naughty and you can weep out all your troubles and I will console you."

I did as she bade me. I ordered food—Cook sent hot, tiny, crispy prawns, bathed in sizzling butter. There were other scrumptious things as well, fruits and pastries, and when Aquinas brought the champagne, I noticed he was careful to bring the finest bottle in the cellar. He withdrew, tactfully closing the door behind him, and Portia and I happily commenced to a Lucullan feast. Or at least, Lucullan by our standards.

I told her everything as we ate. Well, nearly everything. If I am honest, it was nothing like everything. I gave her a carefully edited version of the truth, juggling secrets like so many conjurer's balls. In the first place, I did not reveal the secret of Brisbane's parentage. I simply skimmed rather neatly over Brisbane's retrieval of the box, telling her of his pugilistic endeavors at the Gypsy camp, but purposefully leaving out his fluent conversation with Jasper. Naturally I did not mention the kiss—if it could be called a kiss. That seemed a tepid, bloodless sort of word to describe what we had done. But it was private, and I could not bear the thought of recounting to her, chapter and verse, what it had been.

I also neglected to mention Magda's fatal grudge against Valerius. Portia inferred, because I heavily implied, that Magda's trouble had been with Edward and that the arsenic had been intended for him. She assumed that Magda neglected to use the poison before Edward died by another's hand and I did not correct her.

I also omitted the bloody shirts and Val's presence at Carolina's grave the night Magda was banished from her camp. I had not spoken to him myself yet, and I did not feel it quite sporting to spill his secrets to another member of the family. I owed it to him to hear his side of the story before I threw him to the wolves. Besides, I was desperately afraid Portia would run straight to Father, and that was a complication I could do without.

So I presented her with a bowdlerized version of events, stressing the tangle surrounding Edward's death and my own sadness at Simon's impending loss. Puggy snored, but Portia was very attentive.

She sympathized over Simon for a moment, then steered the conversation back to the investigation.

"You must keep yourself busy, Julia," she advised. "I know that Simon's passing will grieve you, but it comes as no shock. He has been unwell for so long, and surely it is a blessing in itself that he is shortly to find release."

I murmured something in agreement.

"So," she went on briskly, "you must have a thought to life after Grey House. You must bring this investigation to an end as quickly as possible and move on with your life."

I drained my glass, licking the last drops of champagne. Delicious. I poured another. "I know. I do have plans, you must believe me. I wish to travel, perhaps even to write a book. I thought of selling Grey House, as well. It's really far too big for me." I stared at the fizzy gold bubbles of the champagne racing one another to the top of my glass. "But I feel that if I do not know the truth about Edward, however painful, that I cannot move forward. Can you understand that?"

"Yes, of course." She popped a prawn into her mouth, then selected one for Puggy. "And what of Brisbane? Shall you see him again when all this is finished?"

I shook my head and immediately regretted it. Champagne always left me dangerously light-headed. "I do not see why I should. I mean, I think it highly unlikely. I would have no need of him in a professional capacity, and socially…"

I let the thought hang there unfinished. It was provocative, really, the notion of meeting Brisbane in a social setting, with none of the complications of an investigation. "No, I think our paths will not cross again."

"Pity. I think you rather like him."

My first instinct was to deny, but I realized the futility before I even said the words. Ever the elder sister, Portia liked to think that she understood me better than I knew myself. I merely smiled at her.

"What if I did? I have found him enigmatic and tempestuous. You yourself said he was too much of an adventure for the likes of me."

Portia snorted. On any other woman, it would have been vulgar. On her, it was roguishly charming.

"Too much for the little mouse you were then, creeping about in your blacks and greys. Look at you now," she said with a sweep of her hand toward my vivid violet gown and its daring neckline. "You've come quite a long way since then, my pet. All bold colours and alabaster décolletage. Too delicious. And as for Brisbane being enigmatic and—what was the other?"

"Tempestuous," I supplied, thinking of the faint black-plum bruise on my back, a bruise just the shape of his hand.

"Tempestuous. Most interesting qualities, Julia, and you would call them liabilities. Tell me, what did he look like at the Gypsy camp? Was he really naked to the waist?"

She leered at me over the top of her glass and I could hardly speak for laughing.

"Ninny. He looked like a man, what do you expect?"

"Descriptive details, please! It's been ages since I saw one, and I likely never will again, at least if Jane has anything to say in the matter. Now, reveal all!"

I settled back against the cushions and described in lurid detail.

"Goodness," she said when I had finished. "Are you certain you are not embellishing? You always were prone to exaggeration as a child."

I shrugged. "It is all in the eye of the beholder, is it not?"

She was thoughtful as she reached for a raspberry tart. There was a scratching sound at the door then and we exchanged looks of surprise.

"Another bottle already? Aquinas is a gem, Julia. Whatever you are paying him, double it instantly."

I rose. "It is not Aquinas. There would have been footsteps." I opened the door cautiously. No one. I stepped back and there was an odd ruffly sound from the floor.

"Ah, thought you would invite yourself to the party, did you?"

The raven made a whirring noise in his throat and toddled past me, grave as a judge in his little black robe.

Portia gave a little cry. "What the devil is that?"

I closed the door and resumed my seat. "A raven, and not just any raven, my dear. This gentleman happens to be one of Her Majesty's own."

Portia's eyes were enormous. She reached for Puggy protectively. "You don't mean it! Not a Tower raven…what on earth is he doing here? How?"

The bird was pecking comfortably at the lace-edged hem of her gown. I distracted him with a tart, waving it in front of his bright black eyes. "Val. He won him off of Reddy Phillips on a lucky hand at cards."

Portia, clutching Puggy to her bosom, leaned over and watched the raven, tearing daintily at the tart.

"He's rather handsome, but something of a macabre sort of pet, don't you think? Especially with a dying man in the house?"

"Don't be ghoulish," I said sharply. "Simon has not seen him, nor will he. It might upset him in his present circumstances."

Portia agreed, then tossed another tart to the bird.

"That's for me," he said pleasantly.

Portia's eyes rounded even more. "He speaks?"

I nodded. "Apparently Reddy took him for a jape, substituting another bird in its place. No one at the Tower seems to have noticed, which I find ridiculous. I mean, one would think that if one's job is the care and well-being of these creatures, one could have the diligence to tell them apart."

"One would," she agreed. "Do you mean to keep him, then?"

"I mean to give him back, only I don't quite know how. Reddy plagued us for a while, but I did not want to turn the bird over to him."

"Why ever not?" Portia's voice rose in exasperation, the perquisite of an older sister. "You want to be rid of him, who better to take him off your hands than the little half-wit who stole him in the first place?"

"I cannot explain it, except to say that I do not like Reddy Phillips. I did not wish to make it so easy for him."

Portia regarded the raven a moment longer. He had finished his little treat and was sitting, looking from one of us to the other, as if he understood each word perfectly.

"You know, I am not surprised Reddy has business with ravens," she said thoughtfully. "His elder brother was quite obsessed with them."

"Was he?" I was keeping a wary eye on the bird. He was eyeing Puggy a little too intently for my liking.

"Yes, you must remember Roland. I was obliged to dance with him sometimes during my Season thanks to Auntie."

We grimaced at each other. Aunt Hermia's rule that one must dance with any gentleman who asked was ironclad. She made exceptions only for the most outrageous cads. She had some notion that it would give us an opportunity to widen our acquaintance, but as we always tried and failed to make her understand, there was a reason we were not acquainted with such people in the first place.

"I remember him vaguely. Whatever became of him?"

"Dead. Married some thin, weedy girl from the Duke of Porthchester's family. She was only sixteen, if memory serves. Piles of money on his side, a lineage to the Norman Conquest on hers. Unhappy marriage, by all accounts." As always, I was deeply impressed with Portia's ability to remember the minutest details of other families' misfortunes. She was a walking catalog of gossip, and although I deplored it, secretly I was rather glad. It saved me the trouble of talking to people. "Roland was quite apparently indiscreet with his affairs. He was actually on his way to an assignation when there was an accident. Train, boat, carriage, I can't recall. Something to do with transportation. Anyway, I don't think the child-bride mourned him very long. She married some Continental, a count or some such creature, the next year. Not a farthing between them except for her jointure from Roland, but they seem quite happy."

I sipped at my champagne, wondering how differently my life might have turned out if Edward had left me a widow years earlier. Might I have found a Continental count to ease my widowhood? Portia was still talking, reminiscing about the Phillipses.

"He was a member of that awful club, do you remember? They formed it the year you made your debut. Fashioned themselves after Cousin Francis' Hellfire Club."

I preferred not to remember. Sir Francis Dashwood, a cousin on our father's side, had been the founder of the infamous Medmenham Club, often referred to by its more descriptive—and accurate—sobriquet, the Hellfire Club. The members had been notorious for their exploits, both in the bedchamber and in the chapels of the occult. In the years since its dissolution, a number of other reprobate youths had attempted to revive it, with varying success.

Portia was musing aloud. "What did they call themselves? Something very like it…Brimstone! Yes, that was it. The Brimstone Club. They had all of these nasty little rituals, deflowering virgins together, that sort of thing. And all of that superstitious nonsense! They used to drink out of virgins' skulls to cure diseases and things. You must remember—it was all the talk for the entire Season. Such speculation about who might belong. They were so secretive about their membership, no one ever knew for certain. Except for Roland Phillips—he went on and on about it. Of course, that family has never been one for discretion. Roland talked about how they always had ravens when they met, for effect, I suppose. His father bought that estate the other side of Basingstoke. They used the old folly there as a meeting place for the club, almost a ruin, I think it was. Very atmospheric and eerie. Tried to conjure the dead, I think."

I stared at her. "You are making all of that up. You are quite drunk. Give me the champagne."

She snatched up the bottle and held it out of my grasp. "I am not making it up. It was most entertaining. And profitable," she said with a wicked gleam in her eye. "I managed to blackmail Bellmont into giving me a tidy little sum of money by threatening to tell Adelaide he was a member."

"Never!" I did not imagine that Portia would scruple at a little good-natured extortion within the family. What shocked me was the idea that our eldest brother might actually have done something worth concealing.

"Do not let me shatter your illusions, dearest. Monty is lily-white, I promise. But you know what a Polly Puritan Adelaide is. If there had been a breath of scandal touching Monty she never would have married him. I thought it might be amusing to touch him for a little pocket money. Fool that he was, he paid me."

"Portia, that is disgraceful. How much?"

She flashed me a smile. "I shall never tell. Suffice it to say that my domination over him came to an end when he discovered me in a compromising position with Daphne Pascoe."

"No! I thought that Jane was…that is to say, I did not realize…" I struggled to find the proper vocabulary. My attempts at tact sent Portia off into gales of laughter.

"My poor sweet, my life does not fit very easily into the proper pattern, does it?"

I shook my head. "No. But then none of ours has."

She shifted Puggy comfortably on her lap. "Oh, I don't know about that. You did what we were supposed to. You married your childhood sweetheart, lived in a quiet house in a quiet street, going to quiet parties, wearing—"

"Yes, I have got that. Quiet clothes. How depressing you make it all sound. Well, I mean to make a proper scandal of myself just as soon as I have the chance. In fact, I may have already begun. I was quite thoroughly rude to Doctor Griggs this week."

Portia gave me a pitying look. "My precious pet, you must do considerably more than snub that old fusspot to atone for a decade of normalcy."

"It is a beginning," I replied mildly, thinking of all I had not told her. "At least it is a beginning."

THE THIRTY-THIRD CHAPTER

The proclamation made for May,
And sin no more, as we have done, by staying;
But, my Corinna, come, let's go a-Maying.
—Robert Herrick
"Corinna's Going A-Maying"

The next day Morag brought the early post with my tea. Propped against the silver teapot was an envelope, thick and creamy, covered with a deep black scroll of now-familiar handwriting. I slit the seal with my butter knife.

My lady,
I have met with the proprietress of the establishment in question. This lady, Miss Sally Simms, declined to offer any useful information on the grounds of client confidentiality. I was only able to confirm that the box had been in her possession at one time, and that items of that type are usually given as tokens of esteem to clients of note. She declined to say whether this touched Sir Edward, and suggested that it was possible that the box passed through many hands before coming into his possession through quite innocent means. I will pursue this matter further, but at present I am obliged to leave for Paris on a matter of business. I shall write again upon my return, which I anticipate will be in five or six days—certainly less than a week. In the meantime, I must em-

*phasize that you are not to involve yourself in this inves-
tigation in any capacity.*
Yours sincerely,
Nicholas Brisbane

Morag was bustling about the room, humming to herself.
I resisted the urge to crumple up the letter and throw it at her.
If I did not know his hand so well, I would have hardly
believed him the author of this missive. It was cool and
arrogant and pedantic—very like his manner when we first
met, but I had thought, hoped, that we had progressed beyond
this. I was thoroughly annoyed with him, not least for scam-
pering off to Paris when we clearly had unfinished business
in London. Sally Simms, indeed!

Pouting, I munched a piece of toast and considered my
course of action. I could maunder about the house as I had
been doing, or I could get out into the town and pay a few calls,
refreshing myself and keeping well out of trouble until
Brisbane's return. Irritated as I might be, I had no desire to call
down that temper on my head. I would wait patiently until his
return, then call upon him and sweetly press my case. I had
little doubt that his abrupt departure for Paris was due in large
part to his vexation with me. So be it. I would win back his
good favor by following his instructions, much as they chafed,
and clearing up a few little mysteries of my own. I would
confront Valerius at dinner and force him to tell me the truth
about his antics. And in the meantime, I would find out what
was in Madame de Bellefleur's mysterious, luscious rose
salve….

She received me with all the warmth and charm I had come
to expect, throwing open her arms and enfolding me like an
old friend.

"What a delicious surprise! I was perishing of loneliness,
and here you are, an angel of mercy," she said, tucking her arm

through mine. She took me into the little parlor with its lovely bee-strewn upholstery. She rang for Therese to bring cakes and a delicately scented citrus drink that was lusciously cool, perfect for the sultry warmth of the morning.

"What weather we are having," she commented as she handed me a plate stacked with tiny orange cakes. There was a candied violet sitting prettily on the top. "I was just telling Therese this morning how lovely it was going to be. Such heat for May Day!"

I looked at her, startled. "Is it May Day? How extraordinary. I had no idea."

She smiled at me. "It is much celebrated in the country, is it not? With ribbon poles and queens of the May?"

"Oh, yes. There are festivals and flowers—it is quite something. Somehow one loses track of that in town. I wish I had remembered, I would have brought you a basket of sweet peas. It is traditional to hang them on someone's doorknob and run away before they see you."

Her eyes were dancing. "How charming! Tell me more."

I did. I told her about bringing home hawthorn branches, and the morris dancers, and cricket matches, and found myself growing terribly homesick for the countryside. Abruptly I changed the subject.

"This drink is quite delicious, Madame. You must tell me how it is made."

She wagged an elegant finger at me. "It was Fleur, do you not remember? The drink is very simple. I will write it out for you later. One of my little receipts."

I fetched the little pot from my reticule. "This is all I have left of the last concoction you shared with me. My maid attempted to re-create it, but I am afraid she lacks your skill. The most she managed was a pale pink syrup."

Fleur laughed and clasped her hands together. "Then you shall have more. I am always so happy to share."

And I believed she was. I could see the genuine pleasure she got from giving to me, and I wondered if it was because she had rather made a living out of receiving. Accepting the jewels and bibelots and money of her admirers must be rather tiring after a while, I reflected. It must satisfy some primitive, nurturing side of her to be able to give something instead.

"You are pensive," she said suddenly. "Forgive me for prying, but I think you are thinking too much."

I smiled at her. "Yes, I am thinking rather too much. I wondered if you had heard from Brisbane."

She nodded, her sleek dark head barely touched with silver in the strong morning light. "Yes, he goes to Paris today. I am very wicked. I know he goes on business, but I still say to him, 'Nicky, please go to Guerlain and get my favorite perfume, and then I must have some chocolate and ribbons and fans and stockings…'" She trailed off with a laugh. "I am too awful to him, but he is very good to me, and I do so love my little treasures from my home."

I hesitated, taking another sip of the citrus drink to smooth the way. "Fleur, I know about his past. About his being Gypsy, I mean."

She lifted a delicately plucked brow. "Indeed? Did he tell you?"

"Not precisely." I thought it likely he had told Fleur himself. I could picture him, sleepy and warm, tangled with her in a twist of heavy, crested linen sheets, murmuring confidences he would never share with me. Ruthlessly, I dragged my imagination back to its proper place. "You see, I followed him—it was during the course of the investigation," I said hurriedly. "No, don't look at me like that. I did not mean to pry, truly I did not. I thought he was in danger, but then…"

She smiled, the brief shadow of disapproval dispelled.

"I understand. He is very stubborn, you know, stupidly so. I imagine he did not take it very well when you learned his secret."

I pushed away the memory of the rough tree bark digging into my back, his fingers twisting into my hair…it had been a worthy distraction. Had it been a tactic, a stratagem to lure me from the discovery I had just made?

I wrenched my mind back to Fleur and the question she had put to me.

"No. He was quite angry at the time. We made it up after a fashion, but I know he is still put out with me."

She shrugged. "Men are prideful creatures and Nicholas is prouder than most. He will forgive you before he forgives himself."

"Perhaps. I tried to make him understand that it does not matter, not a bit, but I know he thinks that it does."

Fleur leaned forward, focusing her eyes so intently on mine that I began to wonder if she practiced mesmerism.

"But it does matter. Not to me, and not to you, but we are enlightened women, my dear. We judge him by the man he has become, not the child he was, and not the blood he bears. But there will always be those…" She paused, shivering slightly. "I remember one time, in Buda-Pesth, it was quite horrible, my dear. I truly thought he was going to be killed. He made the mistake of saying something in Romany to the wrong person, a powerful person with friends, and with a grudge against his kind. I do not think Nicky would have told me about himself if it were not for this man. But he needed help to get out of the city. He turned to me, I turned to my husband, and together we managed to smuggle him to safety."

I was staring at her, stupefied. It sounded like something out of a picaresque novel. She gave me her little enigmatic smile.

"I know, it sounds fantastic. But that is how it ended, between Nicky and me. He fled for his life and I owed his salvation to my husband. I was so grateful to Serge, he risked so much to save Nicholas, just to make me happy. Do not worry,

I repaid him amply," she said, falling into a fit of warm, honeyed laughter. "So much has changed since then, but so much is still the same. Nicky is proud. No matter what he says about not caring, he does. Those little thorn pricks hurt—sometimes more than the sword."

I nodded, remembering his bitter words about the taunts of his cousins. "I think you are right. I know it was difficult for him as a child, and is still so with his family. He told me he is not angry that I discovered his birth. Perhaps he is growing more comfortable with it."

"Perhaps. He is more than thirty-five now. Men begin to change then, to grow more serious, more wise about the things that matter."

"You are right, I am sure. He said he does not care if the truth comes out and he is finished in society. He said he merely cultivates respectability because it brings him more lucrative business."

Again that sweet, warm laugh. "That sounds like Nicky. A bit of a pirate at heart, no?"

I grinned at her. "More than a bit, I should think." I felt my smile fade as I thought of something else I had long wanted to ask her. "Fleur, when Brisbane came here to you to convalesce—that is, I wondered if his health—I mean, his headaches…"

She gave me a pitying look, understanding, I think, what I was trying to ask and why I wanted to know.

"I only ask because he seems to suffer so, and his man, Monk, said he has been to doctors. His remedies are unorthodox, dangerous, I fear. I hoped something could be done for him. Please do not tell him I spoke to Monk. He does not know. I just thought that if I knew more about them, if we could discover the cause, perhaps I could help," I finished lamely.

"My poor child, you really do not know?" Her eyes were

warm, pitying, the same expression I had seen in Father's eyes when I was nine years old and he had to tell me that my favorite cat had been struck by a cart. "There is no help for Nicky because he does not wish it. He knows perfectly well what causes them."

I put down my glass, careful not to shatter it although my hands were shaking. "He knows what causes them? Then why does he not take steps? Surely something can be done."

She was shaking her head, resigned. "No, for Nicky the cost is too high. To fight the headaches would mean embracing what he truly is, and this he cannot do."

"Fleur, you mystify me. Stop speaking in riddles!" I demanded, angry and a little frightened now.

Her eyes were fixed on my face, still pitying, but now I found it condescending rather than kind. I was growing tired of Fleur and her enigmatic conversation.

"It is very simple, my dear. Nicky has the second sight."

Out of kindness I did not laugh. But I did smile.

"Fleur, surely you are jesting."

Her face was composed and serious. "I am not. Nicholas has the sight. He comes from a long line of Roma with the same gift. Or curse, as he calls it."

I shook my head. "I cannot believe it. The second sight! That is a fairy story for children. Surely you do not believe it."

"But I do. I was as disbelieving as you at first," she assured me, "but there is no other explanation." She hesitated, weighing her words. "I will tell you the truth now, my dear, about why Nicky had to leave Buda-Pesth. It was not because he spoke Romany in front of someone he oughtn't. The truth is much worse. There was a child, a little boy, perhaps five years old. His father was a very important man, a count—very wealthy, very well connected. The boy disappeared one day when he was in the park with his nurse. She looked away for a few minutes, and *poof*—" she snapped her fingers "—he was gone. The father was in agonies, he drew upon all of his influential friends. The entire city was searched, but they did not find him. Two days went by and still he was not found. That night Nicky had a dream, a terrible dream. He woke screaming, bathed in sweat—he was wild-eyed, like a child waking from a nightmare. He did not even know what he was screaming."

My mouth had gone dry, but my palms were wet. "What was he screaming?"

It might have been a trick of the light, but for a moment her face fell and I could see every one of her sixty years. "He was screaming, 'No, Father, don't let him kill me.' He was screaming in a child's voice, you see."

"A nightmare," I said firmly. "It proves nothing. Anyone might have dreamed it."

Fleur went on, her voice flat now. She told the rest of the story plainly, without emotion. "Nicholas was getting by in Hungary with his excellent French and a bit of German. He never bothered to learn Hungarian," she said, watching me closely.

I swallowed hard. "And that night—"

"He spoke perfect Hungarian. In the voice of a child," she said softly. "When he woke, he was able to give a perfect description of where the boy had been taken—a place he had never been and did not know existed."

We were silent a moment. "That is extraordinary," I managed finally. She smiled thinly.

"That is not all. His description was a child's as well. He told of what a child would see, what a child would remember. It was as if he *was* that child. When they followed the directions he gave them, they found the boy. He had been murdered, savagely, at the hands of a madman. And the first person they suspected—"

"Nicholas," I breathed.

She gave a Gallic, offhand little shrug. "Of course. It was only logical. Who else could have known where the child would be found but the man who put him there? It was all I could do to get him out of the city before they came for him. It was another fortnight before the true murderer was discovered in the act of attempting to take another child. It was proved beyond doubt that he killed the first boy. He even confessed to it before his execution."

"They might have hanged him," I commented softly.

Fleur shook her head, her expression profoundly sad. "It was not that which nearly destroyed him. It was the dream itself. It was real to him, as real as if he had lived it. He *did* live it. He was as terrified, as tormented as that boy had been. He told me that he had had such dreams, sometimes while sleeping, sometimes awake, for many years. He had tried to control them, to push them away. He took things—sometimes to make him sleep too deeply for the dreams, sometimes to keep him wakeful for days at a time. He always felt them coming on, often days in advance, he told me, like storm clouds gathering in his brain. Sometimes he was successful in keeping them at bay. But there were other times…the dreams were simply too strong. And when he was fighting them, pushing them down, the headaches would come. Solomon's choice, no? The vicious headaches, or the horrible dreams. He hates those dreams. They are a legacy of his Gypsy blood. His mother's people are famous for them. Perhaps that reason, more than any other, is why he has turned his back on his own kind."

I sat, feeling limp and exhausted by her story. I could not imagine what it must be like to live such a life, seizing any means of escaping from one's own mind…like a wounded animal gnawing at a trapped leg.

"That was what was wrong with him, when he came to you. He was recovering from one of those dreams."

She nodded. "It was. He had tried desperately to keep one of those visions at bay."

"Was he successful?"

"Not entirely. He saw enough to frighten him deeply." Her eyes were guarded. Much as she appeared to enjoy my company, her loyalty was with Brisbane. I do not think she would have told me the full truth, not even then, had I not already known. She must have seen the fear in my face, for I knew I could not mask it. I did not want to ask her, but I did.

"What did he dream of?" I asked in a thin, bloodless voice.

"My dear…" She stretched out her hand and touched mine. "He dreamed of you."

THE THIRTY-FOURTH CHAPTER

Though this be madness, yet there is method in it.
—William Shakespeare
Hamlet

She could tell me nothing more. When she had asked him about the dream, Nicholas had murmured my name. That was all. Whether I was in peril or simply a bystander in his vision, she could not say.

I was not comforted. The details she had given me about his time in Hungary left me chilled and nervous. In spite of myself, I cast glances over my shoulder as I returned to Grey House. No one lurked there, but I felt better when the door was shut and I was safely locked behind my own door once more.

Fleur had apologized of course. She had not meant to alarm me. She pointed to Brisbane's absence and insisted that he would never have left London if he believed I was in any true danger.

This did not ease my mind. I thought of what he had told me when we began our investigation. He had warned me of the danger, but I had not heeded him. I had thought it all a marvelous game, a parlor trick to winkle out a murderer before he guessed I was on his trail.

I had been very, very stupid. I could see it now. I had confided in a few trusted souls. But should I? Were they worthy of my trust? Or were they simply waiting for that perfect moment when my attention faltered to give me a gentle nudge down a steep staircase? An innocent glove, laced with poison…a box of chocolates, envenomed with a pin… I sat in my study, torturing myself for the better part of an hour before I came to my senses. Honestly. I was no better than that stupid girl in *Northanger Abbey,* seeing danger behind every bush, villains behind every door. The only thing to do, in spite of Brisbane's warning, was to proceed with the investigation. The sooner the murderer was unmasked, the sooner the danger would be past.

Resolute, I pulled out a little notebook, wrote down everything, laying out all of the clues we had discovered, noting each of the developments that had led us to this point, and the blind alleys that had led us nowhere. I wrote tirelessly, knowing that if I just put it all down, somehow, something would leap off the page at me.

And there it was. So simple I could not believe it had not occurred to me or to Brisbane before. The Psalter. We knew the text of the message I had found because it was still in our possession. But what of the others? They, too, had been scissored from the holy book. Was there a reason those particular passages had been chosen? The scripture we had seen referred to wickedness. Were the others more specific? Did they point to a particular wrong that Edward had committed against the sender?

Fired with new enthusiasm, I fetched the ruined Psalter and an old Bible from the bookshelves. Comparing them carefully, I noted down the exact verses that had been fashioned into threats for Edward. There were eight of them altogether, including the last, the one I had found hidden away in Edward's desk. I wrote them out onto a single sheet of paper and studied them.

The first was a warning, it seemed.

The face of the Lord is against them that do evil, to cut off the remembrance of them from the earth.

The second was much in the same vein.

For lo, they that are far from thee shall perish; thou hast destroyed all them that go whoring from thee.

Three and four were grimmer.

God shall likewise destroy thee forever, he shall take thee away, and pluck thee out of thy dwelling place, and root thee out of the land of the living.

Let death seize upon them, and let them go down quick into hell; for wickedness is in their dwellings, and among them.

Five and six continued, more vicious than the ones before.

But thou, O God, shalt bring them down into the pit of destruction; bloody and deceitful men shall not live out half their days, but I will trust in thee.

As smoke is driven away, so drive them away; as wax melteth before the fire, so let the wicked perish in the presence of God.

I hardly had the stomach to read the last two.

But the wicked shall perish, and the enemies of the Lord shall be as the fat of lambs; they shall consume; into the smoke shall they consume away.

Let me not be ashamed, O Lord; for I have called upon thee; let the wicked be ashamed, and let them be silent in the grave.

I sat back, the words running like mad squirrels through my mind. So much talk of wickedness and destruction. Clearly the sender was accusing Edward of some evil, but what? There was talk of shame and deceit and destruction by fire, all vague enough. But there was one word that caught my eye. *Whoring.* Was it significant that the sender had chosen this verse, perhaps the only one in the entire Psalter to contain that particular word? If so, it pointed very clearly in one direction. The brothel.

The one place that I could not investigate while Brisbane was out of town. I cursed him inwardly, as well as my own inability to get the information I required for myself. I could again assume a disguise and attempt to go myself, but I had taken Brisbane's warning to heart. I felt, with some appalling certainty, that Brisbane would have had far more experience with such places than I. If he said there were thugs outside whose sole purpose was to inflict torture on the curious and the unruly, I had little doubt there were. I did not need to see them for myself. What I needed was a man. And I knew precisely where to find one.

THE THIRTY-FIFTH CHAPTER

Many will swoon when they do look on blood.
—William Shakespeare
As You Like It

"Absolutely not," Valerius said when I presented my plan to him. "You must be barking mad."

"I am not. I simply want you to go to Pandora's Box and ask a few questions for me. Surely that is not too much to ask."

"But it is! Putting aside for just a moment the wild impropriety of what you are asking, it is dangerous."

I sighed and pushed away my dessert plate. I had not expected him to be so difficult. I had presented him with a definite plan, beautifully conceived and completely financed by me. All that was required of Val was a little pretense. He had only to present himself at the brothel and request the company of a young lady. Once in private, he could ply her with a handsome gift of money to answer a few questions I would provide. It all seemed quite uncomplicated to me. He need not even scruple to undress the poor girl. She would earn her fee for nothing more strenuous than a little conversation, and the proprietress need never know. I pointed all of this out to Valerius. He said nothing, but sat, contemplating his pudding.

"I cannot," he said finally. His eyes did not meet mine. "I

wish I could oblige you, but I cannot, Julia. Please do not ask me."

"No, no, of course," I said, my voice chill with anger. "I have asked too much of you. A few questions of a poor prostitute, that was all. But there are other questions, you know, Valerius. Questions that I could ask you. Questions about the night you came home with a bloody shirt and a feeble explanation. Oh, I believed it the first time. But not the second."

He had gone very white, his lips bloodless where they pressed tightly together. He said nothing, and I went on, keeping my voice low and smooth.

"I did not ask, Valerius, even though I realized then that there were many such nights, many such shirts. And I did not ask about Magda, even when I found arsenic in her room and she admitted that she wanted to poison you—even then I did not ask."

He started, his complexion draining to white. "What? What do you mean about Magda?"

I took a sip of my wine. "She kept arsenic in her room. She meant to kill you with it because of what you had done to Carolina."

"Carolina! You cannot think I had anything to do with that awful business!"

I did not listen to his words. I had expected a denial. Instead I watched his skin, observing the warm flush of colour into his pale cheeks, the wildness of those lovely eyes. I had always known when Valerius was lying as a child. His neck would grow spotted red, even to the tips of his ears. But now, as his natural colour came flooding back, it did not deepen. His neck and ears were pale and unblemished.

"She said that you…" I paused. Had she ever named him? I thought back on our conversation. Had either of us?

Val leaned forward, earnest but not pleading. "I promise you, Julia, I had nothing to do with Carolina's exhumation. What I have done is terrible enough, but never that."

I looked at him sharply. "Valerius, we must have truth between us. Tell me. All of it."

He nodded, and I saw a gravity in his face I had not seen before. For the first time, I saw the man and not the child.

"I cannot go to Pandora's Box for you, because I am too familiar there. They know me."

I took another sip of wine, rough against my dry throat. "Go on."

"You know that Father will not permit me to open my own practice. You cannot imagine what that means, to be denied the chance to do the only thing that I can do well. And I can do it. I could be a very fine physician, Julia."

He spoke quietly, without pleading. I gave him credit for that much. There was no petulance in his tone, only the sober dignity of a grown man.

"Are you saying that you do not patronize this place as a client? That you are their physician?" I tried to mask the incredulity in my voice, but I heard it, and so did he.

He smiled faintly. "Julia, if you could but see them, you would understand why I am not tempted. They are pitiful creatures, most of them. Pretty enough, for a few years, when they are young, before disease and rough trade coarsen them. That life ages them quickly. And there are so few people like Aunt Hermia who care to help them. She gives aid to those who have already left the trade. I do what I can for those still in it. I spend a few days each week at Pandora's Box, administering treatment to their prostitutes and to those from the other brothels run by the same owner. Sometimes I am called in the evenings, if there is an emergency. The proprietress pays for their medical care, but I give the money to Aunt Hermia for her mission. It is all I can do."

He paused, gauging my reaction. I did not give him one, for I did not yet know what to think.

"Does Aunt Hermia know?"

He turned his wineglass around in his hands, strong, capable hands—a healer's hands.

"No. She thinks I am lucky at cards."

"Probably best not to tell her. She would enlist you to physic the penitents at the refuge."

Val smiled sadly. "I would have liked that, being open and aboveboard about the whole thing. Believe me, Julia, I never meant for it to come to this. I did not intend to deceive Father. I was offered the chance to work and I took it. I know it was stupid and rash, but I knew better than to ask Father. He would never have agreed."

"Better to ask for forgiveness than permission," I said quietly.

He continued to roll the wineglass in his palms, watching the wine turn through shadow and light, changing colour with the reflection of the candles.

"We've always found that the best way to handle Father, haven't we?"

"I suppose. But what of the prostitutes? What do you do for them?"

The wineglass rolled to a halt, then resumed its slow revolution. "Whatever I must. Sometimes the men are rough and there are bruises, even broken bones to treat. Many of them are diseased, and must be dosed for it. Some are pregnant, and must not be."

I held very still. "Abortions," I said flatly.

He nodded.

"Oh, Valerius, how could you?"

It was a question, not an accusation, and he knew it.

"Because someone will if I do not, and likely it will be a drunken, ham-fisted old butcher who would perforate their wombs and kill them. At least if I do it, they don't die."

"No, they live to go out and get pregnant again!" I hurled at him before I could stop myself. I held up my hand before he could reproach me. "I am sorry. That was unkind."

He shook his head. "No. It was true. That is the most difficult part, you know. Trying so hard to save them from themselves—healing the bruises and stitching up the wounds, hoping that this time, just perhaps this time, they will gather up whatever shreds of human dignity remain to them and leave while they still can. I always thought Aunt Hermia was daft for caring so much what became of her charges. I remember her coming home, weeping or creating a ferocious row with Father because one of her penitents went back on the game. I never understood why she couldn't simply shrug and go on. There are so many of them to save. And yet I find myself doing just the same. I remember the faces and the names and the stories of every girl I have ever seen in that brothel. Sometimes one of them does not come back and I pretend it is because she's gotten away. More likely it is because she died, or failed to please and was sold to a cheaper, rougher sort of place. And I always hope, when one of them comes to me because she is with child that this time will be her last—that she will listen and learn. I do my best to educate them, to help them prevent it from happening again."

"Are you successful?"

There was that faint, heartbreaking smile again. "Once in a while there is a girl young enough to listen. And I hope that she will remember what I have taught her. And one day, if she leaves the game and marries and settles down to a respectable life, she will be able to have children, unlike many of her sisters."

"Oh, Valerius. Why this? Why not the workhouses? Or the orphanages?"

The smile fell from his lips and his expression was one of raw, unblunted grief.

"Because of Mother."

"Because she died in childbed?"

"Because I killed her," he said very quietly.

"Don't be stupid," I told him sharply. "You were an infant. It was hardly your fault."

He shrugged. "I know that now. But there was a maid at the Abbey, one of the local girls who worked in the nursery. She always used to look at me slyly and whisper to me how much everyone loved the countess, and how she had died because of me."

"That was stupid and cruel—backstairs gossip, and completely untrue."

"But you believed it," he said softly.

"I was six years old! I also believed in fairy rings and wishes on clovers. As you say, I know better now."

He nodded. "Well, when I began to study medicine, I wanted to know—everything. All about birth and why some women, with no medical care at all, can have a child as easily as breathing and why others, even with the best doctors, die from it."

"You were her tenth child in sixteen years," I pointed out. "Perhaps she was simply exhausted. In that case, blame Father."

"I did, for a while, once I stopped blaming myself," he said blandly. "But I did not much like that, so I decided to blame God."

"When did you stop doing that?"

"Oh, I haven't. It's rather easy to blame someone you don't have to see over Sunday dinner."

"Yes, well, I shan't criticize you on that score. I have been guilty of it myself."

We were silent for a while. Val rose and went to the sideboard, pouring us each a glass of port. Usually, I did not drink it as it was a gentleman's drink, but this was a vintage Aquinas had selected, rich and dark, and it suited my mood to be a little rebellious.

"So that is my truth," he said finally. "What is yours?"

I told him. This time, unlike my narrative to Portia, I neglected nothing. I even told him the truth about Brisbane's indisposition and his Gypsy blood, warning him strictly against sharing either snippet of information with anyone.

When I had finished, he poured us each a second glass of port.

"We must have been utter dolts not to have seen it before," he commented. "And even when I saw him speaking Romany I never made the connection. It was all so fast, and then he started to chase you over the Heath, and then—"

He broke off and I let my eyes slide away. Val and I had shared many confidences this evening, but there were some things I was still unwilling to discuss. I cast around for a new subject.

"Val, did you ever see Edward at Pandora's Box?"

He hesitated, then nodded. "I did. In fact, he was the one who brought me to the place. Miss Simms, the proprietress, had complained to him about the difficulty of finding a physician who was willing to treat prostitutes and would be discreet about the business. He thought of me and asked me to accompany him to meet Miss Simms. I thought he was a benefactor," he explained quickly. "I did not realize he was a patron. I suppose I must have known, but I did not want to think about him betraying you. So, I convinced myself he was simply there to see to their well-being. As I was."

"Perhaps he was, at first," I said with a shrug. "It seems a pointless sort of thing to gnaw one's heart out over now." It sounded convincing at least, to my ears, anyway.

"I think you are quite correct," he went on. "The verses about whoring probably refer to his visits to the Box. But if Brisbane got nothing from Miss Simms, I will not either, I can promise you that. She is hard as nails and twice as sharp. But there might be others…"

He trailed off and I put my hand on his. "Try, Val. Please."

He nodded. "I have a case there, a girl with a broken arm I set just yesterday. She's started a fever and I wanted to look in on her. I suppose I could ask a few questions—but I must be discreet, so discreet that I may not even be able to discover what you wish to know. I cannot jeopardize the trust I have gained, you understand?"

"Yes, of course. Thank you."

He rose and so did I. For the first time since we were children, he enfolded me into an embrace. And since this time he was not attempting to toss spiders down my dress, I rather enjoyed it.

I went to Simon's room after Val left, thinking to read to him for a little while. But he was sleeping quietly, with Desmond sitting nearby. I smiled at the boy.

"How has he been this evening?"

He rose noiselessly. "The doctor was here earlier, my lady. He said that Sir Simon had rallied a little. His temperature is down and his pulse a bit stronger."

"Really? Well, so long as he is comfortable, that is the important thing," I said, watching as Simon moved a little in his sleep. "Is he warm enough?"

"Oh, yes, my lady. Doctor Griggs gave very specific instructions as to his care."

His face was troubled and I hastened to soothe him. "I am certain you are doing an excellent job, Desmond. I know it is not the most rewarding of tasks, but it is an important one, and you have the family's thanks."

For a moment he blushed deeply, his eyes downcast. His shyness was almost palpable. Before I could speak again to reassure him, he gathered hold of himself, dipping his head in a bob of respect. "Thank you, my lady. I have done my best."

I smiled again and slipped out, thankful that there was at least one situation I had left in capable hands. I was not so certain about Val.

I need not have worried on that score. Val did not return to Grey House until very late, but I had left the light in my room burning, a signal to him that I had not yet retired. He scratched at the door and I called to him softly to enter.

He gave me a tired little grin. "Success."

I patted the edge of my bed and he sat next to me so that we could talk without disturbing anyone. The last thing I wanted was Morag bustling in, asking pointed questions.

"You cannot imagine how simple it was," he said, marveling. "I was about to knock at Miss Simms' office, as I do every time, to let her know that I have arrived. Just as I raised my hand to knock, I heard her speaking sharply to one of the girls, warning her that a man had been about the place asking questions about Sir Edward Grey and that she was to tell nothing of what she knew."

"Brisbane," I said excitedly.

Val nodded. "Simms threatened her with a beating if she talked. The girl swore that she would never reveal anything, then Miss Simms dismissed her."

"But if she promised—" Val's smile cut me off.

"A promise to Miss Simms is a promise to the devil. All I had to do was offer the girl, Cass is her name, some coin. Although she hates Miss Simms enough that I think she might well have told me everything simply for spite."

"What did you discover?"

"Not everything. She confirmed that she often saw Sir Edward and spoke to him. And when I explained to her that his widow had questions, she asked to speak with you directly."

I stared at him. "Surely you told her no."

"I did not," he stated roundly. "You want answers and Cass is willing to give them to you."

"Val, I appreciate this Cassandra's—"

"Cassiopeia," he put in.

"I beg your pardon?"

"Cassiopeia. All the girls are given a *nom de guerre,* for lack

445

of a better phrase, from Greek mythology. To carry out the Pandora theme."

"Yes, well, that is commendably thorough. All the same, I do not think it at all suitable that I should meet this person."

But even as I said the words, I regretted them. Val risked his good name and his personal safety to give these squashed blossoms medical treatment. Aunt Hermia provided a refuge for those willing to give up the game and live a more conventional life. And Morag herself, well, it was best not to dwell on Morag. But I could not be happy instructing Val to do that which I could not. I had been attempting to prove myself a worthy partner in this investigation from the very beginning. It was time to show my mettle.

"I am sorry. Of course I shall meet with her. Have you made the arrangements?"

Val did not disappoint me. Knowing the impossibility of meeting either at my home or her place of business, Val had arranged a rendezvous in the Park for the next morning. He had provided Cass with enough money to procure herself a bit of incognita, and he had told her I would be thickly veiled and wearing black. He promised to escort me himself, in spite of Cass' warning that she would speak only to me.

"You have done rather well for your first foray into investigation," I told him.

He smiled wearily. "Is it? You have forgotten the Heath."

I felt myself flush, remembering the way that adventure had concluded. "You had best go to bed now," I said in my best bossy-elder-sister voice. "We must be out early to catch our little bird in the Park."

He left me and I retired, but sleep came slowly. Val's reminder of the adventure on the Heath had caused me to think of Brisbane. I wondered what he was about in Paris. I remembered his cool detachment, his thinly veiled anger the last time we met. I thought of Fleur, and her elegant, dazzling charms, how he confided in her so willingly and turned to her in times of trouble. And by the time I finally dropped off to sleep, I was fairly certain that he thought of me not at all.

THE THIRTY-SIXTH CHAPTER

When sorrows come, they come not single spies,
But in battalions.
—William Shakespeare
Hamlet

The next morning I would have just as soon stayed abed. A chill, nasty wind had blown up, with a dark canopy of gray cloud that threatened rain. If I had looked to the weather for a portent, I would have been highly disappointed. But Cass, the obliging young inmate of Pandora's Box, proved more informative than I had dared to hope.

She found me, almost as soon as I entered the Park, Val pacing discreetly behind me. She was dressed as a flower girl in a worn coat of threadbare green velvet and a straw hat wreathed in yellow blossoms. She approached me, calling her wares and offering me a fistful of lavender.

"Good morning, your ladyship," she said, smiling broadly. Her accent was the commonest sort of London speech, at times almost unintelligible. But her face was roundly attractive. She had a charming, winsome manner and a smile that seemed to illuminate her entire face. Her colour was high, and I wondered if she found the whole exercise to be some sort of grand enterprise.

"Good morning," I returned civilly. "Are you Cassiopeia?"

She smiled, revealing rather good teeth. "That's what they call me at the Box. My real name is Victoria, just like the queen. Vicky, they called me at home."

"What shall I call you?"

"Oh, Lord, I don't care, my lady. Whatever you likes."

"Very well, then, Victoria."

She snickered, not unkindly, and I realized that probably no one in her short, chaotic life had ever addressed her by her proper Christian name.

"Victoria, my brother, Mr. March, tells me that you have some information for me."

She nodded, her expression dark. "I do. I've no call to keep my word to that Sally Simms. She's kept back my wages twice this month for nothing. I do my job, my gentlemen are all quite happy."

"Hmm. Yes. Suppose we walk for a bit and I will ask you a few questions."

She nodded, moving down the path that I indicated. The Park was quiet. It was too early and too chill for most visitors, but I did not like being so near Rotten Row. The path wound us in the opposite direction, away from the faint noise of the streets and farther into the dark gloom of the sheltering plane trees.

She shivered a little in her thin coat.

"Are you warm enough, Victoria?"

She nodded. "I don't much like trees. I always fancy they look like giants, with great big arms waving about."

"I presume you are not country-bred then?"

She puffed with pride. "I am a proper Cockney. Of course I don't get home to my mam very much on account of Miss High-and-Mighty Simms working me all the time. I had to feed her a tale this morning about my mam being sick to get out of the Box. But she was good enough about it. Sent for a hackney to bring me. The driver seems a good sort. I'll give him a copper and he will never tell he didn't take me to mam's."

I was shocked. I knew that the prostitutes lived in the brothel, but they could not be prisoners, could they?

"Surely she does not hold you there against your will?"

The girl laughed, a dry, grating sound so unlike Fleur's gentle bells. "Bless you, no, my lady. It's just that Simms makes us sign a little book telling where we're going and when we'll be back. She had a few girls disappear on her, pinched away to other houses, and she doesn't mean to lose any others. And some girls will fix a plan to meet with one of the gentlemen outside the Box, to keep the money for themselves. But I've never thought that was worth my trouble."

"Indeed?"

"Not at all. What's a girl supposed to do if a gentleman won't pay after he's had his fun, or turns nasty-like, if there's no Tommy about?" she asked reasonably. I nodded, remembering what Brisbane had told me about the men who committed cheerful violence to keep customers and prostitutes in line at the Box. Doubtless these were the Tommies.

"Besides," she went on blithely, "I like clean sheets for my business and a bit of a wash in between. Some gentlemen are none too fresh, if you take my meaning."

"Oh, dear," I murmured. In spite of my pretenses to independence and bold thinking, I was beginning to understand how very conventional I really was.

"I suppose we had better come to business. My brother tells me that you knew my husband, Sir Edward Grey."

"Oh, yes, my lady. That is why I wanted to speak to you, personal-like. Some ladies get all in a twist when they find out their gentleman was a customer. I wanted you to know that Sir Edward, well, it was different with him. He paid me for talk and he talked about you quite a fair bit of the time."

I stopped and stared at her. We were of a height, Victoria and I, both of us fairly diminutive, but appearing taller. My carriage was nearly perfect thanks to Aunt Hermia's rigorous schooling. I wondered where Victoria had learned hers.

"Sir Edward paid you for conversation?"

"Oh, yes. He had awful nice things to say about you, my lady, and I do say they were the truth. He was always talking about how nice you were, how ladylike. He did say he regretted marrying you something terrible, but that it was not your fault, you'd been a proper good wife."

"How flattering," I said faintly.

She nodded. "He said you were so pretty, he just liked to look at you, that he didn't need to be a proper husband to you."

I said nothing to this, but Victoria did not require a reply. She went on, chattering as if she did not know each word was a lance to me.

"He didn't mind about the children, you know. He never blamed you for not having them. He blamed himself. Said if he had lived a better life, he could have made you a better husband and not taken such a risk with your health as he had his own. Of course, he always said—"

I put a hand to her sleeve. "What? What risk to my health?"

Her eyes widened. They were beginning to wrinkle at the corners. She could not have been more than twenty, and already the signs of her hard life were etched in her face.

"The pox, my lady. He felt right terrible about it."

I moved away, groping for a bench. Val, sensing my distress, came closer, but I waved him back angrily. Victoria sat next to me. She did not ask my leave, but I did not care.

"The pox. Edward had syphilis?"

"Why, I thought you knew, my lady. The way he talked and all, he said that you couldn't have children because of his syphilis. I thought he meant he gave it to you."

I shook my head. "No. He must have meant that he could not—"

I could not bear to say the words.

"Ah, you mean, he couldn't go with you, because he was afraid of giving it to you when you'd not had it?" she finished for me.

I nodded.

"Well, that does make sense. He was always so cruel about himself, saying such terrible things. Called himself a ruination, and a devil. I used to feel sorry for him, with his pretty manners and nice clothes. He had such a nice way of speaking and all. Hard to credit he'd feel so low about himself."

I nodded again. My hands were shaking, so I clasped them firmly together, the glove leather creaking a little.

"Did he say when, how he contracted the syphilis?"

She tipped her head, thinking. "Before he married, I know that much. He said he hadn't realized he had already got it when he married, but the doctor told him he would not have been contagious right then. He explained it once, but it was confusing. I think he said there was a first bit of it, when he was ill, but didn't know what with. Then he felt better and married your ladyship and everything was all right. Then he got sick again and the doctor told him what he had and to stop laying with his lady, lest you get it as well."

"Christmas," I said softly. "That would be when he moved into his own bedchamber."

"That's right, he said that. He said he just couldn't tell you. He thought you'd be so disappointed about the kiddies and all."

How perfectly sweet, I thought bitterly. Edward had not bothered to tell me about this vile disease, leaving me to wonder all these years at our barrenness, blaming myself. And all the while...

I looked over at the girl and smiled weakly. "It must have shocked you to hear such things. It shocks me now."

She returned the smile and reached out, to my astonishment, patting my hand. "Not much shocks me, my lady. I've seen a hundred men or more with their trousers off."

I nodded and looked away. She had given me much to think of. I did not know if any of it was connected to Edward's death, but I was glad to know it just the same.

I squared my shoulders. "Thank you for your frankness. I hope that you will not suffer for it at the hands of Miss Simms."

"Oh, no. She warned me off talking about him, but she doesn't really think I'd spill. She knows he hadn't been to see me for nearly two years before he died. He had taken to going upstairs, to the attic, for his entertainments."

I smiled at her. The notion of Edward seeking his pleasures in a dusty lumber room amused me for some reason. "The attic? Whatever for?"

"Why, yes, my lady. That's where they keep the boys."

THE THIRTY-SEVENTH CHAPTER

If you have tears, prepare to shed them now.
—William Shakespeare
Julius Caesar

"Edward went with boys?" To my ears, my voice sounded normal enough, casual, as though I were inquiring about the health of a mutual friend. But my thoughts…even now, I cannot quite describe the chill, the numbness. How could I not have known?

She was nodding. "He did. Said he'd always liked them better. But he quite loved you, my lady," she said hastily. I think she meant it kindly.

"Was there a particular boy?"

"No, my lady. He did not use them very often, you see. But Miss Simms was always glad to see him. Some gentlemen like a bit of the rough, but not Sir Edward. He always treated us kindly. Simms likes that—it doesn't do to damage the merchandise, she always says. She gives all the regular gentlemen boxes, pretty porcelain things, for keeping sheaths in." She threw a doubtful look at Val. "Mr. March does say that it keeps infection down, of the pox and other things. Some of the gentlemen complain, or just won't wear them at all. Not Sir Edward. He were always most particular about wearing them. And Simms thanked him for that. Fastest way to drive off business, she says, is with pocky whores."

I was only half listening now. Brisbane had been correct about the box and its purpose. But even he had not guessed the awful reason behind it.

"Thank you for your time, Victoria. I believe my brother gave you half of the fee yesterday. Here is the remainder."

I took a wad of notes from my reticule and thrust them at her. I had no idea how much I gave her. It must not have been less than the agreed amount, though, because after she counted it, she tucked it away in her bodice and flashed me a smile. She was missing a few teeth, but those she had kept looked strong and straight enough.

"You are indeed a real proper lady. Thank you."

I removed something else from my reticule—a card.

"Take this," I said, holding it out to her. She took it and looked at it curiously, as though it meant nothing to her. I realized then that she likely could not read.

"It is the address of a refuge. It is maintained by my aunt, Lady Hermia March. Should you decide to leave the Box, there would be a place for you there. They could teach you to read and write, and eventually secure you a position."

She laughed. "Doing what? Serving? Scrubbing floors and blacking grates? No, my lady, I think not. I am what I am. I'll not change now."

She made to hand the card back, but I refused to take it.

"You may have need of it yet. Keep it. You will always be welcome."

She shrugged and the card went the way of the money. But I thought it quite probable that the card would find its way into a dustbin before the day was through.

I put out my hand. "Thank you, Victoria."

She blinked, then dropped her hand into mine, shaking it slowly.

"Thank you, my lady."

Then the training of her early years returned and she

bobbed her head at me before moving back the way we had come. I watched her, for lack of anything better to do. She moved quickly, and as she reached the end of the path, a figure stepped out, a grizzled older man, dressed in an elegantly impoverished coachman's cape. He doffed his hat to her and she gave him her basket and a smile. The hackney driver, no doubt. He walked with a hunched back and a twist-legged limp. Victoria was careful to match her pace with his, and he in turn guided her around a puddle, patting her arm solicitously. I was pleased that at least someone had a care for the poor creature. I doubted that she would come to Aunt Hermia's refuge. And I doubted she would live out more than another half-dozen years. I heard my brother's steps crunching softly on the graveled path as he came near.

"Oh, Val, why did I ever marry?"

"Because you loved him?" he hazarded as he sat next to me.

"Did I? I can't remember now."

He covered my hand with his own large, warm one. "Was it very terrible, what Cass told you?"

"Yes, actually. It was. Did you know that Edward had syphilis?"

His hand clenched mine and it was a long moment before he replied.

"No. How did Cass—"

"They made him wear condoms at the Box, to protect the prostitutes."

"Dear God," he said softly, giving a sad, heavy sigh. "Miss Simms is quite protective of her staff. An outbreak of syphilis, a rumour of it, can be devastating to the kind of trade she plies. Clients expect that in a certain kind of brothel, but not in Mayfair."

"Did you know that that is why she gave Edward the box?"

"No. Like Brisbane, I thought it a token of regard. I suppose that is why there were never children."

"Yes. Edward did not wish to infect me. Apparently his first attack was before we married. He did not realize then what it was. Afterward, when he learned of it, he quit my bed."

We were carefully not looking at each other. I think, for all his medical training, he was embarrassed. And for my part, I only knew I could not bear to look into those wide green eyes, so like my own, and find pity. Or worse.

"Sometimes it is difficult to diagnose," he said softly. "He might easily have mistaken the first attack for a touch of influenza. The second time, it is usually more certain. In the interim, he would not have been contagious. It was best he left your bed, you know. It is possible he would not have been able to father children in any case once the disease set in. It takes some that way."

I think he meant to comfort me, but I barely heard him. All I knew was that the man I had grown up with, married, thought I knew, had in fact been a stranger to me.

"There is more," I told him. He tightened his grip on my hand, mooring me to the bench. "He went to the attic."

I heard the sharp, low intake of breath, the muttered curse. I thanked God I did not have to explain it further. From his association with the brothel, Val knew exactly what to infer.

"Oh, Julia. Little wonder you cannot remember loving him. He must seem a stranger to you now."

"Yes." I felt my earrings swing against the silk of my veil. I must have nodded, but I do not remember moving at all. I felt nothing but the pressure of his hand on mine and the light whisper of the earrings brushing the veil. "I thought I knew him, Val. We grew up together, for God's sake. How could I not know that he preferred boys?"

"Men," Val corrected. For the first time I looked at him. He met my eyes squarely, to his credit. I doubt many could have under the circumstances.

"Victoria—Cass, said there were boys in the attic."

He shook his head, his dark hair glossy even in the gloom. Why did he never wear a hat, I wondered inconsequentially.

"They call them that in the Box, but they are men. Young ones, seventeen, eighteen and older. There are no children kept there."

"Thank God for that," I said with feeling. "I thought she meant—"

"No. Edward's preferences might have been unorthodox, but they were not criminal."

"But they were," I pointed out quietly. "Sodomy is against the law."

"We condone Portia's behavior. Is this so very different?"

He was trying to be fair and evenhanded—probably with an eye to making me feel better about the situation. I did not.

"Portia is in love with Jane," I hissed at him. "She does not pay strangers for their favors."

"Does that mean that you would find it more excusable if Edward had loved one person, instead of satisfying himself with prostitutes?"

I snatched my hand back. My breath was coming quickly, puffing out my veil in little waves. "It is not excusable in any event. He broke his vows to me, vows he never should have made, given his proclivities."

Val made to speak, but I continued on, ranting him to silence. "A year ago, I buried him, and I was relieved, I confess. His health had grown so poor, and his temper so uncertain, that I had learned to fear him. He even struck his valet on occasion, and once, just once, he raised his hand to me. He did not hit me, but I saw the struggle within him to stay his hand. He had become violent, Val. And every day after that one I wondered, was this the day he would lose that last, desperate bit of control? Was this the day he would beat me or kill me?"

Val did not try to speak now. He simply sat and listened,

letting the pain pour out of me as poison will from a lanced boil. "By the time he died, I was prepared to let him go. I had mourned the boy I loved because I had already lost him. But at least I had the memory of what he was, what he had been, to console me. But now, when all his sins have come to light, I have not even that small solace. I cannot ever again grieve that he is gone, miss his ways and his smiles, without thinking of the lies and the deceit. Do you not understand, Valerius? Every memory I have of my husband is a lie."

I rose, shaking off his protective arm. "Leave me. I will make my own way home."

"Julia, please. I did not wish to hurt you. I thought only to console, and in my clumsiness I have wounded you. I am truly sorry."

He was penitent, but not pleading. He had learned pride and he wore the dignity of the Marches like a mantle.

I nodded in acceptance. "This is too raw, yet," I said by way of explanation.

He enfolded me in his arms, the second time in two days, I marveled. I stepped back, feeling marginally better.

"There is a call I must make now."

"Shall I come with you?"

I opened my mouth to refuse, then thought better of it.

"Yes. There is someone I should like you to meet."

THE THIRTY-EIGHTH CHAPTER

Canst thou not minister to a mind diseased,
Pluck from the memory a rooted sorrow...
—William Shakespeare
Macbeth

Mordecai Bent's rooms were exactly as I had expected. Tiny, overwarm, and so cramped with books and medical equipment that it was difficult to move. But the fire was cheerful and Mordecai was hospitality personified, as if entertaining angels unaware.

"This chair, my lady," he said, sweeping up a pile of papers and an errant sock. "It is the most comfortable and nearest the fire. Mr. March, may I offer you the bench by the bookcase?"

Val, mesmerized by the contents of the bookcase, barely waved a hand. "If you do not object…"

Mordecai flushed with pleasure.

"Oh, no! Please, look at anything you like. It is so seldom I have the pleasure of speaking with another medical man."

This time Val flushed, and it occurred to me that introducing them might have been a tiresome mistake. If I was not quite careful, the conversation could easily move into deeper and duller waters than I could navigate with patience. I cleared my throat delicately.

"Doctor Bent, we have called because I recently discovered something concerning my husband's health. Something that might have bearing upon this case."

Bent's eyes flew to my brother's tall figure, silhouetted against the bookcase. "He is entirely in my confidence," I assured him. Bent smiled. There was a dot of custard on his lapel, and a button swung gently from a single thread at his waistcoat.

"I shall be too happy to help," he told me. "But Nicholas wrote that he was going to Paris, and that the investigation was in abeyance until his return."

"Oh, of course. But this information just fell into my lap, most unexpectedly, and I thought I might save him a bit of time by consulting you in his absence." The lie fell smoothly from my lips.

He seemed satisfied with that and sat forward, his eyes gleaming with interest behind his spectacles.

"It appears that my husband suffered from syphilis, Doctor Bent. He had had it for some time."

He considered this a moment.

"Hmm. Yes, that does complicate matters," he said, his brow furrowing. If I had not been so humiliated by having to tell him, I might have been amused. He did not consider the personal ramifications of the syphilis, only its application to the case—a true medical man.

"Do you know how long he had the disease?"

I shrugged. "He contracted it sometime before we were married, a few months, perhaps. I am told he experienced a relapse of sorts some months after we married."

Bent nodded. "Yes, although it isn't precisely a relapse. From what we understand of the disease, it normally follows a pattern—an initial infection, then a period of dormancy, followed by another outbreak. Then a second period of dormancy. These quiet periods can last for years, during which time the patient is completely asymptomatic."

I must have looked blank, for he amended the word quickly. "Without symptom. The second phase of dormancy can even last the duration of the patient's natural life. But in most people, the second dormancy is followed by the most extreme symptoms of the disease—a breakdown in general health, uncertain temper, that sort of thing."

I thought of Edward's turns, his periods of malaise, his little black rages, and that short, terrible moment when we had looked at each other, the bits of broken vase littering the carpet between us, his hand raised, poised and twitching at my cheek....

"Doctor Bent, is it possible that Edward did not suffer from heart trouble?"

"But he did," Valerius put in quietly. "He'd had it from boyhood, don't you remember? Old Cook always saying he'd never make old bones, just like all the Greys?" I did remember. I had told Brisbane of it only a few weeks before. But I had felt the ground shift under me when Cass had bestowed her revelation, and I found myself wondering which memories were true and which were lies. And I knew I would continue to do so for many years to come.

I turned to Bent, who was nodding, his eyes shrewd.

"Yes, sometimes syphilis will lodge in a patient's heart or lungs, especially if there is an underlying ailment. It is possible that the disease worsened his heart condition, or perhaps it affected it not at all. It is impossible to say without a proper postmortem, and of course, it is too late for that."

I shuddered, thinking of Edward's corpse, moldering away, the evidence quietly decaying during the months that I had wasted.

"Is it possible that Edward was not poisoned, after all? Could not the disease have accounted for his symptoms and the, er, discoloration?"

Val looked away and Doctor Bent reddened slightly. "No, my lady, I fear not. His symptoms were clearly those of poisoning. In fact, I think I have discovered the cause."

He put his hand out to rummage through the papers stacked precariously on his desk. After a moment he grunted in satisfaction. He extracted a single paper, an illustration of a flower. He handed it to me and Val came to look over my shoulder. There was a Latin inscription at the bottom of the page.

"*Aconitum napellus,*" I read out. "Monkshood."

Bent nodded. "It is the only natural poison I could find that fits both the symptoms and the method. It is absorbed through the skin, and ferociously deadly in quite a short period of time."

"Wolfsbane," Val murmured, peering at the tall stalk of the capped blue flower.

"I remember it," I told him. "Do you? The werewolf stories they used to tell at the Gypsy camp." I turned to Doctor Bent. "My father always permitted Gypsies to camp on his lands in summer. One of the old men used to tell us tales of werewolves on the nights of the full moon."

"To what purpose?" Bent asked, smiling. "Simple campfire pleasures?"

"Hardly. His wife sold charms—little bags stuffed with flowers of wolfsbane and a silver coin for protection. As I recall she charged a fine price for them and always sold quite a few. But we always felt better for walking home with those little bags tied around our necks. Nanny always made us throw them away, of course. She was quite right to do so, I imagine, if the stuff is really absorbed through the skin. How stupid we must have been!"

Bent shrugged. "Safe enough, if the flower only was used, and it was kept in a bag. No, the greater danger by far is the root. When it is dried, the poisonous effects are greatly heightened. It can be reduced down to its most venomous components by careful preparation. Dangerous, of course, for the hands preparing it, but quite simple so long as certain elementary precautions are followed."

"So you are saying that anyone could have done this," I said slowly.

"I am afraid so. All it would take is a little privacy, a spirit lamp and some time. The rest of the ingredients would be perfectly innocent to procure from a chemist—a compound to dissolve the aconite into to spread it onto a sheath, and so forth. As for the monkshood itself—" he shrugged "—it grows in nearly every garden and often without."

"But the knowledge," I protested, "surely someone would have to have specific knowledge of deadly plants to attempt such a thing."

"You would be surprised, my lady. Such knowledge is not hard to come by, nor particularly difficult to understand. I warrant any good herbal would give the specifics on monkshood—and nearly every household I know possesses at least one herbal."

"Even mine," I said ruefully.

He smiled, a bright, comely thing in his dark face. "Just so. Of course, mistakes can be made, quite easily. If our poisoner was not careful, he could have poisoned himself without difficulty. I think you must look for a cautious but audacious man. An interesting combination, I should think."

I thought of Brisbane's observations about poison being a woman's weapon. "A man? Are you convinced it was a man?"

"No, I—"

There was a rustling sound from the next room and I saw Bent start a little, his eyes flicking to the barely open door. "The cat, probably after a mouse…pardon me, my lady."

He rose and went into the adjoining room, speaking sharply. He returned a moment later, carrying a large white Persian cat. He closed the door behind them, scolding her softly. She looked up at him with wide, cool eyes the colour of seawater.

"What a lovely creature!" I exclaimed. I put out a hand to pet her, but she swiped at my glove, hooking it with a claw.

"My lady, I am sorry—she is an ill-tempered beast, and not worth her keep."

Gently, he unhitched her paw from my hand and dumped her onto his desk where she sat, watching me, flicking her plumy tail with disdain.

"No matter, Doctor Bent. It was my own fault for attempting to pet her without asking. Cats never seem to like that, do they? No, do not be so hard on her. She must be worth her keep if she brings you mice."

"She is an aristocrat," he said, putting a finger out to rub her under the ears. She purred softly. "She eats better than I do and looks down her nose at the world."

"But she is pretty, surely that is reason enough to keep her."

She squeezed her eyes at me and I thought I might be forgiven for my initial faux pas. I glanced at Val, who had wandered off to the bookshelves again and was fingering a gruesome-looking volume on skin lesions.

"Valerius, would you wait in the carriage, please? I would like a few minutes more with Doctor Bent, nothing that touches the case, I promise."

He replaced the book he was perusing and came forward to shake Bent's hand. They made pleasant noises at one another, and after several attempts, I finally succeeded in getting him to leave us in privacy.

We resumed our seats and Bent fixed his attention carefully upon his cat, avoiding my eyes. He knew what I was about to ask.

"Surely, you are not concerned," he began.

"Of course I am. How am I to know without a proper examination?"

He shook his head. "My lady, you have complained of none of the symptoms. Sir Edward, for his faults, was careful to avoid passing the contagion on to you once he knew of it."

"That does not mean I am free of it," I said softly. "Surely you do not expect me to take my good health for granted. I cannot sit and wonder, waiting for the symptoms to appear, wondering if I shall go mad."

He looked up sharply.

"Yes, I know that much," I told him. "Edward was barely spared that. I might not be so fortunate. I must know."

He rose suddenly. "My lady, I cannot. Not now, it grows late. I have patients I must attend to. If you are troubled, certainly Doctor Griggs must be the physician—"

"No," I said sharply. "He knew of Edward's disease and did not see fit to warn me. I have no trust in him."

His warm brown eyes were sad as a spaniel's. "I am more gratified by your trust than I can possibly express. I cannot, not today. But if you are still determined—tomorrow, perhaps. I could come to Grey House."

I rose and extended my hand. "Thank you. I know you do not wish to do it, but I also believe that if you discover the worst, you will tell me. I have no such faith in the honesty of others."

He nodded sadly and let me out. Neither of us was anticipating our next meeting with any pleasure, but I knew I could rely upon him and I was determined that we would keep our appointment for the following day.

But Fate, and the murderer, had other plans for me.

THE THIRTY-NINTH CHAPTER

When men a dangerous disease did 'scape
Of old, they gave a cock to Aesculape;
Let me give two, that doubly am got free
From my disease's danger, and from thee.
—Ben Jonson
"To Doctor Empirick"

*T*he last person I wished to see upon entering Grey House was Doctor Griggs. But there he stood, retrieving his hat and stick from Aquinas. He regarded me coolly.

"Good afternoon, your ladyship," he said with exaggerated formality. He was marginally more cordial to Val.

I returned the greeting and flashed Val a meaningful look. He withdrew at once and I turned back to Griggs.

"Doctor, I hope you can spare me a few minutes. There is something I should like to discuss with you."

He assented, reluctantly, I fancied, and followed me into the drawing room. It was cold. No fire had been lit, but I did not wish to receive him in the comfort of my study. It seemed an intrusion even to have him in my home now, and I hoped the chill formality of the drawing room would convey the disdain in which I held him.

I turned to face him as soon as the door shut behind us. I did not bid him to sit.

"Doctor Griggs, I shall be brief. How long have you known that my husband had syphilis?"

He blinked slowly, as a tortoise will, and gave a deep sigh, of resignation or perhaps annoyance. It was impossible to tell.

"Five years, more or less."

"I suppose I must thank you for your honesty, if nothing else. I rather thought you might try to deny it."

"There would be little point in that," he said, his expression sour. He was finding this distasteful, at the very least. "Clearly you have discovered it for yourself. And your manner makes it quite apparent you have lost any ladylike scruples that would have kept you from pursuing this highly inappropriate matter."

I lifted my chin and drew myself up as Aunt Hermia had taught me.

"Inappropriate? The question of Edward's syphilis touches on my own health, health that you endangered by your silence."

He opened his mouth, aghast. "But I could not tell you! Such things are private between a man and his doctor."

"But not a man and his wife," I said bitterly.

He cleared his throat and attempted a mollifying tone. "It was an unfortunate thing that Sir Edward contracted this disease. I did not feel it warranted distressing your ladyship by revealing it."

"Do not, I beg you, dress your cowardice in the cloth of compassion. You kept your silence because it was the simplest thing to do. You told Edward to abandon my bed and any hope of an heir, but you never once thought what it might cost me. For him to leave my bed on the grounds of mortal illness is a thing I could have borne. For him to have left it, left *me* thinking it was because of my barrenness, was too cruel."

"It might have cost you your life or your sanity if he had not!" Griggs returned hotly, his plump cheeks trembling with rage. "Would you have rather he kept at you, trying for a child that would surely have been diseased and infecting you in the process? For that is what would have happened, my lady. I see it was too much to think that you might appreciate my efforts on your behalf."

We stared at each other a long moment, so far apart that we both knew the gulf could never be bridged. There was anger and bitterness and righteous indignation on both sides. Finally, I took a step backward, my hand on the doorknob.

"You may continue to treat Sir Simon until his death. After that, you will not come here again."

He gave me a bow from the neck, coldly furious. His mouth worked, as if he wanted to say something, but resisted it. I stepped aside to let him pass. I did not want even my skirts to brush against him as he left Grey House.

After Griggs left, I sat for a long time in the dimly lit drawing room, thinking over everything I had learned that day, none of it pleasant, perhaps some of it useful. I had been dealt a number of blows, to my pride, my vanity, my smug sense that I knew those about me. I had been so secure in my certainty, and yet there had been secrets, swirling about me like fog-bound shadows the whole time, while I stumbled, blindly oblivious to it all.

But after a while I grew tired of feeling sorry for myself and I rose, intending to go and change for luncheon. At the door I collided with Desmond, his head down, looking neither right nor left. He collected himself with a shudder.

"My lady! I am so sorry—please, I was not attending."

I brushed at the crease in my skirt. "It was nothing, Desmond. Do not trouble yourself. How is Sir Simon today? I thought to look in on him after luncheon."

The comely face clouded a little. "Not well. Doctor Griggs was discouraged at his lack of appetite."

"Well, I suppose that is to be expected." I looked closely at Desmond. His own face seemed thinner to me, his eyes ringed with shadow. "Are you eating enough yourself? I daresay your rest is broken with caring for Sir Simon. Perhaps the task is too great for one person. We could engage a nurse."

Desmond swallowed thickly. "No, my lady. I am quite well. The city air does not always agree with me."

"Ah, yes. You are country-bred, I know. Well, we shall soon have you back in the countryside. I have spoken to his lordship and he is very happy to have you come and tend the dogs for him at Bellmont Abbey."

Desmond bowed his head. "Thank you, my lady."

"Are you certain you don't mind the duties? Tending the kennel is a bit of a comedown from a footman's lot. And you won't have any livery to lord over the rest of the staff," I said, smiling.

He smiled back, blushing a little. "I do not mind that, my lady. I am out of my livery now, and the more comfortable for it. I look forward to tending his lordship's dogs. I think the country is where I belong."

"Well, it is settled, then. When your duties here with Sir Simon are concluded, I will send you down to the Abbey."

He looked distraught for a moment, doubtless thinking of the difficult days ahead as Simon's life drew to a close. I moved on, leaving him to his errand, and went to luncheon, making a mental note to myself to make certain that Aquinas had raised Desmond's pay. He was working himself to death for the Greys, and the poor boy should be compensated for it.

Luncheon was dull, or perhaps I was. I had no taste for the salmon and left the fish almost untouched on my plate, picking instead at my peas. Aquinas clucked softly as he removed my uneaten food, but did not scold. We talked briefly of Desmond and other household matters, but I had little interest in any of it. I was still quite overwhelmed by all that I had learned of Edward. I was thinking of Edward, in fact, when Aquinas brought my pudding, and something else.

"A list of supplies that Desmond has drawn up at Doctor Griggs' direction, my lady. With your approval I shall dispatch Henry after luncheon to the chemist."

He busied himself whisking crumbs from the tablecloth while I looked over the list. "It all seems in order, I suppose." It was written in Desmond's simple, painstaking hand, a holdover from his days at a village school, no doubt. His writing was plain and serviceable, meek even, nothing like Brisbane's bold scrawl. But Brisbane's hand would have left no margin at all, I thought with a smile, where Desmond's had left him a good four inches for a bit of doodling. He had a fair drawing hand, but his subjects were a touch morbid—understandable, I supposed, given his current post in a dying man's room. There was a tiny horse, plumed in funeral black, and a hideously accurate undertaker's mute with large, sorrowful eyes. It must have taken tremendous skill to infuse the little drawing with such mournfulness, I thought, raising the paper to scrutinize it more carefully.

Aquinas set his mouth in disapproval. "I know, my lady. I already spoke to the lad about using house paper for his drawings. That is the trouble with country-bred servants. They none of them know the cost of things in town."

"It isn't that, Aquinas. Look at the figure of the mute. He's obscuring something, but you can just see it, there."

Aquinas bent swiftly, peering at the page.

He paled, as white as the table linen.

"It is a gravestone, my lady."

I nodded. "Exactly like the one in the last note Edward received. I think I shall keep this, Aquinas."

He came near to me. "My lady, I shall send for the police."

"No!" I did not mean to thunder at him, but I think the silver rattled on the table. He stepped back sharply.

"As you wish, my lady."

I rose. "This must not become public, Aquinas. I could not bear that. I will speak to him myself first."

"My lady, you must permit me to be present when you interview him. For your own protection."

"You may wait outside. He will not harm me." I still do not know what made me so certain of that, but I believed it then.

I rose, having no appetite for pudding, and beckoned Aquinas to follow me out of the door and up the stairs to

Edward's room. Once there, in those still, quiet rooms, where Edward seemed to linger, I hesitated, then gave Aquinas his instructions. He raised a brow, but did not demur. I moved across the hall and waited. After a moment, there was a soft scratch and Desmond entered. He did not look about him, but stood, staring at the floor.

"Does it make you uncomfortable, to be here? In his room?"

He swallowed, his Adam's apple bobbing sharply in his slender throat.

"My lady?"

"Do not pretend with me, Desmond." I held out the list of supplies with its tiny testimony of his guilt. "You should never have put one of your drawings on the note you sent to threaten Sir Edward. It was foolish."

I do not know what I had expected. Angry denials, violence, insults? Instead he crumpled inward, folding himself over like a wounded animal. He hugged himself tightly with both arms, as if to contain the pain.

"I never meant it," he said, so softly I had to move nearer to hear him. "Not really. I meant only to frighten him, to make him see what he had done to me."

"What had he done to you?" My voice would not go gentle. It cracked, and through the cracks, I could hear my own anger and disgust. But there was pity there, too, in spite of myself.

He shook his head angrily and scrubbed at his tearing eyes. "Oh, do not make me say it, my lady. You must know."

I did not make him say it. I did know, and that was enough. "When did it begin?"

He took a deep, shuddering breath and his head fell back, tears slanting backward down his cheeks. "Two years back," he said finally. "I did not wish it, but he was so kind when he wished to be. It was as if he cast a glamoury over me."

I started at the word, so old-fashioned. But then I recalled where Desmond came from—a tiny village, buried in the countryside. They still believed in such things, I had seen it in my own village of Blessingstoke. We even had our own white witch there. Why should Desmond not believe that Edward could ensorcell him into lovemaking against his will?

Of course, if he believed himself bewitched, it excused him from the greater crime of wanting it, I thought cynically. I looked at him carefully, from his pretty hands to his lightly-limned profile and wondered. How much force had Edward had to use? Persuasion, certainly, but force? I did not believe it.

"Why the notes? Was it really necessary to torment a dying man?"

He went all sorts of unnatural colours. White about the nostrils and fingers, red everywhere else. He wiped again at his eyes, shaking his head. "I was angry, my lady. There is no excuse for it."

"Angry? Why, then? By your own reckoning you had been his lover for a year already. Why then?"

He gave a shudder, like a tiny convulsion of pain.

"Because it was then that I fell ill," he said softly.

I felt my own breath leave in one sharp exhalation, as if I had been struck hard and fast in the stomach.

"You have syphilis." It was not a question; I stated it flatly, knowing it.

He nodded. "We were not always careful about using the sheaths. Sometimes, we were overhasty together."

If I had doubted this boy's passion for the affair before, I did not now. He had convicted himself with a pronoun. We.

"Were you angry enough to kill him?" I asked blandly. He stared at me, as if I had suddenly begun speaking another language, a foreign tongue he had never heard.

"Kill him? My lady, I loved him. I could not raise my hand against him enough to leave this house as I should have done, as I prayed to do so many times. How could I want to kill him?"

He still had not grasped the truth, and I watched him carefully as it was borne in upon him. A paleness washed over him, and a stillness with it, of so profound a shock and despair that I knew it could not be feigned.

"My God," he said softly. "Tell me this is a poor jest, my lady, for pity's sake."

"I wish that I could," I said evenly. "But my husband is dead by another's hand."

He started, violently, but I raised a placating hand.

"Not yours," I told him, holding his gaze with my own. "Not yours, you have not the stomach for it. But you must tell me this. Were you with him, as lovers, the night that he died?"

He hesitated, biting at his lip. He would have liked to refuse the question, but he knew that he could not. Finally, he nodded slowly, fresh tears coursing slowly down his cheeks.

"Half an hour before," he said softly. "The house was in such a bother about the party, it was easy to slip away. We had not been together for months. I had missed him so."

I remembered then what I ought to have recalled before. Desmond had been at Grey House while Edward and I wintered in Sussex, at my father's estate. We had only been in London a few days before we planned our entertainment. There would have been little opportunity for these tempestuous lovers to have renewed their relationship. But this brought a new question.

"Why did you lie with him if you were angry enough to send those notes?"

He flinched at my plain speaking, but he answered quickly enough, smiling a little at the memory.

"I was angry before because I had just learned of my illness. I learned I had not been the only one for him. I was jealous and angry. We were parted for the winter, and my bitterness was everything to me. I sent him the notes, but smiled to his face. He never suspected I was angry with him. But when he came back, and still wanted me—" He paused, his face rapturous. "I could not believe he had chosen me. He said we would be together, that he was finished with the others. I loved him, my lady," he ended on a sob.

I turned my face away as he wept softly. There was only one thing more to ask. "Why the sheath that last night? Both of you were infected, why bother?"

"The doctor had told him it was necessary for him to use them, even if he was with someone who already had the disease. Something about it making the disease more virulent if he were exposed again. I did not understand it entirely."

But I did. Edward's constitution was already weakened, almost fatally so. Even without the poison, he would have likely lived only a matter of months. But with his declining health, he could not risk a fresh infection of the disease—having it already was no protection against a new infestation of it, an infestation that could prove quickly fatal in his condition. It was ironic that the very device he used to preserve his health had been the means of destroying it.

I squared my shoulders and faced Desmond. "You will speak of this to no one. When your duties here are at an end, we will see you settled into a proper nursing home, where you will be looked after."

He nodded, his face awash with misery. He did not attempt to apologize again, and for that I was glad. I had dealt with him calmly enough, but I realized my hands were fisted damply at my sides. I needed a few moments to compose myself. I dismissed him with a jerk of the head and he left me. I sat woodenly on the side of Edward's bed, feeling raw with emotions I could not entirely identify.

Humiliation was only the first. How many others had there been? Who had known? Who had watched me with pity and scorn and the secret knowledge of what Edward was? I felt sick to my stomach with it, and I sat there, swallowing it down. I thought of the conspiratorial smiles Edward had given me, and wondered how many others had received them as well. The little jokes, the charming ways—I had thought them mine, at least for a while. I had been so bloody stupid, I told myself savagely. How could he have done such things, under my very roof? But more importantly, how could I not have known?

I looked about the room, silently hating everything in it. I had not been here since Magda and I had made an attempt to clear it. There were boxes, still only half-packed with suits of clothes. There were still sheets on the bed, a few shirts in the drawers. His ring and watch were still in a box on the dresser, his cologne still scented the air. I looked around at the little statues—a shepherdess, a flute-playing youth, a Roman warrior. I saw the invitations still tucked into his mantel mirror—from the wealthy and respectable. How many of those men—a cabinet minister, a vicar, a duke—had been party to his visits to the brothel? Were they all privy to that? Did they occasionally catch one another's eyes over the saddle of mutton at dinner parties, winking discreetly and thinking of other delicacies they would enjoy together as their wives sat, pretty and oblivious?

I wrenched my eyes away from the invitation cards and looked about the room, seeing Edward through his things. It was like reading a stranger's palm. His brushes, just so and painfully clean, without a single blond hair to mar their perfection. His books, clean and unmarked, because he preferred things fresh and new. His pictures, some good copies of famous pieces, some little paintings done by friends to commemorate happy times. There was a view of the Colosseum bought when he toured Rome, and another of a country folly, Gothic and dark, with autumn leaves curling at the foot of the stones....

I stopped there, my progress arrested by this little sketch. I stared at it, scrutinizing the twisted branches and crumbling leaves, the carved stone and the pointed arches. I had seen another picture, very similar, but done by another hand. Between them, they linked two people to one shared moment, one place where they had been together, long enough to make separate sketches of the same courtyard, sketches they both kept as a memento. The sketches linked them to each other and to this place—and to a motive I had never guessed at.

In that minute, as I stared at the lightly penciled lines and arches, everything I had heard and learned over the past weeks came rushing back at me. I stood, letting them wash over me as I heard the voices, as clearly as if they were speaking in my ear. Whispers about mysterious travels, ravens and follies and thwarted, poisonous love, jealousy and disease, and a virgin's skull. Everyone had contributed something; their voices threaded and tangled, merged and knotted, but I could still hear them, saying the things that I had heard but not understood until just this minute, when it all fell into place and I simply *knew*, as one knows that fire is hot and sleep is sweet. It was just that sudden, that elemental, and it occurred to me then that the truth is precisely that—elemental. It is the essence of itself; it cannot be argued or winnowed down to something less than what it is. It simply is.

To be certain, I removed the sketch from the wall. The wallpaper was bright behind it. In all the years I had lived at Grey House, I had never seen this picture moved from its place, a significant place, I realized now. Edward would have been able to see it from his bed, the first sight of his morning, the last sight of his evening. I opened the frame and slid the sketch out. There was an inscription penciled on the back, very brief, but it was enough. I knew now who had killed Edward. And more important, I thought I knew why.

There was not much to be done. I made my arrangements for that evening, telling no one, not even Aquinas, what I had discovered. He went smoothly along with them, thinking that

I was still pursuing poor, pathetic Desmond. I let him believe it because I had no choice. I had to face the murderer alone. I was not afraid, although I know now that I should have been. And as I dressed myself that night, I began to wonder if I had in fact known it all along....

THE FORTIETH CHAPTER

Water, water I desire,
Here's a house of flesh on fire;
Ope' the fountains and the springs,
And come all to bucketing.
What ye cannot quench, pull down,
Spoil a house to save a town:
Better 'tis that one should fall,
Than by one to hazard all.
—Robert Herrick
"The Scare-Fire"

I did not announce myself. I had taken care no one else would be about, and I slipped in quietly, hoping to catch him unawares. I do not know why, except that I wanted to watch him one last time, before this thing came between us. I wanted to see if his eyes were still innocent, those eyes that had looked into mine, closing just as he had kissed me, a kiss that I could feel on my lips still. It would brand me, I thought a little hysterically, this murderer's kiss. No matter how many others should kiss me in my life, I would remember his lips on mine.

It was a moment or two before he looked up and saw me there, motionless in the doorway. He smiled and I marveled. He did not know, still did not realize that I saw him for what he was. My heart turned within me at his smile and I faltered. I could not do this. I could not say what must be said. I made up my mind then to be silent, to make no accusation, but leave him alone with the knowledge of what he had done. It would be so easy, simply to smile back and ask him how he had been. I could make some pretext for coming to him now and he would not know, not entirely, that I had ever suspected him. It might lie between us, but not for long. Perhaps I could pretend.

But in the end, I could not. I stood there and simply held out the sketch to him. He stared at it, and for a moment, I wondered if he was going to lie about it, hoping that I had not read the inscription, that condemnation written in his own hand. He might yet have bluffed, taken the chance that I had not put the pieces together. But he read my face swiftly, and clever and destructive as he was, he was too tired of it all to pretend with me. I think he felt in that moment that I would understand him, and so he confided. I suppose it was a sort of compliment, but perhaps it was not. Perhaps he simply wanted to tell it to anyone, after all this time.

"So you know," he said softly. "Come and sit down. No, do not linger there in the doorway. You are perfectly safe with me. You forget, I have kissed you," he said with a seductive smile. "I have tasted your lips on mine, Julia. I could not destroy you, although I think the memory of it may well destroy you in any case." His laugh was mirthless. I sat as he bade me.

He looked at me awhile, his eyes searching my face. "Yes, you do know, I see it there. So much knowledge, so much bewilderment. You cannot understand it, can you? Even now, you cannot imagine why?"

I shrugged. "You were lovers and he betrayed you. You loved him, but he fell in love with someone else. It is simple enough. A story as old as time, is it not?"

His smile was wolfish. "How very progressive of you, my dear. You make it all sound so conventional. I might almost believe you approved of our sort."

His eyes were lively, snapping and bright with some private malice. He might claim to savor the taste of my kiss, but he wanted to hurt me, that much I could sense, as a hind senses a wolf in the wood.

"Your sort is not my concern. I merely supplied you with your motive as you asked."

His smile deepened, but I saw the lines of cruelty about the mouth and eyes that I had never noticed before. I had spent so much time with him; how could I have not seen it?

"Sweet, innocent Julia. I often thought it might be fun to tell you, to take you into our confidence. I suggested it once, but he got quite angry. A pity that my tastes do not extend to women...." He broke off a moment, and I looked down at my hands, feeling sick. "Oh, yes, we might have made quite a game of it. Or at least that is what I used to tell him. The truth is, I don't think I could have borne sharing him, not even with you. But Edward could be tiresome in his misguided loyalties—and shortsighted, you know. He wanted to protect you. And the boy. I warned him about the boy, you know, but he did not listen."

"You killed him because of Desmond."

The predatory eyes sharpened. "I warned him. He could toy with others, but he loved me—only me. I even permitted him to marry you because I knew he did not love you, not really, not in the ways that mattered. I warned him he was getting too close to the boy, but he did not hear me. So I simply crafted a little test."

"The condoms," I said flatly. The eyes danced a little.

"Oh, she knows the word! Imagine that, the earl's little Dresden china daughter, knowing about such things!" He laughed but did not move near me. I thanked God for that. I could not have borne it if he had touched me. "Yes, just like the knightly contests of old. If he was worthy and faithful, as he promised, he would not die. But if he failed me, if he was not worthy, if he were faithless, his own treachery would be his undoing. An elegant little solution, I thought."

His mask of savagery slipped a little then, and I knew what he had suffered when Edward died. Knowledge not only of his own guilt, but of his lover's infidelity.

"Oh, Julia," he said, with his sly, beautiful smile, "have you never known me?"

"I begin to think not. You have kept yourself well guarded. I did not suspect what you were until this very evening."

I knew it was a mistake as soon as the words were spoken. But I could not bring them back. If I hesitated now, he would spring some trap of his own devising, something I had not been clever enough to foresee. I had no choice but to go forward, but carefully.

His voice was silky. "You have not discussed your suspicions with anyone? Not even the clever Aquinas?"

"No," I said truthfully. I did not believe that he would hurt me, not even then.

He smiled again, those white, wolfy teeth gleaming in the dim light.

"Julia, do you trust me so well? And do you regret it now? How delicious to have you here at last, as if...ah, sweet mouse Julia has wandered into the tomcat's lair...whatever shall we do with her?"

It was difficult to believe I had ever seen a sign of ill health on this man. His voice was strong and alive, his eyes fairly glowing with pleasure. He radiated strength and vitality, and I think he might have been capable of anything in that moment.

With some great effort, I kept my voice level. "You will not harm me. You are sick, that is all. It is your illness that speaks so. This is not you. You have cared about me. I know it. Perhaps you even loved me. You will not harm me," I repeated, as much for my own sake as his.

He reached a hand out to take up a box of matches. He said nothing while he struck one, lighting a lamp. It flared, then settled to a warm glow, bathing us both in soft light.

"That is better," he said, settling himself comfortably even as he scrutinized my face. "You have changed through all of this," he said at length. "You have grown up. You have me to thank for that. You were so delightfully appealing in your innocence. I wanted to take you in hand, you know. I wanted to educate you, to strip the scales from your eyes. Perhaps that would have been a better revenge on Edward than killing him," he said thoughtfully, tilting his head to eye me better. "Yes, I think it would have been. I could have given him an infidelity to match his own. And it would have hurt him, you know. He did love you—or at least he tried. But I could not bear touching you any more than he could."

"What makes you think I would have complied?"

He gave a short laugh, but it had no power. I suddenly realized that the newfound strength and vitality, the awesome glitter in those savage eyes, was due to some drug. He had dosed himself, perhaps to assuage his ailment. Or perhaps he had grown accustomed to needing it simply to survive. But he had not taken enough, or had taken it too soon. It was wearing off, and soon he would be weak and puny with the aftereffects of it.

"You would have lain down for me," he said softly. "You have been ripe for it for years. All you want is the right man to say the right words and you will open like a well-oiled lock."

I said nothing. The accusation was too crude to merit a response. It was only later that I acknowledged that he knew me better than I ever suspected. I did not like to admit it, but it was possible that I would have lain with him, only just possible, but it was there. I had been lonely and unappreciated. Who was to say what I might have done, if the circumstances had been just so? If he had caught me at a vulnerable moment, if he had looked at me in just the right way, with murmured words of love and seduction, his hands gentle but eager, urging me…I like to think I would have had the strength to resist that. But I knew better.

"But I could not do it," he said regretfully. "My quarrel was with Edward, and there I kept it."

"When did you prepare the poison?" I asked curiously.

This might well be the only time I would have to question him, and I wanted to ask everything. I did not want to wonder later.

"The autumn before he died." He laughed at the memory. His voice was softer than it had been, a little thready. "I nearly killed myself in the process. But it was easy enough. A few books, a few basic precautions, and the thing was done. Too easy, really. It's a wonder more people don't do it."

"And you put the sheaths into the box and left it in his room."

He nodded, his gaze distant.

He had been cautious, and yet audaciously bold, I thought with some admiration. It had been cleverly executed and brilliantly conceived. He had gotten away with it for a year. How much longer might he have kept his secret had I not gone meddling? And, more to the point, how long would I live, knowing what I knew?

As if reading my thoughts, he stroked the side of the lamp, studying the flame, and said, "You were a brave girl to come here and plan to accuse me of murder. And braver still to hear my confession."

I watched him watching the flame.

"I am tired," he said suddenly, the drug having spent itself quickly. "I wish I could play with you a bit longer, but I am tired now."

I made to rise. "You should rest now. You are not yourself. I will go."

"No," he said sharply, and the sheer power of his voice held me to my chair. "We must finish this. I cannot live," he cried, "not now. I don't even want to live, not without him."

"You are not thinking clearly," I said, edging to my feet. "You are ill and tired. Sleep now." And, thinking to reassure him, I added, "I will tell no one."

His eyes flashed and I knew I had made a critical miscalculation. "No, you will not tell. Not now. Not ever."

With his last words, he picked up the lamp in both hands and hurled it at me. I ducked, shielding myself with the chair. The lamp crashed against it, breaking and spilling oil and fire over the silk and wood. Flames rushed to the floor, racing over the carpet to the bed and to the hem of my skirts.

I screamed and batted at the fire licking my skirts. It extinguished immediately and I turned to where he stayed, smiling at me, though the fire was rising between us.

"Will you save me, Julia? And risk your own life? Or will you run away?" His voice was mocking, even now. I reached for him. God help me, I would have saved him even then. But the smoke and the fire were rising hotly and I was thrown back. I turned at the door and saw the bed, engulfed in flames.

"Simon!" I screamed. But there was no reply.

I took the stairs of Grey House two at a time, my scorched skirts high in my hands. My lungs, constricted with stays and smoke, were screaming by the time I gained the ground floor. The servants were gone, sent away for the evening at my insistence, and the empty house echoed with the sounds of the fire, the taffeta rustle of flames, and the shriek of shattering glass. The hall was filling with smoke and I could barely see my way.

Suddenly, above me, a black shadow swooped from above. In my terror I thought it was Simon, risen from his burning bed, but it was not. I nearly sobbed in relief as the raven wheeled before me, leading me on to the door. He screamed, flapping in front of me as I followed him. I reached the door, but the locks were fast, secured for the night as the staff were still out. I wept as I struggled with them. The smoke was billowing down the stairs, blackening the hall in a thick, sooty fog. My hands were slippery on the locks and I could not manage them.

Behind me, the raven continued to wheel and scream, scolding me, I thought. I cursed as I turned the first lock, snicking the bolt back. I moved on to the second, both hands wrapped around my skirt to grip it better. I took a deep, choking breath of the black smoke and nearly swooned. I was light-headed with it, scarcely able to see the lock in my hands. The raven screamed and I tried and failed, tried and failed again.

I took another breath and felt myself grow suddenly dreamy and tired. Another breath and I would not keep my feet. If I did not turn the lock now, I would never do so. Panting out the suffocating smoke, I tightened my grip one last time and the lock turned in my hands. I stumbled back in relief, yanked at the doorknob and felt the rush of sweet, cool, coal-gritted London air. My clothes and face were streaked with soot, my skirts charred where they had been afire, and I was red-faced with weeping and panic. But I was alive, I thought to myself exultantly. I staggered out onto the front step, feeling the rush of wings as the raven passed me to light on the iron railing.

I clung to the railing next to him, weeping and coughing. I felt a hand, slapping hard at my back, and looked up, straight into the face of the Ghoul.

"Good Lord, Julia, you look a fright. What is all the smoke about? Did Cook burn dinner? I just heard about Simon's bad turn. Am I too late?"

I stared at her, from her neatly flowered hat to her trim little boots. She had a carpet bag in one hand and a hatbox sat on the ground. She was freshly arrived from Twickenham, unex-pected, and so much more than welcome. She was perfectly, utterly normal, and I felt laughter, hysterical and sharp, bubbling up as I looked at her.

I opened my mouth to speak, but I could not make the words happen. Instead I watched as the street, dotted with soft, glowing lamps, began to spin about me. I let go of the railing, my feet floating free of the earth. I heard a voice say, "Oh, dear, I believe she is going to faint."

And I did—straight into the arms of Nicholas Brisbane.

THE FORTY-FIRST CHAPTER

But whether Julia to the task was equal
Is that which must be mentioned in the sequel.
—George Gordon, Lord Byron
Don Juan

I awoke a moment later to the pungent smell of the Ghoul's vinaigrette. Brisbane was no longer holding me. I had felt the sensation of lips on my brow and I tasted salty wetness on my mouth, like tears. But they must have been my father's, for it was he, with Aquinas, who held me up between them as I turned and retched up smoke. They held me up and kept me well out of the way as we listened for the bells of the fire brigade.

The Ghoul fluttered about, taking sniffs of her vinaigrette and wailing. "Why does he not come out? What does he mean, going into that place? Is he quite mad?"

I shook off my father's arm. "What is she talking about?" I asked him. At least, I thought I did. The smoke had roughened my voice and I could barely speak. He patted my arm absently.

"Brisbane has gone inside. To see if he can rescue Simon."

I thrust him away and made to sit up. "He cannot! The first floor is in flames—he will be killed!"

The more I protested, the more they held me. Finally, I gave in, spent, and sagged against my father, silent tears channeling through the smoke on my face.

"He came to me tonight," my father said softly. "He insisted you were in danger, only he could not tell me why. It was not until we were halfway here that he began to scream."

"Scream?" I croaked at him. He nodded gravely.

"He did not even realize what he was doing. He beat the glass of the carriage windows like a madman, screaming that he smelled smoke. Aquinas and I thought he was deranged. But he knew—my God, how did he know?"

"He has the sight," I told him, whispering in my smoke-thickened voice.

"Ah. That explains much." Father was country-bred as well. He could believe in such things, as did Aquinas, who nodded, his eyes fixed upon the open door of Grey House. We waited, it must have been only a few minutes, until the fire brigade arrived, all snorting horses and clanging bells. I watched, never taking my eyes from the open door, lit with the unholy glow of that fire. I watched until my eyes burned and my lungs clouded again with that smoke. I watched until my father finally forced me into the carriage and out of harm's way. I watched, but Brisbane never came.

They found him in the back garden in the end. He had made it nearly up the stairs before the heat had beaten him back. But his way through the hall had been cut off by then, and he had only escaped by kicking out a window and hurling himself through the broken glass into the garden. He had cuts and bruises, a few small burns to show for it, and a voice they said rasped as badly as mine.

I did not hear it for myself, for he did not come to me. I waited, as I had waited outside of Grey House that terrible night, but still he did not come. So I convalesced slowly at March House, under the care of my family, and Crab, the mastiff, who lay on my bed with her litter of pups and refused to budge, and Mordecai Bent, who was also doctoring Brisbane and sometimes brought me news of him.

It was not until nearly a week after the fire that I was strong enough, and Mordecai brave enough, to tell me all.

"He never went to Paris," he told me. "He followed you instead."

I thought back and made the connections I had missed.

"The old man with the twisted leg, in the Park."

Mordecai nodded. "He was the cat in my rooms, as well," he confessed, shamefaced. "I did not like to deceive you, but he insisted. He said that he must know."

I shrugged, stroking Crab's silky ears. "He had lost faith in me, and with good reason. I lied to him and I concealed evidence to protect someone. If he did not trust me, it was because I did not trust him first."

"Even so, he did not like it," Mordecai put in. "He followed you as much because he feared for your safety as to observe your movements. He knew you would object to being kept under surveillance, but he felt very strongly that you were in danger. He just did not know from what quarter."

"He did not suspect Simon."

Mordecai shrugged. "There was no reason to. The girl from the brothel told him what she had revealed to you. Nicholas decided to pursue Sir Edward's valet instead and make inquiries at his club. He believed that so long as you were at Grey House you were safe."

I gave a smoky little cough, halfway between a laugh and a sob.

"I did not suspect Simon, either, not until that very day," I told him. "But the pieces all fit, however unlikely the picture."

We talked, quietly, of things that had passed. It felt good to unburden myself, and I knew he wanted to tell me things, things I needed badly to hear.

"He had dreams of you, you know," he said softly. "Terrible dreams. He believed you were going to die if he did not stand watch over you. But how could he tell you? He did not know that Fleur had told you about his gift—his curse. He has never willingly told anyone about it—not Fleur, not me. I found out by accident, much the same way Fleur did, when we were boys."

"Little wonder you are so close," I said with a smile. I could smell the smoke on my breath still as I spoke. Mordecai's smile was warm and nostalgic, but sad.

"It has been very difficult for him, trying to fit in, to be normal. He is an extraordinary person, in a very ordinary world."

"That he is," I agreed readily.

"And you will not forgive him," he said, the humour dying quietly out of his eyes.

I shook my head slowly. "Do not say that. I do not like to think that I should harbor ill feelings for him. No, I will forgive him. In time. And perhaps he will forgive me."

"He already has," Mordecai protested. "You will never know the panic, the battle-rage, he felt when he knew you were in that burning house. My lady, he—"

"Do not," I warned him sharply. "Do not declare anything for him that he will not say for himself. Whatever his feelings for me, he is not easy about them, or he would have come to me. Do you deny this?"

He shook his head woefully. "No, I cannot."

"Very well. He will get on with his life, and I with mine, and we shall see where that leaves us."

Mordecai left me then, sad but resigned. There were no tidy, happy endings here. There had been too much pain and too much mistrust for that. And if Crab minded the tears I wept into her neck, she did not say.

But there was some satisfaction, if not happiness, to be had. Desmond, ailing now, was removed to a nursing home in Kent. There were gardens where the patients might be permitted a little occupation at their leisure, and I was told he settled in quickly. Mordecai, having examined me from top to toe, pronounced me fit enough, in all respects, including the one I was most troubled about. He recommended a spell in a warm climate to restore my lungs, and my thoughts turned again to Italy. I made preparations quietly, to take Aquinas and Morag, and no others. I had had enough of family entanglements to last some time. We would travel slowly together, and after a while would meet with my brothers in Italy.

The only other development of note was my father, and his preoccupation with my sickroom. I noticed he was most often present when Fleur made one of her many calls, bearing salves and sweetmeats and armfuls of flowers. She read to me and brought me magazines of the latest fashions and tempted me to eat the little delicacies she had Therese concoct for me. Father always made some excuse to linger when Fleur was perched charmingly on my bed, laughing her pretty laugh and pampering me with her kind attentions. He looked a bit bemused by her, and I fancied I saw a spark there that I had never seen in him, but I resolutely made up my mind not to worry about it. If Father took up with Fleur, he could do far worse, I thought pragmatically. For that matter, so could she.

To his credit, Father managed to sweep all the ugliness of Grey House under the carpet with the rather prodigious March broom of privilege and influence. Grey House, uninsured, was a total loss, as were the contents. My sisters came forward with photographs and sketches, books and albums, piecing together for me the remnants of my childhood. Nothing could replace all I had lost, but their efforts helped, as did the extraordinarily generous check from Lord Porlock for the grounds on which Grey House had stood. Before the ruins were even done smoking he had teams of men shoveling out the rooms and architects on the site drawing up plans for his new town house.

The fire itself was recorded as a tragic accident, and everyone viewed it as a coincidence of divine order that the staff had all been given the evening off. Aquinas lied smoothly, saying the boon had been his idea, a treat for the servants so that they could enjoy the Queen's Jubilee celebrations, and no one could budge him from that. He knew that if the truth were known, if people understood that I had told him to dismiss the staff, it would cast suspicion upon me and my possible motives for wanting Grey House empty that night. Aquinas himself never reproached me for not confiding in him, but I knew that my failure to do so had broadened a breach between us, one that might only be healed with enough time. He had suspected what I was about, and that was why he had gone to March House, to beg my father to intervene. But he blamed himself for not acting sooner, and no matter how I tried to reassure him, I knew he felt he had failed me.

I castigated myself bitterly for not seeing what the consequences of my actions might be, but I had one consolation. In my stubborn insistence on confronting Simon alone, I had possibly saved lives that might otherwise have been lost in the fire. It was a very little consolation, but I clung to it like a drowning woman. It meant something to me that at least I had done one thing right.

Val confessed his own actions privately to Father, who took it rather handsomely and made arrangements with Mordecai for Val to work with him in his practice and under his direction. I thought this new gentleness of Father's might perhaps be Fleur's doing, but I could not be certain. In any case, Val moved back into March House, and their quarrels were largely a thing of the past.

Even the matter of the raven was settled, its presence at Grey House becoming public knowledge thanks to an enterprising newspaper reporter. Father was summoned to the palace, but Her Majesty, who was in a rather good mood due to the Jubilee celebrations, and who it must be said always had a fondness for handsome men as well as a natural sympathy for another widow, insisted upon writing out an order making me a gift of the raven in recognition of the bird's valorous conduct. My letter of thanks was answered with a somewhat terse reply from her secretary. I think she had begun to regret the impulsive gift by then, and I heard later that she had had a rather severe interview with Reddy Phillips' father. No one knew the exact details, but I did not think it an accident that a sizable statue of Prince Albert was immediately commissioned by the Phillipses to be placed on the village green near their country house.

Free at last to enjoy my new pet, I bought him a handsome cage and applied myself to thinking up a proper name for him. Not surprisingly, the staff of Grey House was dispersed save the handful I retained for myself, some going to the country, most being found new posts in London.

So everyone settled into the same, or more comfortable, circumstances than before. Everyone except me. I found myself brooding, silent for long periods of time, and thinking thoughts best left to darkness. I thought often of Simon and his terrible love for Edward. There had been a house party at the Phillipses' country house the same summer I had gone to the Lakes with my aunt, the summer before Edward and I wed. I had not wondered about it before, but now, when I thought of the melancholy sketches of the Gothic folly, and Portia's revelations of what the Brimstone Club had done there, I guessed. They had been lovers there, perhaps for the first time. That whole group of young men, so eager to be thought devils. Was this the worst of their secrets? Affections that would never be accepted? Love that could never be revealed?

But then I remembered what Simon had told me once, about fearing death so much that he had tried anything to save himself. And I thought of Portia, chattering on about the Brimstones and their belief that drinking from the skull of a virgin could cure diseases. Magda came to me, quietly, simply appearing in my room at March House late one evening. We talked for some time. She stroked my hand, murmuring endearments and lamentations in Romany as I spoke. I had worked it out for myself by then, but she confirmed it. It had been Simon who despoiled Carolina's grave, not Valerius. In his desperation to find a cure for his syphilis, he had exhumed Carolina to take her head for a drinking vessel. He had taken to his heels when Magda had appeared, probably quite relieved when she did not reveal his filthy secret. But she had plotted her own revenge, even then. And Simon's suffering at the end was not entirely due to the advanced stages of his syphilis, she admitted to me through her tears. The arsenic I had discovered in her room had not gone completely unused, in spite of her claim to me that she had harmed no one. I sent her away again then, sickened, but more sympathetic to her than I would have liked. I had forgotten to ask her about Mariah Young, the one mystery I had not solved, but I found it difficult to care. I had unearthed too much misery in my meddling, and I did not have the stomach for more. I dreamed of Carolina that night, as I dreamed of all of them, Simon, Edward, even my mother sometimes.

In an effort to end the dreams, I went to Highgate one afternoon, alone and heavily veiled. I walked through the cemetery, grateful for the quiet, broken only by the soft dripping of the rain onto the gravestones. I stood for a long time by Edward's grave, thinking over all that had passed, all that we had been to each other and all that we had not. I said goodbye that day, for the first time, and the last. And just before I walked away, I laid a small wreath of laurel at Edward's feet and another just next to it, at the stone whose inscription read only "Sir Simon Grey." There was no body there, and no poetry to mark where his body should have lain. But I had given him a place next to Edward for all of eternity. That should have been enough to appease any ghosts who might have lingered. I knew as I walked away that I would not come again.

But still the dead came to me. I dreamed of them, nearly every night, waking shivering and alone, and often weeping. Morag brought me warm drinks and bathed my brow, but we both knew it was time for me to move on.

"I shall speak to Mr. Aquinas about packing," she said one night, after a particularly unspeakable nightmare. "It is time to go."

I nodded, and between the two of them, they made all the arrangements. My father helped, and it was soon settled. My clothes had been replaced, thanks to Portia and the Riche brothers, and some new things ordered, suitable for travel.

"You will go to your brothers," Father advised me. "Ly writes that they are most concerned for you and would be happy to meet you in Florence."

I nodded, listlessly. "That will do."

He talked on, detailing things I did not care to know, before he reached down suddenly and took my hand.

"Julia, listen to me." I looked up and saw him, really saw him for the first time in days. "You have suffered a terrible blow, but you shall recover. You are young and strong, and you will feel this pain acutely because as yet in your life you have not suffered much. But you must believe me when I tell you that this will be blunted, the edge will not cut so deep after a while. You will enjoy life again, and you will laugh and love and weep for others."

He held me then and I wept against his shoulder, sobbing out an entire marriage worth of betrayal and pain and despair into his jacket. He simply held me, stroking my hair until I had finished. Then he pulled back and smiled at me.

"A good wet weep is always just the thing. You will feel better soon. Not just yet, but soon. And when you do, enjoy it. Life is too uncertain, my dear. You must seize happiness where you find it."

I nodded, and after he left, I thought for a long time on what he had said. But I was still not ready to face Brisbane. He had not written to me, or attempted to call upon me, and I woke the morning of my departure feeling grateful for it. I did not think I would have the strength to go if I saw him just then. How could I tell him that when I saw Grey House, blazing up into the evening sky, my regrets were for him, for what would never be between us? I had not mourned Edward then, or Simon. I had mourned him.

But there was time now to sort my feelings, and understand myself better, to ponder questions still unanswered. I still did not know quite where I stood in Brisbane's estimation, or for that matter, he in mine. Italy would be a new beginning for me, I thought exultantly. A renaissance in the land of rebirth, I decided as I walked out of March House, into the warm June sunshine. I had just stepped to the open door of Father's carriage when a messenger ran up, panting and holding a hand to his side.

"Lady Julia Grey," he gasped out. I motioned to him.

"I am Lady Julia."

He extended his grubby hand, bearing a small package, wrapped in brown paper and scrolled with my name. I gestured to Morag to give him a coin and settled into the carriage, glancing out the window as I did so. Across the square, barely visible through the leafy shade, I saw an old man, twisty-legged and very still, with a stout white cat with a plumed tail perched quietly on his shoulder. A breeze tossed the leaves, blocking my view, and by the time they had blown back again, the spot was empty.

I sat back and thumped the roof of the carriage with the end of my parasol.

The driver sprang the horses and we were off, Aquinas mounted with the driver, Morag seated opposite me. We would take Father's carriage to the station, then the train to the coast. We were sailing to Italy, through the Strait of Gibraltar, and I was very nearly numb with anticipation. Morag busied herself taking inventory of our reticules and boxes, certain that we had forgotten something. I waited until her attention was engaged before I unwrapped the little package. There was a box inside, but no message. Just a bit of soft cotton wool and a thin silver pendant, struck with the head of Medusa, strung on a black silk cord.

I turned it over, running my finger over the new engraving, freshly incised onto the reverse of the gorgon head. It was a series of letters and numbers, a code, but perfectly decipherable to one who had been fed Shakespeare with mother's milk. *2HVIIIIii362*. No child of Hector March could mistake that attribution. It was from *The Second Part of Henry VI,* the third act, the second scene, line 362.

For where thou art, there is the world itself.

I threaded the cord under my collar, tucking the coin into the hollow of my throat, where it had lain so often on him. As I did so, Morag looked at me suspiciously.

"What was that, my lady?"

I passed the wrappings to her.

"A going-away present," I remarked lightly. I settled back against the cushion, anticipating my year away and the sharp pleasures that might await me at the end of it.

Of course, I did not realize it at the time, but it was to be nothing like a year before I came home again. I did not know when I would see Brisbane again, but I knew that I would. Someday.

And indeed I did. That is when we found the body in the chapel. But that is a tale for another time.

* * * * *

511

Turn the page to read an excerpt from

SILENT IN THE SANCTUARY*,

Featuring Lady Julia Grey and Nicholas Brisbane
By
Deanna Raybourn

*Available January 1, 2009 wherever fine books are sold.

THE FIRST CHAPTER

Italy, 1887

Travelers must be content.
As You Like It

"Well, I suppose that settles it. Either we all go home to England for Christmas or we hurl ourselves into Lake Como to atone for our sins."

I threw my elder brother a repressive look. "Do not be so morose, Plum. Father's only really angry with Lysander," I pointed out, brandishing the letter from England with my fingertips. The paper fairly scorched my skin. Father's temper was a force of nature. Unable to rant at Lysander directly, he had applied himself to written chastisement with great vigour.

"The rest of us can go home easily enough," I said. "Just think of it—Christmas in England! Plum pudding and snapdragon, mistletoe and wassail—"

"Chilblains and damp beds, fogs so thick you cannot set foot out of doors," Plum put in, his expression sour. "Someone sobbing in the linen cupboard; Father locking himself in the study after threatening to drown the lot of us in the moat."

"I know," I said, my excitement rising. "Won't it be wonderful?"

Plum's face cracked into a thin, wistful smile. "It will, actually. I have rather missed the old pile—and the family as well. But I shall be sorry to leave Italy. It has been an adventure I shall not soon forget."

On that point we were in complete agreement. Italy had been a balm to me, soothing and stimulating at once. I had joined two of my brothers, Lysander and Eglamour—Plum to the family—after suffering the loss of my husband and later my home, and very nearly my own life. I had arrived in Italy with my health almost broken and my spirit in a sorrier state. Four months in a warm, sunny clime with the company of my brothers had restored me. And though the weather had lately grown chill and the seasons were turning inward, I had no wish to leave Italy yet. Still, the lure of family and home, particularly at Christmas, was strong.

"Well, who is to say we must return permanently? Italy shall always be here. We can go to England for Christmas and still be in Venice in time for *Carnevale*."

Plum's smile deepened. "That is terribly cunning of you, Julia. I think living amongst Italians has developed a latent talent in you for intrigue."

It was a jest, but the barb struck too close to home, and I lowered my head over my needlework. I *had* engaged in an intrigue in England although I had never discussed it with my brothers. There had been an investigation into my husband's death, a private investigation conducted by an inquiry agent. I had assisted him and unmasked the killer myself. It had been dangerous, nasty work, and I told myself I was happy to be done with it.

But even as I plunged my needle into the canvas, trailing a train of luscious scarlet silk behind it, I felt a pang of regret—regret that my days were occupied with nothing more purposeful than those of any other lady of society. I had had a glimpse of what it meant to be useful, and it stung now to be merely decorative. I longed for something more important than the embroidering of cushions or the pouring of tea to sustain me.

Of my other regrets, I would not let myself think. I yanked at the needle, snarling the thread.

"Blast," I muttered, rummaging in my work basket for my scissors.

"We are a deceptively domestic pair," Plum said suddenly.

I snapped the threads loose and peered at him. "Whatever do you mean?"

He waved a hand. "This lovely villa, the fireside, both of us in slippers. I, reading my paper from England whilst you ply your needle. We might be any couple, by any fireside, placidly whiling away the darkening hours of an autumn eve."

I glanced about. The rented villa was comfortably, even luxuriously appointed. The long windows of the drawing room overlooked Lake Como, although the heavy velvet draperies had long since been drawn against the gathering dark. "I suppose, but—"

What I had been about to say next was lost. Morag, my maid, entered the drawing room to announce a visitor.

"The Count of Four-not-cheese."

I gave her an evil look and tossed my needlework aside. Plum dashed his newspaper to the floor and jumped to his feet.

"Alessandro!" he cried. "You are a welcome sight! We did not expect you until Saturday."

Morag did not move, and our visitor stepped neatly around her, doffing his hat and cape. They were speckled with rain-drops that glittered in the firelight. He held them out to Morag who looked at him as though he had just offered her a dead animal. I rushed to take them.

"Alessandro, how lovely to see you." I thrust the cape and hat at Morag. "Take these and brush them well," I instructed. "And his name is *Fornacci*," I hissed at her.

She gave me a shrug and a curl of the lip and departed, dragging the tail of Alessandro's beautiful coat on the marble floor as she went.

I turned to him, smiling brightly. "Do come in and get warm by the fire. It has turned beastly out there and you must be chilled to the bone."

He gave me a look rich with gratitude, and something rather more as well. Plum and I bustled about, plumping cushions and making him comfortable with a chair by the fire and a glass of good Irish whiskey. Alessandro had never tasted whiskey until making the acquaintance of my brothers, but had become something of a connoisseur in the months he had known them. To begin with, he no longer made the mistake of tossing his head back and drinking the entire glass at one gulp.

After a few minutes by the fire he had thawed sufficiently to speak. "It is so good to see you again," he said, careful to look at Plum as well as myself when he spoke. "I am very much looking forward to spending Christmas with you here." His English was terribly fluent, very much better than my Italian, but there was a formality that lingered in his speech. I found it charming.

Plum, who had poured himself a steady glass of spirits, took a deep draught. "I am afraid there has been a change in plans, old man."

'Old man' was his favourite nickname for Alessandro, no doubt for its incongruity. Alessandro was younger than either of us by some years.

The young man's face clouded a little and he looked from Plum to me, his silky dark brows knitting in concern. "I am not invited for Christmas? Shall I return to Firenze then?"

I slapped Plum lightly on the knee. "Don't be vile. You have made Alessandro feel unwelcome." It had been arranged that Alessandro would come to us in November, and we would all spend the holiday together before making a leisurely journey to Venice in time for *Carnevale*. There was no hope of such a scheme now. I turned to Alessandro, admiring for a moment the way the firelight licked at his hair. I had thought it black, but his curls shone amber and copper in their depths. I wondered how difficult it would be to persuade Plum to paint him.

"You see, Alessandro," I explained, "we have received a letter from our father, the Earl March. He is displeased with our brother, Lysander, and wishes us all to return to England at once. We shall spend Christmas there."

"Ah. How can one argue with the call of family? If you must return, my friends, you must return. But know that you will always carry with you the highest regard of Alessandro Fornacci."

This handsome speech was accompanied by a courtly little bow from the neck and a noble, if pained, expression that would have done a Caesar proud.

"I have a better idea, and a very good notion it is," Plum said slowly. "What if we bring Alessandro with us?"

I had just taken a sip of my own whiskey and I choked lightly. "I beg your pardon, Plum?"

Alessandro raised his hands in a gesture I had seen many Italians employ, as if warding something off. "No, my friend, I must not. If your father is truly angry, he will not welcome an intruder at this time."

"Are you mad? This is precisely the time to bring someone outside the family into the fold. It will keep him from killing Lysander outright. He will behave himself if we cart you back to England with us. The old man has peculiar ideas, but he is appallingly hospitable."

"Plum, kindly do not refer to Father as 'the old man'. It is disrespectful," I admonished.

Alessandro was shaking his head. "But I have not been invited. It would be a great discourtesy."

"It would be a far greater discourtesy for Father to kill his own son," Plum pointed out tartly. "And you have been invited. By us. Now I must warn you, the family seat is rather old-fashioned. Father doesn't hold with new ideas, at least not for country houses. You'll find no steam heat or even gaslights. I'm afraid it's all coal fires and candles, but it really is a rather special old place. You always said you wanted to see England, and Bellmont Abbey is as English as it gets, dear boy."

Alessandro hesitated. "If I may be so bold, why is his lordship so angry with Lysander? Surely it is not—"

"It is," Plum and I chorused.

Just at that moment, sounds of a quarrel began to echo from upstairs. There was a shout and the unmistakable crash of breaking crockery.

"But the earl, he cannot object to Lysander's marriage to so noble and lovely a lady as Violante," Alessandro put in, quite diplomatically I thought.

Something landed with a great thud on the floor above our heads, shivering the ceiling and causing the chandelier above our heads to sway gently.

"Do you suppose that was one of them?" Plum inquired lightly.

"Don't jest. If it was, we shall have to deal with the body," I reminded him. Violante began to shriek, punctuating her words with tiny stamps of her heel from the sound of it.

"I wonder what she is calling him. It cannot be very nice," I mused.

Alessandro gave an elegant shrug. "I regret, my understanding of Napolitana, it is imperfect." He dropped his eyes, and I wondered if he understood more than politeness would allow him to admit.

"Probably for the best," Plum remarked, draining the last of his whiskey.

"Do not finish off the decanter," I warned him. "Lysander will want a glass or two when they have finished for the evening."

"Or seven," Plum countered with a twitch of his lip. I gave

him a disapproving look. Lysander's marital woes were not a source of amusement to me. I had endured enough of my own connubial difficulties to be sympathetic. Plum, however, wore a bachelor's indifference. He had never said so, but I suspected his favourite brother's defection to the married state had rankled him. They had traveled the Continent together for years, roaming wherever their interests and their acquaintance had directed them, exploring museums and opera houses and ruined castles. They wrote poetry and concertos and painted murals on the walls of ancient abbeys. They had been the staunchest companions until Lysander, having left his thirtieth birthday some years past, had spotted Violante sitting serenely in her uncle's box at La Fenice. It was, as the Tuscans say, *un colpo di fulmine*, a bolt of lightning.

It was also a bit misleading. Upon further investigation, Lysander discovered Violante was Neapolitan, not Venetian, and there was quite simply nothing about her that was serene. She carried in her blood all the warmth and passion and raw-boned energy of her native city. Violante *was* Naples, and for a cool-blooded, cool-headed Englishman like Lysander the effect was intoxicating. He married her within a month, and presented Plum and I with a *fait accompli*, a sister-in-law who smothered us in kisses and heady jasmine perfumes. For my part, I found her charming, wholly unaffected if somewhat exhausting. Plum, on the other hand, was perfectly cordial and cordially perfect. Whenever Violante stepped from a carriage or shivered from the cold, Plum would offer her a hand or his greatcoat, bowing and murmuring a graciously-phrased response to her effusive thanks. And yet always he watched her with the cool detachment one usually reserves for specimens at the zoological garden. I often thought there might be real fondness there if he could unbend a little and forgive her for coming so precipitously into our lives.

But Plum was nothing if not stubborn, and I knew a

straightforward approach would only cause him to dig his heels into the ground like a recalcitrant pony. So I endeavoured to distract him with little whims and treats, cajoling him into good temper in spite of himself.

And then we met Alessandro, or to be accurate, I met Alessandro, for he was a friend of my brothers of some years' duration. Rome had been too hot, too noisy, altogether too much for my delicate state when I first arrived in Italy. My brothers immediately decided to quit the city and embark on a leisurely tour to the north, lingering for a few days or even weeks in any particularly engaging spot, but always pushing on toward Florence. We settled comfortably in a tiny palazzo there, and I began to recover. My fire-roughened voice smoothed again, never quite as it had been, but not noticeably damaged. My lungs were strengthened and my spirits raised. Lysander felt comfortable enough to leave us to accept an invitation for a brief trip to Venice to celebrate the debut of a friend's opera. Plum pledged to watch over me, and Lysander departed, to return a month later after endless delays and a secret wedding, his voluble bride in tow.

Alessandro had kept us company while Lysander was away, guiding us to hidden *piazzi*, revealing secret gardens and galleries no tourists ever crowded. He drove us to Fiesole in a beribboned pony cart, stopping to point out the most breathtaking views in that enchanted hilltop town, and introduced us to inns in whose flower-drenched courtyards we were served food so delicious it must have been bewitched. Plum always seemed to wander off, sketchbook in hand to capture a row of cypresses, stalwart and straight as a regiment, or the elegant curve of a *signorina*'s cheek, distinctive as a goddess out of myth. Alessandro did not seem to mind. He talked to me of history and culture and we practiced our languages with each other, learning to speak of everything and nothing at all.

They were the most peaceful and serene weeks of my life, and they ended only when Lysander returned with Violante, bursting with pride, his chin held a trifle higher from defiance as much as happiness. With his native courtesy, Alessandro withdrew at once, leaving us to our privacy as a newly-reformed family. There were flinty discussions verging on quarrels, where we all went quite white about the lips and I could feel the heat rising in my face. Lysander had no wish to inform Father of his marriage, thinking instead to make a trip to England sometime in the summer, bringing his surprise bride with him then. Plum and I argued forcefully against this, reminding him of his duty, his obligation, his name. And more to the point, his allowance. If Father was made to look foolish, angered too far, he could easily slash Ly's allowance to ribbons or halt it altogether. Lysander was an accomplished musician, but he was a conductor *manqué*, a dabbler. He had no serious reputation upon which to build a career, and without a formal education, without proper connections, his situation was impossible. He relented finally, with bad grace, and Plum penned the letter to Father, writing in Lysander's name to tell him there was a new addition to the family.

The reaction had been swift—a summons to Lysander to bring his bride home at once. Lysander, in a too-typical gambit of avoidance, rented the villa at Lake Como, insisting we could not go home before *Carnevale* season and that we might as well spend Christmas in the lake country. But he had under-estimated Father. The second letter had been forceful, specific, and brutal. We were expected, all of us now, to return home immediately. Lysander had masked his dread with defiance, dropping the letter on the mantelpiece and shrugging before stalking from the room. Violante had followed him, accusing him of being embarrassed of her, if I translated correctly. The Napolitana dialect had defeated me almost entirely from the beginning, and I think our inability to understand one another most of the time explained why Violante and I had learned to get on so well.

Suddenly, Plum cocked his head. "Listen to the silence. Do you suppose one of them has finally done the other a mischief?"

"Your slang is appalling," I told him, taking up my needlework again. "And no, I do not think one of them has done murder. I think they have decided to discuss the matter rationally, in a mature, adult fashion."

Plum snorted, and Alessandro pretended not to notice, sipping quietly at his whiskey. "Adult? Mature? My dear girl, you have lived with them some weeks now. Have you ever seen them discuss anything in a mature, adult fashion? No, and they will not, not so long as they both enjoy the fillip of excitement that a brisk argument lends to a marriage."

I blinked at him. "They are newlyweds. They are in love. I hardly think they need to hurl plates at one another's heads to enjoy themselves."

"Don't you? Our dear Violante is a southerner, who doubtless took in screaming with her mother's milk. And Lysander is a fool who has read too much poetry. He mistakes the volume of a raised voice for true depth of feeling. I despair of him."

"Do not worry, Lady Julia," Alessandro put in gently. *Giulia*, he said, drawing out the syllables like poetry. "To speak loudly, it is simply the way of the southerners. They are very different from those of us bred in the north. We are cooler and more temperate, like the climate."

He flashed me a dazzling smile, and I made a feeble effort to return it. "Still, it has gone too quiet," I commented. "Do you suppose they have made it up?"

"They have not," came Ly's voice, thick with bitterness. He was standing in the doorway, his hair untidy, his colour high with righteous anger, his back stiff with resentment. It was a familiar posture for him these days. "Violante is insisting we obey Father's summons. She wants to see England and to 'meet her dear papa', she says." He flung himself into the chair next to Plum's, his expression sour. "Hullo, Alessandro. Sorry you had to hear all of that," he added with a glance toward the ceiling.

Alessandro murmured a greeting in return as I studied my brothers, feeling a sudden rush of emotion for the pair of them. Handsome and feckless, they were remarkably similar in appearance, sharing both the striking green eyes of the Marches and the dark hair and pale complexion that had marked our family for centuries. But although their features were similar, their clothes stamped them as very different men. Plum took great pains to search out the most outlandish costumes he could find, outfitting himself in velvet frock coats a hundred years out of fashion, or silk caps that made him look like a rather dashing mushroom.

Lysander, on the other hand, was a devotee of the spare elegance of Brummell. He never wore any colours other than white or black, and every garment he owned had been fitted a dozen times. He was particular as a pasha, and carried himself with imperious grace. When the pair of them went out together they always attracted attention, doubtless the effect they hoped for. They had a gift for making friends easily, and more times than I could count since my arrival in Italy, we had entered a restaurant or hotel or opera box only to have my brothers greeted by name and kissed heartily, food and drink pressed upon us as though we were minor royalty. They could be puckishly charming when they wished, and delightful company. Until they were bored or thwarted. Then they were capable of horrifying mischief, although they had behaved themselves well enough since I had joined them.

I flicked a glance at Alessandro from under my lashes. He was still placidly sipping his drink, savoring it slowly, his trousers perfectly creased in spite of the filthy weather. He was an elegant, composed young gentleman, and I thought that with a little more time he might have been a noble influence on my scapegrace brothers.

I smoothed my skirts and cleared my throat.

"My dear," I told Lysander, "I think it is quite clear we must return to England, and you must face Father. Now, we can sit up half the night and argue like thieves, but we will talk you round eventually, so you might as well capitulate now and let us get on with planning our journey."

Lysander looked wonderingly from me to Plum. "When did Julia become brisk? She has never been brisk. Or bossy. Julia, I do not think I much care for this new side of you. You are beginning to sound like our sisters, and I do not *like* our sisters."

I said nothing, but fixed him with a patient, pleasant look of expectation. After a long moment, he groaned. "*Pax*, I beg you. I am powerless against a determined woman." I thought of his tempestuous bride, and wondered if I ought to share with her the power of a few minutes of very pregnant silence. But there was work at hand, and I made a note to myself to speak with Violante later.

"Then we are agreed," I said. I rose and went to the desk, seating myself and arranging writing materials. There was a portfolio of scarlet morocco, stamped in gold with my initials, and filled with the creamiest Florentine writing-paper. I dipped my pen and gave my brothers a purposeful look, the tip of my pen poised over the luscious paper. "Now, we have also had a letter from Aunt Hermia, and I have managed to make out that she is intending to hold a sort of house party over Christmas. We must not arrive without gifts."

"Oh, for God's sake," Lysander muttered. Plum had brightened considerably, thoroughly enjoying our brother's discomfiture. Clearly the return of the prodigal son as bridegroom was not going to be a quiet affair. Knowing Aunt Hermia, I suspected she had invited the entire family—a not inconsequential thing in a family of ten children—and half the village of Blessingstoke as well.

"Come on, old thing," Plum said. "It won't be so bad. The more people there, gobbling the food and drinking the wine, the less likely Father is to cut off your allowance. You know how much he loves to play lord of the manor."

"He *is* the lord of the manor," I reminded Plum. "Now, I thought some of that lovely marzipan. A selection of the sweetest little fruits and birds, boxed up and tied with ribbons. I saw just the thing in Milan, and we can stop *en route* to the train station. That will do nicely for the ladies. And those darling little bottles of rosewater. I bought dozens of them in Florence."

I scribbled a few notes, including a reminder to instruct Morag to find the engraving of Byron I had purchased in Siena. It would make a perfect Christmas present for Father. He would enjoy throwing darts at it immensely.

Suddenly, I looked up to find my brothers staring at me with identical expressions of bemusement.

"What?" I demanded. "Have you thought of something I ought to have?"

"You have become efficient," Lysander said brutally. "You are making a list. I always thought you the most normal of my sisters, and yet here you are, *organising*, just like the rest of them. I wager you could arrange a military campaign to shame Napoleon if you had a mind to."

I shrugged. "At least I would not have forgotten the greatcoats on the Russian front. Now, Plum has proposed Alessandro join us in England."

Lysander sat bolt upright, grasping Alessandro's hand in his own. "My friend, is this true? You would come to England with us?"

Alessandro looked from Lysander to me, his expression nonplussed. "As I already expressed to your kind brother and sister,

I am reluctant, my friend. Your father, the Lord March, he has not invited me himself. And this is a time of great delicacy."

"There is no better time," Lysander insisted. "You heard Julia. Father and Aunt Hermia are planning some bloody great house party."

"Language, Lysander," I murmured.

Naturally he ignored me. "Alessandro, our family home is a converted abbey. There is room for a dozen regiments if we wished to invite them. And do not trouble yourself about Father. Plum has invited you, and so have I. And I am sure Julia wishes it as well."

Alessandro looked past Lysander to where I sat, his gaze, warm and dark as chestnut honey, catching my own. "This is true, my lady? You wish me to come also?"

I thought of the weeks I had spent in Alessandro's company, long sunlit days perfumed with the heady scent of rosemary and punctuated with serene silences broken only by the sleepy drone of bees. I thought of his hand, warm on the curve of my back as he helped me scramble over stone walls to a field where we picnicked on cold slices of chicken and drank sharp white wine so icy it numbed my cheeks. And I thought of what he had told me about his longing to travel, to see something of the world before he grew too comfortable, too settled to leave Florence.

"Of course," I said, with a firmness that surprised me. "I think you would like England very much, Alessandro. And you would be very welcome at Bellmont Abbey."

He nodded slowly. "Then I come," he said at last, his eyes lingering on me.

Lysander whooped and Plum poured out another splash of whiskey into their glasses, calling for a toast to our travels. I returned to my notes, penning a reminder to myself to send out for a timetable. As my hand moved across the page, it shivered a little, marring the creamy expanse with a spot of ink. I drew a deep breath and blotted it, writing on until the page was filled and I reached for another.

At length, the gentlemen left me, Plum to show Alessandro to his room, Lysander to tell Violante the news of our imminent departure. I was alone with the slow ticking of the mantel clock and the crisp, rustling taffeta sounds of the fire as it burned down to ash. My pen scratched away the minutes, jotting notes to extend our regrets to invitations, requests for accommodation, orders for hampers to be filled with provisions for the journey.

So immersed was I in my task, I did not hear Morag's approach—a sure sign of my preoccupation for Morag moves with all the grace of a draft horse.

"So, we're for England then," she said, her chin tipped up smugly.

"Yes, we are," I returned, not looking up from my writing-paper. "And knowing how little love you have for Italy, I suppose you are pleased at the prospect."

She snorted. "I am pleased at the prospect of a decent meal, I am. There is no finer kitchen in England than that at Bellmont Abbey," she finished loyally.

"I would not put the matter so strongly, but the food is good," I conceded. It was plain cooking, for Father refused to employ a French chef. But the food was hearty and well-prepared and one never went hungry at the Abbey. Unlike Italy. While I had reveled in the rich, exotic new flavors, Morag had barely subsisted on boiled chicken and rice.

I returned to my writing and she idled about the room, poking up the fire and plumping the occasional cushion. Finally, I threw down my pen.

"What do you wish to say, Morag? I can hear you thinking."

She looked at me with a studiedly wounded expression. "I was merely being helpful. The drawing room is untidy."

"We have maids for that," I reminded her. "And a porter

to answer the door. Why did you admit Count Fornacci this evening?"

"I was at hand," she said loftily.

"Ha. At hand because you strong-armed the porter, I'll warrant. Whatever you are contemplating, do not. I will not tolerate your meddling."

Morag drew herself up to her rather impressively bony height. "I was at hand." She could be a stubborn creature, as I had often had occasion to notice. I sighed and waved her away, taking up my pen again.

"Of course," she said slowly, "I could not help but notice that his excellency, Count Four-not-cheese is coming back to England with us."

"Fornacci, *Fornacci*," I told her again, knowing even as I did so I might as well try to teach a dog to sing. "And yes, he is coming to England with us. He wishes to travel, and it is a perfect opportunity for him to spend time in a proper English home. My brothers invited him."

"And you did not encourage him?" she demanded, her eyes slyly triumphant.

"Well, naturally I had to approve the invitation, as it were. It would have been rude not to do so."

I scrawled out a list of details that must not be forgotten before our departure. The heel of my scarlet evening slipper required mending, and I had left Plum's favourite little traveling clock with the watchmaker to have the hour hand repaired and the glass replaced. Violante had thrown it at Lysander and dented the hands badly.

Morag continued to loom over the desk, contented as a cat. I could almost see the canary feathers trailing from her lips.

"Morag, if you have something to say, do so. If not, leave me in peace. I am in no mood to be trifled with."

"I have nothing to say, nothing to say at all," she said, moving slowly to the door. She paused, her hand on the knob.

"Although, if I *were* to say something, I would probably ask you how you think Mr. Brisbane will like the notion of you coming home with that young man."

A pause, no longer than a quickened heartbeat.

"Morag, Mr. Brisbane's feelings are no concern of mine, nor of yours. I shall retire in a quarter of an hour. See that the bed is warmed. It was chilly last night, and I shall blame you if I take a cold."

She made a harrumphing noise and left me then, thudding along the marble floors in her heavily-soled shoes. I waited until she was out of earshot before folding my arms on the desk and dropping my head onto them. Nicholas Brisbane. The private enquiry agent who had investigated my husband's death. I had not thought of him in months.

Or, to be entirely accurate, I had suppressed any thought of him ruthlessly. I had smothered any thoughts of him still-born, not permitting myself the indulgence of even the memory of him. There had been something between us, some-thing indefinable, but *there*, I had been certain of it. But nearly five months had passed without word from him, and I had begun to think I had imagined it, had imagined the moments that had flashed between us like an electrical current, had imagined the one searing moment on Hampstead Heath when we had both of us reached beyond ourselves and clung to one another feverishly. There was only the memory of that endless kiss to comfort me, and the pendant coin he had sent me by messenger the day I had left England.

I drew the pendant from the depths of my gown, turning it over in my palm, firelight burnishing the silver to something altogether richer. It was warm from where it had lain against my skin all these months, a talisman against loneliness. I ran a finger over the head of Medusa and her serpent locks, mar-veling at the elegance of the workmanship. The coin was old and thin, but the engraving was sharp, so sharp I could imagine her about to speak from those rounded lips. I turned it over and touched the row of letters and numbers he had had incised as a code only I would decipher. I had felt a rush of emotion when I had first read it, certain then that someday, in some fashion I could not yet predict, we would find our way back to each other. *For where thou art, there is the world itself.*

And yet. Here I was, five months on, without a single word from him, his pendant now cold comfort for his indifference. I laid my head back down on my arms and gave one, great, shuddering sob. Then I rose and carefully placed the pen into its holder and closed the inkwell. I tamped the pages of my notes together and laid them on the blotter. I opened the morocco portfolio and dropped the pendant into it. Medusa stared up at me, expectant and poised to speak. I closed the portfolio, snapping the closure with all the finality of grave-yard dirt being shoveled onto a coffin. Whatever had sparked between Nicholas Brisbane and I was over; a quick, ephemeral thing, it had not lasted out the year.

No matter, I told myself firmly. I was going home. And I was not going alone.

* * * * *

BOOK CLUB QUESTIONS FOR
SILENT IN THE GRAVE

Please find a series of questions that could be used by book clubs interested in discussing *SILENT IN THE GRAVE* at greater length.

We hope these questions enhance your enjoyment of the book, and spark interesting and spirited debate.

1. Julia Grey was born into a family of wealth and prestige. How do the Marches resist the confines and expectations of society?

2. How is Julia's role within her marriage reflected in the setting of Grey House? Contrast the setting of Grey House with that of Nicholas Brisbane's rooms in Chapel Street.

3. As an arrangement between friends rather than a love match, Edward and Julia's marriage was typical of the time. Why, then, was it unsatisfactory?

4. The book covers a murder investigation, but also a woman's journey to find her authentic self. Describe the most important ways Julia begins to know herself.

5. At the heart of the book is Julia's relationship with two men: Edward and Nicholas. Compare and contrast these relationships.

6. To what extent is Simon a villain? Are his actions justifiable?

7. In the book, the motive for murder is jealousy. Is it possible to kill something you truly love?

8. Death had its own culture in Victorian England. Compare and contrast this to modern attitudes about death.

9. The happiest relationships in this book are not conventional ones. Describe the happiest relationships and discuss why they are so satisfying.

10. Was justice served by the outcome of the novel?

11. Given their characters and histories, is a romantic relationship between Julia and Nicholas sustainable?

12. Nicholas struggles with flashes of precognition. Is this ability a gift or a curse? How could he make better use of it?

13. What drives Nicholas? How does he differ from the other men in Julia's life?

14. Given the drawbacks of living in Victorian England, and the privileges of wealth and good birth, would you like to trade places with Julia?

15. Discuss how the issue of homosexuality is handled in the book. Are the homosexual characters sympathetic? How are their choices a reflection of life in a more restrictive and repressive time?

A Note on the Typeface

Berkeley (Body Text):
Berkeley Oldstyle is a beautiful and popular text face, distinctive for its elegant ampersand, and spur at the apex of the capital "A." Berkeley Oldstyle was selected for *Silent in the Grave* for its readability and understated elegance. The old-style serifs along with the graceful balance between the vertical and horizontal strokes make it a natural choice. Type set in Berkeley allows an effortless flow, while the face's unique details bring distinction without hindering readability—all of which are great assets in a text face. *Berkeley* also complements Lady Julia—the typeface of the initial caps.

Berkeley Oldstyle was designed by Frederick Goudy in 1938 for the University of California, and later revived by Tony Stan, a type designer based in New York.

Old-style serif:
Normally a left-inclining curve axis with weight stress at about eight and two o'clock, serifs are almost always bracketed; head serifs are often angled.

Lady Julia (Initial Drop Cap):
Lady Julia is a typeface custom designed by Juliana Kolesova for *Silent in the Grave,* as well as for future books in the series. The decorative initial caps reflect the embellishment and attention to detail so reflective of the Victorian era. It is graceful and elegant, much like our heroine, Lady Julia.